There were, of course, survivors…

The world was not destroyed—just a way of life. The global population was cut down to perhaps one-fifth of what it had been. The ecosystems were utterly disrupted. The climate was transformed.

In what had once been North America, the survivors struggled to prevail in a new age of plague, radiation sickness, barbarism and madness. There were days of seemingly endless night, eerily lit by fires in the sky. Pyrotoxin smogs blanketed the earth. Fetid strontium swamps created new and terrible life forms. Two-hundred-mile-an-hour winds hurtled across the landscape, and when by some freak chance a storm cloud swept in from the sea, it was acid rain that fell— pure acid that stripped a man to the bones in sixty seconds of shrieking agony.

In spite of this, life returned.

In isolated pockets, survivors fought back against terrible odds. And won.

Sort of.

JACK ADRIAN

DEATH LANDS

Pilgrimage to Hell

A GOLD EAGLE BOOK FROM
WORLDWIDE

TORONTO · NEW YORK · LONDON · PARIS
AMSTERDAM · STOCKHOLM · HAMBURG
ATHENS · MILAN · TOKYO · SYDNEY

First edition June 1986

ISBN 0-373-62501-4

Printed in Canada

Prologue

THE WORLD BLEW OUT in 2001.

To be precise, at noon on January 20, 2001.

There was an irony that only a very few people fully appreciated. That is, about 0.0001 percent of those who survived.

Back about thirty years or so a science fiction writer called Arthur C. Clarke had gotten together with a movie director called Stanley Kubrick and made a film called *2001: A Space Odyssey*. The film, the beginning of a series of such films, had a message. For many who had seen it and read the story in the last quarter of the twentieth century, the year 2001 had become a symbol of optimism and hope for the future of mankind. Calmer times were only just around the corner. Peace and prosperity were assured.

The world blew out in 2001.

So much for fantasy.

THE FULL DREADFUL REALITY began at noon on that crisp and clear January day with a one-megaton blast in Washington, D.C., power base of the United States of America and political center of the Western world.

The bomb was not triggered above the city, nor was it the result of a preemptive strike by a passel of missiles hurtling in through the air defense screens and hitting the deck.

It erupted without warning in the bowels of the Soviet embassy, in a basement section that was a restricted area even to the ambassador, V. A. Vorishin, who, like just about everyone else within a five-mile radius, was vaporized.

Mr. Vorishin was not actually in the embassy at the time. He, along with a multitude of other foreign dignitaries and a vast assemblage of national and civic leaders, journalists, members of the judiciary, show biz personalities and thousands who were just along for the spectacle, was on Capitol Hill, attending the inauguration of the forty-third President of the United States, a man in his sixties, a man who had first come to fame back in the early 1980s as a dark-horse contender for the Democratic leadership, strongly favored at the time by young voters called "yuppies."

Within the blast area itself a number of things happened inside a very short time. The flash, which grew in brightness to one thousand times the sun's radiance in two seconds, ignited all flammable materials. The blast hurtled outward, pulverizing anything and everything that stood in its way. Tall buildings were uprooted like trees, falling apart as they descended to the earth, the shattered pieces of masonry, stone, steel girders and glass sent whirling in a deadly vortex. A tremendous ball of fire, expanding rapidly and angrily, roared like dragon's breath up into the troposphere and beyond, fed by the thousands of smaller conflagrations that had started almost instantaneously.

Incredibly, a few, a very few, of those in the city survived the initial blast, but they were soon put out of their misery. Within a few minutes two other, smaller, bombs exploded: one, to the northwest of the city in Bethesda, beneath a chic art gallery owned by a man whose father had "defected" to the West from Bulgaria twenty years earlier; the other, to the south, in the basement storage area of a large drugstore situated in Indian Head, across the river.

The effect of these two secondary bombs can only be described as monstrous. The initial shock wave, already losing momentum, was renewed, strengthened, fortified. A firestorm developed. Hurricane-force winds hurled the superheated fire-mass around until the very air itself seemed to ignite. The Potomac River was sucked up into the fiery sky in a vast, roiling waterspout that evaporated even as it rose. Dust and ash and pulverized debris cut off the sunlight, as though someone had thrown a switch. Immense damage was sustained in Baltimore, Hagerstown, Fredericksburg, Annapolis. The city of Washington, along with its inner and outlying suburbs, was wiped off the face of the earth, leaving only a crater large enough to house a few Shea Stadiums and a lot of seared rubble.

IT IS NOW, OF COURSE, CLEAR that this was merely the climax to the first chapter in the grim saga of the end of Western civilization. For the catastrophe was not the result of a sudden mistake on someone's part, an ill-understood order or a chance accident. There had to be a prologue.

Some might argue that the prologue began to unfold when Karl Marx first met Friedrich Engels and began to postulate an alternative political creed to that which held sway in the early nineteenth century. Others might push the jumping-off point further back in time: to the French Revolution, say, or the teachings of Rousseau and Babeuf. Or perhaps the insurrectionary sermons preached by the fiery hedge priest John Ball prior to the Peasants' Revolt in England in 1381 were indirectly to blame. Or even . . .

But this is academic. Although the roots of the virtual destruction of a global way of life must necessarily lie deep in the past, the actual concrete and significant causes clearly took place within a generation of the moment of disaster.

The history of the last fifty years of the twentieth century is one of general gloom shot with stabs of light. Perhaps one could say the same about the history of the world since man first shuffled out of the caves and began to hunt and gather and till the land. But so much happened during the twentieth century, and so much of it happened so fast, that a good analogy might be of a car on a long downward slope whose driver suddenly discovers that the fluid is running out of his brakes. No matter that the slope is a gentle one; once momentum has been achieved, a certain point reached then passed, there is no stopping the downward rush that very soon becomes headlong, irreversible, terminal.

The United States, deliberately isolationist in between the First and Second World Wars and yet historically jealous of Great Britain's high global profile during and before that period, was swift to change its foreign policy and seize the guardianship of the Western world from the 1950s onward.

During this time atomic power became more than just a science fiction cliché; West and East glared at each other during the Cold War; tensions eased as détente became a political priority; pacts were signed, treaties ratified; an arms race began, got out of hand; black-gold blackmail became a hideous reality when the Arab oil states became greedy for power; money markets throughout the world rocked and teetered; enormous economic depression arrived, stayed for more than a decade.

In the 1960s and 1970s America got its fingers burned in Southeast Asia, fighting a war that, despite what later apologists maintained, could never have been won. In the late 1980s to early 1990s, the same old story was rerun in Latin America, for the same old reasons. This time, however, the stakes were higher and the face cards more evenly distributed. For a time the world tottered on the brink of a Third and probably final World War. In the end, both superpowers, Russia and America, backed off. For the moment, mutual face-saving became the order of the day.

In 1988 President Reagan was succeeded by his vice president. The crisis in Latin America had slowly grown during Reagan's two terms of office, but it was his successor who, early in 1992, had to face the Soviet leader Mr. Gorbachev across a table in Geneva so that both could pull back from the brink with as much grace as could be mustered.

One might have expected that a grateful U.S. electorate, later that year, would have returned the Republican leader for a second presidential term with a thumping majority. But the electorate is notoriously fickle. In 1992 the Republicans were skinned by the Democrats, led by an aging Democratic figure, a long-time politician from a family of political stars, a man with a terrible driving record in his native Massachusetts.

The American public had had it up to its collective back teeth with the GOP. Over the previous twelve years there had been too many close calls, too many near disasters. It was time to turn to a symbol of the past, time to revert to a New Frontier style of politics.

But the presidency of this East Coast aristocrat—whose political acumen, never particularly strong in the first place, had been frayed and shredded by years of self-indulgence and self-pity—was an unmitigated disaster. After four years of inept rule, verging at times on the catastrophic, the electorate demanded the return of the devil they knew, and in 1996 the previous President, in any case still regarded by the mandarins of his own party as a sound, even muscular, choice, took the country by a landslide and became, for only the second time in American history, an ousted President who returned to the White House in triumph.

But this had little effect on the global situation, and toward the end of this man's second term, in the spring of 1999, there occurred an event that was to have a shattering effect on the course of world history. Or what was left of it.

In a spectacular and bloody coup the Soviet leader N. Ryzhkov was gunned down, in the corridors of the Kremlin itself, by hardline Stalinist revisionists. Most of Ryzhkov's key associates, inherited from his predecessor, Gorbachev, who had died in a plane crash in the Urals in 1993, were shot, and for six months the USSR was racked by a civil war far more atrocious in the short term and far more damaging in the long term than that out of which Soviet Russia had agonizingly emerged back in the early 1920s. The upper echelons of the Soviet army, in particular, were decimated.

The coup had been masterminded by KGB chief V. N. Pritisch who, it was rumored, had already disposed of the previous head of the KGB, V. Chebrikov, five years earlier. Chebrikov, a close ally of both Gorbachev and Ryzhkov, had died of a brain tumor and been given a full and impressive state funeral; however, some said a lethal injection, administered by Pritisch himself, had helped Chebrikov on his way.

Pritisch was a hard-liner who detested the West, favored the bleaker aspects of Stalinism and was determined to revert to the original Marxist-Leninist line of total world revolution leading to total world domination. On the other hand he was as much of a pragmatist as any serious politician, and although it might be supposed that the bombs that destroyed Washington were detonated at his instigation, this was by no means the case. Pritisch needed time to plan, a ten-year breathing space, after the short but savage mayhem he had inflicted on his own country, in which to develop his global strategies. The bombs that destroyed Washington gave him nothing.

They were the work, in fact, of a secret and even more extreme junta of disaffected senior internal security officers who, for five years or more before the Pritisch coup, had been plotting not simply for revolution but for outright war. This group, headed by two shadowy figures in the Soviet hierarchy, B. Sokolovsky and N. D. Yudenich, were fanatical purists who believed that over the past generation there had been too much humiliation and marking time, too little action. They called themselves *vsesozhzhenie*, or "terrible fire."

Their grievances, real or imagined, were many. The fat-cat corruption of the Brezhnev era had, they felt, never been entirely eradicated, even under the brisk, no-nonsense rule of Gorbachev. The gradual erosion of influence over the lesser partners of the Warsaw Pact and Russia's European satellites during the 1970s and 1980s worried them. The growth of consumerism, the importation of decadent, Western-style petit bourgeois values into western Russia appalled them.

But if the domestic scene was one at which they looked with sour eyes, the international scene, and Soviet foreign policy in general, seemed to these philosophers of the "terrible fire" one of gross mismanagement, a succession of blunders and embarrassments.

The disastrous intervention in Lebanon during the mid to late 1980s had led a number of Middle Eastern allies to back away from Soviet influence right into the welcoming arms of the United States. The tactical retreat from Afghanistan in the late 1980s had been, for them, a humbling experience. And the return of Soviet forces in even greater numbers only three years later had merely resulted in an even more debilitating and long-drawn-out war of attrition with the rebels that still smoldered into the late 1990s.

The bloody holocaust that had swept South Africa in 1988-9, when President Botha, after three years of vacillation, finally offered the black population limited as opposed to universal suffrage: far too little, far too late, had been a shambles politically as well as literally, for the victorious, Marxist-oriented African National Congress had turned its back on its Soviet mentors and accepted aid from the increasingly capitalistic China.

The back-down over Latin America had been, the *vsesozhzhenie* thought, nothing short of an act of cowardice. And the assassination of Fidel Castro in 1993, probably engineered by rogue members of the American CIA, had not been dealt with at all with the firmness—the sternness, even—that was, the plotters felt, required. The subsequent uprising had been put down by the Cuban army with no help from the Soviet Union, who were still uneasy, so soon after the Latin American crisis, about cruising into dangerous waters. The fact that the U.S., for the same reason, had not poked its oar in when for a couple of weeks Cuba had been theirs for the taking, proved that the Americans were just as stupid as those who sat around the mahogany conference tables in the Kremlin.

The gradual spread of Islamic fundamentalism from Iran into Turkmen and Uzbekistan had slowly but surely, like a relentlessly insidious maggot, reached up into the southern parts of Kazakhstan: extremely sensitive territory. On the other side of the Golodnaya Steppe lay some of the most secret military establishments in the whole of the USSR.

All in all, the past thirty years seemed to them to have been a time of confusion and disorientation, a time of feeble men and feeble policies. In spite of the massive strides forward in agriculture, historically the weak link in Soviet domestic affairs, the huge leaps in industrial manufacturing and, more important, technological development in outer space, there seemed to those of the *vsesozhzhenie* to have been a loss of direction. A loss of faith in the old Marxist-Leninist ideologies. A loss of purity.

Purity, it was argued, could only be regained in the heart of the fire. Fire cleansed. The world must be set alight.

And not in ten years' time. Or twenty. Or a hundred.

Now.

In the U.S. there was unease at the Pritisch coup, alarm at the subsequent show trials that dragged on through the spring of 2000, and then a ground swell of pure panic as it was realized that the face of Soviet Russia had undergone a complete and utter transformation, an almost total reversion to the stony, obdurate, uncompromising mask of Stalinism.

The strong feeling in the country was this: the Republicans, in general, were politically right of center; the Democrats, in general, were politically left. Better, therefore, to go for the party that might—just might—find some common ground with the new rulers of Russia than the party whose inveterate and historic belligerence might—just might—upset the Soviets into doing something drastic and irreversible.

The American electorate could well have gotten it right. There could have been some kind of cobbled-together short-term accommodation with Pritisch, although Pritisch himself viewed matters in the longer term and had made up his mind that within a decade the entire world scene must be transformed.

But this, too, is academic. The *vsesozhzhenie*—who also called themselves the *obzhigateli*, or "igniters"—had other ideas. More to the point, they had contacts in what remained of the armed forces. Owing to the Byzantine and intensely secretive nature of the Russian power structure, much could be done with those who hated Pritisch as much as they hated the West.

And much was done in the final quarter of the year 2000. Plans were devised. Preparations made. Secret orders given and carried out. A state of readiness was achieved.

All culminated in the long-range remote-controlled detonation, by a small group of *spetsnaz*—special forces—of the three Washington bombs.

THE PLAN of the *obzhigateli* was, briefly, as follows: once Washington was out, the three main U.S. space stations were the primary targets. These would be destroyed by particle beam weapons from a variety of killer satellites directed by the two central Soviet space stations. A minute at most.

The U.S. and the NATO countries would then have to rely on the rather more antiquated sky- and ground-based early warning systems still in operation as backup to the extremely sophisticated SDI "loop." First priority, then, was the huge 767 Fortress flying in a figure-of-eight pattern above the American Midwest, the DEW Line "golf balls" stretched across the Arctic landscape from Alaska through Canada and across to Greenland, and the new NORAD bunkers situated beneath the dusty terrain of New Mexico—the old NORAD complex, deep within Cheyenne Mountain in the Rockies, had been taken more than a decade previously by a curious and obscurely funded government controlled "energy" department, which also ramrodded a number of other locations to be found—or, it was profoundly to be hoped, *not* to be found—in the continental U.S. and elsewhere. Once these and four key communications facilities in Europe and Turkey had been taken out—the Deluge.

Although "terrible fire" was made up of ideological purists who planned for Armageddon, even they did not wish for total destruction. There were to be degrees of conflagration. Although certain places, mainly in North America, Europe, the Middle East and China, were to be made practically uninhabitable for generations, other locales—in America and Europe—were not to receive a full-scale "dirty" missiling. There had to be something to inherit when the *obzhigateli* emerged from their bunkers.

Once the human command chain had been wiped out and early warning systems rendered inoperable, nuclear forces targets were next in line: ICBM and IRB sites, storage areas, sub bases. After that came the conventional military targets: supply depots, naval bases, air defense installations, marshaling yards, military storage facilities. From there it was logical to move to civilian and industrial targets: factories, petroleum refineries, ports, civil airfields, electronics industrial bases, nuclear reactors, areas where coal was mined and steel manufactured, power stations and grid centers, important cities. Some cities were to be wiped off the map, others neutralized by the latest "squeezed" enhanced-radiation weapons, now capable of delivering a very "clean" and short-term packet to within, quite literally, meters of their targets. Certain areas were to be drenched with chemicals.

ON THE FACE OF IT, all seemed simple enough.

But from the start, things went drastically wrong.

The *vsesozhzhenie* had been aware that whatever happened, a large degree of "knee-jerk" retaliation against the USSR was unavoidable. They assumed, however, that by decapitating the U.S. power and command structure at a stroke, retaliation would be minimal. They knew that once the President was dead, the Vice President would take over; if he died, the Speaker of the House of Representatives would then be in command. And so on down a designated chain of civilian successors numbering—or so it was thought—possibly a dozen. After these had been eliminated, the U.S. would be akin to a chicken with its head cut off.

Unfortunately for the Russians, their intelligence was fatally out of date. Even as far back as the 1970s, command of the U.S. could pass to as many as sixteen civilian successors, as well as a number of top military advisers. This figure had been upped to twenty-five civilian successors during the Latin American crisis of the early 1990s, and the number of military advisers had been raised, as well. Further, it had been decided that one-third of this group could never be within one hundred miles of the President at any given time. Thus, decapitation was virtually impossible.

Not that this made much difference in the long run since, as it happened, the eleventh in line of succession that January day was a certain Air Force general called P. X.

"Frag" Frederickson—a somewhat gung-ho individual who, if the President had survived, would not have held his position of responsibility under the new administration.

But at twelve noon on January 20, 2001, he did hold that position, and at 12:00:46, as he sat at the command console in the windowless 767 approximately one and a quarter kilometers above the city of Sioux Falls, South Dakota, he knew that a mushroom cloud had appeared over Washington. He also knew, as he stared at the flickering kaleidoscope of lights to the left of his seat and at the information clicking on-screen beneath them, that he was now the forty-fourth President, unelected, of the United States.

He did not need to launch into a complex series of button-tapping movements to "find the key," in other words tap out a sequence on the console that would release the lock of a small safe nearby, then tap out another sequence that would spring a drawer containing the authentication codes manual. The general knew all the codes he needed to know off by heart, though he should not have known even one of them. The general had made it his business to know the codes and to keep up with the irregular changes. Although he had absolutely no idea that such a group as *vsesozhzhenie* existed, he was in many ways their brother in hatred.

An arctic smile played on his craggy face as he reached out with spatulate fingers and swiftly keyed into the computer a set of high-priority sequential commands. Thus, three minutes and twenty-nine seconds before the two secondary bombs in Washington finished off the work of the first, the United States had launched.

THE RETENTIVE MEMORY AND FIERCE HATRED of a fifty-six-year-old Air Force general did not save the Western world. But on the other hand they certainly screwed *vse-sozhzhenie*.

Within three heartbeats of Frederickson's keying in his last commands, the three U.S. space stations had shifted orbit. Instead of being destroyed they were crippled; even so they were still able to cripple the two Soviet stations. All contact with both was then lost.

The events of the next hour or so need only be briefly told. Silos of varying sizes across the length and breadth of the U.S., the continent of Europe and the Arctic blasted open, letting loose a terrible mélange of weaponry. Submarines lurking in the oceans of the world shook almost in unison.

Within five minutes, towns, ports and defense installations in Eastern Europe were devastated. Within fifteen minutes the ICBMs swept in over the Arctic Circle, and entire cities in Russia itself began to wink out, to become smoking heaps of radioactive ash. Military bases and missile sites in the Kol'skiy Poluostrov—Kola Peninsula—Novaya Zemlya, Severnaya Zemlya, Novosibirskyeostrova, Chukchi and Kamchatka, as well as those deep in the heart of Eastern Europe, disappeared in a flash.

Too late, of course. Just seconds too late. If Frederickson's strike had been preemptive, it would have turned Marxist-Leninist ideology into a dead philosophy, something to be yawned over in the history books.

But there were to be no history books, for even as Russia was disappearing under soaring fireballs and vast mushroom clouds, so was Western Europe, so was the Middle East, so was China.

And so, to all intents and purposes, was North America.

The commercial East Coast was obliterated by the retaliatory attack, as were the industrial belts around the

Great Lakes and the petrochemical and defense manufacturing zones strung along the Louisiana coastline. The Southwest—most of Arizona, New Mexico, west Texas—became a land of fire. Cities vanished in the wink of an eye; new lakes were created; forests blazed. The area around Minot, North Dakota, was devastated, as was the Cumberland Plateau that stretched across Tennessee, and central Nebraska. Florida, southern Georgia, Alabama and eastern Mississippi were hit by a rain of biological and chemical agents, sub-fired from the Atlantic. Cheyenne Mountain, no longer considered a high priority target, was hit once, just at the moment when a singular experiment was taking place deep in its bowels.

But the most stupendous destruction of all took place on the West Coast. Here the Earth was tormented into giving birth to an entirely new coastline.

Months before, Soviet "earthshaker" bombs had been seeded by subs along fault- and fracture-lines in the Pacific. Now these were detonated. At the same time the Cascades, from Mount Garibaldi in British Columbia down to Lassen Peak in California—that highly unstable stretch of the "Ring of Fire" that encircles the Pacific—were showered with ICBMs and sub-launched missiles. The earth heaved and bucked and burst apart with a succession of cataclysmic shocks. The volcanos from Mount Rainier and Mount St. Helen's in the north to Mount Shasta in the south, and beyond, blew their stacks. Rock and magma blasted into the sky. Huge rifts tore into the mountains, thrusting deep into the heart of the Cascades. Vast areas of land and mountain lurched downward massively and the gap between the Cascades and the Sierra Nevada was breached, the Pacific Ocean boiling through in spuming waves a mile high.

Within minutes the hugely populated coastal strip from San Francisco to San Diego had gone, as though it had never existed. The Black Rock Desert was suddenly an inland sea with mountain peaks as islands. The mighty tremors, the colossal underground explosions, bucketed on down the fragile chain. Death Valley, the Mojave and Colorado Deserts were inundated. Baja, California, racked and tortured by the stupendous quake spasms, literally snapped off, fragmenting westward, disappearing beneath the churning waves. The Pacific lashed at the foothills of the Sierra Madre.

Here, the volcanic explosions went on for some years. Elsewhere there was only silence.

IT LASTED FOR A GENERATION. The Nuclear Winter. Far worse than some had argued; not as horrific as others had theorized.

There were, of course, survivors. The world was not destroyed, only a way of life. The global population was cut down to perhaps one-fifth of what it had been. The ecosystems were utterly disrupted. The climate was transformed.

In what had once been North America, the survivors struggled to survive a new dark age of plague, radiation sickness, barbarism and madness. There were days of seemingly endless night, eerily lit by fires in the sky. Pyrotoxin smogs blanketed the earth. Temperatures dropped to freezing and below. Peat marshes, coal seams, oil wells smoldered and flared fitfully. Toxic rain from soot-choked clouds lashed the land. Billions of corpses decayed and rotted, became as one with the poisoned earth.

Slowly, over the years, the survivors dragged themselves out of caves and bunkers and began to look around them, began to think, as humankind has a habit of doing, that things were pretty goddamned lousy, but not, perhaps, as goddamned lousy as they might have been. Such is the unquenchable human spirit, with its seemingly ingrained philosophy of make do and mend.

Who knows how language survived, but it did, in all its variety. Not only the language of science, of mechanical things and weaponry, but also of prayer, of inspiration, most especially of curses. Concepts of measurement—the shape of time and space—and tattered theories of agriculture, transportation and the strategies of war managed to prevail quite well through the ravages of endless social collapse. Rituals of sex and a taste for organized crime still echoed in one form or another down the years, as did an appreciation of the self, an understanding about mirrors and the search for the superior person. Literature and moral philosophy suffered horribly, history became garbled and formal schooling and worship were lost causes, but throughout the new wastelands glimmered determined traces of intellectual, psychological and emotional human growth, thrusting up from the rubble like wildflowers, though inevitably mutated. And usually, of course, for the worse—usually in the most terrible form imaginable.

There were still roads. No amount of nuking can destroy every road in the entire world. There were still buildings standing. No amount of nuking can destroy every building in the entire world. Lines of communication and dwelling places; that was a start. And the survivors built from that.

There were still animals on which one could ride, and which would pull wheeled vehicles. Then people discovered that, with a certain amount of ingenuity, they could adapt certain large vehicles so they were driven by steam. That was a technological breakthrough. Books were useful here. No amount of nuking can destroy every book in the entire world. Knowledge was power over the darkness, the destroyer of ignorance and fear.

For much of the twenty-first century the survivors lived on a knife-edge. It was a hand-to-mouth existence. Yet slowly they learned how to cope with disaster, take each day as it came, adapt. They began to experiment with what they had, discover new ways of doing old things—and discover *old* ways of doing old things. They began to explore.

Toward the end of the century a man stumbled across an astonishing cache of food and merchandise and survival equipment and weapons. He discovered that this was a Stockpile, laid down before the Nuke by the government of the day. The man learned that there were other hidden Stockpiles dotted across the vast land. He began to trade this material, began to search for more caches, began to travel—at first by steam truck and then, after he'd come across the first of many huge Stockpiles of oil and gasoline, by gasoline-driven vehicles.

At first he did this for purely mercenary reasons, but as the years went by he found that bringing light to dark places had its own reward.

Then others began to trade, others whose motives were by no means as altruistic. This is often the way.

Now, in 2104—old style—just over one hundred years after the Nuke in what had once been known as North America, the descendants of those who had not succumbed to radiation sickness or died by violence at the brutal hands of their fellow men and women, look out upon a vastly altered and for the most part hideously strange world.

To the north lies a cold waste where men clothe themselves in furs the year round. Where once the Great Lakes had been, there is now a huge, sullen inland sea, bordered on the northeast and south by a blasted land. From Cape Cod down to South Carolina lies a ruin-choked wasteland to which only now is life slowly returning, but to the north of this seared terrain—New Hampshire—and below it—south Carolina—there exist bustling Baronies, ruled by powerful families who have clawed out territory for themselves over a period of sixty years or so. Here primitive manufacturing industry can be found, a veneer of civilized sophistication. Even electric light. But there have, of course, been no advances. Weapons, tools, gadgets: all these date from the last quarter of the twentieth century, either as relics handed down from father to son over three generations and kept in as workable condition as possible, or as loot from the various Stockpiles opened up over the years.

Where in the South the rich and evil soup of chemical and biological agents vomited across the landscape, there now exist fetid strontium swamps and near-tropical forest, where new and terrible life-forms lurk.

The Southwest has become a huge tract of simmering hotland, dust-bowl territory for the most part, skinned of cacti and even the most primitive forms of vegetation, where 250 mph winds hurtle in from the Gulf. And when by some atmospheric miracle storm clouds sweep across from the Pacific, it is acid rain that falls—pure acid that can strip a man to the bones in seconds flat.

The resculpted West Coast has now calmed down, although it is still volcanic, and far below the earth's surface and beneath the waves there are still tremendous natural forces simmering in uneasy captivity. Stark fjords stab into the mountainous coastline to the north; steaming lagoons lie to the south.

In the heartland of this huge country there are dramatic changes. The Great Salt Lake, already rising dangerously in the late twentieth century, has extended its bounds because of quake subsidence at the Wasatch Fault and the years' long drenchings caused by intense climatic disturbance. It now covers nearly 15,000 square miles and is roughly the area of the ancient Lake Bonneville of more than ten thousand years ago.

Everywhere there are ruined cities overgrown with noxious vegetation where people, of a kind, still live and battle for survival and supremacy among the brooding tree- and undergrowth-choked urban canyons. A new lake has formed in what was once Washington State; new deserts have appeared; the Badlands are even worse.

Large areas of the country lie under an umbrella of dust and debris that clings to the atmosphere in strange forms: in some places as a boiling, red-scarred belt of cloud maybe a mile thick; in others as a dense blanket of toxic smog and floating nuclear junk. A coverlet of destruction mantling a land of doom.

Little wonder, then, that the entire continent, north to south, east to west, coast to coast, is known to those who inhabit it as *Deathlands*.

THREE GENERATIONS HAVE NOW PASSED since the Nuke, time enough for bizarre, mutated life-forms to have developed, both human and animal. In some mutants the genetic codes have become completely scrambled, giving life to monstrous beings, men and women with hideous deformities; in others, the rearrangement has been far more subtle. Extrasensory perception and the weird ability to "see" the immediate future are two of the special talents typically possessed by certain mutants.

In all the coastal Baronies, mutants are feared and hated; in some they are hunted down and ruthlessly exterminated. Small groups of "muties" have fled up to the far northeast, to where old Maine bordered old New Brunswick. There are no customs houses now. Here, amid the cool, dark pine and larch woods, largely untouched by radiation showers, they have integrated with the Forest People, isolated and secretive folk who rarely travel.

Far more roam the Central Deathlands, where it's still pretty much a free-for-all society. There is no interest at all in what goes on in the rest of the world. Why should there be? Here is what matters. And now. A fight for survival in what is still a hostile and deadly environment, a grim world of danger and sudden death and teeming horrors from which there seems to be no escape.

AND YET, AND YET...

Strange stories have been handed down from one generation to the next. Wild hints circulate. It is said that the old-time scientists made certain discoveries back before the Nuke—bizarre and sensational discoveries that were never made public. It is rumored that there are awesome secrets still to be uncovered in the Deathlands, deep-level "Redoubts" stuffed with breathtaking scientific marvels, fabulous technological treasure troves. It is even whispered that there is an escape route: that somewhere, beyond the Deathlands, there lies a land of "lost happiness."

Absurd, of course. Irrational. A foolishly nostalgic dream conjured up to compensate for living a life of horror in a land of death.

Or is it...?

Chapter One

REACHER COULD SMELL BLOOD.

It was there in his nostrils, a coppery odor, redolent of death and horror. Then it was gone. It had lasted a microsecond, as it always did, and then there was nothing there at all but the memory of it.

That and the icy chill stroking his spine like skeletal fingers and the blood-red haze that clouded his mind. He shivered, groaned softly, clutched at his brow.

Death was ahead. The warning had been given. The weird antennae of his psyche had fingered the future, told him of blood and destruction. But the how and the why of it, the exact where and when, were never granted, not to him. Reacher was not a true Doomseer; exact details were denied him. He could only perceive the psychic smell of it. And he knew it would be soon, very soon. Within minutes. There was nothing he could do about it, nothing on earth he could do to stop it.

McCandless growled excitedly, "The mutie's got something. He's pickin' something up."

Reacher felt a hand shake him roughly on the shoulder. It broke his concentration, scattered the scarlet fog in his mind. He stumbled forward, dropped to his knees, his hands scraping rock and sharp-edged stones at the side of the old tarmac road.

"C'mon, c'mon!" McCandless's voice rose from a growl to a vicious snarl. "On ya feet, mutie. What is it? Whatya seen? Where's the danger coming from?"

Still half-dazed from the effects of the sudden mind-zap, Reacher struggled to his feet, blinking his eyes rapidly. He stared around him as though seeing the terrain, his surroundings, for the first time, as though waking up from a dream.

A cliff face rose up sheer from the side of the road on his left, its summit lost in the hovering gloom that was split, every few seconds, by fierce jagged traceries of lightning darting surreally about the sky. To his right, beyond the road and the bush-matted strip of verge, was the lip of the gorge that plunged heartstoppingly down to the river racing far below. Ahead was the road, rutted and cracked and potholed, unused for generations, devastated by the angry elements that feuded constantly day and night in these blasted and forsaken mountains, winding steeply, disappearing around craggy bends. Behind, the road snaked downward to the river, through grim foothills, past sick forest and leprous meadow out to an even grimmer plain.

"Reacher, dammit! What the hell do you see?"

Reacher wiped an arm across his face, leaned groggily against the black granite of the sheer cliff, stared sullenly at the three men facing him.

First, McCandless. Always first. The leader. The guy who had brought them together, the guy who had succeeded where everyone else, every mother's son over the past three or four decades, had failed. That was his boast. Black bearded, scarred, glaring eyed, hulking in his furs. McCandless was a brute schemer who let nothing get in his way. He wanted power and he bulldozed opponents, anyone who thought differently or acted differently.

Then Rogan. McCandless's sidekick. Tall, craggy, stupid faced and stupid brained. But handy with his shooter—that had to be admitted. Reacher had seen how handy Rogan could be back in Mocsin when the tall, pea-brained man had shot a guy's nose away. Rogan hadn't liked the way the guy had been badmouthing McCandless, calling him crazy for even thinking of heading up into the Dark Hills. Rogan had shot the tip of the guy's nose off—one slug, swiftly done, almost without thinking about it. Last Reacher knew, the guy was still alive. And why not? All Rogan had done was blow his snout away. Nothing to it.

Then there was Kurt. Kurt was okay. Solidly built, stocky, thick reddish brown hair, watchful eyes. Nothing seemed to worry Kurt. He took things as they came, did the best he could in a bad situation. He, too, was handy with his gun, handier than Rogan and McCandless put together. Which was why he was here, on this rutted road that snaked blindly higher and higher into the Dark Hills. McCandless didn't care much for Kurt, but he cared a lot about the way he handled a gun.

"Reacher, I'm gonna cut your heart out unless you tell us what you seen."

McCandless's voice was now low, thick with rage.

Reacher wearily pushed himself away from the rockface.

"Don't see anything, McCandless. You know that. I ain't a doomie. I just smell it."

"I oughta get myself a doomie, Reacher. You ain't paying your way."

"You'd never have got a doomie, McCandless. You know that, too. Ain't too many of them guys around and most of 'em keep dark what they got."

Rogan spat at the road. He growled, "Miserable mutie. Yer all the same. Ain't human an' ain't worth shit."

He cringed back as McCandless suddenly turned on him. The leader lashed a gloved fist across Rogan's face. Rogan grunted, staggered back toward the precipice, then tripped, sprawling only inches away from the drop. He glared up at McCandless with red-rimmed eyes.

Around them the wind howled like a dead soul racked in chilly Hell. Lightning flickered crazily; the air seemed charged with electricity. Even though the wind was a cold and icy blast, the atmosphere was heavy, muggy. Reacher felt his bones had been somehow turned to lead. His body was clammy with sweat under the thick fur garments, even as the wind cut at his exposed face like a keen-bladed knife.

Reacher watched Rogan crawl away from the chasm and scramble to his feet. Rogan didn't look at McCandless. He was breathing heavily, fingering his face where the bulky man had struck him. Reacher didn't need his uncanny power to tell him that danger threatened now. Any fool could see that an explosion was only minutes away.

But that was not what Reacher had smelled seconds before. He did not know what had triggered off his psychic alarm, but it was definitely not Rogan going berserk or McCandless cutting loose just for the hell of it.

McCandless was a psychopath, almost totally unstable. Already he'd gunned down Denning, a man of some education who'd suggested there might be a way into the mountains other than the road, and if there was it might be the wiser route to take. Denning's view, mildly expressed, was that the obvious course of action could often lead to needless danger. The road, he'd said, was too open; cover was negligible. Who knew what dangers lurked hidden, out of sight? Muties, mannies—anything could be up there. On the road you were an easy target. Maybe that was why no one had ever returned from the Dark Hills, though many had set out. Try some other route, Denning had advised; and if there wasn't one, then okay—the road.

It was a reasonable argument, put in a reasonable manner. It made sense. But not to McCandless, who'd not even bothered to debate it. He'd simply pulled out his dented, much used .45 automatic and put a softnose into Denning's face, blowing the rear of his skull out in a spray of blood and pinkish-gray matter. End of argument. McCandless and Rogan had divided up the contents of Denning's backpack, taking gun, ammo, food, other essentials. Then the party had moved on.

No one had argued. Rogan hadn't argued because he knew he'd be sharing the spoils. Wise man. Offing Denning meant at the end of the day that there was one less mouth to feed, one less person to share in the possible treasure at the end of the trail. The fact that it also meant they had one less gun to blow away attackers with did not necessarily occur to him.

Kurt had not argued because he was phlegmatic by nature. He knew he would not get a share of Denning's leavings because he was a hired gun, a blaster pure and simple. Sure, he'd get a share of whatever they found, if anything, up in the hills. But other than that, forget it. He just took orders from McCandless, kept his eyes open for danger, hoped for the best.

Reacher certainly had not argued. He was a survivor. The main reason he'd survived to the age of thirty, give or take a year or three, was that he never argued. With anyone. Especially not with guys who held guns and called the shots.

In any case, his peculiar talent—born out of a blind stew of scrambled genes somewhere back along a kin line a century before—was invaluable to McCandless, however

much the bulky man might rage and fume, and unless he
went stark out of his mind Reacher would survive yet.

On the other hand, thought Reacher suddenly, the way
things were going, the way madness seemed to be en-
croaching on them all, there was a damned good chance
the guy *would* go stark out of his mind.

McCandless said, "So I ain't got me a doomie, I got me
a senser. Why did I get me a senser? To sniff out trouble." His voice dropped menacingly. "And what was the
deal? The deal was this senser'd get food and a share of the
good stuff when we hit it. That was the bargain. Just so
long as he worked his passage." He suddenly screamed,
"So what did you see, Reacher?"

Reacher was on the verge of repeating that he hadn't
seen anything, that he'd made it perfectly clear to Mc-
Candless right at the start that he couldn't see anything,
that he never would see anything, that it was a sheer physical impossibility for him to see anything. And then he
thought, split-second swiftly, the hell with it: a quibble like
that will get me a slug in the skull. Right now McCandless
was not interested in word play.

He gestured up the road. "There. Somewhere up there.
Waiting for us."

McCandless let his breath out in an exploding snort.

"Right! What?"

"Dunno." Reacher spoke carefully, choosing words that
would not touch the bulky man off. "All I get's an
impression." He tapped his forehead lightly, not looking
at McCandless or the other two.

Trying to explain to men like these was always difficult,
and in any case Reacher himself had no real idea why he
was the way he was. It was relatively easy to accept the
physical aspects of genetic mutation—why some mutants
had no mouths, for instance, or three eyes, or scales, or

pachydermatous skin. Especially these days. Those who knew about these matters said that the full effects of the Nuke were only just beginning to come to the surface.

But how in hell did you explain something that went on in the mind? Something that was not at all tangible. Something extrasensory. Something that had to do with the emotions. At least that was the way Reacher figured it, if he thought about it at all, which wasn't very often. There were other more pressing problems to think about and try to cope with in this wacko world. Like a lot of muties, Reacher accepted that he was different and kept his head down. There was no percentage in making waves. Again, the guys who knew about these things had actually figured out a very strange scenario: they said that maybe in another two or three generations—if there was anyone left at all in this hell-world—it could be that mutants would exceed normals. That in fact it would be the muties who were the norms, the norms muties. That was a pretty wild theory. Reacher tried not to think about it, although it gave him a secret twinge of pleasure and satisfaction. Hell of a twist!

He said, "That's all I ever get—an impression. In my mind. Ain't nothing physical, McCandless, but it's never wrong. Somewhere up the road we got trouble. Could be us, could be guys waiting for us. Could be a rockslide. I dunno. But it's there, and I'm warning you. We have to tread careful, real careful."

"Shit!" McCandless spat at the rutted road, his brow a corrugation of leathery lines. "Ya tellin' me nothin'. We gotta tread real careful *where*!"

"I'm warning you," repeated Reacher stubbornly. "This is special, whatever it is. This is death."

McCandless's eyes locked onto the mutie's for a microsecond, then flicked away. The bulky man pulled at his beard.

"An' it's gonna happen, no matter what?"

Reacher bit his lip.

"It ain't as simple as that. Yeah, it's gonna happen, whatever. Doesn't necessarily mean it's gonna happen to us."

"Ya never wrong, huh?"

Reacher fidgeted, shrugged.

"Niney-nine percent."

McCandless's face split into a grin. Reacher thought he looked more insane than ever.

"Well, okay! That's good enough, Reacher, y'ol' mutie!" He stepped forward, thumped Reacher hard across the back. "I'm feelin' lucky today! That one percent is ridin' for me! We're gonna get us the loot and we're all gonna be kings of the mountain! Ain't that right, Rogan?"

Rogan grinned sourly. "Sure is, boss."

McCandless fixed Kurt with his crazed gaze.

"What about the blaster? Whaddya think, Kurt? We ridin' lucky?"

Kurt's face was expressionless, a mask. He was bitterly regretting this whole venture. He had a strong feeling, an unshakable feeling that they were all going to wind up dead. Nastily. Or if not quite that, some disaster was heading their way with no reprieve.

This feeling had been building up inside him for three days. It had actually started about two seconds after McCandless had first clapped him on the shoulder on the dusty drag outside Joe's Bites in Main Street Mocsin and offered him the blaster's job for an eighth share in whatever they found in the Darks. It was an insane proposition, and McCandless had an insane reputation. The only reason Kurt had agreed to it—instantly and without thinking about it much at all—was that the night before he'd bucked one of Jordan Teague's captains, felled him to the floor in the tawdry casino in the center of the Strip, and he was already making panic plans to get out of Mocsin fast. The only snag was, the next land wagon train wasn't scheduled to leave for at least a week and Kurt did not have the cash or even the creds to buy himself some wheels and the necessary amount of fuel that would take him to the next main center of population two hundred and fifty kilometers to the south. The fact that Teague's captain, an ugly son of a bitch with a walleye named Hagic, had been cheating Kurt—and Kurt had spotted it—made no difference. You didn't screw around with a member of what passed for the law in Jordan Teague's bailiwick. Jordan Teague didn't like it, and he had peculiar ideas on how to avenge insults in his own special brand of law. Kurt had spent most of the night shitting himself in a cross-the-tracks cathouse, a real sleazepit not even the grossest of Teague's minions would touch, before sneaking out to get some food at Joe's—and running into McCandless.

McCandless was in a hurry. A hell of a hurry. He was heading out into the Deathlands there and then. The guy he'd hired as blaster had thought better of it and disappeared and Kurt didn't blame him. The very idea of venturing into the Dark Hills was clearly the product of a diseased imagination, and that about summed up McCandless's mind. Even Jordan Teague had never contemplated an expedition into the Darks. Despite the possibility that something weird and wonderful could be hidden among those brooding peaks, the fact was that over the years many had gone looking for it and only one had ever returned.

Kurt remembered that return very clearly. He had good reason to remember it. His brain switched back, the camera of his memory revealing a scene now nearly two decades old, the screen in his mind showing a crazed, babbling wreck of a human being, brain fried, wild eyed, clothes in rags and tatters, crawling toward him along the dusty apology for a once busy blacktop.

Dolfo Kaler. A man with creds in store, real estate; a power in the land. Or as much of a power as one could ever be under the gross shadow of Jordan Teague. Certainly more power than most in Teague's primitive gold-based miniempire. He had his own satraps, his own bullyboys, a fleet of land wagons, a few good trade routes mainly to the East, and fuel-alcohol supplies if not exactly on tap at least regular. Teague let him be. Kaler had solid contacts in the East, some kind of kin who would only deal with him. Teague knew that if he deeped Kaler those contacts would be lost. He kept an eye on Kaler, just in case Kaler started to dream dreams of empire, but otherwise left him alone; there was a wary truce between the two men.

But the fact was that Kaler was not greedy for what Teague had. He watched his back when Teague was around, but otherwise he was not involved with the man. He had other dreams, sparked by whispers that nagged at his brain, insistent ghostly murmurs that urged him to think the unthinkable.

Somewhere up in that vast range of hills that they called the Darks was . . . something. Treasure, they said. A fantastic, unbelievable hoard just sitting there, just waiting for a strong man to claim it.

That was what was said. That was what had been whispered for a generation. Two generations. More. Maybe going right back to the Nuke.

Maybe going back to before the Nuke.

So there had to be something there. It was a hand-me-down tale, a story embedded deep in the recent folk memory. Kaler, a sensible man, discounted stories of gold, jewels, fine raiments, all that stuff. It was so much crap, so much useless crap. Who needed it? So okay, Jordan Teague was starting to create an economy, a life-style, on the gold he was digging out of the seams exposed by the Nuke, forgotten through the Chill—just like *everything* had been forgotten—and rediscovered only a few years back. Teague was moving the stuff very gingerly to the East, and guys out there were sniffing at it, pondering its possibilities, wondering if it would do them any good. And maybe in another ten years gold would be back in fashion, but ten years was a long time and right now the only worthwhile way of doing things was barter, trade, credit. Sure, coin was coming back; it was useful. But thus far it sure as hell didn't beat fresh food, canned food, animals—as long as they were reasonably pure—weapons, ammo.

Especially it didn't beat ammo.

And that was what Dolfo Kaler figured was up there in the Darks. No fairy-tale hoard of goodies, but a Stockpile—a major Stockpile, maybe far bigger than any of the ones that had been unearthed so far.

Anybody who was anybody now knew that, before the Nuke, the government of the day, a government that had ruled the whole land, north to south, west to east, had been rumored to have squirreled away stuff in deep-cast ferro-concrete bunkers. Now it was an established fact. Some had been discovered, opened up. There was a guy who called himself the Trader who'd found two and turned them into a business. He'd started off by chugging around the Deathlands in steam trucks a couple of years before, but now he was using gasoline. *Gasoline!* And trading guns in every direction. He was heavily weaponed himself too, as guys who'd tried to hijack him had discovered to their cost.

The shit was there if you could find it, but from what Dolfo Kaler had learned, the Stockpiles found up to now were small. The nagging suspicion he had was that if there really was something up in the Darks—and if it was a Stockpile—it was a big one. And that was why he didn't give a fart about Jordan Teague's little fiefdom. If what he suspected was true, and if he could get his hands on it, he could turn himself into king of the known world.

Dolfo Kaler's mind lovingly dwelt on boxes of guns in their original greased wraps, pristine fresh, never used. Crates of grenades. Heavy armament. Trucks. Tanks. Oceans of oil.

Power.

So he went out. He took fifty men, all of them hand-picked from his own garrison mixed in with others from his contacts in the East. Hard-bitten dog soldiers. Didn't give a nuke's hot ass about anything or anyone.

It was a mighty expedition. Seeing it, even Jordan Teague got broody. But then it had to be, because others had heard the summons—the siren call that drifted into men's minds from the Darks. Others had hit the road on the hundred-klick or so journey under the sulphuric skies, across the parched earth, through the leprous forests that grew around the foothills of the Darks.

And none had ever come back.

Which meant there must have been a strong contingent of maniacal muties barring the way to it.

Dolfo Kaler knew how to deal with crazies. Blow 'em away. He bartered, he finagled, he called in every long-term debt he had out, and in the end every man jack of his team had an automatic rifle of some description and a stack of rounds. He also acquired seven MGs, four flame-throwers and a supply of precious fuel and two bazookas. Not to mention a box of grenades and a launcher.

And then he set out.

There were six big steam trucks, snorting and grinding and belching black smoke, and they shifted butt one fine spring morning when the skies were not as yellow as usual and a hazy red fireball of a sun was doing pretty well in its struggle to penetrate the haze. There must have been half of Mocsin on the edge of town to see them off, waving crudely fashioned flags and whooping and hollering fit to burst. Maybe three thousand souls to watch the biggest thing to happen to the town in decades.

Kurt remembered it. He remembered it very well. It had happened on his birthday, and his ma and pa had taken him to see the cavalcade as a birthday treat. Kurt remembered yelling with the rest of them. He didn't really know what he was yelling for, except that just seeing those huge, lumbering steam trucks lurching out of town was exciting enough—the most exciting thing that had ever happened to him. And the guys in the trucks, yelling, too, caught up in the glamour of it all, waving their pieces above their heads, all clearly itching to fire a few shots to finish the celebration off but not daring to because ammo was ammo then, and you didn't waste one single round of it.

And Kurt remembered the payoff. The horror of that day, maybe four months later, with the late summer sun blistering down through the haze, a light wind whipping up the dust into the heavy air in thin spirals—and the single raggedy man crawling toward him, blind eyes staring out of a gaunt and blackened face, one desiccated hand clawing and twitching in the air like a mummified insect come to dreadful life. A human skeleton, his clothes in rags and tatters, inching his way laboriously along the ruined blacktop. Muttering and mumbling to himself as his knees and bony legs scraped faintly along the dusty road, he pulled himself wearily forward with the sound of old parchment being gently squeezed.

Dolfo Kaler. A man of considerable will.

Kurt remembered turning and running in blind panic back into town, his bare feet hammering at the hot, dusty ground. He remembered the confused aftermath, the deputation of eight armed men, led by Jordan Teague himself carrying a pump-action, Teague striding out of town toward the blackened, sticklike figure rustling its way along the rutted blacktop. He remembered how they kept their distance from Kaler, well out of reach in a half circle, watching him drag himself slowly toward them. How they glanced at each other, shook their heads, faces showing a mix of horror, boredom, grim ruthlessness. How they all, as one, each of the eight, lifted their pieces and fired.

Kurt remembered that, all right.

He remembered it was Jordan Teague who aimed at the head and blew it off with an ear-cracking roar of sound, automatic fire and pistol single-shot clattering in echo, rounds jerking and smashing the stick man up and down and back along the blacktop in a flailing scramble of limbs and blood and flesh chunks.

They said they had to do it because it was a stone-cold cinch that Kaler was contaminated in some way; maybe he had the Plague itself. That was a popular theory because guys who caught the Plague found themselves driven to the limits of their endurance and beyond before they finally fell apart.

But Kurt knew the sun-crisped ruin of a man did not have the Plague. Even at the age of ten he knew that. Knew for sure. A classic symptom of Plague was that you could not talk, could not articulate words, you could only gargle and growl and foam at the mouth. And Kaler might have been mumbling and muttering when Kurt found him, but there were words coming out of his mouth: most were garbled, incomprehensible; a few were chillingly intelligible.

Kurt could hear the rasping croak now, the words creaking out through those blackened lips: *"Fog...fog devils...tear you...apart..."*

McCandless's voice cut through his dark musings.

"I said, what do you think, Kurt? You listenin' to me?"

And now there he was, trekking through this savage land at McCandless's heels, following Dolfo Kaler's trail and the trail of all those other poor bastards who had never made it back to Mocsin. Never made it back to anywhere.

Sure he was mad. But come to think of it, not half as mad as Jordan Teague would have been if Teague had gotten his fat hands on him. Hiring on with McCandless had been the perfect escape—except of course for McCandless's lousy rep and McCandless's lousy destination. If only he'd headed off elsewhere on the road to the Darks, managed to sneak away on foot or stolen the truck. If only. But there'd been no time, no opportunity. McCandless had already been able to claw some gas from somewhere, enough to fill the tank of the beat-up, rickety truck that had only just managed to get them here before seizing up completely in the foothills. That was where McCandless had iced the fifth member of the party, Denning, and that was where they'd bedded down for the night, and that was where, burn it all to Hell, he should have split.

But he hadn't. And he still wasn't entirely sure why.

Maybe the vision of riches or weaponry beyond his wildest imaginings had held him to this course: an infatuation with power.

Maybe it was just as simple as a belief that when the chips were down he could get shot of McCandless and Rogan and maybe Reacher, too—but maybe not Reacher; Kurt felt a vague kinship with Reacher—and take what was there all for himself. Simple greed. Maybe that was it.

Kurt shrugged, his face still masklike.

"Yeah."

"Yeah what?" rasped McCandless. "Yeah, ya listenin' to me, or yeah, we're all gonna get lucky?"

The thought struck Kurt anew that there was no way McCandless was going to share with him if they struck it lucky. Or with anyone. He had in fact been aware of that all along, right from the start, right from the moment when McCandless had grabbed him.

McCandless—sharing? Even an eighth? Fat chance.

He said, his voice lifeless, his mind filled with the sudden image of Denning with just a bloody mush were the back of his head had once been, "Both."

"Fine," said McCandless, with a grin. "So let's do it. Let's move, huh? Let's get us some of that good fortune."

They stumbled up the road, Reacher in front, McCandless next, then Rogan. Kurt took up the tail.

He gripped his old Armalite auto-rifle with both gloved hands, left under the stock, right around the trigger guard. Every so often he glanced back, but there was no one there. They'd seen no one since they'd left Mocsin. No muties, no mannies, no norms. Nor had they seen much fauna, come to that. The odd snake, nothing much else, nothing that looked at all as if it could wipe out a party of fifty men and all the men who had gone before.

Nor had they seen any sign of the steam trucks. No rusted hulks, no nothing. So unless the area they still had to reach, the high side of the mountains, was inhabited, it looked as if the only thing that could have dealt death to all those pilgrims of the past was the fog.

The fog that Dolfo Kaler had babbled about.

Fog devils, he'd said. Tear you apart, he'd said.

A fog with claws.

The wind was getting wilder, a banshee wail that echoed and reechoed around them. The four men had to fight to keep their balance, to stop from being plucked into the air and hurled over the edge of the precipice. They hugged the granite wall, stumbling and staggering onward, holding on to rocks with their gloved hands.

Kurt had to sling his rifle, a thing he did not care to do in a situation in which a second's delay in pulling it off his shoulder might be all the difference between life and death. But it was either that or be buffeted by the howling gale across the road and over into the black abyss the other side.

Suddenly it was colder. Much colder. Kurt stared upward, saw snow sweeping in from afar, a blizzard of ice and sleet hurled across the wilderness straight at them.

Yet still the lightning flickered and flared, exploding the blackness every few seconds with an unnatural radiance.

Head down, Kurt cursed through gritted teeth as the whirling maelstrom of ice chips exploded over them, battered them like hammers. Blindly he groped in his furs, tugged out heavy-duty Snospex, somehow managed to pull them over his head. He pulled the hood of his furs down hard, then crouched, gripping chunks of rock for dear life as another blast of wind hammered across the road with a demon's roar.

The wind died as suddenly as it had risen. It disappeared as though it had never been. Fat snowflakes softly feathered down through the air.

Breathing hard, Kurt clambered to his feet and unslung his rifle. He stared around, fearful that something might have snuck up on them while the gale had kept them flattened to the rock wall.

Nothing. The lightning cast a cyanic glow over the mountainscape. McCandless turned, stumbled back down toward him.

"Blasted nukeshit storm. Ain't seen nothin' like it. Ain't natural."

Kurt said, "Ain't nothing natural in the whole nuke-shittin' world, McCandless. Not since the Nuke."

"Shit," spat the big man, "yer a philosopher, Kurt." He turned back disgustedly. "C'mon! Move it! Let's go!"

They trudged onward, snow still drifting down from the lightning-slashed blackness all around them. It was hot again, humid. Clammy. Kurt could almost taste the electricity in the air, like a sharp razor flicking at his tongue. He shrugged irritably.

He watched Rogan ahead of him. Rogan, too, had pulled his parka hood over his face, but was now shoving it back up again. The gesture, the movement somehow angered Kurt. He sniffed the air, wondered idly how Rogan would take it if he suddenly cut loose with his piece and blew his head off. Kurt chuckled darkly to himself. Not very well, he thought. Not very well at all.

It was so nuke-blasted hot.

He took a bead on Rogan as he silently swore. Rogan's head filled the sight. Kurt dropped by a millimeter or so. Now the stupid clown's neck. A round in there at this distance would plunge through skin and tissue, shatter the cervical vertebrae, punch out the thyroid cartilage, send the whole head spinning off sideways. In his mind's eye he could clearly see it sailing through the snowflakes, blood spraying out from the torn underside.

Suddenly there was a flurry of movement in the sight, a yell of outrage exploding from the target. Kurt let the rifle down slowly as Rogan's own piece jerked up.

Rogan screamed, "What the hell you doin'?"

Kurt held his rifle loosely and grinned. "Thought I saw a movement."

"Where? On my head?" Rogan's face was red with fury.

"Yeah. Flea or something. Maybe a louse. Who knows?" Kurt was now impassive.

"What's with this stupe? He out of his mind?" McCandless glared at Rogan.

"Shut it. You want the whole mountain to hear you?"

"He was tryin' to kill me!"

Kurt said, "He's overreacting, McCandless. I think he's gone wacko."

Rogan took a step toward him, the rifle jabbing out. There was a crazed expression on his face. Kurt's own gun was raised again, aimed at Rogan's heart.

McCandless jumped forward, banged his left hand down on Rogan's rifle, clamped it tightly. He shoved the piece downward.

"Ya both crazy! Do I blast ya both?"

Kurt dropped his rifle and yawned deliberately.

"Dunno what's eating him. I was just sighting, that's all. Seems to me, McCandless, you want to keep an eye on your buddy or he's liable to do us all in."

"Listen...." Rogan's voice was thick with rage. One gloved hand jerked up, forefinger stabbing toward Kurt. "You listen to me...."

"*You* listen!" McCandless heaved himself at the man, swung him around. He now had his automatic pistol out and was jabbing it at Rogan's face, the muzzle inches from the man's left eye. "Shut it! Just shut it!" McCandless's eyes bugged and Kurt's hands tightened on his own piece. Any moment now, he thought, any moment...

"Hey!"

Reacher. Up front. Kurt's eyes shifted from the two men in front of him and refocused on the senser mutie up the trail. Reacher was standing beside a bend in the road, waving an arm, gesturing frantically. McCandless's grip on Rogan loosened. The .45 slowly dropped.

Reacher was shouting, "Round here. Quick."

McCandless lumbered up the road toward him, still gripping the pistol. Rogan shot Kurt a black look, then followed. On Kurt's face was a dark smile, the eyes narrowed, the lips a thin curved line. Kurt shivered slightly, then wiped an arm across his brow. He was still hot. He moved on up the road, keeping to the left side even though the wind had dropped and was no longer sweeping across in violent gusts.

At the bend he stopped. Reacher was now beside the precipice, pointing. Kurt stepped to his side and stared down.

"Caught sight of 'em," the mutie said. "I was backing away, thought McCandless and Rogan were going to go berserk. Then I'm on the edge and I look down."

"Yeah." Kurt gazed at what the flickering lightning revealed far down into the plunging abyss—heaps of twisted wreckage, rusty metal skeletons, parts scattered far and wide along the narrow rock bank of the raging river. Beside him, McCandless, on his knees, stared down, too.

"So that's where they ended up."

"Yeah." Kurt swung around, to look at the winding road. It narrowed, curved around the rock wall to the left. A blind corner. But there was no one, nothing, no hidden cave mouth from which might erupt a horde of shrieking muties.

He sniffed the air. A strong smell of ozone drifted into his nostrils, sharp and heady. He noticed that the lightning had become forked, crackling with blue-tinged flares, tiny explosions that added eeriness to the already strange lighting effect. The sweat was pouring off his brow and he wiped at it with his sleeve again, inhaling the strong fur smell as if to ward off that other alien and unnerving odor.

"I don't like this," he muttered, turning back to the abyss.

McCandless grunted as he got to his feet.

"They must've been blown off the road. The wind just lifted the whole pack of 'em, threw 'em down."

"Steam trucks?" Kurt raised an eyebrow.

"Sure," snapped McCandless. "It happens."

"All six of 'em?"

"It happens!" The big man scowled at the rusty wrecks far below. Then he glanced at Kurt warily. "How come you know so much about what kinda traction those guys had?"

"I remember when Dolfo Kaler went out. It was only a couple of decades back. I was a kid, but I remember it."

"Yeah?" McCandless's voice was thick with suspicion. "Sure. So what?"

"So nothing," growled McCandless, his eyes flicking back to the scene below. "See any stiffs?"

"Well, I guess they'd be picked bones by now." Kurt stared up at the towering peaks that soared above them, black and ominous. He gazed down again, noting the smoothness of the cliff face below, pierced here and there by tough-looking bushes that sprouted from unseen cracks and crevices.

"The acids would eat 'em up," Rogan put in, staring moodily downward.

"Ain't no acids round here," sneered McCandless. "Look at the rock, stupe. All round ya. Ain't eaten away. Smooth. Look at the road. Acids would tear all that up, dissolve the surface cover." He spat contemptuously into the sullen void below.

Kurt hitched his pack to loosen the straps. McCandless turned away from the brink of the precipice.

"Let's go. We gotta deal of trekkin' to do before we reach the top."

Rogan snarled at Kurt. "Don't you go pointin' that piece at me again, blaster. You hear me?"

Kurt did not bother to reply. He checked his gun, checked above, checked behind. He watched Reacher head toward the next bend, then moved on up the road himself, the ozone smell very strong in his nostrils now, an ugly, steely stink. He thought about the trucks and knew it would need a fantastic blast of wind to hurl them all over, all at once.

No wind, however fierce, had hurled them over into the abyss.

"McCandless!"

Kurt's head jerked up. Reacher was now at the bend, looking beyond it. His voice was not a yell but a hiss of alarm, incomprehension. There was tension there. Kurt began running. He passed both McCandless and Rogan, his gun held in both hands, his boots thudding on the road's hard surface. He reached the senser. He stared up beyond him at what lay ahead.

Fog.

A thick, sullen wall of it, gray-white, impenetrable. And huge. It blotted out the sky above them, loomed hideously high like an immense barrier across the road—a

barrier that seemed to be alive, for it quivered and heaved
gently. Thick tendrils stirred and inched out along the
road's surface at its lower edge, like questing fingers, then
retreated into the main mass. A dull, eerie glow emanated
from its heart, blue tinged, somberly highlighting the immediate area.

Kurt gazed at it, his mouth suddenly dry. His eyes automatically took in the fact that it only extended to just
beyond the edge of the precipice; there it seemed to fade
away to become tattered shreds of whiteness hanging in the
air. That somehow made it all the more unnatural, all the
more terrifying. It seemed to Kurt to be not at all atmos-
pherically created; not at all strange and random, in the
way that much of the weather in the Deathlands seemed
bizarrely random, in the way that here and now there was
snow, heat, wild winds, periods of sullen stillness.

He whispered, "The fog..."

A hand grasped his shoulder and tugged at it. He half
turned to face McCandless's glaring eyes.

"What the hell is this, Kurt? What the hell d'you know
about this?"

"I don't know what you're talking about. I don't know
anything."

"'The fog, the fog'!" mimicked the big man savagely.
"Ya knew this was waitin' for us. Ya knew it. How come,
huh? How come ya know so much about this? What else
ya got up ya sleeve, blaster?"

Kurt pulled himself away from the leader's grasp. He
snarled, "I tell you I don't know anything. Dolfo Kaler
talked about the fog, that's all."

"Dolfo Kaler was shot to shreds while he was still
crawlin' into town. Even I know that, Kurt."

McCandless's .45 automatic was in the big man's hands,
pointing at Kurt's face. McCandless held it two fisted,

unwaveringly, his face behind the gun a mad, glaring mask. Kurt's own gun was held right-handed; he knew he didn't have a hope of jerking it up in time to blow McCandless away before the big man had sent a magful into him.

"McCandless, I told you, I was a kid at the time. I was the kid that found him." The words came tumbling out of his mouth. "He was mumbling something about a fog. That's it. That's all. It didn't make sense then, doesn't make sense now. Except there it is, the fog. All we have to do is walk through it."

McCandless's eyes narrowed. Sweat coursed down his face. He lowered the automatic slowly, almost grudgingly. Kurt breathed out hard.

"That's it," he repeated, his voice hoarse.

"Don't look like no fog I ever saw," muttered Rogan. He shot a scowl at Kurt. "He knows somethin' else, boss, you bet."

"Shut it," snapped McCandless.

The big man moved slowly up the road toward the eddying wall. Above, lightning flickered fitfully.

"Don't smell like fog," sniffed McCandless. "Rogan, take a walk."

The tall, craggy man took a step forward, then hesitated and stayed where he was. He stared at the rippling, gray-white wall, his mouth open.

He said, "Hell, boss, send the blaster. Or the mutie."

"The blaster I need, the mutie I need. Get in there."

Rogan backed away. "I ain't goin' in there. You go."

McCandless exploded, "Ya piece of nukeshit, Rogan, *get in there!*"

Rogan was beside Reacher now. He suddenly grabbed the mutie senser and pushed him, flung him toward the fog. Reacher stumbled. He hit the road and rolled to one side, yelling. McCandless jumped at Rogan, huge gloved hands outstretched, but the tall man evaded him, swinging his rifle and savagely clubbing McCandless's face. The barrel's sight ripped at the big man's right eye, tearing into flesh. McCandless screamed and reeled away. He clutched his head.

Kurt thought, this is it.

He swung his ancient Armalite up but Rogan had danced away toward the senser, who was scrambling to his feet. Rogan's rifle roared twice, on single shot, the bullets slamming into Reacher as a freak gust of wind suddenly roared up the pass. Reacher was bowled over by the impact of the rounds hitting him. Muzzle-flash sparked from Rogan's piece again and with a wail of pain and terror, Reacher jackknifed and sailed backward over the edge of the abyss. His shriek died in the wind's howl.

Laughing crazily, Rogan backed away from Kurt, covering him. He backed toward the fog, seemingly oblivious of its presence. He backed toward a tendril that shimmied out to him like a groping finger.

It touched him.

There was a spark, a flash of angry blue light, and Rogan pitched forward into a somersault, yelling as he spun. He smacked into the road, whinnying in terror.

But he still held his gun.

Kurt sent a shot at him, the Armalite bucking in his hands, but the round ricocheted off rock into the howling, lightning-lit darkness. Before he could center on the tall man again, muzzle-flash flared and an invisible fist pounded at Kurt's shoulder, jolting him backward, cracking his head against the cliff face.

HE COULD FEEL NOTHING except the chill of the wind, a sudden cold wetness on his face. He opened his eyes and saw huge snowflakes whirling down again, driven by the wind. His shoulder throbbed and he stared at it, seeing nothing in the thick fur but knowing he had a bullet somewhere in his upper arm or chest. He found he'd lost his rifle. He was cold and hot at the same time, the sweat freezing on his face. He felt he could stay there forever, propped up against the rock. Focusing on the road, he registered that McCandless now had only one eye.

The big man was wrestling with Rogan, bare-handed, roaring like an angry bull. Rogan had a rock in one hand and was trying to smash it down on McCandless's unprotected head. Where the big man's right eye had been was a red mush that was streaked down his cheek and into his beard, runny with sweat and snow. He was roaring insanely, clawing at Rogan's face. Snowflakes, hard driven, blurred the scene and gave it the quality of nightmare. To Kurt, they seemed like shadow figures backlit by the lightning, their cries torn from them by the driving wind.

Rogan clubbed down with the rock, smacking it into McCandless's head. More blood. The big man staggered and fell to his knees. Both hands now clutched at his face. Rogan lifted the rock once more, then yelled in agony as McCandless head-butted him in the groin. Rogan lost hold of the rock to clutch at himself, his mouth wide, a soundless howl erupting from it.

He booted out at McCandless and rocked the big man backward. He followed this up with another savage, jolting kick. McCandless was on his back, clawing for and then wrenching out a knife. As Rogan grasped hold of the rock again, McCandless stabbed out at the other's nearest leg. The blade sank home; this time Kurt saw blood sluice out through the rent in Rogan's pants, just above the top of his boot. Rogan collapsed onto his adversary, smashing the rock down sickeningly. For a second they lay still,

Rogan atop McCandless, then Rogan pulled himself up into a straddling position, brought the rock down a second time onto McCandless's head. Then a third time. A fourth. Kurt could hear nothing, just the insane shriek of the gale, but he knew that labored gasps were heaved out of Rogan with every smashing blow as he pounded away at the big man.

McCandless lay unmoving. Rogan finally collapsed onto him. The two figures began to blur with the snow that thickly distributed itself across the scene, piling up, whipped into low drifts by the wind.

The fog still quivered and heaved as though alive, the blizzard not affecting it, the snow around it.

Kurt tried to get to his feet but he was still dazed by the crack to the back of his head. His boots slipped on the snow-slick ground; it was too much of an effort to do anything but lie there, go to sleep, drift off into eternity.

A sudden movement caught his eye: Rogan rolling off the body of the big man, staggering to his feet in a flurry of snow. Rogan was not steady on his feet, but this did not seem to worry him. He was cackling insanely.

Kurt watched as Rogan leaned forward and dragged at the snow-covered lump on the road. Snow came off McCandless in a small avalanche as Rogan shook him violently, like a dog with a rat. McCandless had no face, just a red ruin. The wind tore at it, rinsing it with snow, but nothing could wash all the blood away, nothing in the world could clean it up.

Rogan dragged the body to the edge of the precipice. The wind had died yet again. Crazy weather, muttered Kurt, dully watching the snowflakes die until there were just a few big ones tumbling silently down, floating gently out of the lightning-shredded blackness. He saw Rogan heave the dead meat that once had been a man over the edge. And now the bastard's coming for me for sure, he thought.

He watched Rogan limp across the snowy road toward him, watched him suddenly stoop, grab something. The Armalite. So that's where it had landed.

"Hey, blaster! Gonna blast ya!" Rogan seemed cheerful. "Maybe I oughta shoot ya around a little," he added, triggering a round.

Kurt heard the sharp crack of the shot, heard himself yell as it hammered into the rock inches from his face, showering him with rock shards as it whined away.

"You thought you was gonna grab it all!" yelled Rogan. "Ol' Rogan, he wasn't gonna get nothin'."

Again the rifle barrel flamed, again a round tore into the rock face, then careered off into the night.

What a way to die.

The mutie had been right, dead right. Death had been lurking only just around the corner. Their own deaths.

Then he noticed that the fog was on the move.

At first he thought his eyes were playing tricks. Perhaps it was just the effect of the fog's contraction-expansion motion, the breathing movement that made it seem alive. Then he realized the stuff was actually inching its way down the road, in bulk, the whole huge quaking gray-white mass sliding forward with a rippling motion, tendrils of the misty muck questing out along the blacktop.

"It's moving," he croaked.

"You stupe," crowed Rogan derisively. "You ain't gonna get nothin'. You hear me, blaster? Nothin'. All you're gonna get is a load of lead in your innards. Me, I'm gonna get what's up there, up the top of the mountain. All for me. No share-out. Especially no share-out with that prick McCandless. He thought he was the flaming emperor, but he ended up carcass. Just like you, Kurt. A carcass.'' He let out a wild, echoing guffaw.

Kurt watched as the advancing fog sent out its gray-white feelers toward the tall man. He couldn't figure it out at all, didn't know what in hell the stuff was, couldn't imagine its origin.

Something to do with the Nuke; something left over, maybe? That had to be it, had to be the answer. He chuckled to himself as he watched the foggy tentacles reaching out for Rogan, not at all blindly but purposefully, as though the very sound of the tall man's harsh, jeering voice constituted its target. Like thick cables, three tendrils snaked through the air to clutch Rogan's body and curl around it.

Sparks erupted fizzingly, half blinding Kurt. Rogan shrieked aloud. He writhed helplessly as though gripped by a giant's fist. He was wrapped in a huge amorphous cloud that solidified around him . . . then it snatched him up into the air.

Rogan was shrieking with shock and agony, still writhing in its clutch. He had been gathered up in some sort of twister. But this was no mere tornado that sucked objects up capriciously, then blew them all over the landscape. This thing had claws.

Fog devils . . . tear you apart . . .

A jolting, destructive, naked power lurked at the fog's heart. It had a mind of its own.

The tentacle that gripped Rogan swung high, long sparks crackling from it, playing around the struggling, yelling figure. Rogan was haloed in fire. With a last despairing shriek, the tall man disappeared into the center of a white wall.

The fog still advanced. Slowly. Inexorably.

Kurt's gloved fingers scrabbled at the rock for a firm handhold. He shoved himself forward and sideways, scrambling to his feet, staring at the advancing mass. More fog tendrils were extending out of it, groping in his direction, questing around. Kurt backed away from them, their acid stink almost overpowering him.

Lightning flared and crackled, revealing the mountaintops ranged all around him as grimly frowning peaks. Kurt glanced over his shoulder, back down the ruined road.

The wall of fog shifted onward relentlessly.

Kurt let out a mewing croak of terror, turned, one hand clutching at his shoulder where now blood seeped through the fur. He began to stagger like a drunken man down the rutted road, back toward the Deathlands.

Chapter Two

SAVAGE EYES WATCHED the line of lights that bobbed gently up and down in the far distance; preternaturally sensitive ears caught the dull roar and rumble of powerful engines. There was forward movement there, an onward surge. The lights were getting closer by the second.

The watcher had greenish skin that looked, at a distance, as if it were faintly scaled, though it was not. The scale effect was just that—an odd skin effect, something he could not wipe off, something he had to live with, some genetic eruption whose exact origin was unknown. It didn't bother him. He was known as Scale and that didn't bother him, either. Nothing bothered him. Mutation was a matter of complete acceptance among mutants; it was only norms who got twitchy.

He had overlarge eyes, black rimmed, deep hollowed. His mouth was wide and thick lipped. His nose was a slight bulge above the mouth, with two tiny orifices; his sense of smell was almost nonexistent.

He rose to his feet, snapped long slender fingers. Another figure, overtall and with very long arms, slipped from behind to hand him a pair of powerful glasses. The man with the faintly scaled skin took the glasses and put them to his eyes and adjusted them.

There were maybe fifteen vehicles in the convoy, including three big war wagons. The man nodded. The Trader. Only the Trader carried that amount of punch.

The Trader was a hard nut to crack. No one had ever managed to take him, though many had tried, both muties and norms. In many ways the Trader was the most powerful man in the land. He had hardware, high powered and deadly, and plenty of it; he had fuel supplies, secret and well hidden, known only to him and his captains, his closest and most trusted confidants; he had contacts, from the civilized East to the primitive West, from the suspicious North to the outright barbaric South. He dealt in weapons, a trade built up over twenty years or more. But he bartered and sold other merchandise, too: food, clothes, gadgets, fuel, generators, wisdom, knowledge. He even dispensed justice in the more outlying regions, in the tiny scattered hamlets hundreds of kilometers from the huge Baronies of the East and South.

He was trusted and he was fair, but he was no simp and his revenge could be devastating. All who knew of the Trader knew the tale of the Eastern town that had tried to mess with him, a town of low morals run by an ambitious madman. The exact nature of their mistake had been lost over the intervening years, but the outcome was retained in the memories of most who had dealings with him. The town had been destroyed, razed to the ground, wiped from the face of the earth. He had spared no one. Such had been his fury that he had massacred the inhabitants to a man, woman, child. And animal. He had not even spared the animals, had not taken them for himself but instead had slaughtered the herds and left the carcasses, and then moved on.

It was a lesson. You did not mess with the Trader.

Sure, there were other traders, men and women who traveled the Deathlands in convoy, bartering and haggling, stealing and slaving, picking up merchandise here, selling it there. But none of them traveled the Trader's routes, none had his expertise, and none had his nose for the hidden Stockpiles that the pre-Nuke military men had laid down more than a century before.

Those were the plums that everyone wanted to pick, the hidden man-made caverns scattered across the land, stuffed with hardware, fuel, weaponry; the secret silos that the governments of the day had ordered to be constructed against a time when the world might be in ruins and power shifted solely to those with the muscle and the guns to hold on to it. The irony was that the Nuke had been so devastating, so ferocious, so unbelievably swift that chains of command all over the world had been destroyed more or less at a stroke, and their secrets had been lost with them, lost for nearly a century.

Now they were being uncovered slowly, very slowly—secrets hidden from most of those who had inhabited the land once known as the United States.

And mostly they were being uncovered by the Trader, who traveled the land, north, south, east, west; who probed and poked and dug and excavated; who journeyed far into regions no man had trod for a century, regions no sane man wished to tread. It was said that the Trader had trekked deep into the heart of the fiery southwest where hurricane-force winds howled across a moonscape where nothing grew, no man lived. It was said that his land wagons had specially reinforced and adapted roofs because he journeyed deliberately into regions where the acids could strip a man to his bones in a second. It was rumored that he had even penetrated the mountains overlooking the bleak western coastal strip, had viewed like a conqueror of old the steaming lagoons, the long jagged fjords thrust deep between craggy peaks, and had sailed the simmering seas below which vast cities lay crumbling and rotting as they slept an eternal sleep.

All this was said; much of it was true. And the proof was the hardware, the strange and incomprehensible artifacts, the sealed crates of exotic foodstuffs he brought back time and again after each trawl through the Deathlands.

The man called Scale handed the glasses back to his companion. He gazed up at the dark sky broodingly, calculating that there was an hour to dawn. No hint of a smile crossed his face, but his dead eyes had come alive.

He said, "Trader."

Not "a trader," noted the man with the very long arms.

"We take him?"

"Sure."

"We take the Trader?" The long-armed man was dubious.

"Sure."

The man thought about this, staring at the line of lights wobbling far away. It seemed to him that Scale was about to bite off more than he could chew. It seemed to him that Scale was in danger of choking himself to death.

"He's heavy."

"So are we."

"Not like him."

Scale shrugged.

"We hit him in the dark. Three war wags. Front, middle, rear. Can't turn in the pass—too narrow. So go for them and hit 'em hard. We got the muscle. We disable the middle so it blocks the road. Rear trucks can't go forward, front can't go back. We hit both ends, simultaneous. Ain't got a prayer."

The man with the long arms pondered this. In principle it sounded good, the perfect ambush. But—the Trader? He bit his lower lip with three sharp, filed-down teeth, the only ones in his mouth.

"He got muscle. Plenty muscle."

"Sure. So have we."

"Not like him."

"We do it."

The long-armed man turned to stare down into the darkness cloaking the patiently waiting band of men below.

"Hellblast, Scale, we already got us a catch. Two land wags, truckin' out to the Darks."

The man with the faintly scaled skin shook his head irritably.

"Ain't enough. Any case, it's the ammo. Trader, he's got plenty ammo, plenty guns. Big mothers."

"Plenty men, too," the long-armed man pointed out.

"Nah. He travels light, from what I hear. Lot of big wind about his manpower. These days, he travel light."

"Where'd you hear that?"

"Fat Harry. Last time there. Said the Trader was gettin' to be an old man, thinkin' of quittin'." He chuckled suddenly, a dry, sour sound. "We'll hurry it along. Quit the fucker ourselves."

"I dunno, Scale. The Trader." The man shook his head glumly.

"Don't forget," said Scale, "what we got."

"We ain't got nothin'."

This time the man with the faintly scaled skin laughed aloud, his eyes wide and crazy.

"We got the stickies, idiot! We got the stickies."

IN THE LEAD WAR WAGON, in a small toilet cubicle to the rear, the Trader was being sick. He knelt on the swaying floor, gripping the sides of the aluminum bowl, and heaved four or five times, finally slumping back on his heels against the wall of the cubicle. He was sweating. He wiped his brow with a rag, then wiped his lips, carefully, almost delicately. The noise of the war wag's powerful engine thundered in his ears and he was glad of it. It meant no one could hear him or what he was doing. He clambered to his feet, a powerfully built man with stiff, grizzled hair, and stared down at the contents of the bowl dispassionately. He knew exactly what to expect.

Blood. But this time more of it than ever. Almost looked as if he was hawking his whole nukeshitting guts up.

Hanging over the can was a mirror that bounced gently, clacking with every bump and lurch of the vehicle's wheels and tracks over the rutted road. The Trader stared at himself thoughtfully, a face he saw every day of every week of every month of every year. But older, definitely older. Much older than yesterday, a hell of a sight older than last week. White, too. Unhealthy looking. Once his face used to be red-brown, vigorous, alive. He breathed out slowly, then kicked the flush pedal beside the bowl. The hell with it.

He reached up and opened a small cabinet fixed to the wall. Inside were shelves of bottles and jars. His eyes took in the various colors, considered the positions of each container. As he could neither read nor write, it was the only way he could distinguish their contents.

He took down a bottle of green liquid, uncapped it, wiped the neck with his rag, took a long swig. He shook his head, washing the stuff around his mouth, then threw his head back and gargled noisily. The bellow of the engine drowned all sounds. He spat into the small hand-basin beside the closed gunport and twisted the tap, and water from the tank in the roof washed the green liquid away.

He put the bottle back and lit a cigar. That would take the smell of peppermint away, right enough. The Trader chuckled, forgetting for a second the terrible ache in his guts as the thought hit him that the mouthwash, plus the other bottles of the same stuff from the same cache, was probably the only mouthwash within a few hundred thousand kilometers of him. Weird stuff. Stuff that had been stored deep down someplace, freak material survivors of fire and ice, and often to be found in huge amounts, "factory fresh" it sometimes said on the labels. There weren't many of these finds, but there were some, and they were mighty strange in their bright packaging and their huge quantities. Such caches were usually buried deep under rubble, and if it was a huge, sparkling supply of mouthwash that you found after all that digging, you were more than likely to think it not worth the effort. Except the Trader. He liked the stuff. He liked the joke inherent in luxury products suddenly found in quantities far out of all proportion to their usefulness.

He slapped at his face, his cheeks, hard, to get some color back, breathing in sharply, squaring his shoulders. He took a long pull at his moldy old cigar and let the smoke drool out of his mouth. Then he pulled open the door.

The Trader moved fast down the narrow passageway outside. On his right was a machine-gun blister, occupied by a dark-skinned youth who briefly nodded to him before letting his eyes flick back to the port above the gun and to the rushing darkness outside the bulletproof glass.

The Trader, cigar firmly clamped between uneven yellowed teeth, walked on, climbed some steps, pulled himself into the main cabin area of the vehicle.

It had once been a mobile army command post—long, long ago, back when there'd been an army to command. It had been his very first acquisition, maybe a score and a half years ago. He and Marsh Folsom had discovered it while escaping from a bunch of cannies in the Apps, or the Applayshuns as some old folks insisted on calling them. A rockslide, old, maybe triggered originally by Nuke tremors, had uncovered a vast man-made cavern, reaching deep into the heart of the thickly wooded slopes. Inside was Golconda. That was what Marsh, a man who'd read books, had said as they'd stared in awe at the rows and rows of parked vehicles, all kinds, all types, that stretched away from them into the gloom. The MCP had been the nearest, a huge mother, though not as huge as she was now.

Over the years the Trader had added to it, fixing gun ports here, rocket pods there, machine-gun blisters everywhere. His engineers—once he'd started up in business, recruited reliable men, using the Applayshun cavern as his main HQ—had fixed pierced-steel planking double thickness all around it, modified the interior and rewired it to his specifications, adapted and strengthened it. It was now a death-dealing juggernaut, capable of considerable speed on the flat, with retractable tracks for the rough terrain over which it surged with incredible vitality for its bulk. It was also the flagship of the Trader's fleet of war wags, land wags, trucks, powered vehicles and personnel carriers.

The Barons of the East had their ramshackle armies, their trucks, their matériel, their war wags. But it was pretty much penny-ante stuff, and in any case most of it had been supplied by the Trader directly, and although he could not stop—not that he wanted to—the slow march of a manufacturing industry that had started in a small way a generation back—the crude electrification of small plants in certain places, mostly based on the utilization of hundred-year-old equipment that had survived; knowledge gained from old manuals and handed-down memories and skills—he could still see to it that he, and he alone, controlled the heavy hardware that had been salted away so many years before. He still had his secrets, though there were many who plotted and schemed in smoke-filled rooms to wrest them from him, many who saw him as the ultimate block to their own acquisition of power.

The Trader's philosophy had changed through the years. At first he'd sold, bartered and traded damned near anything and everything he could lay his hands on, for gold, coin and creds. His success was due solely to his own natural vigor and energy and the smartness of Marsh Folsom, who could read and write and because of this could go some way to deciphering some of the meager clues they had found in the original Apps caverns and other Stockpiles.

Folsom knew from his reading that the old-timers used incredibly complex pieces of machinery called computers, and he figured that much of the paperwork they had found in the Stockpiles had a lot to do with those things, but unless you had been trained how to use them there was no way you could crack the code. Although both he and the Trader had actually seen these computer machines in their travels around the Deathlands—mostly wrecked, unsalvageable, though there'd been some that had appeared intact—you also needed power, a lot of power, to turn the blasted things on. And even if you could somehow work it, Folsom knew they'd still be useless because no one could comprehend how to handle them. A live machine you didn't understand was as redundant as a dead one you did. Maybe more so.

Still, they'd persevered. Folsom had followed up clues on military maps, had pinpointed locations, areas of possibility. The Trader had gone out to those locations and dug around, sometimes hitting pay dirt, more often than not drawing one big fat zero. The percentage against them over the years was depressingly high. In every ten tries, maybe one was on target.

Their second major find had been a sea of gas in vast containers hidden below the peaks of the mountain range that stretched toward the cold zone to the north, maybe two hundred kilometers beyond the ruins of Boston. It had been a bitch to transport shipments of it the enormous distance back to the Applayshuns through rugged and dangerous terrain, frequently fighting a running battle with muties, mannies, cannies—the muties with pre-cog powers even more eerie than the doomies'—and sheerly vicious norms who attacked from crazed blood lust alone. But out of that terrifying odyssey had grown the Trader's band, for although Folsom played around with his maps and files, the Trader recognized the more immediate need for satellite recruitment, a nucleus of hardcase guards and blasters who would fall in with his ideas, obey orders, keep their mouths shut tight.

That had taken time. You couldn't simply grab the first guys who came along. The Trader wanted—needed—integrity in his followers: fearlessness, nerve, a resolute loyalty and maybe something approaching devotion. And once he'd got what he wanted, or as nearly as he decided he was ever going to get, he ran a tight ship.

You wanted creds? You worked for them. You wanted a life that, hard as it might be, was a hell of a sight easier than that experienced by the vast majority of the Deathlands dwellers? You had to earn it. You wanted sex? You either got yourself a solid partner, or you paid for it. It was readily available; there were plenty of burgs in the Death-lands that were simply open brothels. What you did not do, however, was grab it any old damned where. You did not use force. You did not kill to get it. Anybody who did, and was caught, faced summary execution, no reprieve. It was one of the Trader's iron rules. Even when he'd destroyed Cooperville, there'd been no rape.

It was one of the things that had bolstered his rep, given him the key to all those small towns that were tight little enclaves, well defended, well manned—all those small towns with their strong guard units who turned away other, lesser, traders who were not so choosy in the way they conducted their business; who were, when you got down to it, little more than marauding bands of killers and cutthroats, looters and pillagers. That was not, and never had been, the Trader's way, and most recognized this in the Deathlands, and welcomed him with open arms instead of gun barrels.

Still, his methods had changed over the years. Whereas before he'd been willing to get shot of all he came across for the best price he could find, now he held back on much he discovered in his foraging trips. In his early days he'd let too many guys have too much hardware, too much high-powered hardware, and it seemed to him now that such a practice had been not merely unwise but an outright disaster whose hideous ramifications lingered with him still. He had come to realize that unwittingly, thoughtlessly—greedily—he had armed groups whose aims were by no means altruistic, whose ideas were in fact solely concentrated on power for its own sake.

As the years had gone by the Trader had brooded long on the guns problem and had still come up with no firm solution. You had to have weapons to defend yourself. In an ordered world, maybe, you relied on those forces you yourself set up to guard your rights and liberties, hold the peace, defend the weak against the strong. And even then, even in the most orderly society there might ever have been, there would still be those who secretly sought evil and who therefore preyed on the less fortunate.

And what if those who carried the weapons, those whom you'd set up, turned against you, were corrupted by the very power you had bestowed upon them? It happened. It always happened. Marsh Folsom, who knew about these things, had said it had happened all the time, throughout recorded history.

Because the trouble was that for some people power was a heady drug. The more they had, the more they wanted. It was that simple.

And yet it seemed to the Trader, thinking about such things, arguing the problem out with his captains through the long watches of the night, over many years, that though in a sense he'd been dead wrong to let loose all that vicious ordnance he'd discovered, in a sense he'd been dead right.

There was no denying that he had armed certain communities, deep in the wilder reaches of the Deathlands, that, because of him, had stayed intact and had flourished when by all rights they ought to have gone under, been ravaged by the fireblasting drivers and muties and crazies who roamed the land. At least with weapons they'd stood a chance.

The fact was, whichever way you cut it, a weaponless burg didn't have a hope. Not now. Not in these wild times. The Trader has seen what could happen to such communities too often to deny this. There had been many towns, mostly of a strong religious persuasion of one kind or another, that had denounced violence, renounced weaponry; that had proclaimed a new era of peace and harmony following the Apocalypse. All had fallen prey to the men of violence who had renounced nothing. Sometimes they had merely been invaded, enslaved. Sometimes, dreadfully, serfdom had been the least of their woes.

The Trader acknowledged to himself and to those closest to him that the blame for many of these atrocities had to find its way back to him. He sometimes wondered how in hell what passed for civilization these days had managed to make it through the past hundred years or so, not only through the Cold, which by all accounts had been grim enough, but beyond, when folks had started crawling out of their holes to grab what was left after the collapse.

It was true that the Nuke had not destroyed everything, and it was equally true that somehow thousands had managed to make it through those long years when it was said that the sun had died. From what the Trader had heard from that generation, it was a time of horror and a time of terror, and in many ways it had gotten worse when, especially in the East, the seasons had slowly begun to return and people had started to drag themselves into the daylight of a new and terrifyingly transformed world.

But having acknowledged his culpability in the matter of trading in the kind of materials that might better have been left undiscovered, he nevertheless felt that in some small way he had also been able to lift people back onto their feet again by rediscovering creation. For in these strange and secret Stockpiles were generators, survival equipment, processed food that could last for centuries if necessary, tools, fuel, the means to learn, the means to expand, the means to grow. All this, too, the Trader had hauled around the Deathlands, leaving communities better equipped to battle with the ever-looming dark that still threatened to overwhelm what was left.

And whereas before he'd been greedy, careless in his dealings, now he was more scrupulous, more circumspect. Now there were things he discovered, then swiftly reburied. He still broke out in a sweat when he recalled the time, five or six years before, when Ryan and Dix had followed up a lead left by Marsh Folsom and found, buried in the hills of what had once been a place called Kentucky, an immense collection of sealed airtight drums, tens of thousands of them, all neatly tabbed and docketed, all with that deadly and unmistakable symbol stamped into their casings.

The juice they called nerve gas. Hundreds of thousands of liters of it.

The same kind of shit that had rained down during the Nuke, from both sides, leaving an appalling legacy behind it, a legacy that still lingered and would still linger for decades, maybe generations, far into the bleak future.

They'd closed down the cavern, the Trader and Ryan and Dix, buried the entrance under a controlled landslip, destroyed all the paperwork that had led Marsh Folsom into pinpointing the area as a Stockpile possibility in the first place, and hoped for the best. It was all you could do, but it still gave the Trader nightmares when he slept, still gave him the shakes when he awoke.

Because there was always the outside chance that some other guy might just fall over it, even buried as it was…somehow, sometime. There was always that chance. Some guy by no means as scrupulous, some guy who might well figure out a way actually of using it, of bringing even more horror to a world already stuffed with horror up to the gullet.

There were times when the Trader felt burdened with the immense weight of secrets he had uncovered, the vast power he had but could not use, the huge guilt load he—

and he alone now that Marsh Folsom had gone—inescapably carried.

Sure, he had Ryan and Dix. The situation was tight with them as with no one else he could think of. But they had only arrived in the past ten years. Less. They had not been with him since the beginning, all those years ago. The weight they carried was lighter by far than the tremendous and often crushing burden that seemed at times ready to pulverize his soul.

And now the blood. That was a new and special weight on him because, apart from anything else, it put a horizon to his life . . . a horizon that he was inevitably getting closer to by the month. By the day.

By the hour.

He sucked at the cigar, took it out of his mouth, blew smoke into the air. His head buzzed, his arms and legs felt as though they'd been fashioned out of lead. He felt old. He felt he knew what it must be like to be 110.

He was only fifty-three.

"You okay?"

"Sure I'm okay. Can't a feller take a crap once in a while?"

The Trader glared at his war captain as he strode across the wide cabin. Raven-haired, the young man called Ryan Cawdor stood just over six feet in his boots yet seemed far taller. The Trader had known instantly, the first time he'd seen Ryan, that here was a man he could not only entrust with his life, but one who could inspire trust in others, a man for whom other men might well lay down their own lives.

That was a dangerous power to own, and there was no denying that Ryan could be a dangerous man. Rangy, limber, yet powerfully muscled, with that shock of thick night-dark curly hair, that single eye, intensely, chillingly blue, able to penetrate to the very core of a man's being, and the long scar slash from corner of eye to corner of mouth that no amount of sunlight could burn brown and that at times of stress and fury seemed almost to glow with a livid fire—this man was a fierce and relentless war captain. Yet that was by no means the whole story, as the Trader well knew, for Ryan was no mindless human bludgeon intent on berserk savagery to gain a particular goal, but a cunning, wily fighter, a realist, a pragmatist who would battle against all odds, yet knew to the instant when to retire in good order, when to conserve his forces.

The circumstances of their first meeting had not been auspicious. It was hard to think about trusting a person when that person had a heavy-caliber automatic jammed into the back of your skull and was whispering in your ear that one stupid move would bring about instant dissolution of the brain pan.

At the time the Trader had been sitting at the wheel of his personal war buggy, and in fact just five seconds before had unlocked it and climbed in after checking that all the locks were secure and no one had been tampering with them.

So much for security. So much for the antipersonnel device that ought instantly to have taken the arm off any guy who so much as touched the outside of the damned door.

But Ryan was good with locks—although even he now acknowledged the superiority of J. B. Dix when it came to the lock-picker's art. It was one of Ryan's finer points, the ability, if a guy was more skillful than he, to recognize the fact and admit it. And also, of course, he was on the run. These elements combined meant that the Trader's supersecure and seemingly impregnable war buggy was easy meat.

The Trader had been finishing some business in one of the then typical roaring towns in the center of the Deathlands—not that the situation had changed much in a decade; there was still an abundance of such pest holes scattered about the land—and he had been only too willing to put his foot down when ordered and, in the muttered words of the unseen man crouching behind him, "Get the hell out" fast. The land wag train had been waiting for him and ready to go a couple of klicks out of town. This was clearly no surprise to the stranger, who had chosen his getaway vehicle with great care.

And when they'd both climbed out of the vehicle and the Trader had turned and gazed at the man who was still covering him, he'd made his mind up on the instant. Had known with complete and utter certainty that this was the guy he wanted, the guy he'd been unconsciously searching for for years. With the automatic still pointed unwaveringly at him, at a point just below his heart for maximum incapacitation without, quite, the finality of instant death, he had offered the unknown man a place in his organization. The unknown man, just as swiftly, had shrugged his shoulders, holstered the shooter and accepted.

He called himself Ryan, but had offered nothing else about himself—not his background, close kin, place of origin, taste in women: nothing. In particular, he had not explained why he was on the run or who he was running from. It had taken the Trader some time—about five blasted years—to piece a pattern together, put Ryan into some kind of context. Even now there were blank pages, areas where information was not so much sketchy as entirely absent. But at least he had come to know who Ryan was and why he had landed up in the Deathlands as a runner, an outcast. At least he now knew why the guy refused trips to certain of the Eastern Baronies, why he never spoke about his past, why at times he never spoke, period.

Why he lacked an eye.

It was difficult for the Trader to identify why he had trusted Ryan on sight, and it was especially difficult—almost impossible, in fact—to sustain that trust when he discovered who Ryan really was and what he had done, or at least what he was supposed to have done. That was so grisly a crime, so appalling, so outright wicked an act of sheer malevolence and evil that even by the pretty abysmal standards of what passed for civilization in the late twenty-first century, it had hit an all-time low.

A man who did that wasn't fit to live.

And yet, and yet . . .

Instinct—his prime, and priceless, asset: worth more to him than all the jack, all the spare change in the known world because it had never yet let him down—told the Trader that this was a man of probity, a man of honesty and integrity, a man of high courage who would never stoop to a mean act or betray a trust.

And so it had proved. From day one of their now-decade-long association, the Trader had not regretted taking the guy on, not for a second. He'd had moments of doubt, one or two—such as when he'd fitted that highly significant, not to say shocking, piece into the jigsaw that portrayed the man's past—but they'd not lasted long. The Trader had backed his instinct and, as far as he was concerned, once again it had not betrayed him.

The war wagon bucked violently and lurched to one side, then righted itself under the skillful hands of its driver, Ches. Things slid off shelves, clattered to the metal-plated floor. Cohn, the radioman, who also handled the navigation, muttered a curse and bent to retrieve protractors, pencils, a steel rule.

J. B. Dix, seated in the co-driver's swivel chair, smoking a long thin black cheroot that looked as unappetizing as the Trader's cigar, half turned to stare impassively back at his chief.

"You want to complain about this road, boss. It's a disgrace."

Despite the gnawing fire in his stomach, the Trader chuckled.

"Teague's territory, J.B. Or what he claims is his. Road care's a low priority around here. He's got other things to occupy his mind."

"Or what passes for his mind."

"Yeah, like how to dig up more of the yellow stuff at less cost," Ryan said. "Or no cost at all."

Dix lifted an eyebrow and Ryan nodded at the unspoken question.

"Slaving."

"He's getting to be a big man. Gotta lotta boot," muttered Dix.

"Come a long way," agreed Ryan.

J. B. Dix sucked on his crudely rolled cheroot. He was the Trader's main lieutenant, known as the Weapons Master. Whereas the Trader was merely a businessman, it was Dix who had the knowledge of weaponry, booby-traps and so on. A thin, intense, bespectacled man with a receding hairline, a penchant for thin black cheroots, a fast but very devious mind and a terse, monosyllabic conversational style, it was Dix the Weapons Master's destiny to become a close personal ally of Ryan's.

The war wag's engine bellowed throatily as Ches took her up the dial. In front of him, across the front of the cab and below the narrow, bulletproof see-through windshield was a bewildering array of screens and dials, button sets and circuit breakers. Not many of these were in use. Originally all, including the huge vehicle's weaponry, had been linked to a central control computer, but as no one had ever been able to figure out how it worked, the Trader's mechs had ripped the guts out of everything and started over. Only the fascia remained, to confuse any hijacker who through some incredible stroke of good fortune might manage to get inside the war wag's cabin.

"The way I see it," said Ryan softly, "he's come a damned sight too far." He stared accusingly at the Trader.

"We've been through this a thousand times, Ryan. My word is my bond. You ought to know that by now. It's the only reason I've stayed in business. Two years ago I took Teague's hand and promised him a fat delivery. That's what we have here, and I can't back out. Fireblast it, man!" he suddenly exploded, "you know damned well I've pulled back on everything! He wanted twenty cases of auto-rifles. He's getting eight. He wanted fifteen boxes of grenades. He's getting six, and those are stun not frag, and he knows we know the difference. I've pared the whole consignment to the bone and he's not going to be happy."

"Too bad. The guy's a leech. He's getting more greedy and more dirty by the hour. He'll screw us if he thinks he can and the way things are, that's exactly what's going to happen."

"I know that," barked the Trader. "I know all about Jordan Teague. Hell, I traded stuff with the son of a bitch from the very first cache, twenty-five years ago." He took a pull at the cigar, coughed a little. "Or thereabouts. He was a rat then and he's a rat now. I know it. But I shook his hand. The deal goes through."

The Trader swung around and glared at no one in particular. Dix was staring at the radiant ribbon of road, picked out by the twin spotlights located high above the cab, protected by wire mesh against a sniper's bullets.

Darkness clung to the light's penumbra. The highway unwound before them, potholed and rutted.

Ryan leaned against the steel ladder that led up to the MG-blister built into the roof of the cabin. He shrugged, glanced at Cohn.

"How long?"

Cohn said, "'Bout a half hour to dawn. Hills ahead. The road goes up. That'll slow us. Pass through the hills, and beyond that, maybe two hours to Mocsin."

The Trader said, "We stop five klicks out. Take this one and the two big trucks in. If I know Teague, we'll have to wait a day before the bastard'll see us."

"He's getting fancy as well as greedy."

"He's a rich man, Ryan. He knew folks'd come back to gold, knew it'd be in demand someday. So he created the demand, he hurried things along. Smart businessman."

"And prime shit."

"Sure." The Trader grinned suddenly, his face a waxy pallor. "Like every businessman since the world began, or so I'm told. Like me."

Cohn snickered. He checked his pocket watch, reached out a hand and flicked a switch in front of him. Atmospherics crackled loudly, then died. Cohn leaned across the table and began checking out the rest of the convoy.

Ryan walked to the rear of the cabin. There was a passageway that led to the armory, the bunk rooms, the kitchen facility. Over the roar of the engines he could hear Loz, the cook, bawling some piratical song or other as he prepared breakfast. To his left were steps leading down to the toilet. He stared down the short shaft up which the Trader has so recently emerged jauntily, waving his cigar. He could still smell the fumes trapped down there, the fumes that, on the Trader himself, powerful as they were, had not quite hidden the even more powerful smell of peppermint.

The Trader was dying.

Ryan knew the Trader was dying. J.B. agreed with him. Both men—war captain and weapons master—had made a compact to say nothing to anyone else, least of all to the Trader himself. The Trader was a proud man; he refused to admit to any physical weakness or debility, and death was the ultimate, final debility.

Ryan had noted the evidence: the racking, lung-shredding cough in the mornings, the sickness he thought no one knew about, the grayness of face, splashes of blood he'd not noticed. It all added up. The disease was eating the Trader up and it was getting worse, heading inexorably toward the final dreadful extremity.

And although there were medicos back in the Apps, the old bastard refused to see them, under any circumstances. Didn't trust them. He'd had a kid brother who had been shot up in the legs years back and had been put to the knife. But the doc had bungled. The kid had gotten gangrene, had died in terrible agony, rotting away before the Trader's eyes. Since then, forget it—no quacks.

Ryan didn't know what to do. For once in his life he felt helpless, useless. The Trader had taken him in, had given him back something he thought he'd lost forever, and now, when the Trader needed help desperately, there was no way of giving it to him.

Ryan went down the steps, clinging to the rail as the big war wag lurched. Crouching in his gun port, the dark-faced kid called Ell glanced around at him as he approached and shook his head.

"Nothing. This is an easy one, Ryan. No problems."

Ryan's mouth twisted slightly.

"Don't put the hoodoo on us, kid. We're not there yet. These hills we're entering..." He made a thumbs-down gesture. "Bad muties. Full of them."

"They won't bother us. Ain't no marauders got half what we got. We could cream 'em up."

"Hasn't stopped others from trying."

Ryan stared bleakly out of the gun port. It was still dark, but dawn raced up behind them. And Mocsin was getting closer by the minute. His mouth twisted up again as he thought of the gross figure of Jordan Teague, self-proclaimed Baron of these territories. Ryan hated the thought that they were carrying arms to him, but he acknowledged that the Trader was right: you kept your word even to scum, unless they really crossed you. If you began breaking your word, folks'd start getting edgy with you, even if they knew all the circumstances. If you broke your word once you could do it twice.

Trouble was, that fat bastard Teague was probably buying guns from other traders, was probably building up an awesome armory. Rumor was strong, too, that in the past couple of years Mocsin had become a hellhole, a dirty beacon that beckoned only the most viciously depraved of men, rad-rats, cannibals, barely human creatures who because of their terrible mutations and deformities had been squeezed dry of any kind of humanity whatsoever.

It sounded to Ryan as if Jordan Teague was gathering muscle for some grim purpose, and the more you traded stuff to the guy the more quickly that purpose would be achieved.

He said, "You keep your eyes wide open, kid. First moving shadow you see, hit it. Hit it hard. Take no chances."

He turned abruptly. He moved back toward the steps and began mounting them. And froze as he caught the sudden shrill squawk from the radio in the cabin above, the glitz of atmospherics, the harsh yell of shock that cracked across the airwaves.

Even as he vaulted up the last remaining steps, the alarm started howling and he heard the Trader shouting, *"Brake!"*

Ryan slammed across the cabin, reaching up for and grabbing his automatic rifle as he did so, flicking the selector to three-shot and slinging it as he reached the driver's area, clutching the back of Dix's chair as the huge vehicle lost its forward motion.

Cohn was gabbling into his mike, men were tumbling down from the upper chambers and Ryan could hear the thud of boots behind him as more men disgorged from the bunk rooms, the jittery MG-like rattle of rifle checks and mag slams.

"Teague?" he snapped.

"Who knows. Doubtful. Muties, more like." The Trader was ramming a mag up into a battered-looking Armalite rifle as he spat the words out, his face drawn, his eyes flickering around the cabin.

Ryan stared forward. The road ahead, seen through the narrow windshield, was empty of movement—human movement; otherwise, it was alive with tracer streams from the cabin-roof machine gun as the gunner sent firelines exploding up and down the potholed surface, hammering into the rocks that loomed all about.

They were still moving slowly forward, but then Cohn said tensely, glancing around from the radio, "She's out of it. Maybe immobilized."

"Tell 'em to hold on." The Trader gestured to Ches. "Close down." He turned to Ryan. "Number Four truck. Blown, that's what's happened. Land mine maybe. The rear end, I understand. Now they can't move, and neither can the rest of the train. Can't pass 'em, either. Too damned narrow.''

Ryan sprang up the steel ladder into the MG-blister, squeezed himself up behind the gunner's chair. O'Mara, the gunner, was training around, weaving short-burst tracer patterns up and down the road and across, kicking up dust and blacktop chunks, then easing himself back to angle high into the rocks each side. Ryan stared back along the war wag's roof, saw the convoy as a drunken line of lights stretching away and down, those vehicles at the rear still moving slowly, closing up. Three vehicles back from the war wag, fire could be seen, not strong, a dull red glow that flickered feebly against the bright spot shafts from the cab-mounted searchlights on each land wag and truck. But Ryan could see nothing else. No movement, no human presence. No sudden and erratic stabs of red muzzle-flash. He turned to stare frontward again. The road was picked clean for yards ahead, empty of anything.

He said, ''Cool it. Don't waste ammo.''

He scrambled down the ladder and strode to the radio op.

''What gives?''

Cohn shrugged, puzzled.

''No alarms. Just Number Four's blown. Lost all traction. Everyone else is saying no problems. Four's starting to burn but they reckon they can contain it. They'll have to step outside. I'll tell—''

''No. Wait.''

''Hell, Ryan. S'just an old land mine is all. Coulda been there since the Nuke. Been waiting for years. Or maybe fell off a land wag, I dunno. Into a chuckhole. That dink McManus just happened to steer his truck right atop it. Wham!'' Cohn stared up at him. ''Number Four's gonna burn up unless they get outside to it, and—'' he gestured at a clipboard of papers by his side "—she's got bang-bangs on her."

"Wait!"

Cohn shrugged and went back to his mike as the tall man swung away. Ryan didn't like the explanation about a land mine waiting all that long a time before deciding to blow. It was perfectly possible, but he didn't like it. This pass was too damned narrow. It should have blown years ago. There must have been a hundred vehicles of one kind or another traveling this stretch over the past century. This was the main trekline to Mocsin. It ought to have been triggered before.

Nor did he like the idea that a mine had fallen off a truck grinding up this wrecked road in the recent past. Because if it had simply bounced off somehow, it wouldn't have been primed and ready. In any case, landies were too expensive, too valuable, to leave on a truck where they could pitch over the side or off the back.

"Still nothing?" he said.

Cohn said, "Still tight. 'Cept for Number Four. They're getting a mite twitchy, Ryan."

"Tell 'em to hold on."

There were six exit points on the war wag. One, a hatch to the roof; one at the rear, presided over by two MGs; two toward the rear, one each side, above the back portions of the port and starboard rocket tubes; an escape hatch below the driver's chair, very tight, very secure; and one that opened out, portside, opposite though back from the radio table.

Ryan knew without needing to check that now all four main doors were surrounded on the inside by weaponed-up men, ready to sell their lives dearly, five-man squads for each. Nor did he need to check whether all of these doors were primed, for he knew that Ches would automatically have triggered the internal locks electrically as soon as the alarm, now silent, had started yowling over the sound system. That killed the carefully engineered boobies set into the locks themselves. But still no one could simply open up from outside and walk in—door control was on the inside.

The Trader was seated in Dix's chair, ready to take over if Ches caught it somehow. Dix was at the rear, in command there. Two runners were ready, two kids in their late teens, positioned one each end of the long vehicle, in case radio contact died on them or was knocked out. And above, another man had gone to join O'Mara, with a signal lamp. And in each of the massive war wags it would be the same: men jumping to their places smoothly, fluidly, without thinking about it for a second.

Here the five-man squad was flung out around the cabin area: one crouched in the well that dropped to the head, an MG trained at the door; two men in the passageway leading to the bunk-rooms, one lying on the floor, the other flattened against the wall angle; one man beside the radio table, auto-rifle fixed on a point about a foot above the bottom of the door itself; the fifth behind the door, the first to fire, ready to jump into the opening and pour steel-jacketed death into the night. Cohn crouched over his wall transceiver, whispering at it, uncomfortably aware as always that he would be literally a sitting target once the door was open.

Ryan killed the lights, turning the large cabin into a place of shadows weirdly lit by the driver-control lights and lamps in the bunk-room corridor. He pressed two buttons on a small console beside the door, flicked two long bolts, twisted at the handle with his left hand while stabbing a finger at another button on the panel. A small bulb in the panel remained dark.

"External lights've gone, or been blown. This could be it."

He shoved the door open with his boot and sprang back, to be greeted by darkness outside, darkness that was not night darkness but deep dawn-gray. As his eyes became accustomed to the near absence of light he could just make out a jumble of rocks near the edge of the road where nothing moved. His auto-rifle was held two handed, trigger ready. Adrenaline was boosting into his bloodstream. He could hear nothing. Every vehicle in his land wag train had rolled to a halt.

Then he glanced down. He saw the hand, long fingered and bony, appear as though by magic at the bottom of the doorway, something clutched in it. The hand jerked, unclenched, disappeared. A steel ball clattered fast across the floor toward him.

Without conscious thought, he reacted so his right boot hit the object on the bounce, sent it sailing back out into the night again, his right finger squeezing off two 3-round bursts of automatic fire that angrily highlighted the face of the man flattened against the wall beside the door. The he was diving to his right and screaming, *"They're under us!"*

His yell was lost in the cracking blast of the grenade as it ripped itself apart among the boulders, sending steel shards and bits of rock whistling in through the door.

Ryan rolled, shot to his feet almost in one fluid movement and lunged at the doorway, his rifle flicked to full automatic and spewing rounds, hot brass clattering against the steel wall nearest him. As he reached the doorway, two shadowy figures vaulted up into the space, only to be punched back shrieking, their chests slug-stitched, their backs spraying blood and bone. Ryan grabbed the handle, pouring more lead down into the road, and yanked on it, slamming the door tight. He shot the bolts, breathing hard, then swung around on Cohn, his brain already working out survival details.

"Get hold of Four. Tell 'em to abandon ship. Up through the roof and jump for Three. There's probably guys crawling all over the place, so watch the hell out. Tell 'em the last man out must leave a four-minute booby as near as possible to their cargo. Tell Two and Three we're shifting butt right now. Tell the rear trucks to backpedal fast."

Cohn went into smooth automatic, playing with his switches, muttering inaudibly into his throat mike.

"Move it, Ches!" snapped Ryan, and grabbed for a handhold as the huge war wag lurched forward with a mighty howl, gathering speed and lumbering onward.

The Trader said, "Must've been well hidden in those rocks. Didn't see a nukeblasted thing."

"They were on the road. Crazies!" Ryan told him. "We probably flattened a score before the guy who mattered managed to grab hold of Four. Suicidal fuckers!"

Now they could hear bullets slamming into their armor, a steady muted rumble of lead on steel as though little men with hammers were drumming up a crazy war dance. The war wag bucked and crashed along, its engine roaring as the slope steepened.

"Nice place to die," muttered Ches, then yelled, "I don't believe it!"

Ahead, far ahead, the road had opened up, a part of it revealing red flashes, tracer lines soaring toward them. Rounds hammered over the front of the lurching vehicle, banged on the bulletproof glass of the windshield.

"Tunnels! Tunnels under the road! When we slowed for the slope, that's when they jumped us, grabbed our underside."

Now the MG-blister above their heads awoke into deadly life and tracers curved down toward the flapped tunnel trap, smashing into it, ripping it apart, sending it bounding away into the shadows beyond the searchlight's glare. O'Mara poured fire straight into the hole, the angle of fire steepening as they roared nearer and nearer.

Cohn said, "Four's out but seems like there's a hand-to-hand atop Three. It's getting rough out there..."

Then he broke off as Ches, his voice a hoarse croak of panic, said, "Hellfire, they got stickies!"

Ryan swung around, saw with a chill of horror four fingerlike appendages appear from out of sight below the windshield, slap hard on to the glass and flatten out slimily, suctioning to the smooth surface. Another four-finger hand whipped up into view, this one clutching a flat black object, which was slammed against the glass. The two hands vanished from sight.

Ches screamed, *"Limpet mine!"*

Chapter Three

RYAN STOOD LOOKING AT THE OBJECT clinging to the outside of the windshield for only as long as it took to blink an eye, but thought and images torrented through his mind.

The window was a goner; nothing could be done about it. If he had armor-piercing rounds in his mag he could blast the window, punch the bomb away. But that would still open them up to the outside, and in any case he didn't have APs up the spout and by the time he banged a fresh mag in, that limpet would have blown and they'd be holed anyhow.

He wondered for an instant whether Ches, one of the newer drivers, only recruited in the past twelve months and lacking the experience of some of the older guys, had, as soon as the alarm had erupted, stabbed a forefinger at one very special button on his console beneath the war wag's massive wheel—and then he bawled, *"Back!"*

The Trader plunged past him, Ches and Cohn tumbling after. Ryan's men were already diving for cover. Ryan jumped for the bunk room passage, hit the deck, found himself lying beside Ches.

"The E-button!" he shouted—but the driver's reply was lost in the roar of sound from up front. Flame bloomed, the shock wave sending debris hurtling through the air.

Ryan brushed glass shards off himself as he scrambled to his feet and ran for the front of the cabin.

The screen was out except for thick, jagged ridges of glass poking up through swirling black smoke. The metal surround near where the limpet had been placed was sagging up top, buckled below. Two of the team began spraying foam at the flames, killing them, and Cohn was already at his radio again, throat mike in place, his fingers working switches.

"She's okay. We're still on line, still connected."

Ryan crouched in the dying smoke, squeezing short lead-bursts out into the night and downward, at a high angle, trying to clean off any stickies that might still be hanging to the war wag's snout, although he guessed that whoever was hitting them would almost certainly be back underneath, clinging on, waiting to make the next move.

"Get the gas masks ready, but don't put 'em on."

The smoke was clearing fast, the flames dead. Ches was back at the wheel again, body armor now buckled over his chest. The spotlights still lit up the road ahead, and now Ryan could see what looked like fireflies dancing up in the rocks to each side—snipers homing in on them. Above, O'Mara's MG began stuttering, trying to keep the bastards' heads down.

Ches said calmly, "I've been meaning to tidy up that shelf below the window. It was getting clogged up with all kinds of crap. Those guys did a sweet job."

"You hit the button?"

"Sure I hit the button—and we're still in business. Far as I can tell the worst damage is to the glass and frame."

"That figures."

"Yeah, well you'd better pray it ain't gonna snow, Ryan, because I don't like driving in a blizzard, specially if that blizzard's coming in at me." He glanced around, and Ryan could tell that although the kid had shifted the vehicle into automatic, he was still putting on a show. "Do I clean 'em off now? Fry them out?"

"No. Not yet. Wait."

The E-button. A nifty device dreamed up by J. B. Dix for just such an emergency as this. Plate-metal strips around each war wag, topside and underside, were connected to the powerful generators at the rear but insulated from the rest of the chassis and frame. The E-button was a failsafe. Now all it needed was the tug of a lever and anyone or any thing touching those innocent looking rods got instant heartburn. Not to mention everything-else burn.

But Ryan did not want to blow that one until they had reached a last-ditch situation. It used up far too much power.

He could hear bangs and cracks outside, short rattling bursts of auto-fire, the hammer effect of rounds pounding the exterior. It wasn't exactly a standoff, but he figured their attackers were conferring somewhere, probably in the tunnels below the road. He idly wondered if they were new tunnels or old tunnels, tunnels maybe dug out by the guys who'd built the Stockpiles. They were more likely new ones, excavated for just such ambushes as this. He half turned, snapping his black-gloved fingers.

"C'mon, c'mon!" His voice was laced with urgency.

Two men shoved past him holding a wood frame that enclosed a crisscross of fine steel mesh. They leaned over Ches, ramming it into place over the buckled screen frame, and clipped it.

"Now let 'em try lobbing a gas can in."

Everything was smooth, thought Ryan, relaxing slightly. He checked his watch, noted that there still remained two and a half minutes to go before the booby in Four blew.

"Lint. Hooley. Up top."

The two men who had carried the wire barrier followed him at the run down the cabin. They threaded into the bunk room passage, waited while Ryan slid open a side door into a ladder well. Ryan mounted the ladder fast but silently, checked out the view ports at the top. Nothing. He began flicking at well-oiled bolt levers in the darkness, slicking them back. Then he slid the hatch sideways softly on its specially fixed runners until it would go no farther, and stuck his head out into the cool air.

Far to the east the gray twilight was gradually easing into milky dawn, but here a wash of flame from the now fiercely burning truck was the only light that mattered, casting a lurid glare over the scene, causing shadow dances on the blacktop, highlighting lurking figures among the roadside rocks and boulders.

There was a gap in the convoy. It was now split into two distinct sections fore and aft of the blazing truck. Ryan's war wag had pulled well forward, and Trucks One, Two and Three had followed. Far down the road Ryan could see the snub-nosed bulk of the second war wag, with the rest of the convoy trailing behind it.

Auto-rifle fire rattled, weaving its high-pitched chatter around single-shot cracks and the roar of the flames. Ryan focused his one eye on the roof of Three and saw that it was clear. Either the guys from Four had managed to tumble down through the truck's roof hatch into comparative safety, or they were dead meat on the road. He could see no one on the other trucks, but that didn't mean there weren't stickies clinging to the sides.

He crawled out into the roof gully, which ran the length of the vehicle, front to rear, wide enough for two men to lie side by side and be hidden from view except from above. Another idea of Dix's: it enabled a war wag commander under ground attack to slide men up unseen into sniping positions. On each side of the roof, maybe less than a meter in from the edge, were clamped two long metal rods running the length of the vehicle—on the face of it a stupid piece of construction since it allowed attackers climbing up the sides an easy handhold to enable them to pull themselves on to the roof, where a surprise awaited them.

Ryan crawled to the rear, hearing Hooley follow him. Lint would stay in the ladder well, rifle ready.

He reached the end of the roof and stared down at Truck One below him.

Truck One was a big trailer rig, its rear end converted in a very special, but unobtrusive, way. Truck One always followed the Trader's war wag in convoy: Strict Rule A. Strict Rule B was that it closed up tight to the war wag whenever the convoy stopped anywhere. Real tight. Strict Rule C was that Truck Two always pulled well back from One, giving it plenty of space at the rear.

Just in case...

Ryan grinned a feral grin. The jump from here was an easy one, no more than a couple of steps. And once he'd landed it would not take two seconds before he'd be sliding through the instantly opened hatch above the rig's cab to drop into the interior.

Still smiling, Ryan edged himself over the lip of the gully and began to crawl across the flat roof toward the port side of the vehicle. He wanted to get a better look at the roadside, see if there was much congregating going on below. He had an idea there probably was. He half turned his head to check back on Hooley, but the guy was still in the gully.

He looked back front again—and the smile froze on his face as a head popped into view only meters away.

A head out of a nightmare.

Huge eyes, two tiny nostrils in a moist, flabby flesh, no mouth, no ears. Hairless.

Four fleshy suckers slapped suddenly onto the roof edge, squishing tight. A squealing snort of rage erupted from the nostrils. Another suckered hand whipped up and around, shot toward Ryan's face with the velocity of a striking snake.

A sticky.

A severely mutated being with sucker pads for fingers and toes with which it could cling to any surface like a leech so tenaciously that it required main force to pull them off; even in death there was little relaxation. Once those fingers smacked onto flesh and exuded their glutinous ooze there was little chance of being able to tear them off.

Ryan had once seen a man attacked by a sticky. The guy hadn't known what hit him. The creature had kneed him, clutched him around the throat left-handed, grabbed his face with the right. The finger pads had slapped home, then retracted, taking the man's face with them, the flesh literally suctioned off the bone in bloody, doughy strips as though the sticky was tugging his hand out of red molasses. Eyeballs had popped. Faceless, the man had collapsed shrieking to the ground.

Bullets hurt them, a heart or head shot could finish them, a razor-keen blade could sure mess them around more than somewhat, but otherwise their wet, rubbery flesh seemed able to absorb the heaviest punishment. And in a battle situation they were like beings possessed.

No one seemed to know where the hell they came from, how they'd mutated. No one could even figure out quite what bizarre combination of genetic malfunctions had created them in the first place. The first sticky that Ryan had seen, a couple of years back, had been in a traveling carny, a weird and horrifying collection of freaks and savagely mutated beings that rode around the Deathlands ramrodded by a fat ringmaster called Gert Wolfram, something of a freak himself as he weighed well over one hundred and fifty kilos and had to be carried everywhere in a special construction chair born by six giants. The sticky's act had consisted of walking up and down high walls, no hands, and pulling the heads off dogs and wolves. Literally pulling them off.

When asked where he'd found the creature, Wolfram had zipped his lip, become extremely edgy. Not long after, sticky sightings came in from all over. Soon they became accepted; hell, a mutie was a mutie. Still, how they ate, for instance, was just one of the many mysteries about them discussed by Deathlanders with nothing else of importance to chew the fat over on an evening when the chem clouds were low and it looked as if the acids were about ready to drop.

Right now, however, the manner in which stickies ate held no interest for Ryan at all. All he could think of, as he rolled desperately to one side, was the incredible sucking power of those oozing pads lunging for his face.

He rolled so fast, so unthinkingly, that before he knew it he was on his back and lying atop his rifle as the hand squelched down on the roof surface inches from him.

That didn't panic him. Already his right hand was at his belt, grabbing for the hilt of the deadly panga sheathed there at his waist. Smoothly the blade came out and just as smoothly, just as fast, he was rolling back to his original position, the panga gripped tight then stabbing outward in a savage, power-packed lunge. The blade thudded into the creature's throat, just above the clavicle, or what passed for a collarbone in the rubbery body. It jammed, which was exactly what Ryan wanted.

Still holding the hilt of the wickedly sharp half sword, he jerked himself to his knees. Two-handed, his muscles cording into cables along his arms, he tugged at the wriggling, squealing creature. Brute force, it was the only answer. With a sloppy, plopping sound one hand came loose from the war wag's roof, then the other. Ryan scrambled to his feet, heaved at the sticky, pulled him over the metal rod, booted the creature in the side of the head.

The sticky was trying to grab for him, its squeal something like a butchered hog's, but unheard by anyone below because of the chatter of auto-fire. Ryan used all his strength to slam the creature down on the roof. He smashed his boot onto its chest and tugged at the blade. Dark red ichor was squeezing out of the rubbery folds of its flesh, and the panga came out soggily. Ryan danced backward as the beast fluted its fury, its wide blank eyes red rimmed. It sprang at him.

Ryan swung the panga two-fisted, felt it bite satisfyingly into oleaginous flesh, watched grimly as the head flew off like a kicked ball, sailing away into the surrounding gloom.

The torso sagged on suddenly limp legs. It collapsed sideways and rolled across the roof before finally slumping against the rail.

Ryan turned to jump back from the roof gully and cursed savagely. More stickies were hauling themselves up and over the other side of the war wag's roof. A brief glance at his right showed shadowy forms crowding onto the nearest trucks in fluid, rippling waves, arm over arm, seemingly inexorably.

Hooley, in the gully, was already throwing up his rifle, and flame was stabbing from it in short bursts. A stammer of fire from the ladder well told him that Lint, too, had opened up.

Ryan scabbarded the panga, then unslung his own piece. No point in silent killing now. He let rip a long jolting burst, left to right, at the bobbing line of heads that had suddenly appeared to his right, over the rear end of the war wag, watching dispassionately as they burst apart like so much rotten fruit. Then he leaped for the gully as more squealing figures came over the side behind him like an ugly tide.

He thought, this is going to be close. It flickered through his brain that no way was he going to be able to make it to the hatch before he was overwhelmed by the monsters.

He opened his mouth to scream at Lint, and then a vast, soaring gout of flame fireballed high into the sky to his right and a tremendous cracking roar, half deafening him. The shock wave of the explosion blew him over, sent him tumbling into the gully where he slammed into Hooley, already a sprawled and dazed figure.

"Number Four!" Ryan gasped. "Hellfire, I forgot how much bang-bang we piled into that one! Must've been most of the dynamite for the trip!" Groggily, his ears ringing, he got to his knees and bawled at Lint, half seen in the hatchway, "Tell 'em now! *Now!*"

Lint's head disappeared. Ryan clambered to his feet. The stickies had come to a halt, were gawping back down along the convoy at what was left of the once blazing truck, now only bits of burning debris scattered about among the rocks and boulders. There was a crater where the vehicle had once stood.

"Even more reason for that bastard Teague to send his road gangs out now," Ryan muttered. Hooley gaped at him as though the massive explosion had turned his brain to jelly.

"Never mind," snapped Ryan, then growled, "If that was a four-minute fuse I'm a dogface."

The stickies had come out of their daze. They were advancing over the edge of the roof again, squealing in rage and triumphant anticipation. Ryan counted at least twenty of the brutes with almost certainly more on the way. And that was just on this war wag.

But it didn't matter now. The beasts were all so much dead meat.

Calmly he watched as the roof-long rods suddenly glowed into life, triggered by Ches in the war wag's cabin below. In a second the entire picture was transformed into one of utter carnage as several thousand volts flowed into the roof rails, along the metal strips that lined the vehicle's side panels and hung along the length of the war wag's underside.

Seared flesh smoked and blackened. Shrieking figures were jolted into the air.

Ryan turned his eye to look along the length of the convoy, seeing the side panels of each war wag, land wag and truck glow eerily white, almost in sequence as, in each cab, a lever was thrown, power was generated, death created.

He saw bodies flung away from the parked vehicles, others adhering to side panels, scorched dark brown and then black. He saw bright, vivid flashes of light. He heard the sizzling, crackling stutter of electrical power jolting flesh, and the squeals, now no longer furious but tormented, agonized, of stickies that were mere microseconds from heart stoppage.

The air held a solid reek of cordite, smoke and something akin to roast pork, stomach-churningly strong.

All along the convoy the panel glow faded, to die as abruptly as it had come to life. Blackened bodies, glued to panels, now fell to the ground like overripe fruit from a tree, littering the roadside in jumbled heaps of starkly, stiffened limbs.

There were survivors, those who had not been swarming over the vehicle, those who had not been in contact with plates or rods. But they could be mopped up easily enough. And quickly enough. Right now, in fact.

Ryan gestured to Hooley. "Tell 'em I'm off on a buggy ride."

He ran to the rear of the roof and jumped for the cab of the closely parked truck behind.

THE MAN CALLED SCALE watched the carnage from the shelter of a small cave overlooking the road. His face registered no emotion—it rarely did—but his mouth was dry. He could not believe what he was seeing. The stickies had been the mainspring of his great plan. Now that plan had collapsed like a house of cards. No one had even hinted that the Trader had electrified his war wags and rigs. And the power! The power they must have used up in maybe fifteen, twenty secs would have been colossal. How could they afford to waste so much? It was like pissing it away.

That weirdo prick, the Warlock, was not going to be pleased when told that all his stickies had been grilled to a crisp, were just so many lumps of fried bacon lying around on an old wrecked blacktop. Not pleased at all. In fact, thought Scale, it might be wiser not to tell him. All things considered, it might be a hell of a lot wiser not to go within a thousand miles of him ever again, avoid him like the plague.

"Scale."

So much for Fat Harry and all his shit about the Trader's winding his operation down. Scale had a good mind to drive to the tubby bastard's trading post and do extremely unpleasant things to him. Like, for instance, flay the skin off him, a layer at a time, then salt the nukeshitting piece of human-shaped garbage down. There was so much flesh on the bastard that it might take some sweet time. And maybe he'd salt him after every crapping layer.

"Scale. Listen!"

And if it wasn't for the fact that right now he didn't have enough gas to make such a visit possible, and in any case that sneaky fat man had built his trading post like a fortress and regularly cleared scrub, shrub and bush from all around him so he could always see who was coming, and had ass-licked the muties who lived in the region so they were all well disposed toward him, Scale reckoned he fireblasted well *would* go take a trip and sort the fat lying sweaty hog out. As it was...

"Scale!"

Scale swung around savagely, one arm extended like a steel rod. It hit the man with the long arms on the side of the throat and slammed him over sideways, making him gag and splutter. The long-armed man felt gingerly at his throat as he scrambled to his feet.

"No need for that, Scale."

"Every need."

"Scale, we gotta get outta here. Damned fast."

"Yeah."

"Maybe we could regroup, huh, Scale? Hit these bastards when they least expect us!"

Scale stared at him, no expression on his face but cold fury in his eyes.

"I ought to kill you. Kill you now." His voice was an icy whisper.

Scale would do no such thing for the simple reason that big as he was, powerful as he was, kingpin of his own group of mutants as he certainly was, by force of personality and force of arms, he could not drive a powered vehicle, and the long-armed man was his personal wheelman. Scale had simply never bothered to learn the mechanics of driving. From the time he was a child, Scale had always been able to make others do his chores for him, and driving was something he left to the long-armed man.

Scale stared down at the scene below.

Mouth gaping, the long-armed man watched, too—watched as the high back of the big trailer rig behind the leading war wag suddenly swung away and down, crashing to the road and forming a long ramp down which surged a small armed personnel buggy.

A second buggy roared down the ramp after the first. Then a third. The rig was a massive buggy pen.

Not for the first time in the past quarter hour, the long-armed man cursed the crassness of Scale, the vaulting ambition that had driven him to take on the Trader. The Trader and his men were legends in the Deathlands. Attacking them had been an act of sheer madness from first to last.

The long-armed man knew what was at the heart of it, and *who* was at the heart of it. The strange and sinister being who sometimes called himself the Warlock, sometimes the Sorcerer, sometimes the Magus, who made fleeting visits to the Deathlands bearing weird old-world artifacts: sometimes weapons, sometimes gadgets whose exact purpose often took a long time to explain. The long-armed man was afraid of the Warlock, with his terrifying half face and his steel eye, and his two tightly leashed companions.

It was the Warlock who had let loose the stickies, maybe three, four winters back. He had brought a couple to a small township to the west, suddenly appearing one day in his armored truck with them in tow. One had died—had suddenly sickened, just wasted away, much to the Warlock's displeasure—but Wolfram the carny man had taken the other, taught it tricks, carried it off. Free, of course;

the Warlock did not take coin or cred for any of the merchandise he brought to the Deathlands, possibly because most of it was of no use to man or beast. Even so, the Warlock gave away everything, useless or not. The long-armed man could never figure out how the Warlock existed, or even where he existed. Some had tried to discover that, but they'd never come back with a location. In fact they'd never come back, period.

And then, the long-armed man recalled, maybe a year after they'd first appeared there suddenly seemed to be stickies everywhere. Some said the Warlock had created them, but that was just foolishness. No one could create men. Except God. And it was well-known that God did not exist. You only had to look around you to see that.

Whatever, a small army of stickies had come out of the northwest and that was it. Most had attached themselves to Scale's troop of marauders, and the long-armed man was dead certain that was entirely because of the Warlock. There was the time Scale had ordered him to drive over two hundred klicks to a tiny hamlet in the foothills of the Darks. The long-armed man had been told to stay put, sit in the land wag for as long as it took for Scale to conduct his business, ostensibly a visit to this real high-class cathouse the ville boasted. But two hundred klicks for a screw? Hell, Scale must've thought his brains were addled. The man with the long arms had never discovered the real reason for that somewhat clandestine visit, but shortly thereafter the stickies had appeared, and you didn't have to be a genius to connect the two events.

So, he thought now, the Warlock was sure as hell behind the stickies and now this particular bunch of stickies was no more, were just lumps of fried meat, and the Warlock, if the long-armed man was correct in his assumptions, was gonna be oh so *pissed*.

The Trader's buggies were converted panel trucks, drastically converted. The lead buggy seemed to bristle with weaponry. There was an MG-slit for the front passenger seat, another MG rear-mounted in the roof. Two stubby barrels jutting out of the front looked like cannon. Poking out of the enclosed rear was what seemed at a distance suspiciously like a mortar barrel, and running along the driver's side, underneath the door, was a long tube.

The long-armed man watched gloomily as the buggy hurtled along the narrow space between trucks and roadside, its front-MG sputtering flame. Rounds flayed a bunch of semi-fried stickies trying to regroup beside the huge bulk of the war wag in the center of the convoy. Stickies seemed able to take handgun bullets, even automatic rifle fire, but they didn't have a hope against the jolting velocity, the flesh-rupturing force, of nearly point-blank MG tracers. The buggy cleared a path, jolting on its shocks as it careered along the rutted road, its bulk smashing into dazed survivors, hurling them to one side.

The three buggies raced and weaved around the parked trucks as a murky Deathlands dawn crept up from the east, sharpening the picture, turning the shadows of tall rocks into pointing, accusatory fingers. Men were now disgorging from the trucks, heavily armed and grim visaged. Pockets of resistance were being mopped up swiftly and professionally, and the long-armed man knew that time was running out, that any moment now the Trader's death-dealing squads, angry and vengeful, would be opening up the tunnel under the road, scouring the rocks for snipers.

And heading up here.

''Scale! We *gotta* blow!''

Parked in the cave behind the two muties was a jeep and two small trucks, and what remained of Scale's force, tense and nervous, knowing that everything had gone disastrously wrong, that it was a shuttleup of the first magnitude. A narrow rocky track ran from the cave mouth, dived through wind-sculpted boulders, paralleled the blacktop far below before curving around to the south and slicing through the hills down toward the ugly seared plain and their campsite, maybe five klicks away. Once there…

"Scale!" The long-armed man's voice was high pitched with panic.

"Quit yappin'. Let's go."

Scale swung around and headed for one of the trucks. A man with deep, hollow eyes and a nose that drooped to his upper lip, joining with it in a flabby mass of graying skin, said in surprise, "You not takin' your jeep, Scale?"

Scale shook his head.

"You take it, Burt. You and Koll. Get outta here fast and warn the camp we're shiftin'. We'll hold the norms off and kill those buggy riders."

The man with the drooping nose made an O with his forefinger and thumb.

"Yeah, Scale. You get us some fresh norm meat, huh?"

"I'll get us some fresh norm meat," muttered Scale, his tone colorless, his eyes unblinking.

He jammed open the passenger door of the nearest truck and climbed in. The man with the long arms jumped into the driver's seat, sweating, not looking at his leader. He said in a low voice, "Smart, Scale. Take the heat off us."

Scale did not bother to reply as the jeep in front started up, revved hard, roared away in a swirl of dust, its sound like a heavy MG jabbering, its muffler long gone. The long-armed man eased the panel truck slowly toward the cave entrance. He braked just inside the opening, then jumped out and ran to the boulder-screened edge of the track.

In the distance the jeep was already at the bottom of the short hill and was now bumping and jouncing along the track at high speed. Farther on was a bend to the right, into the hills. That was where another track, from the road below, joined it. The long-armed man watched as the jeep powered along the straight to hit the bend at speed. It screeched out of sight. The long-armed man turned his eyes to the road below, and for the first time in a long while a gap-toothed smile creased his face.

The lead buggy had clearly spotted the jeep. It was way beyond the feeder track, but suddenly its driver threw her into reverse and stormed back along the road. Then the driver hit the brakes and dust clouded. He geared up, yanked hard at the wheel, trod on the gas again and the buggy, engine howling, roared up the high-incline track.

The long-armed man dodged back into boulder cover as the little vehicle appeared at the top of the track and hurtled out of sight after the jeep. Another buggy followed. The long-armed man frowned: one was okay, two was not so hot. He kept his eyes on the track but no more buggies appeared. He couldn't hear any more engine roar through the heavy chatter of MG- and auto-fire still ripping out below.

He plodded back to the truck, hauled himself in.

"Two of them 'stead of one."

"We can hit 'em."

Scale sounded supremely confident, utterly sure of himself, and the long-armed man shuddered silently. He drove fast but warily. While on the parallel track he kept glancing to his left, down to the road below, to see if he could catch any sign that someone down there had spotted them. But it looked as if luck—or some damn thing—was on their side. Someone down there had let off a smoke grenade and that, together with all the dust and shit that was still being kicked up, had dragged an obscuring pall over the proceedings.

He swung right, checked out the rearview mirror. The second truck was on their tail but not too close. He began to feel relief seeping through him. Maybe they were going to make it out of this one alive, after all.

His thoughts turned suddenly to the red-haired girl. She was certainly one sweet receptacle for his meat! After Scale was done with her, of course. Always after Scale. The long-armed man felt no resentment toward his leader in this or any other matter. Scale was one strong hombre and he went first in all things, and the long-armed man was perfectly content to remain in his shadow. He was not ambitious.

He flicked back to Red Hair. Man, that was going to be something.... He felt himself stiffen as he thought about her. He wondered idly why there'd been no other women on that two-wag train—the one they'd hit and mauled the crap out of yesterday. Kind of weird, that was; he couldn't figure it out at all. Young, too, and that was weird as well, because all the others had been oldies. Dead meat now. And useless. Tough and stringy. Took days to boil up an oldy for soup. No good at all unless you were starving and it was the only meat around. And with Scale you were never starving. Smart shit, was Scale.

Except when it came to thinking he could take the Trader.

As the long-armed man slowed to take a bend he felt a couple of thumps on the side of the truck, tremoring through. He glanced at the rearview mirror, saw nothing out of line his side, then noticed the driver of the following truck had an arm poked out his window, was waving frantically.

He said, "Anythin' your side, Scale? We hit somethin'?"

Scale shrugged, heaved down the window, stuck his head out.

Then yanked it back in again with a yell, jammed the window up.

"Stickies!" he snapped. "Two of 'em. Must've beat it back here, waited for us—I dunno."

"Shit, Scale, they're with us. Let 'em in."

"They don't look too fuckin' happy."

Hands gripping the battered wheel, the long-armed man glanced at his leader, saw that Scale didn't look any too happy, either.

"You can talk to 'em, Scale. About the only one that can."

Talking to stickies was a tiring business. They understood words but you had to yell at them, enunciate each sentence, each word, each separate syllable, extremely clearly. Some kind of lip-reading process, as far as the long-armed man understood it. Once you'd got it into their noodles what you wished them to do, you let them get on with it, let them create the mayhem you wanted. They were very good at creating mayhem.

Scale eased the window down halfway. He pushed his head out and began screaming at the top of his voice. The words were lost in the roar of the truck's engine. Then his head whacked back inside the cab again, and he thrust the window up. A microsecond later a suctioned hand thudded against the glass, spread out, glued itself on. A hideous face suddenly appeared, eyes in frenzy. The glass shook as the sticky jerked at it furiously, one-handed.

Scale yelled at the men crouching in the rear of the bouncing vehicle.

"Blast the fuckers off! Through the panels!"

The long-armed man felt sweat begin to soak his face. He squawked, "Nuke that idea, Scale. We get slugs zippin' around in this space, we're gonna get scalped if nothin' else!"

"Do it!" snarled Scale.

More thuds, sounding like kicks delivered with strength. The sticky at the window had disappeared. One of the men in the back said, "They's on the roof, Scale, an' we ain't all that tight up there."

Part of the roof had been pierced at some point during the truck's history. Wooden panels had been fixed over the gaps.

Scale grabbed for his rifle, squirmed around in his seat and sprayed at the roof, the sound deafening in the confined space. Yelling, the long-armed man ducked as hot brass flew past his head. Angry ricochets burned the air, snarling around his ears.

Scale fought with the wheel, boot-jabbing at the brake as the truck careered down the sloping track. In front, a misty panorama revealed itself. An angry sun endeavoring to pierce the thickening chem clouds shot scarlet light lances through the murk. A seared and dreadful landscape beckoned, stretching into the unseen, unfathomed distance, dotted with stunted trees, their foliage a sickly yellow.

A short distance away, three clouds of dust choked the already turbid air. Ahead, the buggies were chasing the jeep sure enough.

Scale blazed more lead up at the roof and ricochets whined and buzzed.

"Scale!" screamed a man at the back, blood dripping from his face where something sharp had sliced him—a ricochet or a shard of metal. "You're opening the roof up! Bastards'll get in through the hole!"

Scale had indeed opened up most of the wooden panels, had shattered them with ripping auto-fire. A face appeared in the torn space, greasy skinned, with angry eyes glaring downward. It whipped back out of sight as Scale fired again.

A bulky man grabbed at the rifle, roaring, "You'll kill us all, you shitstick!" and tried to drag the weapon away from the demented mutie leader. Scale triggered a burst at him, point-blank, and slugs chewed him apart, punched him away in a spray of scarlet that paint-licked the walls and most of those in the immediate vicinity.

They flung themselves to the floor of the truck, hands over heads, yelling and screaming curses. In the front, the long-armed man prayed and wondered what would happen if he just jammed open his door and threw himself out of this madhouse. But they were going too fast, and the faster he went and the more he swung the wheel right and left, the greater the possibility that the stickies would not be able to batter their way in.

Ahead the dust had cleared. The speeding vehicles had hit a stony patch of ground. Now the buggies could clearly see their prey, and those in the jeep must know that they were doomed.

The lead buggy was firing. Tracers from its passenger seat MG flamed at the bouncing jeep. Rounds hammered at the jeep's rear.

The tires exploded. The buggy hurtled past at a wide angle, raking the bucking vehicle fore and aft. A line of fire caught the jeep's passenger and the long-armed man saw the guy's head burst open, the driver ducking under the hail of lead. The jeep swerved toward the nearest buggy, hit its rear, caromed away but stayed on an even keel. The long-armed man could almost hear the tortured clang and scrape of metal on metal, the boosting roar of acceleration as the jeep plowed on.

But it could not last, and it did not last. The buggies were coming at the jeep from two different directions, MG fire from both converging. Blazing fire lines met, crossing on the ancient, crudely armored jeep. Metal struts flew away, the front tires were shredded to rubber strips, and the hood blew up and sailed high into the sky. The driver was caught by two sets of fire lines and they tore him apart bloodily, throwing chunks of him up into the muggy air. Tracers sought the juice tank, soon found it. Fire bloomed, punching the jeep spectacularly apart, sending it cartwheeling in all directions.

"Holy nukeshit," muttered the man with long arms. The Trader's men had used nothing but MGs for their kill. They hadn't even started on the twin cannon, mortars and rocket tubes yet.

He wrenched the wheel, pulled the speeding, bucking truck onto a side track that dropped away from the track he'd been on. They entered a narrow, gloomy canyon, high cliffed, stretching away from them, undeviating, straight as an arrow before it rose again to trees, vegetation and less dust.

The long-armed man shot a glance at Scale, who was still twisted around in his seat, his gun pointing up at the roof. In the back huddled the others, four of them now. The fifth lay in a widening pool of gore.

The stickies seemed to have calmed down somewhat, maybe mesmerized by the explosion of the jeep. Stickies liked explosions—the bigger, the more eruptive, the better; they liked looking at the flames. But the bastards never gave in. They'd be up there now, waiting their chance, waiting to create more mayhem. He glanced at his rearview mirror, saw the other truck still clinging to his tail, but his own and its dust obscured the entrance to the canyon. He couldn't tell if the two buggies were coming up behind.

The truck hurtled along the flat of the canyon, swooped up and out of it into a grove of trees that drooped with dirty yellow foliage. They were in a wide natural valley, a part of the mountain's foothills, and the camp was almost dead center, a small hamlet of old huts and cabins clustered along one end of what had once been a huge lake but was now only a dirty little pond of muddy, brackish, just about drinkable water. In the distant past it had been a thriving community, a summer resort for wealthy people who came there to fish the lake and climb the mountains for fun. But of course the long-armed man knew only rumors of such things, was in fact puzzled by the notion that people once crawled up steep precipices as an enjoyable relaxation.

He said, "What we gonna do, Scale?"

Scale, still gripping his piece, muttered, "Gonna fuck me the red-hair."

The long-armed man shot a startled glance at his leader. Had he heard right? The noise and clatter of the speeding truck was not good for conversation but the long-armed man could usually get the gist of something that was not yelled at him. He could have sworn that Scale had said something about fucking the red-haired girl. But that couldn't be right. There were priorities, for God's sake.

"Scale?"

"Uh?"

"What we gonna do? Them buggies bound to find us. They're gonna cream us."

Scale's head jerked around, his thick-lipped mouth gaping, his eyes wide and crazy, the gun in his hands suddenly jammed into the side of the long-armed man's head.

He shouted, "So you do what you wanna do! I'm gonna get me the red-haired bitch!"

The long-armed man slewed the truck to the right and into a narrow bush-lined tunnel. The vegetation all around them was parched, but it was still alive; it seemed able to survive, just, in this hostile environment, fed perhaps by the tiny trickles of water that still infiltrated the earth from off the hills. There were no birds in the valley and the long-armed man had never seen any animals. Anything on four legs automatically got eaten. Just about anything on two, as well.

The truck shot out of the tree-lined avenue and the long-armed man swung the wheel and skidded around into what had once been a blacktopped parking lot next to a ruined building that, a century ago, had been a shop selling guns and fishing tackle. A weather-faded signboard was fixed to the facing wall on which the words McPartland Brothers could just be discerned, if there had been anybody there who could actually have read them.

But this was a decaying ville; the art of reading had long departed it. The roofs of cabins were holed, although that didn't matter much since rain was no problem in this part of the Deathlands. Walls of some of the shacks sagged, unmended. Others had no walls at all, were simply wood frames with rotting bits of blanket draped around them, or tarps, or old animal hides brought from elsewhere when Scale had discovered the place and moved his band in. Maybe a few human hides, too. Smoke drifted from some of the chimneys.

The lake lay a few hundred meters to the north, most of it parched, just cracked mud now, the dark water far away toward the center. Across the other side the hills rose up sheer, a frowning, gloomy mass of peaks that brooded over the valley.

Sluttish women in filthy robes wandered toward the truck, most of them at some stage of pregnancy or other, although childbirth here was even less of a problem than the rain. Most of the babies were stillborn. Those that survived were usually sickly and weak, with a variety of ugly ailments and, often, limbs where no limbs were supposed to be. There were some healthier-looking children but these, without exception, were what remained from various land wag trains once the adults had been massacred. Scale saved the females, if they were young and looked strong, kept them as a kind of harem until he grew tired of them, when he tossed them to the men. And if the women thought they got it bad from Scale, they got it a hundred times worse from the men—usually a hundred times at a time.

The long-armed man brought the truck to a halt and shivered. Most of those hundred men were dead now, those in the two trucks probably all that were left. Maybe a dozen men, unless there were a few stragglers in the tunnels still, or hiding out in the rocks above the highway. Hellblast it, he thought, the women outnumber us.

He said, "The stickies, Scale. What we gonna . . ."

Scale jabbed at him with the automatic rifle.

"Out."

"Scale!"

"Out."

"Scale, I'm your wheelman! They'll kill me, they'll suck me apart."

Scale was smirking, licking his rubbery lips.

"I'll get me another wheelman. Out."

Completely over the edge, thought the long-armed man wildly. He was suddenly dying to urinate.

He jammed down the door handle, smacked the door open and flung himself out of the cab, diving to the parched and sparsely grassed earth. He hit the ground, somersaulted, was up on his two legs and running, charging through a group of women who were staring at the truck with lackluster eyes. His breath coming in great wheezing gulps, he came to a stop and swung around.

Nothing. The stickies were no longer on the truck's roof nor clinging to the sides nor, as far as he could see, underneath either. He stared at the other truck, which was braking in a cloud of dust behind the first. Nothing there. Maybe, he thought, they'd hopped off as the trucks were speeding through the trees. In which case they were still around. He glanced fearfully at the wooded area they had come through, but he could see no unnatural movement in the trees. Maybe they'd simply beat it, got disgusted with the whole jig and cleared out. Hah! he said out loud. No way. No way, my friend. Stickies had one-track minds.

And what about the Trader's buggies? Where in hell's name had they got to? No sign of them. No sound of them, either. Had they just given up the chase, turned around and headed back the way they'd come, to the road, satisfied after their single kill?

But that didn't seem too likely. In one respect the Trader's warriors were akin to the stickies: they had one-track minds.

RYAN'S NOSE WRINKLED. The stench from the camp below was like a fist between the eyes. Months, maybe years, of rot contributed to that smell: bad food, excrement, urine, dead bodies flung anywhere to decay. A stomach-churning stink, a monstrous miasma that, he thought grimly, if you could distill it and bottle it, would probably be as efficient in destruction as strong poison. Not that those who existed down there would notice anything. They were surely used to it by now, and worse.

"Hell, Ryan, we're gonna need masks to go down there."

"Yeah, pretty ripe."

"Ripe ain't the word."

"Don't worry, Abe. Couple of mortars should do it. We don't need to go in blazing."

They were crouched on a low, bush-topped bluff that overlooked the pest hole of a camp from the south. Ryan had spotted the two trucks while dealing with the jeep, but then held back from following them too closely. It was easy enough to watch where they had gone, even more simple to follow at a distance and hide the two buggies in the trees that grew this side of the canyon.

"See." Ryan pointed down at the cluster of buildings, to one building in particular, larger than the rest and built away from the center. "That one. Seems to be in better shape than the others, and it's bigger. Old storehouse probably. That'll be where the honcho hangs out, and that'll be where the weaponry and fuel will be stored. And the explosives. The honcho'd want to keep an eye on all that valuable shit. Hit that and we solve the problem."

"What about all those guys? We let 'em live?"

"They aren't going to be zipping around attacking land wag trains now. They'll be lucky to survive out the year. Winter comes, no food..." He snapped his black-gloved fingers.

Abe, a tall, lanky individual with a thick mustache and long, flowing hair tied up in a knot at the back of his head, nodded. He knew Ryan's rules. The Trader's rules, really. No killing for the sake of it. No killing unless you or your buddies were in danger, or unless other, innocent, folk were in danger.

"We can back one of the buggies up here fast, before they catch on to the noise, and just take out that storehouse," Ryan was saying. "If I'm wrong she won't go up like a firework display and we'll maybe have to think again, because they must have matériel somewhere, and that's what we have to destroy. But I don't think I'm wrong."

"Could use a rocket."

"Waste of a rocket. We got plenty of mortar shells."

"Hmm. Okay."

Abe half rose and turned when Ryan suddenly swore. The tall man stooped, turned back.

"Gimme the glasses."

Abe handed over his binoculars, saw what Ryan had spotted. Ryan saw the scene below spring into hi-mag definition through his one remaining eye. The man with the faintly scaly skin, whom he'd already tagged as the leader, was emerging from one of the cabins dragging a woman. But this was not, by any stretch of the imagination, one of the mutie women. This one was dressed in a clean, pouched combat suit with good boots. She was long limbed, full breasted, with a high-boned face. Her most startling feature was her hair: rich, deep magenta in hue, a thick mass of it, flowing over her shoulders and halfway down her back. The mutie leader was dragging her by it, two fists deep in its chunky mass, pulling her along the ground. Her hands were tied behind her and her legs were hobbled at the ankles. Even so she was putting up a struggle, jerking and squirming as she was tugged toward the large storehouse.

Ryan put the glasses down, shot a bleak look at his companion.

He said, "They got prisoners. We go in."

Chapter Four

KRYSTY WROTH WINCED HER EYES CLOSED and pushed her face deeper into the filthy blanket on which she was huddled. All of her body ached, her arms most of all because they were wrenched behind her, tied tightly at the wrists. Her head felt as though someone with abnormally callused hands had reached inside her skull and was clutching at her brain, squeezing it tight then letting it go; squeezing, letting go. Waves of pain washed over her and receded, then surged and fell away again. Her breasts hurt, her nipples hurt. Her ribs and kidneys throbbed where the man with the faintly scaled skin had kicked her viciously, not once but three times, in swift succession. At the moment she was trying desperately not to be sick because in her present position, if she were sick she had no means of avoiding her own vomit, and this would add enormously to her misery, her feelings of mental despair and physical wretchedness.

The sickness slowly receded, leaving her with sweat dewing her skin, her brow clammily cold. She fluttered open her eyes, eased her head sideways, her left cheek away from the verminous blanket. The sudden itchiness she was now experiencing all over her body she could cope with. The odd flea here and there had very little relevance to her present stark situation or the outrage that threatened her, the gross invasion of her body.

She closed her eyes again, breathing out slowly and silently as another, subtly different ache spread through the pit of her stomach, a soft sharpness that was at the same time a feeling incorporeal, a shift in the mind as much as in the body. She winced again, but this time her grimace was halfway an exhausted smile tinged with resignation, as she felt her blood flowing gently out of her, the cyclical clock in her body insistent, relentless, even at such a time, in such a place, at such a dreadful pass.

She almost felt like laughing. Really, it was so absurd. Of course she knew almost to the minute when she was due, had always known, since menarche. Her periods were as regular as night falling, day dawning. And of course she had been aware that she was due, as ever; but the events of the past twenty-four hours—by turns confused, horrifying, violent, ghastly—had torn her own reality apart, had indeed almost shattered it. And now, so near the onrushing moment of terror, of violation, her body had shown her that, blind to all externalities, the secret rhythm of life continued its perpetual motion undisturbed.

Into her mind there flashed again that sickening scene after the ambush, when the two burning land wags had lain drunkenly at the side of the pitted highway and the mutants had been at their bloody work, slaughtering and raping the two old ladies from Harmony, dear Uncle Tyas, Peter Maritza and the rest of the passengers. She heard again thunderous shotgun blasts and the hideous ripping chatter of automatic rifles and shrill, agonized screams. Then the ultimate degradation: the hacking off of the heads, the shoving and kicking and the heaving of the twisted torsos into a tangled heap at the side of the road, fodder for the birds and strange beasts, or perhaps worse, any human carrion that might happen by.

That she had been spared offered no comfort. She knew precisely why she had not been subjected to physical abuse and assault. She saw again, in her mind, the mad eyes of the man the others called Scale as he stared at her in hideous appreciation, literally licking his lips, one hand slowly and obscenely rubbing his crotch. She had surrendered to an engulfing wave of blind panic that threatened her sanity.

Yet even then she'd still had the psychic strength to pull herself away from the black abyss on the edge of which, for a microsecond, she teetered. The mental discipline that had been her mother's strongest bequest came to her aid just when she most needed it. She had divided off her terror and revulsion, forced an almost alien calm to take their place. "Strive for life" her mother had dinned into her at an age when she had not even known what the words meant, and Sonja Wroth had never stopped repeating that blessed motto. It had become a part of Krysty's psyche.

As now, she thought. Uncle Tyas, old Peter and the rest of them were dead. The fantastic dream they had been pursuing had died with them. Only she was left, faced with a lingering horror—a weary death in life, here in this plague pit of slavery and torment and monstrous pain.

Calm. She must become calm, must strive for a measure of tranquillity. Only when she was calm, even if only for a few seconds, was she fully in command, mistress of herself. Of her body. Of, most important of all, her mind.

She knew, now that she was at last alone with a single opponent, that she had a chance, slim as it might be. She *could* escape from her bonds; she *could* destroy the man called Scale. And after that there was the means here, in this huge storehouse converted into an armory, for her to explode out of the building, guns blazing, if that was the way she wanted it. And on reflection, maybe it was: maybe she should exact a devastating revenge upon these animals.

Krysty felt her blood weeping out of her, felt the warm flow of it between her legs, and this heartened her. It signified an untapped energy of vast potency.

Slowly, warily, she swiveled her head to peer across the huge room. This part of it had been transformed into crude living quarters. The wide double bed she was lying on—in fact an old bed frame with a filthy, torn mattress covered by the blanket—filled the angle of one corner. There was a table nearby littered with candle stubs and loose rounds of ammunition. There were a few broken-backed chairs. Opposite her was a grimy window through which nothing could be seen, then a wide planked door, now closed, then another window as filthy as the first. The ceiling was high, high above her. It was dark up there.

Arranged around the walls, jammed down over angled hooks, was a grisly assortment of heads, male and female, hundreds of them, young and old, some fairly fresh, others in the final stages of decay. Sightless eyes gazed vacantly upward at nothing.

The heads of those slaughtered yesterday had not yet been trophied. Krysty did not know where they had been stored, and did not want to know. Their spirits had departed. In her mind she had said prayers for them to the Earth Mother, although Uncle Tyas had not believed in any gods at all, only science. Gods, he'd said, were capricious, whereas science was fixed and immutable. To the old argument that it was science that had virtually wiped out the world a century ago, he had testily pointed out that it was not science at all but people. People misusing science, using it for their own ends, to further their own greedy or stupid or insane ambitions. Krysty was with him in that, at least.

Her eyes moved on.

The rest of the storehouse had been divided at some time into two separate stories, but some of the floor of the upper chamber had long since rotted away. The partition, too, that had once separated the main two-level store from the living area had disappeared. Only a few planks here and there showed that a wall had ever existed.

On the lower level, the ground floor section, she could see Scale's armory and store. Guns were everywhere, some in piles, some stacked against the outer wall: MGs, rifles, shotguns. Some of the weaponry she could identify. There were rows of crates, mostly still sealed, stacked along the inner wall, three or four deep, five or six high. Many, she knew, contained canned food looted from land wag trains. There were other boxes she recognized. A crate of grenades, open, its top wrenched off, stood near the door. She had noted that one almost at once. She knew very well how to use a grenade. She knew very well how to handle an automatic rifle, too. In this, as in so much else, Uncle Tyas had been more than thorough when he took her in after her mother's death.

From where she lay, Krysty could not see the very farthest part of the building. That was where the man called Scale was. She could hear him muttering to himself as he kicked things over, wrenched at cardboard boxes, seeking something.

She wondered how much time she had.

She tried to relax. Forced herself to relax. To do what must be done required calmness, peace of mind. Not for long, however. Only as long as it took for her to be at peace with herself, and at one with herself. Under the circumstances, not easy. But she had to become like the invisible clock in her body, blind to everything but herself.

She closed her eyes, drifted. She felt as though she was on the edge of... what? Difficult to say. She tried to imagine a huge soft mattress, of the kind owned by wealthy folk in the East, one of the symbols of their status. Very thick and very, very soft. And she was lying atop it. What she must do was sink into it. But at the moment it was nothing but unyielding, as firm and obdurate as a tabletop.

Or... maybe not quite as hard as that. Not quite...

She could feel a yielding.

She blocked off all noise, all outside sounds, everything that was not a part of her.

And in her mind, she smiled....

And began to sink into the feathery, cotton-wool softness.

And as she began to sink, so she could feel, within her, a... *stirring*.

SCALE MARCHED BACK DOWN the long room, smacking the coiled bullwhip against the side of his leg. The feel of it was reassuring, as though it was a trade-off for the power he had so swiftly, so devastatingly, lost less than an hour ago.

He would do her now, do everything to her he could think of. Then having assuaged the raging fire in his loins he would flay her, destroy her with the whip. Then he would leave. That was it. He had no idea where he would go, what he would do, because he was not thinking that far ahead. In his mind was a confusion of images—fireballing explosions, red hair, stabbing rifle-flashes, white flesh, soaring tracers, skin that was slick with blood. He marched like a robot, cackling to himself, muttering disjointedly, not even knowing himself what he was saying. Smacking the whip against his leg.

He strode out from under the sagging beams that supported rotting planks and headed for the bed. He did not see the woman as a woman, as a flesh-and-blood human being. Merely as a shape. He threw the whip down on the trash-strewn floor and grabbed at the shape, his hands fumbling, then yanking the loose clothing, ripping it, tearing off long strips of it, clenching fingers at her panties and pulling. He reached for the knife at his belt, sliced the cords that bound those limbs, wrenched them apart, heard the shape screaming... screaming....

SCREAMING! It was as though someone had thrust a spear deep into her soul. Such agony! The psychic shock exploded through her, jolting every nerve end in her body.

She came alive. Her eyes burst open. She saw Scale looming over her, staring down at her, his mouth wide, his jaw spittle flecked.

He whispered "Blood." His voice was thick, the sound coming from the back of his throat. He said, "Bleedin'. Ya bitch. Y'evil fuckin' slut. Ya bleedin'."

His eyes slowly focused on her face and locked on to her eyes. He was breathing stertorously, his brutish frame trembling. Then a frown spread slowly across his scaled face, a frown half of bewilderment, half something else. Half...recognition. Krysty shivered uncontrollably at that look. She knew it for what it was.

He suddenly thrust his face down at her and his foul breath gusted over her face. His left hand shot out, clutched her throat, pulled her half up from the bed. She gagged in pain and terror. He started to smile as he peered into her eyes. Then he began to chuckle, a harsh, rasping sound, the ugliest sound.

"Yeah," he breathed slowly. "I know you, ya bitch."
Triumph suddenly flooded into his voice. "I *know* you!"
He unclasped his fingers, shoved her back against the bed,
his body shaking as the huge storehouse echoed to the
harsh, jarring, malevolent noise of his cackling.

He flicked open his belt, kicked off his boots. He unzipped his pants, thrust them down. Still laughing, he exposed himself, his penis thick and erect. He stroked it, held
it firmly, his eyes suddenly narrowing as he stared at her,
a crafty expression sliding across his face.

"Yeah. I know you. I got who you are. Hell of a thing,
huh? You know—" his tone had become bizarrely conversational "—I was gonna kill ya. But not now. Oh, no,
not now. Gonna keep ya all for myself!"

He stepped forward, his tongue dragging across his thick
lips.

Krysty thought, I was just on the point of it; I was nearly
there, so nearly there. Then she thought, I can still do it.
All I need is just a little more time. Once he's inside me,
then I can do it. It's the only way. It's the only blasted
way...

Then she saw his attention had been caught by something else, something above her. He was staring upward at
the ceiling, at the gloom high in the rafters, his mouth
gaping ludicrously, his features frozen into an expression
of stunned shock.

She wrenched her head back, her eyes penetrating the
shadows, felt horror and loathing flood through her as she
glimpsed what he was looking at. A glimpse was all she
needed, all she wanted. Clinging to a beam by one suckered hand, its twin free, the suckers writhing as they
groped for the wall, was something she had never seen before, only heard about.

A sticky.

Scale jumped back frantically, his face livid, his arms swinging wildly. He shrieked curses as he turned and dashed for the door.

And howled with frenzied fury as another sticky dropped from the shadows above.

At any other time the sight of this half-naked man in a state of near terminal panic, with his rapidly softening erection, would have been comical. Hilarious. But Scale was throwing off psychic waves of unadulterated terror. Krysty could feel it as though it was something physical. He saw death and agony clawing at him and he wanted neither.

Scale sprang toward the crates, grabbed the nearest weapon to hand, a .45 automatic. The gun stabbed flame, the thunder of the shots filling the barn. He emptied the mag into the sticky by the door and the sticky took every round, was thumped back against the wall with their jarring impact.

Krysty saw, with fright-flecked eyes, the slugs slam into greasy flesh around stomach and thighs. Then saw the creature stagger to its feet, red stuff oozing from wounds that were not gaping holes but mere liplike slits, already closing as though sucking the bullets in. The sticky squealed with rage, snorting its fury down its half-formed nostrils, and lunged at Scale, its sucker hands outstretched.

Scale tore a box from one of the piles and heaved it at the thing. The creature's fingers caught the heavy object and held it, almost as though the box had suddenly become a part of it, a clublike extension of its arms. It swung the box and smashed it into Scale, slamming him over into a stack of crates, which swayed, teetered, crashed to the ground.

That saved Scale. The crates rolled and tumbled, some splitting open and sending cans of food spraying out. The sticky blundered into the avalanche and was hammered off balance, going down under what for a normal being would have been a bone-crushing weight of tins. Scale scrambled up and darted to one side, then disappeared down the long storehouse toward the far end.

Krysty, her mouth dry with fear, risked another glance upward. Another sticky was bounding along the wall, high up, like a crazed spider, hand over hand, its long arms supporting its weight with only an occasional kick with its suckered toes to keep balance. Both creatures were naked save for tattered pants. The sticky made it to the upper chamber and vanished into the gloom.

Breathing a prayer, the red-haired young woman closed her eyes again. Concentrating, she let her mind do the work, let it dive into itself so that the light within increased even as her focus became smaller and smaller. Her ankles were now free from her outstanding new strength, her magic, and she could run for it, but her wrists were still tied and without the use of these she might just as well be hobbled again. All she wanted were a few seconds, just a few. She felt the familiar lightness in her head, a feeling like that of bare electric wires of almost no voltage brushing her wrists.

This was power. Woman power in earth: the mind as place. This was strength over material things, a power so strong and so centered in one place that it commanded all it touched. But she wanted desperately to open her eyes, to check for new threats, new horrors that might even now be looming over her. It seemed to her, in the power state, that she had been in a totally vulnerable position for literally minutes on end.

Then she got up, her hands free though her wrists throbbed, the torn cords falling away, her eyes darting to the pyramid of cans so very close to her.

Nothing stirred. She could hear no sounds from the other side of the barn. She put her legs over the side of the bed and sat on the edge for a few seconds breathing in deeply, oblivious of the general stench of the place. She got to her feet, shakily. She was still wearing her boots but her jump suit was in shreds, ripped and torn from breasts to knees. It looked like an animal had been at it, which was pretty much the truth. Glancing down, she saw streaks of blood staining the insides of her thighs and was aware of the dull ache in her womb. She gathered up what remained of her panties—flimsy shreds of cotton—and screwed up one strip. Squatting, she inserted it deftly into herself as a makeshift tampon. Then, still breathing quickly and managing to control the shivering fit that threatened, she hurried across the room to the open box of grenades.

She grabbed four, stuffing three of them into various untorn pockets, keeping the fourth in one hand. She backtracked to where five automatic rifles leaned against the outer wall, and selected one. No mag. She cursed, picked up another. Same again. Desperately she picked up the remaining three. None had mags. She stared around. This was insane. There was an MG lying on the floor, but she wasn't sure she'd be able to control the kickback on that. There were many more rifles but she could see now that all were empty. Then she noticed that one of the crates had burst open, revealing mags aplenty. They didn't seem to be greased and factory fresh, but had been piled in willy-nilly, all kinds, all types, straight, banana, long curve, short curve. More loot from a land wag train. Her eyes flicked at the leaning row of rifles and SMGs and she picked out a Heckler & Koch 9 mm. Good weight, short, a nice death-dealing compactness. She took it up, checked it, went back to the box and tensely fingered through the jumbled mass of sticks, clattering them aside until she found two 30-slug curved mags. One she stuffed into a back pocket, the other she held against the gun while she began cramming the fourth grenade into an already over-stuffed pocket over her right breast.

The pile of cans burst apart in a wild spray of tin. The sticky, squealing viciously, had erupted from the ground.

Krysty gasped. Her heart felt as if someone had just kicked it.

She sprang back, dropping the grenade. She also dropped the second mag. The sticky came at her like a flying fury, and she had to dance away and flee back to the living area of the barn, her right hand fumbling at the re-maining mag jammed into her back pocket. It wouldn't come out, had somehow gotten entangled with the pocket lip. She felt as if she could scream, but didn't. Instead she turned for the door, but the creature was already there, its eyes almost popping with rage and blood lust.

Krysty yanked the mag and it came out, tearing the pocket open at one side. But now she was all fingers and thumbs and the mag would not slot in. The sticky, hoot-ing nasal fury, jumped for her and she felt its wind as she stumbled aside, saw the sucker pads of its right hand lunging at her. She raced away across the room, still trying to shove the mag into the SMG but in her desperation only jamming it. Her heart was pounding like a trip hammer and sweat was coming off her like glistening pearls. Adrenaline boosted her body and desperation boosted her brain.

In a microsecond she took in the fact that one of the pillar supports that held up the upper chamber had heavy nails sticking out of it. Thrusting the mag between her teeth, she grabbed hold of one of the higher nails and thrust a foot at a lower one—the H&K stuffed under her left arm and held tight to her body—and she began to pull herself upward. The nail heads were sharp; they tore at her flesh. She didn't give a damn, didn't even think about it. The fact that her fingers began to bleed and the nail heads became suddenly slippery merely acted as a further booster. She reached the second floor and rolled over onto what remained of the floor planks just as the kill-crazy creature slammed into the pillar.

She stared down at its fearsome, horrific ugliness as it, too, began to climb, hissing and snorting through its nose. She pushed herself up into a kneeling position and once more endeavored to cram the curved mag up into the SMG, but in her terrified haste she fumbled more than before and the mag suddenly became a living thing in her hand, flying out of her grasp. The sticky's head rose above the floor and blindly she smashed the useless gun into its face, crashing the snub-nosed barrel repeatedly into one of its eyes and transforming it into a crimson jelly before the creature was jolted off its perch, tumbling back to the ground. Panic rose like nausea within her, and without thinking she clutched at one of her grenades, yanking the pin and screaming, *"Fuck you!"* as the sticky, shrilling its pain and rage, leaped for the pillar again. She dropped the grenade on it and flung herself backward, scrambling as if demented away from the floor edge.

The roar of the detonation nearly deafened her, and all at once the floor was rocking then bursting apart and she was sliding toward the edge and tumbling over. She fell, still clinging to the H&K, and hit the ground, automatically rolling on the trash-choked floor. Beams and planks thudded down and dust rose chokingly. She staggered to her feet, her ears ringing, her eyes prickling and smarting.

Miraculously the whole barn had not collapsed, and after a moment she could see why. The sticky had taken most of the blast. Unaccountably it had fallen across the grenade, hunched over it, acting almost like a sandbag. Except a sandbag would not have hurled gobbets of flesh and bloody entrails all over the place.

The pillar she'd squirreled up had gone and that part of the upper chamber's floor now sagged drunkenly to the floor, unsupported. Other pillars nearby looked about ready to collapse, and she glanced up at the roof fearfully; it seemed safe enough from what she could see through the dust and the gloom. Steel splinters from the blast had flayed the surrounding area, scoring the wooden walls, tearing the table apart. Heads now lay about the floor in macabre confusion. Miraculously, none of the windows had blown.

She thought, I've got to get out, got to get out.

She wondered why no one had burst in on her from outside after the explosion. Where in nukeshit were Scale and the second sticky?

Among the mess she spotted the first mag, the one she'd dropped, and hastily bent to pick it up. As she did so she was dimly aware of sounds from outside: the muffled roar of engines, accelerating; the stammer of automatic fire and the heavier punch of MGs; shrill cries of panic. Suddenly she could smell smoke.

Confused, she stood up and glanced to her right and saw that something was burning under the sagging floor of the upper chamber. Delayed action from the grenade blast. Had to be. Even as she watched, a tongue of flame caught a rotten plank and leaped up it, gathering strength as it gathered height. In two seconds or less, the single flame had become a leaping wash of fire, greedily engulfing the tinder-dry beams, soaring toward the roof. Dense white smoke, caught by drafts, billowed around, mushrooming upward. Shadows trembled, became distorted by the lurid glare of the flames. The smoke caught her and buried her in a swirling fog, the acrid fumes choking her.

She bent again, groping for the mag, her right hand that held the SMG thrusting outward as she stooped. She grasped the curved shape of the magazine, but the H&K 9 mm was snatched from her hand.

She sprang upright, swung around.

Screamed.

The second sticky was only a rancid breath away from her, starkly outlined against the blaze, its eyes glittering.

She flung the mag at its face, sobbing with terror.

And the door to the barn burst open with a thunderous crash.

Krysty caught sight of a tall man, black garbed, dark haired, an autorifle in his hands. The man had stormed through the doorway and now the sticky turned and moved with astonishing, horrifying speed, dropping the H&K and leaping for the newcomer.

The man fired a 3-round burst, but was off balance from the follow-through jump after kicking in the door. The slugs burned air, hammered the wall opposite. The sticky flew at him, enveloped him, both figures crashing to the floor close to the blaze that had volcanoed monstrously from the open door's in-draft.

Blazing timbers crashed down to the garbage-strewn floor, which caught in seconds, flames leaking everywhere. The heat was corrosive, clawing at exposed skin.

For what seemed long moments Krysty stood like a statue, her green eyes taking in the struggling figures as they rolled and jerked on the floor. The sticky had suckers to the tall man's face, was pulling its arm back, the face seeming almost to expand outward. Hoarse cries mingled with the thunder of the flames as they eagerly devoured the timber beams and tarred roof.

Krysty came out of her trance and grabbed up the fallen mag and the dropped SMG. She felt calm now, completely in control of herself. Perfectly in control of events. She slipped the mag up into the Heckler & Koch and moved across the struggling pair, her hands working the gun.

She went around to one side, deliberately pushed the stubby barrel of the SMG toward the mouthless face of the sticky and squeezed off a controlled 3-round burst. The slugs tore through flesh and bone, smacking the head sideways even as they punched it apart in a greasy explosion of brains and glutinous blood. She fired another burst at the neck, this time uncontrolled, and the bullets tore through ligaments, cartilage and the cervical vertebrae, taking what was left of the head off the trunk in an eruptive, scarlet spray.

The creature slumped off the tall man, the complete disruption of its central nervous system causing it to loosen its gluelike grip. It fell away, sideways, a lump of unmotivated meat.

The man shoved the body away from him, breathing harshly. He got to his feet. Krysty saw by the glaring light of the fire that over his left eye was a black eye patch. A long scar throbbed whitely from the corner of his right eye to his mouth. Two red patches on his cheeks glistened where the mutated being's finger pads had slapped home, exerting their tremendous sucking power. His hair was raven black, thickly curled.

He stared at her, suddenly grinned.

"Timely. Thanks."

She held the SMG limply in her right hand, feeling utterly drained. She couldn't say a word, felt as though anything she did say would come out as an incoherent gabble. Every dull ache in her body became a throb; her limbs, her head, her womb, her chest. The man's face blurred, and it seemed to be falling toward her. Or was she falling toward it?

Strong hands caught her, held her gently.

He said, "You don't look as though you've been having a very good time."

She found herself with her face buried in the exposed fur lining of his black parka, where it was open at the zipper. It was warm and soft, its odor not unpleasant. She felt she could stay there for quite a while, and then thought, Oh, Mother-god!

She jerked her head away.

"The fire. Explosives. This place. Armory."

The tall man looked startled. He grabbed an arm, pulled her into the cooler air outside. Her eyes took in two small armored buggies, one of which was firing indiscriminately at cabins and huts. The nearest buggy had a side door open and the tall, dark-haired man hustled her toward it. Faces peered out at her, and she was suddenly aware that she was half-naked. The tall man had picked up his weapon and was holding it one-handed, butt into the side of his gut, his other arm around her shoulders. As they neared the buggy he lifted the rifle and waved it, and the farther buggy ceased firing.

He said to her, "We couldn't find anyone else, although we could've missed . . ."

"I'm the only one," she said. "The only one left."

"Okay. Up with you."

He pushed her inside the door and as she ducked her head, she heard the other buggy roar into a tire-shredding turn before hurtling off toward the outskirts of the camp. The man banged the door shut.

"Abe!" he yelled. "Get us of here! That barn's full of explosives."

It was cramped. The rear of the buggy seemed packed with armed men, and there was a strong smell of sweat and hot oil. There were two steps up to the narrow doorway that led out to the driver's area, which looked to be equally cramped. The driver revved the bus, swung the wheel. Krysty glimpsed the storehouse with flames roaring around the roof, sparks jetting high.

"Trade this for one of your grenades...?"

A fat man with a stubbled face was grinning at her, holding out a flask. She was conscious that the weight of the grenade in the upper pocket of her jump suit had caused the torn material to sag away, exposing her right breast. She closed her eyes, chuckled tiredly, then thought about which was the priority, thirst or modesty? She took the flask, put the neck to her teeth and took a hefty slug. Neat brandy. She spluttered, most of the raw spirit sluicing down her throat and warming and fortifying her. She took another slug of the brandy and handed it and the grenade to the fat man, smiling gratefully. Then she pulled her jump suit together.

"Always the loser, Finnegan!" shouted someone from the rear.

The fat man grinned like a kid and shrugged, then nearly fell off his seat as the buggy bucked forward, jolting along on its shocks as though smacked by a giant hand.

"No more barn!" yelled the driver.

The tall dark-haired man squatted in front of Krysty, clinging on to a metal projection to hold his balance as the buggy accelerated, jouncing over potholes on the rough track.

"You're safe now. We're the Trader's men. I'm Ryan. I look after things for him. Who are you?" His voice was deep and warm, immensely reassuring.

She leaned back wearily against the two steps. Not even the sharpness of their edges could make her feel uncomfortable.

"My name's Krysty," she said. "Krysty Wroth."

Chapter Five

"IT'S A MYTH," said Ryan. "Will-o'-the-wisp."

"A land of lost happiness," said Krysty.

"Crap. Ain't no such thing."

"That's what Uncle Tyas used to call a double negative. What you just said is, There is not no such thing. And that means, there *is* such a thing."

Ryan leaned back in the swivel chair, his fingers frozen in the act of lining tobacco along a paper, and gazed at the young woman seated opposite him. Almost unconsciously he let his single eye drift across her eyes—large, profoundly green, slightly almond shaped—down to high cheekbones that curved softly around to a firm chin, the nose long, the mouth full-lipped and generous. There were laugh lines there, an imp dancing in those emerald eyes. He thought it would be delightful to dive into their depths, sink slowly down, drift. Still staring, he slicked his tongue the length of the paper and deftly twirled the result.

"Finished?" There was a definitely a sardonic edge to her voice.

"Yeah." He firmed up the cigarette, the best he could do with such crude materials long ago dug up from a buried warehouse site, though the packages had at least been airtight, and he tapped an end against his thumbnail, then fished around in a top pocket, pulled out a lighter tube and flicked it. A flame sprang up, quivering slightly in the draft. Ryan grinned and pointed at the lighter. "A miracle. You know, we got maybe about a million of these little bastards. A billion. Maybe—what's the next one up?—trillion? Found 'em in a military dump down south. Crates and crates and crates of the suckers. Guys who found 'em didn't know what the hell they were to begin with, couldn't figure out how to use 'em. Thought they were antipersonnel booby bombs." He grinned again, shot a glance across the war wag's swaying cabin at J. B. Dix, who was busy greasing one of his pieces—one of his many pieces. "That's not to say that some of them aren't booby bombs," he added. "The ingenuity of man in the causing of destruction to his fellows is boundless. I read that somewhere, or something akin to it. Education, you see. Like you. Dub-ull neg-a-tive." He rolled the words out slowly, frowning mildly as though judging them. "Yeah, that surely is education. It's still a crock of shit, though, this land of lost happiness."

"A paradise beyond the Deathlands," said Krysty. She was rolling her own cigarette from the tobacco supply, her long fingers dealing nimbly with its creation. She was so fast that they seemed almost to flicker. Ryan watched, fascinated.

She had cleaned herself up, now wore a green jump suit taken from Stores. It fitted her in all the right places yet was loose and comfortable looking. She had even polished her boots; the interior lights reflected off the buffed leather. Her hair was just as lustrous, a shining flame-red cascade over her shoulders and halfway down her back. To Ryan, when she moved her head, even if gently, her hair seemed to be wildly alive, to shimmer with a restless motion.

"There is no paradise beyond the Deathlands," he intoned mock-judiciously, sucking smoke. The ancient, preserved tobacco was faintly sweet-smelling as it burned. He wasn't entirely sure what it was, although it wasn't a relaxant like happyweed. Ryan left that kind of thing for off-duty periods. "Only death. This is a world of death. There is no other world."

"Too pessimistic," she said.

"I'm a realist. It's the way it is, the way it'll always be. There's no escape. They screwed us a century ago, and we're left with the pieces. That's it. You make the best of what you've got."

"But wouldn't you like to escape?"

He stared at her, smoke from the cigarette drifting across his blind eye so it did not cause him discomfort, and he thought to himself, very odd question.

"Escape what?" he said. "What else is there? We know a little of what's going on—" he made a vague gesture that took in the entire world "—though not that much, communications being what they are. Even so, it seems that out there is much the same as it is around here. Pretty shitty. Listen." He leaned forward, jabbing the tip of his cigarette in her direction. "I'll tell you. A person gets around with the Trader. I've been with him for maybe ten years, and we've been all over. We've been as far west as you can get without falling off the edge, up through the mountains and down to the Hot Seas. There used to be a wide coastal plain there—cities, highways, millions of people—but it sank. Plain sank. Seems there was a fault or something in the earth and it was a number-one target and they hit it and it just tore the earth's crust apart and the whole deal just slid into the sea. Goodbye, that particular part of civilization."

She said, "California. That's what it was, that's what they called it."

"Well, there's no such place anymore. Hasn't been for a hundred years or more. Not since the Nuke. We thought of trying to salvage something from the seabed—there must be riches down there! A lost world! But it's too far and we don't have the gear. And the sea is hot and bubbling and scummy, and there's things down there only a crazy man would dream up."

"You could say that about everywhere."

"Sure. Doesn't alter my argument, though. Which is— the West? Forget it. Okay—" he warmed to his theme "—the Southwest. Maybe you know this, maybe you don't. There used to be desert down there, out of everyone's way. They were doing things they didn't want people to know about. Only snag was, the other side *did* know about it—they must have known about it because they pounded it, flattened it. Took it out. There's only the wind there now, and sometimes that just literally sears what's left. And where there's no wind, there's nuclear garbage floating in the sky in great clouds as thick as mountains. Sometimes it flares up and sets the night on fire. I've seen it. The sky burns." His voice was softer now, his eye unfocused. "Burns for days and nights on end. And then—" he snapped his fingers "—it stops. Just like that. You don't know why, and you'll never know why. But it just stops, the fire dies, and all you have left is floating nuclear junk." He cocked an eyebrow at her. "You figure that's paradise?"

"No, that's not what I'm—"

"So what about the North? It's cold up there. Hellish cold. There's guys up there, they don't take their furs off more than once a year. If that. Didn't used to be so all-fired warm before, so it's said, except for plains where wheat grew, but it's cold all over now. It could be that the ice from the far north has shifted south, and maybe it's still on the move, maybe it won't stop until the whole world is covered with it—a new ice age. Not in our lifetime, I guess. But it's a frozen hell up there, believe me. I've seen it, I've tried to trek through it. The guys who live there, the Franchies, they'd love to trade, but we don't have the means, the proper equipment. You go up there and your gas freezes in the tanks and gets like jelly.

"So let's try South. I'm easy. Like this, just you and me, we can go anywhere. So—South. Deep down south." His tone darkened. "Now that's a place, let me tell you. A dark locale. Far as I can tell it used to be an area of mainly grasslands, woodlands, all over. But now it's jungle, swamp and rot. There's more mutants per acre down there than any place I've seen. I don't know why. Maybe the chem stuff got out of hand, maybe the opposition went over the top, dumped too many toxins down there. Or maybe it just got hotter anyhow, the climate—something to do with the sea. Who the nuke knows. All I can tell you is that it's a poisoned land and I can do without it. Paradise it ain't."

"Hey, now. You don't seem to—"

"And then we shift to the East. Well, sure. That's civilized, I guess. Parts of it." He paused, took a final drag on the cigarette, butted it. "I guess it's civilized because everyone there says it is. And sure, they got industry of a kind, and they know how to produce electric power better than anywhere else I know, and they got lines of communication that don't break down every three hours, and they can grow their own food, and they read and write, and..." He stopped, stared down at the floor as though a memory had twitched at the outer edges of his mind. He looked up again, his one eye suddenly bleak. "But it's uncoordinated, lady. And beneath a thin skin of culture it's as much of a hell as it is out here. There's maybe a dozen families in the Southern Enclave in an uneasy truce, all

secretly lusting after what the others have got, all about
ready to swoop in and grab any territory that looks to be
weaker than they are.

"I read once about a country out there," he continued,
almost wistfully. "Hundreds of years ago. It was a large
slice of land split up into little territories, all ruled over by
individual princes and barons or dukes or whatever. All
feuding with one another, greedy for land. Everyone else's
land. And if they weren't fighting one another, they were
figuring out how to stab one another in the back in the
smartest way possible so some other guy would get the
blame. And at the same time as all this is going on, they're
busy inventing and creating and painting pictures and
writing books and fashioning crazy models or castles out
of pure gold with all the towers and turrets and draw-
bridges and even arrow slits in the walls, all in proportion, and when you lifted the roof of the tallest tower,
inside was a little glass jar for putting the salt in. Now *that*
was civilization. Sure, I guess the peasants were treated like
shit on the rich man's boots, but even so it was a busy time,
everything going on, an upward surge. They had ambition. There was always something beyond the next horizon, and the next, and the next."

She said, "Italy."

He laughed. "You did read books!"

"My mother. She made sure I knew as much as there
was to know, as much as she could cram into me. She said
it was important."

"She was a wise woman."

Krysty nodded slowly, her head bowed. "Yes," she said.

Ryan did not pursue that. It was not the time. He kept
his eyes on the scarlet glory of her hair, watched as she
brought her head back up again so that they were once

more face-to-face. The imp had gone from her eyes; now they held only grief, a sense of profound loss.

Ryan said, "Well, anyhow, the East Coast has nothing I want. It's an armed camp of greedy madmen. The muties are the peasants and no one is creating paintings that will last for half a millennium and the only gold that's coming in is from that fat rat Jordan Teague, and sure as nukeshit no one's making salt containers out of it."

"If it's an armed camp," Krysty said, "who armed it?" She stared at him clear-eyed.

Ryan held her gaze for maybe six seconds, then looked away, shrugged.

"Yeah. Okay. Point. Maybe we all realize now that our trade routes have been built on orders we should maybe never have delivered."

"'Maybe'?"

"Okay. We should never have delivered." He stopped, stretched, sat back down again. His hands plucked at the crimson scarf tied around his throat and he loosened it. The ends hung heavily down to his waist. "One doesn't always think ahead. You don't plan for the future, figure out the pros and cons of what you're doing. The present is all, lady. The here and now. It's the only thing you have to wrestle with. And that in fact is the history of the human race. Always too frantic worrying about what was happening in the here and how. We forgot that the future is created in the present, that whatever is done in the here and now has an influence on the years to come." His voice drifted low as he stared at his boots. "Too late, lady. Too late..."

Krysty said accusingly, "You could make a start by not delivering all this heavy shit to Mocsin." She didn't know anything about the load they were carrying, but she knew all about Jordan Teague and his miniempire out near the Darks.

Ryan grinned sourly.

"Funny thing," he said. "Teague ain't gonna be—and you can take that as a nondouble negative that's a great big positive—he ain't gonna be too fireblasted pleased about this load."

"That's funny?"

"Well, you see, it just so happens that most of Teague's consignment went up when Truck Four blew. *Boom!*" He spread his arms high. "All those grenades, all that high explosive, all those old armor-piercing shells. Sent most of his delivery to glory in a great big blaze-out. Lucky for us, though, because that's what creamed most of the stickies and other mad muties that had us in a terrible, terrible fix. And that means that Teague's gonna be getting short supplies. Pity."

"And did it?"

"Did it what?"

"All go up."

Ryan chuckled.

"As it happens, no, of course it didn't. But Teague's not to know that. It's the perfect scam. You may not believe this, but we do have a code. Of sorts. I mean, listen—we don't spend sleepless nights gnawing away at the problem, it's too late for that, way too late. The Old Man did it to survive."

Krysty wrinkled her nose. What Ryan had said sounded to her like special pleading. "You still didn't answer the question," she said. "Would you *like* to escape?"

Ryan shook his head helplessly.

"To what? There *is* no escape from the Deathlands."

"Uncle Tyas thought there was."

"You mean, get a boat, take a trip, sail across the ocean? You don't know what's out there or under the waves, just waiting for you. You don't know what's waiting for you on the other side, either. Could be worse than here, though that's hard to imagine."

"No, he didn't mean that."

Ryan pointed up at the dull metal ceiling of the swaying war wag.

"You mean up there? How? *Why?* All there is up there is free-floating garbage. We know the old guys had, I dunno—" he groped for words "—kind of settlements out in space, huge constructions with their own air supplies. That kind of thing. But how the hell d'you get to them? All the places where they had vehicles, aircraft, what have you, were blitzed in the Nuke. We've stumbled across launching grounds with wrecked machinery, incredible rusting hulks lying around, chunks of dead metal. But there's no way you can get this shit off the ground, believe me. No way at all."

"No, that's not what I mean, either. Uncle Tyas knew. He'd found something out. But he wouldn't tell me. He and old Peter..."

"Who?"

"Peter Maritza, his buddy. His close buddy. They did just about everything together. They were always poking into old books...and papers..." Her voice drifted off.

"And?" he prompted her.

"I remember when it happened," she said. "But I was only a kid at the time—maybe fourteen or fifteen, that kind of age."

EVEN AS SHE SPOKE Krysty could see the scene in the candlelit, tightly caulked log cabin that stood at the edge of their hamlet, hidden deep in the rolling hills and forests of the Sanctuary.

She saw again the hawk-faced man, with the deep-set, piercing eyes, then only in his early fifties, striding around the main room muttering to himself as she sat beside the fire quietly watching him with solemn, uncomprehending eyes.

She was still a little afraid of him. His tone was harsh, his manner abrupt. She had not as yet been allowed to plumb the depths of kindliness and generosity that were essential parts of his character. You had to know Tyas McCann a long time before you could get past his guard, the steely barrier of his ingrained reserve and suspicion. And to young Krysty Wroth, then, he was still an unknown quantity, for she had only lived with him since Sonja had died and that was less than eighteen months before. Sometimes she still cried at nights, the image of her mother wasted by the sickness for which there was no cure, from which there was no escape, etched into her mind. And she was lonely—soul-achingly lonely. Her mother had been everything to her, and her mother's brother could never take her place.

Now of course she knew better. Now she knew that it was not a question of Uncle Tyas taking Sonja's place in her love and affection. Uncle Tyas supplied what Sonja had not supplied, and would not have supplied even if she had lived. They were two different branches of the same tree. Her mother had taught her to keep the Secrets; her uncle, how to use them. Her mother taught her knowledge of the Earth Mother; her uncle had expanded and extended this knowledge dramatically, to include just about all he knew about the real world outside, and all he had learned about the catastrophe that had overtaken it: what had happened, how it had happened and why it had happened—though there were more theories than hard facts on that.

And he had taught her how to survive in a world that had been insane for a century. Her mother would never have taught her how to use a firearm. Uncle Tyas had taught her just that.

She could see him now, outside the large, airy, seven-roomed cabin, holding a squat and ugly-looking metallic shape in both hands—she realized now that it must have been the Detonics Pocket 9; it was the smallest handgun Uncle Tyas had in a wide-ranging collection gathered over the years—and saying, "This is a bad thing, little one, but you have to know about it and you have to be able to use it one day, because there are worse things waiting out beyond the Forest, and you have to sometimes use bad things to deal with worse things, worse situations." Krysty was fourteen when she'd heard this.

Almost as soon as she had come to stay with him he had begun his instruction, not only in the use of all kinds of weaponry, but in unarmed combat, as well.

There had been two of them, she and young Carl Lanning, at fifteen the eldest son of Herb Lanning, Harmony's ironsmith. Herb was a big, potbellied, gruff man who had taken over the forge and ironsmith's shop built by his father forty or so years back. He did odd jobs for Uncle Tyas, made strange-looking metal artifacts that Uncle Tyas created on his drawing board from books in his vast library, objects that sometimes worked as Uncle Tyas said they would, and sometimes didn't. And when they didn't, Uncle Tyas would rant and cuss and call Herb the biggest blockhead in the entire Deathlands, say that he couldn't construct a simple metal object when it was handed to him on a set of detailed and meticulously finished drawings. And Big Herb would grin good-naturedly and point out that everything he'd done was from the drawings, and if the thing didn't work it was because the guy who drew it up hadn't got it right in the first place. They used to argue for hours, Uncle Tyas raging, Big Herb smiling complacently, filling a rocking chair with his bulk, both hands clasped across his gut. It had to be said that more often than not Big Herb was right. More often than not, there had been a slight error in transcription from book example to drawing board, because Uncle Tyas worked fast, too fast, often in a white heat of creation, his eager brain far ahead of his fingers, nimble though the latter were. The trouble was, Uncle Tyas invariably wanted things done about half an hour before he thought of them.

Big Herb's eldest boy, Carl, helped him in the ironsmith's shop. He was a tall, lanky kid with a shock of black hair, an explosion of freckles on his face, an inquiring mind, but a gentle nature. That was why Uncle Tyas had chosen him to partner Krysty in his unarmed combat lessons. Krysty remembered overhearing Uncle Tyas talking enthusiastically to Peter Maritza—not "old" Peter Maritza then; by no means "old," even though he was a good ten years ahead of Uncle Tyas—out on the porch one night when she'd been preparing dinner, his voice an excited hiss, a new idea clamoring in his brain.

"You get it, Peter? There's Krysty—she's a girl."

"Tyas, I'm not an imbecile. I know she's a blasted girl."

"Okay, okay. But she's a girl, right? Weaker sex, right?"

"Not around here, buddy. Not in Harmony. Talk like that'll get you strung up from the—"

"All right! In general, Peter! Generally speaking! Weaker sex in quotes, right? Then there's young Carl—"

"You saying he's weak? You saying he's some kind of milksop? Why, I've seen him at the forge—"

"Peter, will you listen to me! Okay, he beats the shit out of all that red-hot metal in his daddy's ironshop, but he's no great shakes when it comes to anything else, right? Sure he's no weakling, but he's not what you or I'd call positive, you get me? Got no drive in him. Just like his father. He's faced with a raving canny, y'know what would happen? He'd just let himself get eaten up, sure as hell. Well, I aim to change all that. Change 'em both. Damn right."

And he had. Changed them both. Especially Krysty. At the age of fourteen she'd learned how to throw a guy to the ground in one second flat, how to disable an adversary with a single one-handed squeeze, how to cripple a man for life with one well-directed punch.

She found that wrestling with Carl in a rough-and-tumble scrimmage was sexually arousing. That in close-quarters proximity to him, in a situation in which both were trying their damnedest to conquer the other, in a fierce and breathless and sweaty scuffle on the ground, rolling over and over each other, first one on top, then the other, each desperate to outtussle the other, she experienced a sudden and overpowering awareness of his maleness, a sharply felt urge to surrender to him yet also a scary and delicious sense of power over him that had nothing at all to do with winning the bout. And the knowledge came to her as, for a split second, they ceased their struggle and stared half fearfully, half defiantly into each other's eyes, that he felt the same. It was partly emotional, she recognized, partly physical. She had never experienced such feelings before.

At fourteen Krysty Wroth knew all there was to know about physical sex—the full details from ovulation to conception through pregnancy and into childbirth itself. But Sonja had also taught her from an early age that sex was not merely an act of procreation but a powerful experience, an expression of heady passion. It could also, if you were lucky enough to find the right partner, be fun. But you had to look after yourself because if you didn't have the luck to find the right partner, you could land yourself in all kinds of unnecessary trouble.

Sonja had also told her that years ago, before the Nuke, there had been religions that preached childbirth almost as a necessity, despite the fact that the world was overloaded with people, a good proportion of whom lived in abject misery and squalor. Those old religions had largely disappeared. Only in the Baronies was religion, in one form or another, used as it had been in the bad old days, as a means of keeping the populace quiet and as a means of keeping the populace growing in number. Down there, you bred for the Barons. Boy children were sent by God; girl children were a damned nuisance, fit only to skivvy and breed—breed more and more boy children: the warrior syndrome.

Contraception was actually banned in certain of the Baronies where the old, ugly Islamic and Judeo-Christian fundamentalist creeds were strong—that women were basically cattle; that they were not only created solely for man's benefit and pleasure but were also inherently sly, lewd and evil creatures and must be kept in a state of subjugation. Although that was not to say that contraception wasn't available. On the contrary, the rich and the powerful could afford the secret and highly expensive prophylactics that did a roaring trade on the various black markets. The poor, as usual, were not so lucky. They had to rely on ill-understood natural methods, altogether a chancy business.

Those who followed the wisdom of the Earth Mother, which was more a free celebration of natural forces than a sharply defined and disciplined religion—an understanding, brought about to a great degree by the often strange effects of genetic and physical mutation over the years, that the power of the mind and the power of nature had rarely been used to their fullest extent—were more fortunate. They had the benefit of knowledge passed down from mother to daughter of medicaments that had been known to a few long before the Nuke—natural specifics, natural ointments, natural oils and unguents, all derived from a variety of roots, tree barks, mashed-up leaves and berries. Now, three generations after the disaster, this information could be said to have become the solid bedrock upon which the slowly expanding worship of the Earth Mother rested.

So Krysty theoretically knew all about sex. It was a natural function and a natural pleasure. And she knew, too, exactly how not to get pregnant. The only thing that remained to be conquered was the act itself, the physical and emotional experience firsthand.

Thinking about her feelings as she'd wrestled with young Carl, and mulling over what her mother had often talked about when she was alive, how if there was any first-time-ever obstacle at all, it was only an insignificant wafer-thin tissue of membrane and it was better to get it out of the way sooner rather than later and when the time came she'd know about it and know what to do, Krysty weighed things up as coolly and calmly as any post-Nuke fourteen-year-old could have and figured that the time had indeed come. She knew what to do, and she did it. Or, rather, she and Carl did it together, and it wasn't the most sensational experience she had ever had, but on the other hand it wasn't half bad, not half bad at all.

It was only years later—maybe seven or even eight, when she returned to Harmony after one of her bouts of wanderlust—that she discovered, to her amusement, that

Uncle Tyas had been deliberate in instigating that, as he was deliberate in most things. That he'd purposely thrown her and Carl together, hoping they'd like each other, because he'd figured Carl for an essentially good, honest, caring kid.

Krysty's amusement at this discovery, which was let drop, again deliberately, by Uncle Tyas, was tinged with mild annoyance. No one likes to find out that someone else has been pulling her strings.

"That was gross interference, Uncle Tyas. What if I hadn't liked him?"

"You did like him," he pointed out, arms wide, an innocent expression on his hawklike face.

"Yeah, but..."

She could find no words of condemnation because none applied.

"Better to let it go to someone you like than by force to a stranger or someone you hate," Uncle Tyas continued. "Virginity means nothing. It's a moralistic ideal from an age that in a certain way was darker and more twisted than our own. But that first time, the way it happens, Krysty, maybe influences your whole life."

Which was true.

The thought and memories and emotions tumbled and shifted around in Krysty's mind as the war wag, like some primeval brute animal, bucked and shook along the blacktop. The images sharpened, then defocused. Became clear again, then vague.

Now Uncle Tyas was dead, he and all his companions on that strange pilgrimage. Rest in peace, she thought.

"YOU WERE REMEMBERING," said Ryan.

He had watched her as she'd stared blank-eyed at the floor. The pause had drifted on for maybe thirty heartbeats, and it was clear from her face, from the shadows that flickered across those drawn features, that memories were flooding into her mind, memories of those now dead. She seemed to him to be a strong person, a woman of courage, a woman who could cope with disaster, yet even the toughest individuals had their limits.

"Yeah, I was." Her voice was low. "There's so much I recall." She gazed at Ryan now, as if deciding whether to tell him one thing more.

"Later, when I was older," she said, "I came back to the house in the afternoon, and Uncle Tyas—I'll never forget it—he yelled something at me as I went in the door. He said, 'They're there! I know it! I can feel it in my bones! It's not a joke! Bastards didn't have a sense of humor!'"

"Which particular bastards?" queried Ryan patiently.

"Scientists is what he meant. Old-time technics. Uncle Tyas was certain they all had no sense of humor. He claimed that was why the world blew up, because the scientists had had no sense of humor, that they were all cold fish without a joke among them."

"Maybe he had a point."

Ryan did not mind her talking on like this, although he doubted very much that there was anything to be gained from her story. He had an idea what the punch line was going to be. He'd heard it, in one form or another, before. Many times. But that didn't matter in the least. It was therapy, he knew—a torrent of words pouring out of her, some kind of emotional release. It was all to the good if it somehow flushed her system of the horror of the past couple of days.

Ryan said gently, "Okay, so what was he talking about?"

She took a breath, bit her lower lip and said, "A couple of months ago I got back to the Forest. I'd been away for a year or more. I've been doing a great deal of moving around myself. Things happen. Change." She shrugged. "I got back and Uncle Tyas opened the door to me. He didn't know I was coming, but as soon as he saw me he said, 'My God, Krysty, I had it all the time and I never knew.' He was shaken, totally shaken. And drawn, too, and ill. He said there was a 'land of lost happiness.' Those were his words. A land of milk and honey beyond the Deathlands. And he'd found the gateway to it, and he knew how to open it.

Ryan thought about what she was saying. He had heard stories like this before, although only stories. Hints, rumors, whispers. A land of lost contentment. No one, to his knowledge, had ever tried to do something about finding the place. Which, in any case, wasn't to be found. It was a myth, a dream. Something to compensate for the horrors of Deathlands existence. Sometimes the stories told of a fabulous treasure hidden somewhere—significantly, always in the most wild and inaccessible places: the Hotlands in the southwest, the icy regions to the north, those mysterious and plague-stricken swamps that glowed in the dark down in the south. Or across the simmering seas to the west. Or even, he'd once heard, up in the sky.

And that was it. Pie in the sky. Heaven. Somewhere—*anywhere*—other than this hell on earth known as the Deathlands.

On the other hand—"more hidden underground than had ever been discovered..." Sure, he thought, that was true enough. He and the Trader and J. B. Dix knew very well that it was so, that there were far more Stockpiles hidden away in man-made caverns than they had stumbled across thus far. That had to be admitted. But strange weaponry? Bizarre secrets? Just a dream. The only bizarre shit they'd ever uncovered was a sea of nerve gas in the hills of old Kentucky, and they'd reburied it in very short order. For the rest—although a manufacturing industry was alive in the Baronies, creakingly primitive as it was for the most part—people were still living with mainly late-twentieth-century artifacts and weapons, and if they were creating new matériel it was based on the old. There were no new kinds of weapons in the here and now. None whatsoever.

"Look," he said gently, "I have to tell you that there is no land of lost happiness. Your Uncle Tyas really was chasing a rainbow, and there's no crock of gold at the end of it because there is no end."

Her head jerked up. She said almost defiantly, "He wasn't a fool and he wasn't crazy. Whatever else he was, Uncle Tyas wasn't crazy."

"I didn't say—"

"He did find something! I know it. It was something important and it was something...outrageous, something completely wild...something that no one's ever discovered before. He wasn't simply some crazy old fucker obsessed with a phantom!"

"Sure."

"And don't 'sure' me, asshole."

"Okay, okay. I'm sorry."

The anger went out of her eyes, the granite hardness from her face. Her body, suddenly tense, relaxed. She breathed in and said "Okay" while breathing out again. "I'm sorry. Hell, you saved my life." All at once she grinned. "You can't be a complete asshole."

Ryan glanced sideways, saw that up front the Trader was watching him, eyebrows raised. Through the steel mesh that covered the blown windshield he could just make out that they were heading through trees, an overlush forest that a century ago had probably simply been pine but was now a moist tangle of humid undergrowth and purplish topgrowth. He remembered the area. They were about five miles out of Mocsin. Talk about bizarre, he brooded. There was enough that was bizarre in the Deathlands without adding to it with all these dreams of fantastic weaponry and who knows what all else. This forest alone was bizarre. How it had grown was beyond him: a random gift from the Nuke. On the other side of Mocsin it was mostly scrub desert to the foothills of the Darks, no purple forest at all.

He suddenly thought, the Darks.

He said, "You were heading for the Darks. Was that where this wild blue yonder all started?"

She scowled at him.

"Still heading," she said.

"You're *what*?"

"Still heading. Still heading for the Darks."

Ryan said, "Come *on*!"

"Don't patronize me," she said through her teeth, the angry look back in wide green eyes.

Ryan held up his hands in mock surrender.

"I'm not patronizing. I'm trying to be realistic. You got any idea what's in between Mocsin and the hills? One hundred klicks of wilderness is what. You gonna walk it?"

"I'll get a buggy."

"How? You got any creds?"

"I'll sell my body."

"As to that," said Ryan, "there's quite a bit of competition in Mocsin. *And* it's regulated. *And* the pay's piss poor. *And* it's a hell of a life. *And*..."

She shot him a withering look.

"You don't maybe consider I have a touch more class than the majority of my working sisters?"

Ryan tapped his teeth with a fingernail and looked her over with amusement.

"Here it is," he said, his eyes locking on to hers. "You have more class than I've seen in five years."

"Only five years? How blasted gallant." Her tone was sardonic. "Don't bother with the honey talk. I can get by."

Ryan stood up and leaned against the steel-faced wall. He went on as though she hadn't said a word. "But that of course only makes it worse. You wouldn't start out in the back-street sleaze pits, you'd go straight to the top. And that means you'd start off with Jordan Teague, the fattest hog in the territory. You'd not only supplant all his harem, which means they'd be gunning for you the whole time, but you'd have to put up with his personal habits and sexual demands, which are by no means couth."

"'Couth!'" She laughed suddenly. "That I like!"

"When Teague's finished with you—only take a month at the most, he has a low boredom threshold—you get passed down to his chief of police, Cort Strasser. Teague's just gross, raunchy. Strasser on the other hand has very strange and violent tastes. Whips, torture, humiliation. I don't believe Strasser likes women very much."

"Okay, okay." Her voice was tight. She said quietly, "Is it any wonder people want to escape..."

"If you've been around," Ryan said, "you know very well that not every city, town or hamlet is the same as Mocsin. Sure there are plague pits all over the place, but you could probably live your entire life out without seeing one."

Krysty stood up, faced him, her deep green eyes diamond hard, defiant. She swept a swath of scarlet hair from her face and it tumbled back over her shoulders. Ryan felt sudden and intense desire for her.

She looked at him and said, "I'm going on to the Darks."

Chapter Six

"AND CHECK YOUR BOOTS," said the Trader through his cigar smoke. He waved the cigar at J. B. Dix. "See they do it, J.B."

"Don't worry. They always do."

"You, as well."

J.B. didn't say anything. He glanced at Ryan, a pissed-off expression on his thin face.

"And don't look like that!" barked the Trader. "I know what I'm talking about! It's the little details. You forget the little details, you might as well be dead. Hell, you forget 'em and you will be dead!"

Ryan reflected that it was ever thus when they were approaching what the Trader invariably referred to as a "pest hole"—a town or area controlled not by men and women with a certain standard of civilized behavior, but by men and women for whom there was no law but their own, no rules but those that they invented on the spur of the moment to satisfy some passing whim or desire. Mocsin was just such a place. It was not the worst, but it was well up—or, depending on how you looked at it, down—the scale.

Back a hundred years or so it had been typical small-town America. A long main street with cross streets cutting it into blocks. A movie house, a bank, a couple of realtors, ice cream and pizza parlors, supermarkets, drugstores, bars, a half dozen greasy spoons, a couple of upmarket but still essentially tacky restaurants, a Lutheran church, a sheriff's office with a small jail facility for drunks to dry out in, two motels. The edge-of-town streets had trees on them, well-shaved lawns in front of medium-sized dwelling places for the moderately well-off. There was a small industrial complex: a machine-tool plant, a couple of lots where electrical components were stamped, a coast-to-coast shipping warehouse, a small plastics factory. Near the industrial part of town the homes were drabber, the streets grimier, the bars grubbier, the night-life darker.

Mocsin dwellers of the past, had they been able to skip a hundred years into the future, would have both recognized the old hometown and not recognized the old hometown. The outline was there. The bank was there, the church, the movie house: everything was still in its place. The Nuke had not hit Mocsin, just the aftereffects.

The bank wasn't a bank anymore, the church wasn't a church, the movie house wasn't a movie house. There were places where you could eat, places where you could sleep, places where you could buy food, but in no sense of the words were these places restaurants, hotels, stores. All were more or less rat pits. What flourished in Mocsin were the bars and the gambling houses and the whorehouses. Perhaps "flourished" was not quite the word: there wasn't a hell of a lot of bartering strength in Mocsin, except at the top.

The top was represented by Jordan Teague, who certainly had his fair share of flesh; and his so-called chief of police, Cort Strasser, somewhat less well endowed in body, though not in brain.

Strasser, nowadays, ran things. Teague still gave the orders, was still very firmly in charge, but Cort Strasser kept the show on the road, did all the hard graft necessary to keep things from falling apart completely. Largely this meant cracking down viciously on anyone or anything that looked as if he, she or it might buck the system, a system that had grown up over a period of twenty years, based on Teague's highly dubious claim but iron grip on the gold mines to the southwest of town.

The road through Mocsin was the main route to the northwest and the north. Travelers, heading into the Rockies in the hopes that there they would find fresh fields, had to pass through Mocsin and consequently had to pay for the privilege, either in creds or in kind. For that reason not a lot of travelers actually made it through the town, the toll being hair-raisingly high. If you argued the toss, you ended up six feet under and your goods and chattels, which included both kith and kin, went straight into Jordan Teague's treasury. If you paid up, it usually broke you, and you either signed on as a miner so that you could earn back what you'd paid out in toll—a laughable ambition—or you simply parked your steam truck and van where a few hundred other hopefuls had parked theirs and tried to find some kind of honest employment in the district. There was now a vast shantytown of rusting trailers, buggies and rigs sprawling out of the south end of town.

Those who resided in the town and its environs did not so much live as exist, and it was a miserable and squalid existence at that. Most took refuge in booze or happy-weed, sometimes both, and brought up their children in wretched circumstances with the ever present fear that one day Strasser's talent spotters would home in on them. Pretty young girls and pretty young boys were always needed for the recreational activities of Strasser's security goons. Then, once the bloom had gone from them, the kids were consigned to the various gaudy houses that lined the streets in the center of town.

Sure, commercial life, of a kind, went on. People made clothes and mended boots and shoes; people reared hogs and horses, built timber-frame houses, had small farmsteads outside of the peripheries where root vegetables, corn and wheat were grown. The mech trade was the real thriver: mechanics, welders, machine repairmen were all highly prized. Men and women who were skilled mechs could command ace jack. Even Jordan Teague had to pay for skill. He had to keep up his fleet of land wags and trucks. Maneuverability was essential in the Deathlands.

"You're not listening to me, Ryan."

"True. I was thinking about Mocsin."

"Don't waste your brain," growled the Trader. "We wanna be in and out of there, smooth and fast."

Ryan laughed.

"Fat chance! Bastard could keep us hanging around for days. Then we finally get the 'audience' with the great man. Then we have to point out that he's only getting less than half because we got hit by marauders. Then he gets mad and stalks out on us. Then we wait around for—"

"Yeah, yeah," the Trader muttered. "I know all that." His face suddenly twisted, his mouth snapping shut like a steel trap as he snorted explosively through his nose. His right hand slid inside his worn leather zip-up and clutched his gut. "Nukeblast this...indigestion."

Ryan stared at him. "See the medics about it," he said.

"Damned warlocks, that's all they are," the Trader grunted. "Piss-artists. The day I let some no-good incompetent get his mitts into me'll be the day after I've kicked it." He wiped an arm across his brow, leaving a smear of grime from the soiled jacket sleeve. "Indigestion is all. Bastard cook. Poisoning me. Needs changing." He gestured at Ryan. "Do something about Loz, Ryan. Get a new cookie. That'll cure me."

Night was falling. Deathlands night. The sky was a lowering bottle green greased with angry flame-red streaks. Dark clouds were boiling up behind them, though it was doubtful that they were rain clouds. In front of them, the mountains were picked out in an extraordinary diamond hard and brilliant radiance, strange luminance backlighting the sharp-toothed serrations of their peaks. A bitter breeze whipped the dust at his feet.

Ryan shivered, closed his long fleece-lined coat, stamped his boots. He said to the Trader, "We still heading south after this number?"

"Yeah."

"Great. It's too near to the Icelands up here. At night you start to breathe sleet chips."

The Trader laughed raucously.

"You're getting soft, Ryan. When you've had twenty years or more of this crap, you don't notice it."

Ryan watched the busy scene below. The land wags, trucks and two of the war wags were parked in a wide circle off the road. Fires were being built outside the vehicles' perimeter, massive constructions of logs and thorn and brush scrub and chunks of long-burning hardwood carried especially for the purpose in one of the trucks. Fires, as such, did not particularly deter marauders or strange animals that sometimes came shuffling around, sniffing for easy kills—dogs as big as steers with tusks a foot long, roaming in packs, bred in secret, truly carnivorous; or hideous, unknown beasts of great bulk that left wide trails of yellow slime behind them—but flames would give light when you didn't want to waste the generators, and psychologically, they were good for the men. What did deter was the immense amount of firepower concentrated in that circle of travel-worn and travel-stained vehicles.

There was enough blast power there to shred anything that might dare to take on the land wag train.

On the road itself, maybe forty meters from the bottom of the hillock on which he and the Trader stood, was the lead war wag, two big container rigs and an armored truck on Ryan's buggy. Men were milling around there; Ryan could see J.B. giving terse orders, checking things out. He yawned, turned, took in the dreary terrain.

This was basically flatland, desert scrub. Behind lay the purple forest, a dark mass only just glimpsed beyond the rises of the semiruined blacktop. To Ryan's right, more forest. To his left, low hills, dun colored, sparsely vegetated with brush and trees picked as clean as ancient animal bones. In front of him, far distant, the foothills leading up to the towering tors and peaks that marched across the dying sun. And between them and Ryan was the road, more woodland and, beyond, out of sight, the mess that was Mocsin.

He glanced northwest. There the hills were significantly darker, blacker. Hence "the Darks." Once, he believed, they had been known by some other name, but what it was he could not say. The Darks suited them: black, brooding mountains, slashed by hideously deep ravines, with a climate and an ugly mythology all their own.

There . . . lay Paradise?

The Trader said, "How's the girl?"

"Great minds think alike."

The Trader glanced at his tall war captain. "Getting yourself in there, huh?" He chuckled. "You young dogs. Make me feel like a real cripple, real old fart."

"I was thinking about what she said. The Darks."

"Most unpleasant locale. Never penetrated it. Nothing for us there, boy. At least nothing marked on old Marsh's plans."

"Doesn't mean to say they're empty."

The Trader laughed.

Had they not once made the long haul through the mountain chain maybe four hundred klicks south of there, and stood looking out over the seething Pacific Ocean, watching it roil and bubble and steam?

Had they not actually managed to sail around the lagoons that lay over what on the old maps once been called "the Black Rock Desert"?

Had they not found a vast inland sea where once had been a lake? Had they not penetrated the peripheries of that dread land of fire and howling wind that lay far to the south of them now, where terrifying gale-force gusts tore across the parched landscape, transforming the world into a hell of dust and whirling grit that shredded bare skin to the bone?

All in search of Stockpiles. All in search of...

Suddenly he stopped laughing, whipped his head around, stared at the tree line toward Mocsin.

"I think I caught a flash." He had turned to the west, one arm flung over his eyes.

"A flash? In this light? What kind of flash?"

"Light on metal. I could be wrong." The Trader shrugged. "Wouldn't surprise me if that fat bastard had guys on lookout for us. But so what? They won't try anything, you bet your life. They'd be outta their skulls. They'd need a few major field pieces to blow our snot away, and Teague's got none."

"That we know of."

Again the Trader's shoulders moved, and he turned full on to Ryan. "Where is the girl, anyhow?"

"Asleep. War Wag Two. She wanted to come with us but I got Kathy to feed her some caps. She's out. She'll stay out for hours."

"And then? Can't keep her on the train if she don't wanna stay, Ryan."

"Kathy'll talk to her, try and persuade her to stay clear of Mocsin and out of the Darks. It's an insane idea to head up there alone. She wouldn't stand a dog's chance."

"Looks a tough cookie to me."

"Not the point."

The Trader pushed a hand back through his grizzled hair, sniffed and spat. He jammed the cigar, now dead, back into his mouth.

"Up to you."

Below, J.B. was climbing the hillock followed by the lanky, long-haired Abe. J.B. stared up at Ryan through his steel-rimmed glasses.

"See the flash?"

The Trader grunted.

"What say we give 'em a little present?" said Abe. "What say a rocket up the ass? Huh? Huh?"

"It's not them I'm worried about," said J.B. darkly.

Ryan caught his eye.

"What's the problem?"

The thin little guy stared at the ground, then glanced to the east where darkness was reaching out toward them.

"Should've made sure of that mutie bunch."

"Man, we destroyed 'em!"

"Could've been more in the rocks. Could've cleared out long before we started looking."

"We were there most of the day, J.B."

Dix's shoulders twitched. "Don't like it. Should've sanitized the place. Scorched earth."

Abe looked uneasy. Ryan felt uneasy. The Trader's face was blank. J.B. looked up, his sallow face coloring slightly.

"Okay. We don't kill for the kill. Even so. Guy who ramrodded that band had brains. Thought he could nail us, which was stupid. But he went about it the right way. That's what counts."

"He's dead," said Ryan. "Gotta be. The girl, Krysty, said a sticky chased him. The sticky came back but the scaly guy didn't. What more d'you want?"

J.B. said, "His head." He added, "I just got a feeling."

Ryan felt he'd known J. B. Dix for a long, long time: an age, a lifetime. He had joined the Trader's band only a year or so after Ryan himself had signed up, and had proved himself utterly indispensable as the Trader's weapons master. Thin and intense, slightly melancholic, he rarely said much; what he did say was short and to the point. Whereas others might yell and rage to push their argument, J.B. just got gruffer, his sentences more clipped. Ryan respected this incisiveness, his singular mind.

Even so...

"Ah, come on!" Ryan punched him on the shoulder lightly. "If that mutie can take the train solo, he can have it. He'll have earned it. We oughta sign the bastard on!"

They began to move off down the slope, Abe veering left, the others heading for the small convoy on the road.

The Trader yelled, "Don't forget. Every hour, on the hour."

Abe waved. "We'll be there."

The Trader said, "Hey, J.B., you tell the guys to check their boots?"

Dix didn't reply.

IN A HUGE, HIGH-CEILINGED ROOM with a gallery running around its walls midway up, and tall windows now cloaked with rich, wine-red velvet hangings, and a door at the far end similarly masked, lit by light lancing down in an intense cone from a single spot concealed in one of the corner angles high above, a man of indeterminate age, clad in a faded and filthy black coat that reached to his thin shanks, and black pants, cracked knee-length boots, a shirt that perhaps centuries ago might have been white but now was a mottled brownish-yellow, and with a tall hat on his head, the brim chipped and worn, the crown sagging sideways as though it had half-snapped off, capered and danced and recited in a cracked tenor:

The shades of night were falling fast,
   As through an, ah . . . something, ah, ah, Alpine—
yes!
   Alpine village passed
   A youth who bore, ah, ah . . . something-ice,
   A banner with a—no, the . . . *the* strange device,
Excelsior!

He skipped a couple of steps, jerked off his hat so that greasy locks trumbled over the back of his neck, and waved it. Then he jammed the hat back on, took it off again and bowed away from the door, facing into the spotlight's glare, sweeping the hat around with a flourish. He straightened slowly, a nervous smile on his stubbly face. His lips came back, revealing unexpectedly white teeth. His eyes were narrowed against the light.

"Come on, come on. That ain't the end!"

The voice came from the darkness, impenetrable to the man in the ragged black clothes, somewhere under the spotlight.

"No, indeed. By, ah . . . no means." The old man's voice was now richer, deeper, more of a baritone. It was clear that the cracked and reedy tenor was reserved for abnormal rather than normal speech.

"Get to the bits about her tits!" bawled another voice. There was a rustle of subdued laughter.

"The, ah...tits. Yes." The man in the black clothes pondered this, a hand to his brow. Close-up, he could be seen to be sweating, the rivulets of perspiration cutting shallow channels through a good deal of grime. "Yes. It is...somewhere...somewhere here. Up in the, ah...cerebrum..." he laughed, somewhat apologetically. "One forgets, my dear sirs. One forgets so easily."

"Get on!"

"Yes. Yes, by all means. Was it not...the girl? The girl warning him? Warning the traveler? Ahh..." He held one hand in the air, forefinger upstretched, pointing toward the ceiling. On his face was a singular expression, the eyes now bulging, a terrible frown concentrated on his brow. He intoned,

Beware the pine tree's withered, ah...branch!
　Beware the, ah...awful *avalanche!*
　Beware...

He paused, squeezed his eyes suddenly shut. His hand dropped to his brow, the fingers digging into the flesh as though trying to claw their way into his brain. He was shaking, shuddering as though in the grip of an ague. His left hand now shot up from his side to his head, the fingers clamping themselves around the hand already there. A sound like a steam whistle came from his mouth.

Near the spotlight muzzle-flashes flared twice. The roar of a handgun crashed through the room, reverberated around it, the sound of the two shots running together. The rounds smacked into the floor inches from the man, whined off into the darkness beyond the light's penumbra. There was a wild yell from the side.

"Nukesucker! Watch what ya doin'!"

At the sound of the shots the man in the ragged black clothes came alive again and skipped backward. It was as if he had been expecting something of the sort, as if the experience was by no means a new one.

"I have it! I have it!" he cried. "The maiden is warning him, warning him of the fearful disasters that may befall a lone traveler amid those eternal Alpinic snows!" Again the hand shot up, forefinger quivering.

"O stay", the maiden said, "and rest
    Thy weary head upon...my breast!"

There was a howl of laughter and a roar of obscenities from the hidden watchers around the huge room.

Which suddenly died to silence as another man strode into the spotlight.

Tall and gaunt, he, too, was dressed in black, though his clothes were not shabby but clean and pressed, his black riding boots sending off a sparkle of highlights from their polished surfaces. His head had a fringe of dark hair at the back but was otherwise bald except for a line of mustache on his upper lip. His skin was yellowish, the flesh drawn over the bones of his face like thin parchment. His eyes were narrowed slits; his lips were drawn back into a grin that held no humor whatsoever.

Reaching the center of the room he halted. The man in the ragged clothes watched him warily, licking his lips.

"Pathetic!" spat out the man with the skull-like face. "You've got it wrong again, you old fool."

The other shook his head, a look of abject terror now sliding across his grimy features.

"No, sir. No, Mr. Strasser, I...I don't believe so." His voice was pitching higher even as he spoke. "I...I may misremember the odd word, sir. Here and there. Now and then. But I don't believe I—''

Strasser lashed out suddenly with his right foot, the toe of his boot cracking into the other's right knee. The man screamed, staggered, collapsed on the floor and clutched his knee in agony.

Strasser bent over him, hissed at him, "We shall have to put you in with the sows again, Doc."

The man on the floor cringed away from his tormentor, his voice a whimper of mingled horror and revulsion. "Please. Not that, Mr. Strasser. Please just tell me, tell me where I went wrong."

Strasser stood and stared down with a cold smile on his face.

"The maiden," he said softly. "You always get it wrong, Doc. The maiden implores the lone traveler—not to put his *head* on her breast, but his *hand*."

The man called Doc blinked up at him, still clasping his knee with one hand, a puzzled expression creasing his face.

"Are...are you sure, Mr. Strasser?"

"Positive! The maiden wants the lone traveler to squeeze her breast. Both breasts, in fact. With both hands. She is yearning for this, you old fool. Her entire body is quivering with lust for him. She tells him that she is wet for him, that only his lips, his tongue, can assuage her desire." He paused, pursed his lips thoughtfully. He said quite pleasantly, "You do remember this, don't you, Doc?"

"Why, yes...yes." The man on the floor swallowed a couple of times, licking his thin lips again, his brow corrugating into a frown. "Yes, I...I do believe you're right, Mr. Strasser. Curious that I should forget Longfellow's immortal lines. So stupid of me..."

"Pathetic."

"Indeed," the man replied, gulping. "Pathetic. Indeed, sir."

"We shall still have to put you in with the sows, Doc."

The man on the floor began swallowing hard. It was clear he was on the verge of tears.

"Please, not that again, don't make me do that again, I implore..." The words came out in a ghastly, whining torrent.

"We shall have to strip you, Doc, and throw you in with the sows. Only when you've done your duty will you be allowed to leave."

Suddenly tears were streaming down the man's face, and his body shuddered convulsively. He began to bang his head on the floor, great choking sobs racking him. He had released his knee and now started beating his clenched fists against the floor in time with his head. He began to howl.

Strasser turned from him, his gaunt face masklike. He snapped his fingers once and two men emerged from the shadows. They bent over the man called Doc and picked him up as though he were garbage.

Strasser said, "Take him to the pigpens. You know what to do."

They dragged him, screaming and howling and kicking, into the darkness.

Strasser watched them go, watched them disappear from sight, heard a door open, clang shut. He turned and stepped from the light into the gloom.

Chapter Seven

JUNKED CARS LINED THE ROUTE into town: rotting, rusting, gutted hulks stripped of every mechanical and non-mechanical item that might be of the slightest use to anyone, fit for nothing but the scrapyard. To Ryan, driving his buggy, his one eye nervously scanning left to right as he lightly gripped the wheel with black-gloved hands, the whole ville seemed like a scrapyard. A gigantic, sprawling and malodorous scrapyard.

Piles of refuse edged into the road, narrowing the way. It would be difficult for two buggies to pass each other without hitting old crates and boxes and rotting garbage in and out of bags; it would be impossible for two land wags.

The buggy went slowly. It was necessary. They passed a narrow street that had clearly been abandoned forever. Garbage filled it from side to side to maybe second-story level and probably from end to end, as well. A street of garbage. Hunaker, who was manning the forward M-60, muttered, "This is nukehell." She stared at the street as they cruised by.

She said to Ryan, "There was a rumor Mocsin was sliding, but it looks to me like it's running out of control."

Ryan reached down with his left hand, felt the reassuring bullpup shape of the LAPA 5.56 mm he'd picked out of the war wag's armory before leaving the Trader and the rest of the convoy on the edge of town. It was thirty inches of compact firepower with a 55-capacity stick mag. They'd found four crates of these in a Stockpile they'd discovered in the foothills of the Ozarks. That had been a very hairy mission: the indigenous population had been distinctly unfriendly, kept to themselves, seemed to be not at all interested in trading of any kind but only in killing anyone who entered their enclave. They'd also found three more crates back in the Apps. The LAPA had excellent performance, and Ryan preferred it to any of the longer autorifles that because of their length were more unwieldy in an urban situation. He carried the LAPA in a looped rig inside his long coat and could pull it fast.

On his right hip was a SIG-Sauer P-226 9 mm, the automatic he preferred even over the ubiquitous Browning Hi-Power that J.B. in particular swore by. Both had considerable punch over a long distance; both were immensely reliable. But in a hot situation Ryan had once had a Hi-Power MK-2 jam on him. That had not been the gun's fault as such, but to Ryan—a mild believer in signals, psychic hints—that was a distinct nudge in the ribs from whatever gods watched over him, and he forswore the Browning and took up the SIG, which had proved to be an eminently satisfactory man-, woman- and mutie-stopper right when it counted. It also, usefully, loaded two extra rounds over the Hi-Power, although J.B. argued that what you could do with fifteen slugs you could just as easily do with thirteen. The logic of this was by no means impeccable, but Ryan knew what the tense, wiry weapons master—a superb marksman—meant. Despite his criticism, Dix had machined one or two extra features on to Ryan's SIG, including a fully adjustable sight.

On his left hip was the panga scabbard, the panga itself now holstered within easy reach on the buggy's door. From his belt hung four grenades—frag—and three mag pouches for the SIG. Inside his long coat, two each side, were four sticks for the LAPA.

Behind the drive seat was an Ithaca 37 pump 5-shot with pistol grip and stock and a Mossberg 12-gauge bullpup 8-shot with sights fore and aft and compacted stock. Canvas panniers on both doors sagged with cartridges.

The buggy itself, like all the buggies run by the Trader, bristled with external and internal weaponry: cannon at the front and a fixed mortar, and two M-60s, one poking out from behind an armored shield at the front, and the other rear-mounted through a roof blister with a wide traverse. Pierced steel planking, double thickness, had been fixed to the buggy's exterior.

In firepower at least Ryan felt reasonably safe, reasonably secure; that was the most you could feel in a hostile situation. And this was most definitely a hostile situation.

The fronts of most of the shops and bars here had been boarded over, glass clearly being in short supply. Where doors were left open, light from kerosene lamps and candles spilled out onto filthy sidewalks strewn with trash. Men stood in the open doorways, staring out at them, faces bleak and cold, uncompromising. He saw a couple of guys spit in their direction as the buggy edged its way along.

There was both tension and hatred here that he could feel even through the pierced steel planking. It was something palpable. He'd had no idea Mocsin had reached such a state, such a grim pitch. He'd been under the impression, if he'd thought about it at all, that Jordan Teague's grip on the town was steel strong, that any hint of opposition to his rule had been squashed flat over the years by Strasser's security force. Now, tooling along this garbage-and car-strewn street, he was not so damned sure.

Hovak, the kid who manned the mortar but who was now squatting behind Hunaker's seat, gazing over her shoulder, said, "Why d'you say that, Hun?"

"Say what?"

"Running out of control."

"Hell! All this crap on the road, on the sidewalks, dummy. Guy like Teague oughta know by now, after twenty years or whatever, you don't let all this shit pile up like this. Asking for trouble. Perfect sniping positions. You wanna hold a town, you have nice wide roads, nice clean thoroughfares so the opposition can't hide."

She reached inside her jump jacket and took out a pack of ready rolled. She offered one to Ryan who grunted and shook his head. She poked one in her mouth and lit it, then pushed a hand through her bright green hair. She said, "Am I right?"

Ryan said, "Yeah, as always."

He liked Hunaker—she was smart and she was tough and she was an excellent shot, especially with the MG— although there was nothing between them and never had been and never was likely to be. It was unnecessary. In any case Hunaker was bi, although she had a leaning toward her own sex. At the moment a particular favorite was a girl called Ange who held the radio op's chair in War Wag Three.

From the back of the buggy, where he was sitting with his feet up on an ammo box, J.B. said, "Oughta have a better intelligence net."

Ryan said, "Who? Them or us?"

"Them. Us. Both. But us particularly. Tighter. Been meaning to talk to the Old Man about it."

"You'll be wanting a secret police net next."

J.B. snickered.

Ryan flicked the wheel a fraction to avoid a mangy-looking dog, then righted the buggy.

They relied for intelligence on live-in friendlies in all of the areas they visited—towns, cities, hamlets, trading posts—and on scuttlebutt that drifted like the wind across the length and breadth of the Deathlands. Often they knew the bad news—massacres, atmospheric devastation, heavy marauder presence—long before those who lived near where it had occurred. Just as often, however, the first evidence of a tragedy was when one of their land wag trains stumbled across it: a ville, maybe, that was a ville no longer, merely a desolation of blackened piles of rubble and a hell of a lot of ash, with a population that consisted mainly of rotting corpses, often savagely mutilated or lacking heads or arms or legs or sexual organs. Or all of these items.

Ryan swung the wheel as something crashed from a mountain of trash ahead of them, picked out by his roof spotlight. "Guns!" he snapped.

The something was a large box. It hit the road, bounced across the road, slammed into the piles of garbage opposite. There was a minor avalanche of muck as its impact vibrated through the pile. The road was now even narrower.

Ryan glimpsed a black shape scuttling along the right-hand garbage line and relaxed. It was a rat, a mutie rat at that, big as a full-grown dog.

"Forget it. A rat."

"Great," said Hunaker, her eyes still narrowed as she glared through the sighting screen. "We eat tonight!" She turned and yelled back to Hovak. "See what I mean? At least there were no mutie rats in Mocsin a couple of years back. Four-legged variety, anyhow."

"Keep by your pieces," said Ryan. "I got a bad feeling about this place."

It was in his mind to turn back right now, get out of town, gather up the rest of the convoy and head out to where the main train was and then beat it.

Ryan took a right after the block where Mocsin's main bank had once stood. Still stood, actually, although now it functioned as a center-of-town HQ for Strasser's security goons. Ryan didn't like to think about what at times went on in the bank's former vaults. It was better not to think about it. Or rather, he thought grimly, more cowardly.

Here the place was a blaze of light from brilliant spots up on the roof. He noted the heavy coils of barbed wire that fenced the area off from the rest of the street. Here at least the garbage had been cleared away. There were three black vans parked inside the barbed-wire perimeters, but Ryan could see no sign of human presence. The windows of the building were all heavily barricaded.

He turned into a side street where there was more light, much less trash. Here was the gaudy house area. Here were the gambling and drinking bars where groups of miners were let loose, in turn, once every six weeks. They came into town in Teague's convoys with jack in their pockets, the younger ones with hope in their hearts, determined to pay off what they owed to the city of Mocsin's tax and toll coffers. Somehow no one ever did pay off what was on the debit side of the ledger. Some went straight to where their wives and loved ones had shacked up, only to find them gone. Vanished. Disappeared. No one knew where. No one cared where. Some might be found in the gaudy houses. It was often the case that a dispirited miner, after a week-long search of the town, in his misery, his need for some kind of affection, even if high priced, would turn to the brothels and discover his missing wife there, all dressed up and no place else to go. Some really had vanished, possibly into Strasser's dungeons, possibly into his perverted half world where they became tormented playthings in the strange and vicious "games" he and his goons initiated. Faced with this kind of horror on top of everything else, the miner would drink himself into insensibility and continue thus until it was time to hop aboard the convoy and head back to the mines once more, care of Jordan Teague. Some went on a smash, a bender, a rampage, and that was as good as committing suicide. And for those who survived, after one bout of heartache and horror, after one "rest period" in which you discovered that your entire world had been destroyed, nothing much signified—so you went back to the mines, worked like a dog for six weeks and returned to Mocsin for another two-week furlough. Only this time you didn't piss around trying to find your nonexistent wife and kids, you went straight to the brothels or the bars or the gambling houses. And that was that.

Yet Ryan frowned as he took the buggy down the long street. He was suddenly aware of J.B. breathing heavily almost into his right ear.

"Funny," J.B. said. Then he said, "Worrying."

"Yeah."

The gaudy stretch of lights, both sides, that they both remembered from the last visit was distinctly far apart. Most of the places here had run on generators, and as the street was one long procession of bars and gaudy houses, there had been no night here at all during the hours of darkness, only brilliant illumination, false day.

But now most of the bars were dark, boarded up, and what lights there were that shone on the road were flickering candles or hissing kerosene lamps. Ryan judged that maybe one in three bars remained open.

"They running out of booze or something?" said Hunaker, brushing a hand through her hair again. The other hand firmly held one of the M-60 grips. She said with a chuckle, "Rot-gut shit, anyway. I had the runs forever last time I was in this toilet of a town," but the chuckle was halfhearted.

"You see Charlie's?" said J.B., craning his neck.

"That's what I'm looking for," grunted Ryan. Then he said, "Yeah. Still there."

Charlie's was on the left, way down. In between it and its nearest lighted neighbor up the street were maybe seven closed and boarded-up bars. The next one down the street was near the end of the block. The two wide windows, on each side of the entrance to Charlie's, were tightly shuttered. Above the closed door was a long panel window, and behind the glass was neon strip lettering spelling out the words Charlie's Bar. The neon was dead. The lettering was lit by five guttering candles, one of which was a mere stub on the point of extinction.

"Hell," muttered Hunaker. "What we gonna find in there?"

"You're not going to find anything in there," said Ryan, pulling over to the sidewalk beside an old rusted post on which was sat something, as he'd discovered some years back somewhere else, that had once been known as a parking meter. A coin in its mouth gave you an hour of parking. Absurd and redundant. "You're sitting here, looking after the store."

"Hellfire," complained Hunaker. "I never get to have any fun when I'm out with you, Ryan."

"You keep your eyes skinned," advised Ryan. "I have a feeling we might be in for plenty of fun before the night's out."

"Do I get to kill one of Teague's sec men? Aw, nuke-blast it, Ryan, please tell me I can do that."

Ryan braked, shifted in his seat. He turned and stared around. There was Hovac, Rintoul—whose boots could be seen but nothing else because he was up in the roof blister—and the three spares: Koll, a tall, bony blonde with an oddly thick mustache; Hennings, a big black with a lacerating sense of humor; and Samantha the Panther, black, too, and a mutant who could see in the dark and had exceptional powers of hearing.

Ryan said, "Rint and Sam. Henn, you take the roof."

He checked his mirrors while the crew made their adjustments, then opened the door and stepped out. J.B. followed him, gripping a Steyr AUG 5.56 mm as though it were a part of him, an extension of his own right hand. Ryan popped his LAPA inside his coat, thought about taking the panga then decided not. He automatically checked the SIG, holstered it, ran his fingers over his belt pouches, feeling their weight, checking their contents; he knew they were all full but did it, anyway. Better to be one hundred percent sure than one hundred percent dead.

"Okay."

He slammed the door, O-ed his fingers to Hunaker through the glass. J.B.'s Steyr was now inside the long coat he, too, wore. The bullpups of the other two had similarly vanished from sight.

A couple of blocks up the street two lurched together, went into a complicated dance routine, arms around each other, to stop themselves from falling over. Or that's what it looked like. Maybe, thought Ryan, they just liked each other. Or maybe they felt lonely in this desolate street. A wind had sprung up, whipping at his hair. He could hear the sound of fiddle music, muted, coming from somewhere.

He turned to the door of Charlie's Bar, shoved down on the handle, walked in.

CHARLIE'S BAR WAS LIKE just about every other bar in the street, just about every other bar in Mocsin, just about every other bar in the whole of the Deathlands. It was a place whose entire reason for existence was booze. It was a place where you went to drink yourself into a stupor, a place where you drank to forget.

The bar itself ran down most of one wall with barrels atop it, strategically placed every three or four meters along, bottles on shelves behind. Tall mirrors hung behind the bar. These aided the lighting by reflecting what was already there. Even so, the long room was murky, a place of dancing shadows, with only three or four lamps and not a hell of lot of candles flickering in the many drafts that struck through uncaulked cracks and crevices in doors and window shutters. It was low ceilinged, drab walled, stale smelling, greasy atmosphered. Smoke hung heavily in the air, a thick miasma that the guttering candles did little to cut through.

Opposite the bar were curtained booths. Small round tables were scattered down the room. The seats were covered in plush that was a century old and looking it. There was chrome everywhere, but it was rusty, tarnished. The booth curtains, threadbare velvet, had once had tassels hanging from them. Early in the reign of Fishmouth Charlie, the current owner, there had been a time when certain captains of Jordan Teague's sec men had taken to wearing fancy epaulettes on the shoulders of their black leather jackets. It was noted by the more sharp-eyed of Mocsin's citizenry that these epaulettes bore a remarkable resemblance to the curtain tassels from Charlie's. Charlie had not made a fuss. Charlie had always had a wise and circumspect nature.

The bar was nearly empty; maybe fifteen or twenty people sitting in the booths or at the center tables, drinking steadily. One or two were eating something that smelled like regular meat stew, and probably was. Charlie had a good rep where food was concerned; you had no worries about suddenly discovering you were gorging yourself on roach mince or putrid hog or prime cut of human when you dined at Charlie's. Many of the drinkers were muties, which, considering the owner, was not surprising.

Ryan went to the bar. He nodded to the woman behind the bar and the woman behind the bar nodded back. Nothing could be gauged from her features. Only her protuberant eyes were at all expressive. From below her eyes, her face bulged out to her mouth, a tiny, thin-lipped orifice like the spout of a volcano. There seemed to be no jawline whatsoever. Although her hair was thick and curly, her eyebrows were nonexistent. She was short, her arms plump, her fingers spatulate. She wore a drab brown-colored shift that had clearly seen better days, yet was clean and well pressed.

Ryan said, "Miss Charlene."

A flicker of amusement darted across the woman's eyes.

She said, "Ryan. Always the gentleman." The voice that emanated from that tiny mouth was surprisingly deep. She said, "What d'you fancy?"

Ryan said, "What else but you?" He put his hands on the bar top and said, "Okay, Charlie, now we got the civilities out of the way, how about a pitcher of wine?" He glanced around, recognized a few faces he knew—Blue Bonnett, Stax with his pointy ears, The Lizard, Hal Prescott, Chevvy the Chase, one-time ace wheelman with a bunch of hog-riders out East and now retired since some joker had blown both his legs off, and Ole One-Eye, grizzled veteran of the short-lived but bloody mutie War of '68, which had flared in what had once been Kentucky. Ryan noted that none looked at all pleased to see him. One or two indeed looked positively murderous. "Then you can explain what's going on, why there were guys spitting at us as we went past, and how come Ole One-Eye there looks like he'd like to pluck out mine to add to his."

Charlie drew the cork on a liter bottle of red and pushed glasses across the bar.

"No one wants you here, Ryan. No one wants the Trader. You tell him to fuck off outta here, get back the hell where he came from."

Ryan poured himself a glass of wine, then shoved the bottle toward J.B. "You say the friendliest things." He sipped some of the liquid, rolled it around his mouth, savored the nutty taste of it. "Tell me more."

"You got weapons, right?"

"Sure. Some."

"Spike 'em."

"As bad as that?"

"The men blew two of the mines three days back."

"They what!"

"I said, the men—"

"Yeah, yeah. I heard you. Deliberate?"

Charlie's tiny mouth closed, then opened. It was her way of smiling.

"Sure, deliberate. They'd have blown the other two, but something went wrong. Fuses, timers—I dunno. So they barricaded themselves in down there."

J. B. Dix's eyelids fluttered. It was his way of expressing astonishment. He said, "I take it you're sure about this?"

"As I am that you're drinking my wine and not paying for it."

"Oh. Yeah." Ryan reached into a back pocket and pulled out some tin. He said, "How blown?"

"Roof rockfalls. Teague's two main sources are now blocked to hell. The other two mines are smaller, easier to defend."

"Defend? They have pieces?"

"They killed a whole squadron of Strasser's sec men. Tore 'em apart barehanded. As you're probably aware—" the deep tones were thick with irony "—Teague's police are well weaponed up. Handguns, auto-rifles, MGs. And plenty of ammo."

"Gas would clear 'em," J.B. pointed out.

Charlie shook her head, black curls dancing.

"Miners have blocked off the entrance to both mines, and the old ventilation system."

"So they just die of no air?"

"Uh-uh. They've been drilling their own air holes. It'd take Strasser's men days, weeks, to find them. Months, maybe."

"Food?"

"Sure."

"Water?"

"Plenty. Pure, too. Can't be got at from outside."

"I suddenly have the feeling," said Sam dryly, "that this one's been a long time in the planning."

Charlie's tone was equally dry. "Right."

Ryan said, "What we have for that fat bastard won't make a piece of spit's worth of difference, Charlie. One, it wasn't a mighty load to begin with. Two, owing to circumstances not entirely beyond our control, the load is damned near halved, anyway."

Charlie shrugged and said, "Makes no odds. You trading with Teague makes you the enemy, places you on his side of the fence. Firmly, buddy. Story goes you helped set the bastard up, anyway."

"Shit!" exploded Ryan in exasperation. "That was twenty years ago!"

A tingle of alarm ran up his spine. There was, it occurred to him, another angle to all this. If Teague was desperate...

He turned to Samantha. "Radio the Old Man. Tell him what's up. Find out if the main train's still checking in on the hour, and tell him to switch to every fifteen minutes."

Sam gulped her wine and made for the door. Rintoul, a stocky, chubby-faced kid, whispered "Shit!" His pudgy fingers clasped at his belt as he glanced around the bar nervously. Charlie made a dry, choking sound through her mouth. Laughter.

"Teague's no fool," said J.B.

"Ten years ago he wasn't," agreed Charlie. "Five years ago he maybe wasn't. But only maybe. Now times have changed. He's sucked this place dry for too long, put nothing back in its place. Maybe the blood was rich twenty years ago, but it's thin as whey now. The assets are stripped. Cupboard's bare. There's nothing left. Teague don't know what's going down half the time. Strasser's king of the shit pile, and he's insane. All he cares about is watching kids killing kids, male and female. You get the message?" She glared at Ryan accusingly.

Ryan drank some more of the wine. Stasis he understood, the stagnation of empire. Evil and greedy men flogging a horse to death but not realizing, not understanding when it was dead, when extinction had been reached, and continuing to beat it and beat it and beat it.

"You telling me the deadline's been reached? Mocsin's ready to blow?"

Fishmouth Charlie stared at him for some seconds, her bulging eyes fixed on his, then she looked down at the bar top, spreading her hands on its shiny, highly polished surface.

"Not as easy as that, Ryan." Her voice seemed, if anything, deeper, certainly gruffer. "Couple of months back we had some kind of epidemic run through the gaudies on the Strip. Real bad. Something internal, rotted 'em out. Teague's medics couldn't cope, so they killed 'em, killed 'em all, girls and boys. First off they needled 'em, but that was too damned slow, so one night they came and took 'em away in vans. Machine-gunned 'em and burned the bodies. Out in the desert. So all the gaudy houses had empty rooms and Strasser blitzed the place, went through Shantytown dragging out just about anyone under the age of twenty, took 'em off. They had to have something to keep the miners quiet, but some of the men cut up more than usual. There was a riot, lotta guys shot. The sec men contained it, put the clamp on, but maybe that was the final straw." She shrugged, gestured around. "You can see how it is. Place is falling apart. Generators going bust and there's nothing to mend 'em with. Lack of parts, lack of interest. Everything in this town is too old, too damned worn out. Unrepairable. Any case, you force a guy to use his wrenches at the point of a gun, he ain't gonna do a prime job. He's gonna do just what's necessary to stop himself getting his head holed and that's all. He's not gonna sweat for you, now is he? So things just get worse. And worse."

Ryan nodded. He said, "But the miners. Stockpiling food, drilling new vents that the overseers don't know about. Shit, Charlie, like Sam said, all that takes time, not to mention a hell of a lot of effort, planning, thought.''

Charlie shrugged.

"Who knows? I ain't privy to everything that goes down in this shithole, Ryan. All I know is that Mocsin's on the edge. It's like there's a button somewhere and there's a finger hovering over it. And once the finger jabs down, once the button's pressed—*Blooey!*''

Rintoul, still casting glances at the hostile faces of the drinkers staring at them, said, "Yer'd think the place'd be an armed camp if all this shit is going on. Patrols in the street, curfew, shoot to kill. Like that.''

"We got a lot of crap at the entrance to town," said Ryan, "and they were nervous, but they didn't seem to be pissing in their pants.''

Charlie reached under the bar and pulled out a cigar. She warmed it over a candle before sucking flame into its end.

"It's like I said, Teague's lost his grip and Strasser doesn't seem to care. I guess they just don't understand after twenty years of tight control. They're blind. It happens.''

Ryan acknowledged the truth of this. All he knew of history told him that often those who had been firmly in control of a potentially dangerous situation for years gradually lost their objectivity. In their rigid and unshakable belief in their own strength, their own power to keep the lid down hard, they were blind to all else, even the most disturbing and concrete evidence of disaffection.

Sure it happened.

And sure it was time Mocsin boiled over. You couldn't beat an entire town into subjection forever.

He took his wine and strode over to the table where Ole One-Eye and Chevvy the Chase—that terrible man crudely named after a suburb of what was once a Washington suburb, according to some ancient map—were seated, Chevvy crouched deep in his mobile chair.

Ryan said, "Look, count me out of this."

There was silence for a moment, then Chevvy snickered and said, "Hey, ya know what? They're crackin' down on muties now."

Ole One-Eye turned on him and rasped, "Don't use that word! How many times I gotta tell you! I don't call you a crapping *norm*, do I?"

Chevvy said, "How many norms you seen walkin' around on no legs, huh? You hideous apology for a human being."

"Pity they didn't blow yer vocals out when they blew yer legs! The shit I hafta put up with!"

The nature of Ole One-Eye's particular mutation was more than merely dramatic. It was clear at once to any observer that at least one side of his bloodline had gotten savagely zapped three generations back by a rabid breed of rad bug. Maybe both sides of his bloodline. That would certainly account for the top of his pate being flat and hairless and made up of flabby, spongy ridges of flesh, and his having only one eye, one glistening ocular orb, dead center of his forehead. From his nose downward, beyond the mouth and the stubbly beard shot with gray, he seemed perfectly normal, though a little on the squat side and with arms maybe a fraction longer than the average. But only a fraction.

It was not known exactly what part he'd played in the Mutie War of 2068. He didn't talk about it much. Mutants escaping serfdom in the Baronies of the East had fled West and gravitated by degrees to the area around old Louisville and built up their own short-lived homeland over a period of four or five years. But there had been too much tension. The people around there, the normals, had grown discontented at what they saw as an invasion of their territory, their "clean" territory, by whole families of those whose indebtedness to the Nuke, genetically speaking, was blazingly obvious. They wanted the muties out. The mutant families, having finally escaped from conditions in which they'd been treated worse than animals, refused to shift. They had built houses, farms, repair shops, set up trade lines. The move toward outright war had a blind and fearsome inevitability about it.

A norm farmer whose steam truck's boiler had burst near a mutie ville had forced a couple of mechs to fix a running repair, then casually shot them both when they'd asked for payment. If the farmer gained any gratification from this act of gratuitous violence, he didn't have it for long. He was followed to his own town and shot outside his home. What followed lasted maybe ten months, during which time hundreds of mutants were massacred, whole villes burned and steam-dozered. They gave as good as they got, but there were too few of them, too many normals who, in any case, called to certain of the East Coast Barons for arms and heavy hardware and reinforcements. The upshot was that in the late fall of '68 the muties had moved out, headed farther into the Central Deathlands, dispersed. Ole One-Eye had turned up in Mocsin and settled there.

Chevvy the Chase grinned toothily, scratching his head. He said to Ryan, "The old bastud's insults are losin' their kick. Time was he could be a mean-assed son of a bitch. Maybe I'm gettin' used to him. Whattya say, Ryan?"

"Yeah," Ryan said,

"Say one thing for this craphole of a town," Chevvy said. "That fat hog of a Teague never used to give a shit if you had one head or two, one prick or three. Know what I mean? But now, hell! Them sec men of his are startin' to beat up on the armless, earless and noseless. They'll be puttin' 'em up agin a wall next, you mark my words." He turned to Ole One-Eye. "They say they aim for the heart, but with you I reckon it'll be someplace else." He cackled, raised his glass of beer. "The perfect target. Here's lead in yer eye, pal."

Ryan said, uneasily, "Look..."

Ole One-Eye made a dismissive gesture with his right hand, drank with his left. He said quietly, "Shut it, Chev," then looked up at Ryan. "Don't mind him. Wind's in the wrong direction. His legs've been giving him shit for days."

Chevvy drank more beer, stared down at what was not there and had not been there for some years. He said, his voice suddenly a hoarse whisper, "Nukeblasted right."

Ole One-Eye smiled gently, gazing up at Ryan. His eye was white irised, pinkish around the edges.

"Speaking as one one-eye to another," he said softly, "I'd say ya better figure out fast which way ya gonna jump, boy. All hell gonna break out soon, and that's a realer feelin' than when young Chev here gets aches in his hocks. Ya gotta choose, boy. Choose damned soon."

Ryan stared down at the guttering flames reflected from the candles in the pools of spilled beer on the tabletop, aware that the buzz of conversation in the bar, muted and desultory as it had been, had suddenly ceased altogether. Even Rintoul, a mouthy kid at the best of times, though a good shot and loyal, had shut up. He could see Ole One-Eye's face, upside down, hideously distorted, in the liquid, could even see that single eye fixed on his. All at once stories he'd often heard on his travels slid into his mind, stories of mutants with the "blazing" eye, the eye that blasted you with a look, the eye that killed. Couldn't be true, of course. Foolish talk. Yet why not? There were sensers, weren't there? Sensers who sniffed out danger, danger that was to come, danger that was just around the corner, short-term, within the hour. And there were those who had an even rarer and more terrifying power, the doomseers: precogs who had sharply defined visions of the future, what was to happen in the longer term. So why not the Eye? Why not a look that could burn your mind out.

He shook his head, looked up suddenly at the reality rather than the strange mirror image. Ole One-Eye's single eye shifted up, too, to follow him. Ryan drank what remained in his glass.

"You're probably right," he muttered.

The other chuckled quietly. "That's m'boy," he said. "One thing about you, Ryan, you're dependable. Known for it."

Ryan rubbed at his face, at the stubble growing on his chin. Weirdly, he felt that he'd just made an important decision, a vital decision, although he was not aware that his conscious mind had done so, and the reply he'd just given had been little more than noncommittal.

He said, "You old bastard, I think you've been trying to hypnotize me."

This time Old One-Eye's chuckle became a wheeze, full of genuine amusement.

"I don't have the Devil's Eye, son, just one good optic that's seen me through a mess of years but it's as straight as yours."

"Yeah. Well. Good luck."

Ryan turned on his heel and made for the bar again. He glanced to his right as the door to the place banged open, but it was not Samantha the Panther. He saw a man whose clothes seemed too big for him, as though he'd shrunk in a shower of rad rain, been not quite eaten up by the acids. He face was gaunt, hollow eyed. His skin was burned nearly black and looked to be so thin that you could poke your pinky through. He shoved the door closed again, his whole body trembling. He seemed to be in a state of near-terminal flap.

Charlie, behind the bar, glared at him.

"Kurt! What the hell you doing out?"

The man said hoarsely, "I had to get out, Charlie. Up in the roof I was going goddamned crazy. The walls were closing in on me. Had to get out. I had to."

Charlie snorted, began rubbing a cloth vigorously over the bar. It was clear she was angry.

"You get back upstairs again, ya stupe. Blast it, I don't know why the hell I bother!"

The man called Kurt staggered toward the bar. He seemed at the end of his tether.

"I met him, Charlie, across the street. Bastard recognized me." His piercing eyes were alive with terror. "Charlie, what am I gonna do?"

"This is all I need." Charlie jabbed the cloth toward the far end of the room. "Beat it. Get back upstairs. Don't make a sound." She snapped, *"Move!"*

The man pushed past them, ran stumblingly along the side of the bar and into the thicker shadows at the end of the room. Ryan heard the rustle of a curtain, a door bang.

J.B. nudged him.

"Let's move. We got the picture."

"Yeah, okay." He turned to Charlie. "What was all that about?"

Charlie nodded in the direction the man had gone. She said, "My lodger." Her mouth opened and shut a couple of times. "I'm looking after the guy."

Ryan knew it would be demeaning to Charlie, whom he liked, but he suddenly had an urge to burst out laughing. He fought to keep the urge down.

"Actually, he's in deep shit. I'm gonna have to sneak him out of town sometime. Got in bad with one of Strasser's gorillas and disappeared. About five, six months back. Then he reappeared about a month ago, looking like he'd been whipped up in a twister, spread all over the landscape then stuck back together again the wrong way. Seems he'd walked back to Mocsin from the Darks."

"The Darks?" Hardin frowned at her.

"Yeah. You remember a head case called McCandless?"

"Sure."

"Ryan." J.B. tapped him on the shoulder.

"Okay, okay. Wait."

"McCandless took off to the Darks with a party of guys including Kurt, who'd signed up on the spur to get out from under the gorilla. The old story. They were looking for the treasure, har har. Only Kurt got back. And he'd stopped one in the shoulder. Had fever, delirium, you name it. Difficult to figure out what was real, what was nightmare. Kept on yelling about a fog with claws, fog with feet."

"Fog?"

"'S what he said."

"Ryan!" J.B.'s voice was urgent.

"Wait, blast it!"

A fog with claws? He'd never heard that one before. That was a wild one. He tried to picture it in his mind but it came out silly. Fever did strange things to your brain, of course...

"Too late," muttered J.B.

The door crashed open once more. Black-leather-jacketed men boiled into the room. Six of them. No, seven including the leader, a beefy guy with a wall eye. Ryan recognized his face about the same time the man recognized him. Guy called Hagic, one of Cort Strasser's upper echelon sec men. A mean bastard, he recalled, although one with no great brain. He hoped there wasn't going to be any trouble, because he was now convinced that beating a hasty retreat out of Mocsin was the only sensible course of action to take, and the quicker the better.

Hagic's men were all armed with auto-rifles, M-16s mostly, which looked to be in reasonable repair. They were shifting themselves into and around the door end of the room, rifles ready, blank faced. Most of them were young, early twenties, raised against a background of violence so that they had become violent themselves, insensible to all but the lowest emotions, icy hearted. Violence was the only way of life they knew.

Hagic stalked down the room, ignoring Ryan completely, even though Ryan knew he'd been recognized as soon as the man had entered the bar.

J.B., next to Ryan, had shifted into his "yawning" mode, a sure sign that he was all too aware that danger loomed. J.B. leaned back against the bar top, yawning a second time, patted his mouth, sniffed as though to clear his nose. J.B. was gearing himself to kill.

Hagic said, "Where is he?" His voice low.

Charlie looked up at him. She had a jug in one hand and was filling it from the nearest barrel.

"Where's who?"

"Don't fuck around, mutie bitch. Where is he?"

Hagic had an H&K 5.56 mm. He was holding it downward, by its pistol grip. Ryan thought he was either very sure of himself or very foolish. More likely the latter.

Charlie repeated, "Where's who?" She sounded genuinely baffled. "Ya looking for someone, we're all here." She gestured around the room at her patrons, all of whom were staring at the sec men with ill-concealed malevolence.

"Listen, mutie bitch," Hagic snarled. "A guy dived in here moments ago. I want him, want him bad. I don't get him, I'll fire this place and you in it. All of you." He didn't look at Ryan. Hagic clearly didn't give a quarter-credsworth of shit if he was nice to the Trader's men or not.

"Whyn't ya say so in the first place?" muttered Charlie. "The Liz, he just came in. Didn't ya, Liz?"

The Lizard, a tall thin mutie with a long nose and blueish squamous skin, stood up at his table. He looked puzzled.

"Sure, M-miss Charlie. Wh-what's ya p-problem, Ca-ca-ca-captain?" The Lizard's speech impediment made it sound as if he was saying "caca" deliberately, and, knowing his sense of humor, he probably was.

Hagic looked murderous. He began to swing the H&K up, and Ryan thought this whole business had gone on long enough.

Ryan said, "You mean the wimpy little fucker who galloped through here just now?"

Hagic paused before turning to face him. Ryan could almost hear the pinwheels of his tiny brain creaking slowly into action. Hagic knew something; more to the point, he knew something was up, was going on—possibly right now, at this very moment. But Hagic was a stupe of the first water. A smile darted across his sallow features. It was probably meant to be friendly but it simply made him look sly. His squint didn't help.

"Ryan. Good to, uh, see ya." He switched his wall-eyed stare to the rear of the room. "You, uh, say you see a guy..."

"Guy come in here, like there were rad rats chewing his ass? Sure. C'mon. Show you where he went."

As he said this he turned away from Hagic, began striding down the room, aware of Charlie's pop-eyed gaze on
his right, but also aware, just, of a flicker of dark amusement fleeing across the ugly features of Ole One-Eye down
the room.

"Shifty little bastard he looked to me."

Out of the corner of his eye he could see the mirrors,
could see Hagic following, three men in tow. And as he
was speaking, his back to Hagic, his open coat cloaking his
movements, his left hand was smoothly cross-drawing the
SIG-Sauer, his right feeling his belt, fingers unpopping a
pouch, drawing from it a stubby little suppressor, screw-
ing it into the SIG's barrel.

"Door here. Yeah, curtain."

That was a pisser. He couldn't not draw the curtain
back, leave it closed. Even Hagic would smell a rat. As he
slid the heavy material to one side he heard Ole One-Eye
berating Chevvy the Chase in a loud voice, Chev's angry
tones replying. Good. Even some noise was useful, attention grabbing just when it was needed. He wondered what
the hell was beyond the door. He wondered how he would
play what now had to be played.

Sometimes a response had to be purely automatic; you
had to work blind and the nature of the killing ground was
in the lap of the gods. The suppressor was tight. He carefully pushed the gun inside his pants but with plenty of grip
available for instant draw.

A door faced him. It opened inward, toward him. That
was a bonus. He pulled it open, smiled. He was in a small
lobby. To one side, carpeted wooden stairs rose to a narrow landing before doubling back. He could see the upper
portion of the staircase through its banister posts. A lamp
hung low on a chain from the lobby's ceiling.

"Stay here," Hagic's voice sounded in Ryan's ear.

Hagic's three sec men pushed past him and began to mount the first flight of stairs.

"Bad character, huh?" murmured Ryan.

Hagic moved closer, inclined his head toward Ryan's. His chin was stuck out and there was a ratty grin on his face. In the light from the lamp it looked like a devil's mask, and Ryan thought the sooner it was destroyed the better for all.

His right hand shot up, hard, the heel of it smashing up into the underside of Hagic's jaw so eruptively that the jawbone cracked, blood vessels in his neck exploded and ligaments tore. Hagic's head rocked back, a gargled grunt bursting out of his mouth in a fine spray of blood, and Ryan's left hand, fist balled, rocked into his stomach with the force of a pile driver. Hagic jackknifed, dry heaving, and Ryan reached past him and pulled the door shut, his left hand yanking up the SIG-Sauer.

He spun around and the SIG spat three times, *fwip-fwip-fwip*.

The first round hit the last man on the stairs in the back, torpedoed him through the rear of his rib cage; it plowed up into his heart and opened his chest in a bloody volcano.

The second round hit the next in line, a head shot that spray painted the wall beyond. The guy spun into the third man, throwing him sideways, his gun thumping down onto the carpet. The third man, too, fell onto his rifle. Ryan's slug smashed into the wall above his head, gnawing plaster.

For a second there was stillness, Ryan gazing up at the third man, who gaped down at him in shock through the banister. The guy clambered to his feet, not yelling, too stunned even to scream, but dragging at his M-16 as a reflex action.

Ryan smacked his right hand into the SIG's butt, switched fingers, hit him with two shots in the chest, banging him back against the wall in the shadows.

Even as this happened, Ryan was leaping up the first flight, booting down on the prone body of the first man and clutching at the corner pole of the banister, yanking himself up and around and grabbing the third man as he tottered forward on the rebound from the wall. He was just in time. Another couple of seconds and the guy would have slammed into the supports and either up-and-overed, crashing down to the lobby below with a hell of a racket, or plowed straight through the posts, making even more of a row.

Ryan pushed him onto the stairs, a slumped heap, then stood up and peered down at Hagic on the floor below. He could see the wall-eyed man glaring upward, clutching his gut, still unable to speak or yell or scream, only wheeze and vomit. Ryan leaned over the banister and shot him, *fwip*, the round powering through his chest and heart, expending itself into the carpeted floor.

Ryan cocked an ear for any untoward sounds from below but could hear nothing through the closed door. He moved lightly downstairs, on the balls of his feet, still on adrenaline burn, the screen of his memory playing over the scene back in the bar. Unless they'd all moved around some, there was a guy standing in front of the entrance door at the far end of the room, and he had to be nailed first and foremost.

He could do it slowly or he could do it fast. If he did it slowly—if he opened the door, wandered casually into the bar, his piece hidden behind his back, and then threw a round at the guy by the outside door (or at least the guy who should be by the outside door)—there was always the chance of something going wrong, possibly badly wrong.

Those goons out there were young, undoubtedly nervy in a situation like this. Just Ryan walking out from the rear and no one else might spook them, then trigger them. There was always that chance.

If he did it fast, on the other hand—erupted into the room and hit at least one of them—the shock factor would be enormous, he knew. The remaining two goons would be thrown off balance. They'd be totally unnerved, ripe for slaughter.

If only he knew what the hell was going on in the bar. And the longer he waited in this lobby, the more twitchy those guys would get. By now they'd be thinking they ought to be hearing bangs and yells and shots.

He bent, peered at the door. But the keyhole was blocked on the other side. His lips came back in a feral snarl. He was still high on adrenaline. He held the gun in his left hand and threw himself at the door.

He hit the wood, the door slammed open, he brought his right hand around to the SIG's grip, slapping it tight, his eye taking in the scene even as he squeezed off.

No one had moved. The man he'd remembered as standing beside the entrance door was still there, his M-16 held in both hands, aimed to his left, at the room in general. Ryan's shot changed all that. It hit the man in the chest and punched him backward, mouth gaping, so that he collapsed against the wall, slumping and leaving a thick red smear as he sank to the floor.

Ryan watched in admiration as J.B., still leaning with his back to the bar, his coat open, his right hand resting on his belt, drew the Browning with shocking speed. His arm jerked up and the Hi-Power barked and spat, its bullet slamming one of the other black jackets over into a table. The table splintered under his weight and the violent impact of his flailing body. His M-16 clattered to the floor.

That was what saved the last man, who was close to the table and to his heart-shot companion. The last man jumped away from the collapsing table and stumbled, dropped his piece, then with a wild yell leaped for the door.

Ryan hammered a round at him but missed by an inch. Or less. In adrenaline-boosted terror, the guy yanked the door and dived through it, the door swinging shut behind him.

J.B. jumped toward the door. Ryan, running to him, yelled, "No bangs in the street!"

J.B. stopped dead, as though mesmerized by a vision only he could see. Ryan, running up the room full pelt, slowed to a halt, SIG raised.

The door had creaked open; in fact, the guy was pushing it inward with his body. The guy staggered in the doorway as the door swung away from him. He teetered on his heels, his arms half raised, his hands clawing feebly at nothing. He fell backward and crashed to the carpeted floor.

Another figure appeared in the doorway. It was Sam, holding a silenced Walther PP Super in her right hand. She stepped over the body, bent and heaved it away from the door. She slammed the door, kept hold of the Walther.

She said, her voice husky but not panicky, "Main train's gone off the air. We were rapping with Cohn in War Wag One when he suddenly reported the convoy was surrounded. Voice came on the net, demanded to talk to the Old Man. Then there was a lot of interference. We relocated, heard this other guy say they'd nerved the main train, they were all dead, finished, kaput, and unless the Old Man threw in, the convoy'd get blitzed, too. Then there was more interference and they cut out."

She stopped, impassive.

"Dead line?"

"Dead as this goon here." She gestured at the man on the floor. "We tried everything. They're off the air."

J.B. shot a look at Ryan and Ryan sucked in air through his teeth, an icy feeling running up his spine like electricity.

Had Teague copped nerve gas? But where from? Then Ryan thought, if *we* found some, why not someone else, somewhere else?

Or was it maybe bluff? Had they merely axed the radio link somehow? But how would they have done that? They could certainly throw in interference fuzz, but not kill it dead unless...

Unless those in the main train really were dead.

And what about the Old Man? Was he dead and those with him, too? On reflection, almost certainly not, and for one excellent reason.

J.B. lit up one of his thin black cheroots, his eyes behind his steel-rimmed glasses narrowed in thought.

Ryan turned to the bar and said, "Do us a favor, Charlie. Get these stiffs outta the way."

"Just like that? I'll wave my wand, Ryan." Then she sighed and said, "Okay, don't panic. We'll fix it. I take it there's more on the stairs?"

"You take it correct."

Charlie's tiny mouth opened and closed.

"You're a real hothead, Ryan." She added, "What if they came in a vehicle?"

"He said he saw them in the street. Across the street."

"Oh, right. Good memory."

Ryan watched as half the bar patrons began dragging bodies toward the far end of the room. J.B. sucked on his cheroot, blew smoke out in a thin plume. He said, "Listen. They used gas on the train. Why didn't they use it on the Old Man?"

"That's a rhetorical question, J.B. You know the answer."

"Hmm. They mortared gas canisters in." He clicked his tongue irritably. "Something we didn't make allowances for. Gas gets in through cracks and tiny holes. So all our people are dead. Nothing we can do there. Say it's a short-term agent. After dispersal they now have to open up all those land wags and trucks and the two war wags. But they can't, because they know that every damned vehicle owned by us is packed with boobies. Everybody knows that. And if they start smashing out window glass or blowing in doors, the whole caboodle could go up and they lose everything. So they're stuck." A dark smile of satisfaction fled across the thin man's sallow features. "They're well and truly stuck."

"So they have to parley with the Old Man," said Ryan. "So they have to take him alive."

"Nontoxic agent."

"Nothing else'd do."

"Yeah."

"So that means," continued Ryan, "the Old Man's out. But he'd have made sure all the vehicles were tight. So that means Teague's goons have got more vehicles on their hands they can't touch, move or do any thing at all with."

"Yeah."

J.B. blew a smoke ring. It sailed up toward the ceiling, shimmying, expanding, drifting out from the center, breaking up.

"And that means," said Ryan, "we're the only free agents in town."

"Yeah."

"But they don't know what we know. No one knows that."

J.B. murmured, "That little extra." He glanced at Ryan. "How long we got?"

Ryan checked his watch.

"Rough timing, I'd say about four hours."

"Gotta work fast. What's your plan, war chief?"

The room was now clear of stiffs. Incredibly those who remained in the bar were drinking and talking as though nothing had happened at all in the past ten minutes or so. He caught Ole One-Eye's single orb, pink rimmed, the eyelid fluttering in a macabre and sardonic wink. He stared at Sam, Rintoul, finally at J.B. He thought of those on the main train, maybe a couple of hundred souls all told. All loyal comrades; some, indeed, close friends who'd shared with him a thousand experiences, a thousand dangers, a thousand joys and carousals. He thought of the flame-haired girl, Krysty, with the deep, the luminous green eyes. Extinguished. Snuffed out. Rage was like a sudden eruption of fierce white flame that licked through his entire system.

He said, his voice taut, "We take the war to the enemy. We pay a visit to Jordan Teague."

Chapter Eight

DESPITE ORDERS, you kept to the shadows. The deep shadows. The deeper the better.

You kept to the shadows despite orders, despite doomy warnings from your unit leaders, despite hideously snarled threats of disembowelment or being flayed alive or having your hands nailed to the wall. Despite all these and more, you kept to the shadows because you were beginning to get...cautious.

A sec man's life in the old days used to be different. It used to be fun, used to be a laff riot. It meant you were top of the pile, king of the ville. Meant you could do what you wanted, when you wanted, for as long as you wanted, and free. Mocsin was open city for the sec men, and you could tool along its streets and whatever you saw was yours. Not for the asking—you didn't need to ask for anything. It was all yours for the taking. Yours by right of conquest. Didn't matter what it was, you had an open license on it. Food, booze, men, women. Whatever was your fancy, it was yours.

And sure, on the surface the situation hadn't changed. On the surface it was still the sec men's paradise. On the surface everything was as it was, as it had always been, since Jordan Teague first hijacked the burg way back when most of today's sec men were brawling brats.

On the surface.

But underneath, paradise was maybe not quite what it appeared to be. There was a tension in the air—something you could almost feel, almost gnaw at—that none of the old-timers had ever known. A population that had once been like rabbits, cowed and submissive, seemed to have changed, seemed to have become insolent. They always seemed to be watching you, except when you looked straight at them and then they weren't watching you at all. Except you always caught that twitch of the face, that nervous flicker of the eyes, that meant they had been watching you. And they always seemed to be whispering about you behind your back, except when you swung around and they weren't whispering at all, their lips were closed. Except you *knew* they'd been whispering about you, insulting you. And you got so mad at this sometimes that you took a whole bunch of them—men, women, brats—and herded them into the trucks and took them back to the Cellars and you stopped them watching you out of the corners of their eyes by taking their eyes out. And you stopped them talking about you behind your back by sewing their lips together.

But the funny thing was, it didn't seem to do the trick, didn't seem to stop the watching and the whispering. And you couldn't herd the whole town into the Cellars.

And then there was the sniping. You'd be in a jeep and heading to the mines or coming back from them, in the line of duty, and suddenly one of the guys with you would keel over, one side of his head blown away, his soft nose and blood and brains splashed everywhere. First time this had happened everyone had thought it was a marauder attack, although marauders around this neck of the woods were in fact very scarce; they'd been dealt with savagely years back and now didn't come around anymore because of Mocsin's heavy rep. But it wasn't a marauder attack.

There were no damned marauders in the near vicinity or the far vicinity, and you couldn't figure out who it was. And then it happened again. And again. And again. And it got to be a regular occurrence, although randomly timed and in different places, different stretches of the road. And so all the open jeeps were laid off and mine patrols only worked from secure buggies and land wags. And now, over the past couple of months, three buggies had been blown to scrap by mines, their occupants so much torn and bloody meat.

And then there were the disappearances. Every so often a buddy would fail to return to barracks. At first this was thought to have been due to drunkenness, perhaps. In the old days there'd been a great deal of drunkenness, but then it was realized that although everything in town was yours, and free, there had to be some discipline in the force, and you only got seriously juiced in off periods, when it didn't matter. But then it was thought that maybe it wasn't the booze because none of those guys ever came back, and at last count, over the past two months or so, there were about twenty guys gone and it was as though they'd never existed in the first place.

And the worrying thing was, no one at the top seemed to be taking much notice of any of this, despite the rumbles of discontent from the lower ranks. And when you put forward the theory to your unit leaders that maybe something ought to be done about this, and it seemed to you that all of these weird occurrences were maybe somehow linked, and it was just possible that there was some kind of underground cell in town intent on sabotage and murder, all that happened was you got bawled out and told to mean up your act, boy, or you'll be on hog duty in short order.

So you shut up.

Of course, you appreciated that the guys up top had their own problems and plenty of them. You couldn't help but notice these things. Power shortages, food shortages, sewer-disposal problems—even the johns in the barracks were beginning to stink up, and no one seemed able to unblock the crappers. And all these epidemics didn't help matters.

And now these miners. It was unbelievable. How in hell had they been able to fix things the way they'd been fixed? Someone wasn't running a very tight ship out there. Some very red faces would be around when it was all sorted out. Not to mention a few summary executions. Probably more than a few, come to think of it, and it was a relief to realize that you hadn't been involved in mine duty for a good four months. So they couldn't blame you.

Best thing to do under the circumstances was keep your head down; don't make waves, don't attract attention. Let the upper echelons sort the mess out. Just do your job and don't talk back and don't come up with wildies about criminal elements in town being behind all this because those at the top knew what they were about, and if they dumped on such theories the reason had to be because they had the matter well in hand.

That had to be it.

Nevertheless, it was wise to take precautions. Even out here, in the north end of town, outside the Big Man's mansion—outside this sprawling, many-roomed pre-Nuke dwelling place that had once belonged, or so you'd heard, to some guy called Bank Manager, whatever that meant—it was wise to be wary.

You always had to stand, when you were on guard duty, out in the light, out in the glare of the spotlights that lit up the area around the house, the lawns, the driveway. That was where you had to be. You had to show yourself, holding your piece, so that any guy who got past the electrified fencing and then the outer ring of sentry hides would see you and shit himself. That was the theory, and as a theory it was fine, although of course the mere idea of *anyone* getting up this far was ludicrous. Laughable. The last time anyone had tried to ice the Big Man was—well hell, it had to be all of a dozen years ago, and he'd been crazy, and in any case what had happened to him had been so bad that anyone trying the same trick would have to be triple crazy. As far as you could remember—and you'd only been eight or nine at the time—they'd kept the sucker alive for two whole weeks, out in the center of town so everyone could see, on a specially constructed platform, and for the last ten days of that two weeks he was screaming to die, begging for it. How the hell they'd managed to keep him alive, with not much skin on him, and things sticking into him and out of him and up him and all, was beyond you. Unreal. Those guys—hell, they'd been real clever, real talented. It was one of the reasons that made you want to be a sec man when you grew up.

So no way was any guy going to be smart enough or brave enough or even stupid enough to get this close to the Big House, and really what you were was a kind of honor guard, and there was no danger whatsoever and it didn't really matter if you stood in the light at all.

In any case, these days the lights weren't so damned bright as they used to be and even here, even outside the residence of the Big Man, there were obviously power supply problems, screwed-up generators and the like. You couldn't help but notice that a couple of the pylons this side of the house were in an alarming state of disrepair, and one of them kept on flickering, which was a nuisance, irritating to the eyes.

It felt safer in the shadows, the deep shadows, where no one could see you—not that there was anyone out there to see you except your opposite number on the other side of the house. You got to see each other every now and again because you arranged it with each other so that that was what happened; so he'd know you were here and you'd know he was there and everything was jake. That way everyone was happy—although, come to think of it, you hadn't seen him for a while now, the creep. He'd probably edged right back to the road and was having a cigarette on the sly, or a woman. And that was exactly what you felt like right now, only this near the House it really wasn't too damned smart, and there go the bastard lights again, right off this time, blackout, and hell, maybe the dark didn't really feel all that safe with no moon in the sky, only the chem clouds shifting in from the west, and here we go again, lighting-up time, flicker-flicker-flicker so it hurt your eyes trying to see across the blasted grass—it made it seem as if there were things out there that couldn't possibly be because your opposite number wouldn't have let them through, and dammit, they really ought to get some sucker to do a job on this system; it was really sloppy, a proper job and no argument. Tell them they'd get their balls bitten off by the dogs if they didn't wire the bastard up the way it should be wired and—shit, that hurt—what the hell is this? Some clown's pissing around, got a knee in your back and a hand over your mouth and you can't yell and your head's being dragged back so you feel your back's going to break any moment and all you can see is this grinning face above you, upside down, staring right at you eyeball to eyeball and then all you can see is some fat blade stroking right into you except you can't see where it's gone, only feel it like an electric kiss on your throat and a sudden shaft of agony that lances straight through you, transforming every single nerve end in your body into an internal live wire, and now the blade's gone and you're sinking backward and there's no hand over your mouth and you want to yell but you can't, you really can't, nothing'll come out and everything's loose and you've shit yourself and there's nothing there, nothing at all, just blackness.

UPSIDE DOWN, in the jittery light from the arcs, the face looked hideous, as though it was grinning up at him with two mouths, one of which had far too much lipstick around it. Ryan knelt, wiped his gloved hands and then the panga on the grass, and thrust the thick-bladed weapon back into its sheath. He glanced around.

Hunaker sidled up and took the guard's legs and they lifted the body and heaved it into the thick shadows at the base of the building's wall, shoving it into the heart of a straggling bush. They crouched beside the bush, waiting, patient.

Out here it was quiet. It was almost as if the rest of the town did not exist. There were trees and lawns and gardens. The gardens were mostly overgrown, a wild and junglelike tangle, although here, around Teague's mansion, some effort had been made to keep the place neatened up, to create not only a setting worthy of Mocsin's lord and master, but also to carve out a loose kind of security zone around the house. There had been other large houses in this part of town, but in the neighborhood of Teague's place they had either been demolished or turned into pens for sec men, so that a weaponed-up enclave surrounded the mansion, small forts around the big one.

That was the theory, and a brief smile twisted Ryan's lips as he thought about it. Actually it was pathetic. Actually security was so damned lax that a single man could have invaded Jordan Teague's sacred precincts with no trouble at all. Sure, there was an electric fence, but the power was on the fritz, as evidenced by the flickering lights, and in any case trees had been allowed to grow over parts of the fence, and it had been a simple matter to swing over. They'd made a few kills, but there were guys out there that they hadn't needed to ice, they were so doped up. In one of the houses every sec man they could see was higher than a bird on happyweed. So high, in fact, that the girls who were also there were utterly redundant, were playing cards and drinking to while away the time.

Decay, thought Ryan moodily, his silenced SIG-Sauer now grip-held in his right hand. The decay of empire. Look back through history and there it was, clearly to be seen. Yet no one seemed to see it. It happened time and time again. Yet nobody ever seemed to learn the lesson. And the chilling thought was that it could happen even to the Trader and his empire, such as it was. All that had to happen was to say the hell with it once in a while, ease up. That was all it needed.

Hunaker muttered in his ear, "Why don't we just take out the light system altogether? Be easier for us."

"Too risky."

"Hell, Ryan, no one'd ever know. It's shot to hell already. Way those damned arcs're blinking on and off..."

"Too risky."

"You're the boss."

Ryan checked his watch. Roughly three hours forty minutes to go. It seemed a lot but wasn't. Not if they got caught up in something, met stiff opposition and had to shoot their way out. It wasn't very long at all.

There was one barrier to success. It was known—it must be known by now—that their little group was outside the net. The guys on the barriers at the edge of town would surely have reported back to Teague or Strasser—probably the latter—that Ryan's buggy had entered Mocsin, unless communications were very sloppy and the guy hadn't bothered to report in. But no, thought Ryan, he must discount that, work on the assumption that right now the alarm was out and Strasser's goons were searching for them. Speed was therefore of the essence. And not only for him but for Strasser, too.

Strasser would need time to think, to plan. A couple of miles outside Mocsin he had a dozen vehicles in a circle—two war wags and land wags, trucks, container rigs—full of stiffs, full of hardware and weaponry and food and all kinds of trade goods, and he couldn't touch them. He had them in his hand, they were his, but they might just as well be on the moon. The only way he was going to be able to get inside them was if someone gave him the key, someone told him how to bypass the boobies and render them harmless. Without the key, the poor fucker was basically up the creek.

Except that he also had the Trader. That was a powerful card. Everyone knew that the Trader's men were fiercely loyal to the Old Man. Strasser's idea would be either to break him or torture him so that someone else would break to save the Trader. What Strasser didn't know was that the intense loyalty of those who worked with the Trader extended into virtually a vow of silence if anything ever went badly wrong. It was impressed into every man and woman never to blab, about *anything*. Sure, there were probably weak links in the chain—in any large organization there were bound to be—but Ryan, running through those who were now spark-out in the miniconvoy, couldn't think of any.

And the Trader himself wouldn't talk. He was one tough old buzzard. The Trader wouldn't talk even if devils from

Hell were peeling his skin off inch by inch, layer by layer. As he'd always said, "If they get me, forget me." That applied to any situation.

Strasser didn't know any of that, of course, and even if he did he would never credit it, would never be able to understand it.

Bastard was in for a shock.

Bastard was gonna pay for so casually destroying so many lives, exterminating without a thought so many good men and women.

And as he thought that, his face bleak, his mouth a thin, tight line, Ryan saw images of the girl, Krysty, in his mind and bared his teeth in a soundless snarl.

Images of her in the mutie-camp barn, smoke smudged, disheveled, her clothes just rags on her, driven by a dynamism he admired in any woman or man; then, having done what had to be done, utterly weary, almost defenseless. And then in the war wag, by turns argumentative, amused, angry, sardonic, sorrowing: so many emotions, so many different facets. A complex and fascinating woman. It had been a case of instant attraction, he had to admit, although that was no big deal in itself. So often it happened, and you took what was offered—if it was offered—and a course was then run to a terminal point beyond which there was nothing else, and that was that. But with Krysty there had been more, far more, even though he had only known her for—what? A couple of hours? Not longer than that. There had been a promise there, a promise of depths he could only guess at, of aggression, submission, self-possession, great intelligence and a deep sensuality that proclaimed itself quietly, with no unnecessary fanfare, in her eyes. Her fathomless eyes.

Well, he thought angrily, the hell with that. The hell with it all. Forget it. Put her out of your mind.

Hunaker whispered, "Here comes J.B., Mr. War Chief Buddy."

Ryan noted grimly that Hunaker was still her usual bouncy, caustic self. She'd said nothing about the massacre, nothing about the loss of one who was to all intents and purposes close to her. But then they'd all lost comrades of one kind or another, and this was not the first time a disaster had occurred, although never on such a scale. Still, he thought, it boded ill for any of Teague's and Strasser's goons who got in her way in this town. And that was fine by him.

He turned on the crouch, saw three figures threading through the gloom toward them, coming around the side of the house.

J.B. eased close, the tall, blond Koll and Samantha the Panther in tow.

Ryan said, "We can either blitz in fast or do it quiet. If we do it quiet, at some point we're gonna hit opposition and we're gonna kill. And although we're using suppressors, they're not. There could be plenty of bang-bang, and even those dummies in town'll get to thinking there's something up when that happens."

"I go for initially quiet," said J.B.

"Same here. Once we have Teague, fuck it. Doesn't matter. Make as much noise as we like. The louder the better because I want Strasser up here and talking."

Built on a knoll, the house was big, rambling. The man who'd owned it so many years before must have been prosperous, a power in the town. In the windows, lamplight could be seen through chinks in the closed shutters beyond the glass, but there was no sound of revelry or celebration. Jordan Teague was having a quiet evening at home. Probably among his loved ones, although that wouldn't include such mundane items as wife and kids. Word was, the Baron was barren.

J.B. said, "Outhouses at the rear and a lot of old garbage. There's two side doors but they ain't been opened in a hundred years. Rear door opens, passageway to it. There were two guys." He didn't bother to mention that the two guys who'd been muttering to each other and smoking beside the rear door were now shapeless bundles among the garbage.

"Main door's not locked," said Ryan. "You go in the back, head upstairs, check that out and hold the upper story. We'll go in the front, wait for you. Two minutes. Any goons, kill 'em quick."

"Women?"

Ryan shrugged.

"If they pull on you, sure. If not, disable 'em, tie 'em up, whatever. We're not animals." He turned to the tall blonde. "Koll, you stay with me."

Most of this, he knew, was unnecessary. All his combatants were highly trained, knew how to act in a crisis or a battle situation. It was simply a matter of working out the approach and after that they were on their own. He'd never yet, in ten years, had one of his men ice another by accident in kill chaos.

He gave J.B. his two minutes, then turned to the porch. As he'd said, the door was unlocked. Hunaker had already checked that out. The door handle was big and round. He turned it, pushed, went through fast, the silenced SIG in his right hand, Hunaker behind him, Koll at the rear.

They saw a large hallway, wide stairs facing them, a passageway to the left diving to the rear of the house. There were closed doors right and left. The hallway was unlit except for chinks of light below the doors.

There was a strong stink of incense mixed in with the burned straw smell of happyweed. Ryan could hear the mutter of conversation from the door on his left. Muted laughter, nothing else. J.B. materialized, moving quickly but silently up the passageway toward him, followed by Rintoul and Sam. Hennings was therefore out back. Good. A murderous bastard at the best of times who stood no nonsense from antagonists.

J.B. and the other two turned to the stairs, raced silently up them, keeping to the side. They fanned out on the landing above and disappeared. Ryan nodded to Hunaker, then gestured at the door on the left. She now held a squat Ingram MAC-11 LISP, a classic weapon. Koll stood by the now-closed main door, a little to one side, a LAPA in his hands.

Ryan moved to the left-hand door, Hunaker at his side. Without hesitation he twisted the handle and shoved the door inward. They both jumped into the room, taking in everything in a split second.

Seven men, black jacketed or in shirt-sleeves. Five sitting at a round table in the center playing cards, one standing beside the table, smoking and holding a bottle, one in the act of walking unhurriedly down the room toward another door at the far end. There were three kerosene lamps, one hanging from a hook on the ceiling. Many candles. The sudden opening of the door caused the flames to sway and gutter, a ripple effect that threw shadows crazily across the room. It also caused the seven men, as one, to gape in stunned amazement.

As Ryan pushed home the door, two of the men at the table sprang up, shoving their chairs back, pulling at shoulder-rigged pieces. It was enough. Hunaker, her body taut, her eyes narrowed, a feral growl at her lips, squeezed off her mag with about as much noise as a dozen guys having a spitting contest all at once might make. A long-drawn-out *Phyyytt-t-t-t*! As she fired she tight-arced the thrust-out gun, casings spraying. The three seated men were punched backward in their chairs, arms flailing, thudding to the carpeted floor. Of the two who'd reached their feet, the nearest was slammed into the other and both seemed to be glued together as they spun across the room, gasping, scarlet holes magically appearing in their chests. Then their feet tangled together and they toppled, crashing to the floor.

As Hunaker had begun her squeeze, Ryan had thrown up his SIG. His prime target was the man at the end of the room, the man near the far door. Ryan bent at the knees and sent two rounds at him. Both hit, the first slamming through the spinal column as he half turned away and punching out the sternum in a wild spray of blood, the second going higher, shattering the collarbone from the side, almost taking the guy's head off on its way out.

Without pause, Ryan swung to the right and heart-shot the man with the bottle. The man choked out an *"Uggh!"* quietly and hit the wall behind him, slid down it, arms wide, coat riding up to his shoulders as he sank. The bottle had already left his nerveless fingers and now lay on the floor, its contents soaking into the worn carpet.

Her right hand remagging the MAC, Hunaker sprinted across the room, silently hurdling the bodies. She reached the end door with Ryan at her heels. Again he gripped the handle, twisted, this time pulling it open. Hunaker sprang through the gap before it was fully opened, Ryan jumping through after her, his SIG left-handed now.

A passage, short, one door at the end half open and light streaming through the gap, though mostly blocked off by a man standing in the opening holding a tray with bottles on it.

Ryan snarled, *"Shit!"* and two-rounded him. It was the only thing he could do. The guy flew backward through the door and the tray crashed to the floor, glass shattering. There was a shout from the room beyond, more of surprise then alarm, but already Hun was flying down the passage, her boots almost not touching down, her short loose coat billowing out behind her like bat's wings. She leaped into the room on the turn and the MAC-11 was spitting even as her feet hit carpet. Ryan, pounding after her, heard glass smash, metal clang and whine, and a sound like someone coughing loudly and very fast.

He reached the doorway, saw Hunaker lowering the machine pistol, a savage expression on her face.

She said "Damn!" in self-disgust and turned away from him.

The room was a kitchen. The only guy there had been butchering meat on a block in the center of the room with a cleaver. He'd taken most of the MAC's mag, had been powered back into a table with glassware and copper pans and skillets on it, and now sagged backward, feet in the air, arms hanging, most of his chest blown out and blood splashed over floor and walls.

Hunaker was muttering curses in a harsh undertone. Ryan knew she was cursing herself as much for butchering one single guy who hadn't even been truly armed as for making such a row.

"You had to do it blind," he snapped. "Could've been a garrison in here."

The room stank of powder and blood. It smelled like a slaughterhouse. Ryan touched the young woman on the arm, then clasped her to him, his eye taking in the fact that the windows all were shuttered and there were three doors off to one side. He could feel her trembling slightly.

Hunaker said in a tight voice, "Shit, she was such a sweet kid, Ryan. I'll miss her, dammit. You dunno what it's like."

"No. Probably not."

She shook herself, clenched her eyes, then opened them again and said, "Okay, let's go. I'll get us all killed at this rate." Her smile was terrible to behold.

Ryan checked out the three doors. Storerooms. Nothing there. They went back along the passage, through the big room, still smelling strongly of cordite, warily out into the hallway. Koll gave them the thumb.

Ryan muttered, "You hear anything?"

"What's to hear?" The tall blonde gestured at the door through which they'd just come. "Good paneling there, Ryan. Thick as hell. You make any noise, then?"

"Clearly not so's you'd notice."

He glanced up, saw J.B. at the head of the stairs, alone, holding up his left hand, four fingers extended. His expression was deadpan.

Four kills. Everything jake.

Ryan shot a look at Hunaker and discovered that she was staring straight at him. He inclined his head toward the right-hand door under which no light could be seen and raised an eyebrow. Hunaker nodded almost eagerly as she slipped a third mag into the guts of the MAC-11.

Ryan said, "You sure?"

Hunaker hissed, "For Christ's sake, Ryan!"

He shrugged. It amused him how people still invoked the name of a deity, or, as he understood it from his reading way back in . . . well, when he *was* reading, some kind of secondary deity who seemed to be a son of the primary deity. But he did it himself, when cussing or expressing shock or anger, often using words that had no meaning for him whatsoever, although that of course was a legacy from his father who'd done exactly the same, and probably his father before him, and so on back to pre-Nuke.

For a second, as he thought like this, the image of his father began to form in his mind. But he blocked it off quickly, the hand that held the SIG clenching involuntarily, so that he nearly squeezed off a round into the floor. He shook his head to clear the image finally, shake the memories away. These days it was easier, thank God.

A brief smile twitched his lips as he caught that. There you are, he thought—*thank God*!

He stepped to the right-hand door, thought about powering in as before but something—he didn't quite know what—stopped him. His gloved hand took hold of the knoblike handle, twisted it firmly, though tugging at it so that no hint of a sound came from the movement. He gently eased the door open slightly. Two inches. There was only darkness beyond. The smell of incense was much stronger here, a positive assault on the senses. He could hear the faint murmur of someone talking, but as if from afar. He pushed the door more, slipped through. He sensed that Hunaker was behind him and half turning his head he muttered, "Close it, but not tight."

He stared at the warm blackness, half closing his eye, then opening it again, wide. Over on his left, in front, was a narrow smear of murky light in the air, which at first he could make no sense of. The light danced, a flickering glow Then gradually he began to sort out details of the room.

Or half room. It was big, high ceilinged. There was no furniture, but the floor was carpeted. Across the room, from wall to wall, hung some kind of thick curtain. Two curtains, actually, pulled together. Hence that chink of light in the center where the inner folds of the two draperies didn't quite meet.

He slid the SIG back down into its belt rig and reached for the LAPA, holding it one-handed as he silently stepped across the room toward the curtain. There was no point now in using a silenced piece. He'd reached his goal. The voice he could hear beyond the thick draperies belonged to Jordan Teague.

He reached the gap in the curtain. It couldn't have been positioned better if some guy had actually set it up for him. Eye high. Breathing through his mouth, the LAPA held down at his side, he peered through.

One bizarre scene.

One bizarre goddamned scene.

There were candles everywhere, their flames fluttering and guttering in the drafts. It seemed as if there were a thousand candles at first, ten thousand, seemed as though the room itself was vast, extending way beyond the bounds of sanity. But of course it was a mirror effect. Long mirrors on all the walls, to the front of him and to the sides, even fixed down over the closed shutters of the windows on the right-hand wall. Ryan glanced up, his eye widening. Even covering the ceiling.

For the rest, there was not much furniture in the room although the place could not be said to be bare. On the floor were thick rugs, all sizes, all shapes and patterns and colors or combinations of colors. There were two potbellied stoves on the right, doors wide, heat belching out; pipes from the top of each rose into the air, sagging drunkenly in badly welded sections, disappearing into the mirrored ceiling. A couple of small tables, both of which seemed to Ryan's mildly discriminating eye to be more than just well-carved—really old period pieces, probably—stood toward the center, smoke rising from large bowls on them. He couldn't see what was burning, but it was sure as hell the source of the rich, cloying stink that permeated the room.

It was what reared up high, center stage but toward the far end, that dragged the word "bizarre" into his mind. A kind of stepped pyramid, twice the height of a man, maybe more, and flat on top. Ryan couldn't see how it was constructed because it was covered with a piece of rich red material, tacked in so that the step treads were tight and thus climbable without getting his boots tangled up in the folds. Atop it, a wide, high-backed wing chair, plain wood from what he could see, although that wasn't much, because of its occupant and the fact that it was partially covered in more material that, as he stared at it, became vaguely familiar, then all at once, after a few seconds searching his memory, became entirely recognizable. He could just make out white stars on a patch of blue, vivid red bars on white. A real relic from pre-Nuke days: a huge version of what they'd called the national flag of this land when it had been a unified country, a power in the world.

Ryan stared at the figure sprawled grossly and grotesquely in the chair, seeming to fill it to overflowing, one foot on the platform, the knee bent back, the other leg hanging over the top step. Except for black knee-length riding boots, worn and dulled, he was evidently naked under what looked to be some kind of fantastic robe, blue in color, thickly lined with soiled white fur, and open at the front. His massive belly bulged in folds, lapping at his thighs. His flesh was pinkish, his face red, the cheeks sagging around a small thick-lipped mouth around which was a fringe of white stubble. The eyes were tiny flesh-choked beads. His head was flung back so that he was gazing up at the mirrored ceiling as he talked, his image gazing back down at him. In his right pudgy hand he held a thick cigar, which, from the look of it, consisted entirely of dry-cured happyweed leaves, rolled tight.

Jordan Teague. Baron of Mocsin.

Ryan almost couldn't believe his eyes, for a moment convinced that the incense that clogged the air was some kind of drug and that what he was seeing was a weird, outrageous vision.

But it was real enough. Two years had clearly made a hell of a difference. Teague had been fat, sure, but this was way different. The guy looked as if he'd need help walking. Or maybe he stayed up there the whole time? There'd been nothing remotely like this in the old days. Teague had gotten around town, done his business, kept a firm hand on things.

In many ways, as Ryan remembered it from the Trader, who knew the background, Jordan Teague had been a typical Baron. He'd come up the hard way. Father and mother had he none—that he knew of, anyhow. He'd cut his own path in one of the southern Baronies and discovered that, as long as he was paid for it—in food, creds or women—he didn't mind killing for his living. Didn't mind at all. He became head blaster for a small-time Baron, supplanted him in a bloody coup and was then, after some years, himself ousted by his own head blaster. There is very often such a symmetry in these matters, although Teague broke the pattern by being slightly quicker on the uptake than his predecessor and escaping with his life. He drifted into the central Deathlands, took up with a band of mutie marauders who had a rather more liberal attitude toward norms than most—that is, they accepted him, instead of spit-roasting him over a slow fire and eating him—and they had a good two years looting, pillaging and raping before the band hit what on the surface appeared to be a sleepy but fairly prosperous settlement ripe for slaughter and rape some distance south of the ruins of the old St. Louis, but which in fact turned out to be a setup by the angry inhabitants of the entire area, who were, after two years of hell, not unnaturally pissed off with the marauders' continual depredations and red-hot for vengeance.

The marauders broke up. Literally. As they drove in they hit a wall of firepower—much of it having been hoarded for years—which destroyed them, their trucks, their jeeps, their women, their bags and traps. Teague, a man of violence but no great brain, for once in his life acted smart by mingling with the normals in the subsequent massacre and distinguished himself by gunning down, with a close-range burst from a hand-held MG, the mutie leader, a guy with a curious piglike snout and the manners to go with it. Actually Teague didn't merely gun him down but cut him in two—it was that close a range. And then blew his head off. Just to be sure. Some days later some busybody with a sharp memory accused him of being one of the band. There was an altercation that Teague won by the simple expedient of icing his opponent with a pump-action. He said it was in righteous rage at such a calumny, but there were those who thought he'd been suspiciously overzealous in pulling his piece and began to get sulky with him. Teague wisely beat it, drifted northwest, landed up in Mocsin. It was ripe for a takeover by someone, and he figured he fitted the bill.

Just about then he bumped into the Trader, who'd recently fallen across his first Stockpile, together with his buddy Marsh Folsom, and had a raft of factory-fresh fowling pieces and mucho ammo to match. Teague had no jack whatsoever, but he did have an astounding stroke of luck. He came across a guy who'd been mooching about in the hills to the southwest of Mocsin and discovered seams of yellow in the rocks. Someone later figured out

that the gold had been uncovered by the last rippling
tremors from the West Coast cataclysm, when Sov
"earthshaker" bombs and missiles back in the Nuke had
carved out a new coastline, taking out half of Washington
state, Oregon and California, and the whole of Baja, California. But such geological pedantry was of no interest to
Jordan Teague, who simply deep-sixed the sucker and
grabbed his nuggets. With these he bought a passel of 5.56
mm M-16A1s modified to handle the M-203 grenade
launcher, crates of mags, plus boxes—assorted—of 40 mm
rounds for the grenade launchers, including HE, frag and
M-576 buck. Teague being Teague, he would have liked to
have had free what he had to pay for, and pay for highly.
But even then, word had gotten around that you didn't
fuck with the Trader, and in any case Teague had the location of the strike—unwisely, the panhandler had made
a map—and it was more than likely that there was more
where the first haul had come from.

There was, indeed, as Teague discovered after he and an
assorted bunch of murderous trash had subdued Mocsin
and set up there in style. In short order he began to mine
the yellow stuff and ship it out East. Slowly at first, but in
the past decade more and more successfully. Jordan
Teague was now an exceedingly rich man although, as
Ryan knew damned well, as anyone knew, none of this
wealth had ever rubbed off on Mocsin.

All in all, a pretty inglorious and unedifying career that,
did he but know it, thought Ryan bleakly, was moving
swiftly to its close.

Ryan still found it barely credible that Teague should
end up like this. He recalled what Fishmouth Charlie and
said about Teague's not knowing what the goddamned
time was these days. Damned right. He looked to be brain-
blasted on booze and happyweed, stuffed to the gullet and

beyond with food. A gross mountain of flab, fit for nothing but the boneyard.

Ryan almost felt sorry for him.

Almost.

There were others in the room. Two women were whispering together at the foot of the pyramid structure, sitting on the lowest step. One was naked, wide hipped with pendulous breasts. Ryan judged her to be well on the other side of thirty. The other was younger; oddly, she wore a top but no bottom, no skirt or pants. They looked bored as they chewed the fat, dispirited. It occurred to Ryan that trying to jolly Teague into raising his flagpole these days must be a full-time occupation, and wearing on the nerves.

Slumped at Teague's feet was a man, a strange and wild-looking guy, at this distance elderly, though Ryan could not be sure. He looked to be medium height though very thin. Sprawled as he was, it was difficult to tell exactly. He was clad all in rusty black except for an off-white shirt. His hair was long and lank and gray. Ryan couldn't see his face clearly because the guy's head was in his hands. He seemed to be crying. Certainly his shoulders were shaking as though he was in the grip of a fit of the ague, although no sounds came from him. Could be he was laughing, but Ryan doubted it.

Hunaker whispered impatiently behind him, "C'mon, Ryan. Let's hit 'em."

"Wait."

His ears were only just beginning to adjust to the wheezy rumble of Teague's voice. He seemed to be talking to himself, with the odd sentence directed down at the crazed old guy at his feet, who took no notice.

Suddenly Teague lashed out with his foot, the tip of his boot catching the old man at the side of his head and toppling him. With a blubbering wail the man tumbled down the steps, a wild sprawl of arms and legs. The younger woman jumped out of the way as he banged past her, landing in a heap on the rugs. Agonized sounds came from him. The girl didn't even turn his way but went around the other side of her companion and the muttered conversation continued as though it had never stopped.

"I told ya!" wheezed Teague. "You listen ta me, Doc, when I'm talkin to ya. An' get up off ya tush."

The man called Doc struggled to his feet, stood with his back to the curtain, his shoulders bowed. He was still trembling.

"Well?" barked Teague.

Though shaky, the old man's voice was rich, deep-timbred.

"I, uh, I fear I, uh, did not hear you, Mr. Teague."

"Don't listen—that's your damned trouble."

"You are, uh, perfectly correct, sir. It is indeed a failing of mine." His voice dropped, as though he wasn't speaking to Teague at all. "I live in the mind, sir. As you know, there is another country there. In the mind. Memories of a better life, a richer existence by far."

"Lotta crap you talk, Doc."

"Indeed, sir. Yes, indeed. Indubitably. I, uh . . ." His voice trailed off.

"Dunno where you fuckin' are, Doc, that's what's wrong with you."

The old man's head came up, his voice stronger.

"Oh, no, sir. Believe me, I know where I am. Indeed I do, sir. I am in Hell. I have often thought it. It is the only explanation."

"Yeah." Teague chuckled throatily, his cheeks quivering. He was still looking up at the ceiling, had not even shifted his gaze even when lashing out at the old man, but now he dropped his head, stared down. "You 'n' me both,

Doc,'' he said. There was a grotesque smile on his face. "Hear Cort had you down in the pens again, ha?"

"Th-that is so."

"Get it up, did ya?"

The old man shuddered but did not answer.

"I said, get it up did ya?" said Teague dangerously.

The lank hair shook slightly as the old guy nodded.

"Well, more'n I can do, Doc," Teague said affably. "Fuck knows when I last got it up. Just lost the inclination. Too much like hard work, know what I mean?"

The old man did not reply.

Teague suddenly barked, "Hey you, bitch!"

Neither of the women took a blind bit of notice.

Teague, grunting and gasping, gripped the chair arms, heaved himself forward. He screamed, *"Bitch!"*

The younger of the two women got up unconcernedly and mounted the pyramid toward him. At the top she stood beside the chair, gazing blankly out across the room as Teague reached out a flabby hand and fondled her buttocks, his fingers disappearing from sight. Grunting, he heaved himself around and thrust the fingers of his other hand up inside her top, began groping at her hidden breasts. Still the woman said nothing, did nothing, her face expressionless. Teague suddenly sank back into the chair with an angry croak, flapped a hand irritably at her. She turned, descended the steps, pulling her top down. She sat on the bottom step and took up the conversation again with her companion.

"Y'know, Cort's gonna kill ya one of these days, Doc."

The old man's hands rose, palms up.

"I am dead already, sir. It is the only explanation."

"He don't like ya, Doc. S'why he likes to humiliate ya. Wasn't for me, you'd be stiff."

"I was taught, sir, that theories must always fit the facts, not facts theories. It is a basic tenet of any academic discipline. And the facts are simple. This is Hell. Therefore, *quod erat demonstrandum*, I am dead. I have been dead, sir, since . . . since, ah . . . ah, dead . . . since . . ."

His voice had become hoarse and he began to tremble again, a terrible feverish shiver that took hold of his entire bony frame, as though invisible hands had gripped him and were shaking him violently. Slowly he sank to his knees, his head held in his hands, his shoulders quaking. Gusty sobs erupted from him.

Teague sucked at his cigar, as though oblivious of what was happening below.

He said, "No way out for ya, Doc. Cort ain't just gonna put ya to the hogs one of these days, he's gonna feed ya to them."

"No. That is where you are wrong." The voice had suddenly become crisper in tone. His head jerked up, dropped to one side, like a bird's. "The locational progressions are simple. There is no problem there. From A to B to C and onward. Or from P to Q and then back to, let us say, G. So you see, there is indeed a way out. Or I should say, many ways out. But finding them, my dear sir, that is altogether a different matter. The Redoubts are there, in situ. Many of them. But—and I put it to you— where is 'there'?"

"Shit," muttered Teague.

"This is the point. And I fear I have to say the answer is for the moment lost." He was talking more quickly now, the words spilling out, a curious excitement in his voice, in his whole bearing. His right hand was raised, the forefinger wagging up at Jordan Teague as though in admonishment. As though the losing of the "answer" was all the gross man's fault. "No doubt it will reveal itself. No doubt *they* will reveal *themselves*. At times the fog clears..."

He stood up suddenly, began to prowl in front of the pyramid, his hands clasped behind him. Backward and forward, backward and forward. His voice dropped to a dreamy murmur that Ryan could only just make out.

"The fog. Sometimes, if let loose, it's quite powerful. Feedback effect, as I recall, though difficult to explain. And quite arbitrary. Of course, they had no real conception of its power. They said they had, but they lied. They lied much of the time." He thumped his right fist into the palm of his left hand, his voice rising to an outraged cry. "They treated me like an animal! It was disgraceful! As though I were a puppet! They had no right to do what they did and I informed them of that fact. And for all their honeyed words I was nothing to them, less then nothing. A subject. An interesting experiment. It was wicked, wicked! God should have struck them dead!" He swung around on Teague, pointed up at him, laughing, his voice cracked, pitching up to a falsetto. "But through the fog, my dear sir! From A to B! And then to R or M or *anywhere*! Find the fog, sir! There is your solution! Your way out! So many possibilities!"

Hunaker whispered, "Shit, Ryan, we're wasting time. Let's *do* it!"

Ryan said "Wait, dammit. There's something..." Then he said, "Lucky we didn't!" as Teague bawled, "Jauncy! Hackutt!" and one of the mirrors on the other side of the pyramid swung open and two goons came through at the run. They had slung M-16s and they went separate ways around the pyramid, right and left, and converged on the wild-eyed old man. They were both grinning death's-head grins.

The old man stopped pacing, seemed to shrivel into himself, his face gray.

Teague said, "Fucker's off again. Take his toys from him."

"No!"

The man called Doc screamed the word. His hands went up toward Teague in an imploratory gesture, silently entreating him not to do what was to be done, and what had been done, probably, on many occasions in the past.

"C'mon, c'mon!" snapped one of the goons. "Take 'em out. Hand 'em over."

Doc stared wildly around, as though looking for some means of escape. Then he swallowed hard, his shoulders slumping. He reached slowly into a pocket of his filthy black coat, then held out his hand. Ryan peered up at the ceiling, the only way he could see what was there: two gray spheroids.

He muttered, "All right, but don't hit the old guy."

"Why not?"

"I'm not sure, but don't. I want him."

"You're the boss."

They slammed through the curtain, Ryan to the left, Hunaker on his right, one target apiece. Simple.

Except that the two women shrieked and bolted. Their ideal course of escape would be off to the side, out of any line of fire. Instead blind panic turned them both into something akin to chickens with their heads lopped off. They dived in front of the two sec men, yelling in a frenzy. One tripped on a rug, the other tumbled over her. Ryan swore and dived to one side as a sec man, quick off the mark, unslung his piece and fired what must have been half a mag in his direction, the rounds flaying the thick curtains behind into wildly flapping cloth shreds. Ryan was firing the LAPA, its butt smacking into his pelvis, but his aim was wild and rounds hammered into the mirrors behind the pyramid, the glass exploding into a million flying shards.

Hunaker hadn't fired at all. She was rolling across the floor toward the wall in a desperate scramble as bullets from the second guy tore air above her head. She was now regretting that she hadn't jumped into this one with a piece—engineered, as this particular piece was, so it fired only in the fully automatic mode—that did not have the ferocious blast power of the MAC, which was fine for blazing out whole groups of targets with a light squeeze of the trigger but lousy when it came to the one-man job, and especially lousy when that one man was surrounded by others you did not want to hit. Sometimes, she thought as she let the machine-pistol go and dragged an H&K P-7 from inside her jacket, you could be *over* overconfident.

She rolled fast and scrambled around onto her stomach, fast-sighting as her head rose from the rug, and the compact snug-gripped P-7 barked twice, the first round missing her man by mere centimeters, the second, because of hand quiver on the roll, whipping at his coat. He yelped, jumped to his left, stumbled and fell, a third bullet from the P-7 tearing air where he'd just been. He rolled, too, and took a dive like a sprinter off the block into the comparatively calmer waters on the other side of the pyramid, joined a half second later by his companion, who'd had the same idea.

That idea was not to face up to Ryan and Hunaker at all but get the hell out of the room in one piece by diving through the still-open mirror door through which they'd arrived.

Except Ryan was ahead of them. Where he was he could not hit them, either of them, but the door itself was another matter. He sent three rounds into it, smashing the glass into a wild kaleidoscope of candle-reflected glitter and punching the door into its frame.

It was a standoff. Neither Ryan nor Hunaker had a direct bead on the two goons, who were now crouched behind the pyramid. On the other hand Ryan, from where he was positioned, could destroy anyone who tried to make for that doorway. The two goons were in a slightly better state, although only very slightly. They at least could snipe if they'd a mind to, or poke their pieces up and over the nearest step treads and blaze off in the general direction of their targets. And by doing that they could at least stop Ryan and Hunaker rushing them from the other side.

Ryan bared his teeth in an icy grin as he stared at the reflection of the two men, one of whom was staring back. Their eyes met. The goon wasn't grinning. He looked as though his bowels were about ready to go. That did not, however, make him any less dangerous.

Ryan's gaze roved. The two women were now trying to burrow under the rugs, shrieking and yelling in total-flap hysteria. The old guy called Doc seemed to have disappeared. Ryan couldn't see him anywhere, had not caught his bolt route. Probably he'd managed to flee through that door. Pity. Ryan would like to have talked to him. He'd seemed a wreck—not surprising if, as it appeared, he was some kind of . . . well, court jester or scapegoat for Teague and Strasser—but he had not seemed completely off his head, which made all that stuff he'd been gabbling about mildly attention grabbing. Or perhaps rather more than mildly attention grabbing. Where had Teague picked him up? He'd not been around two years back. He talked funny, and what was all that shit about "the fog"? The guy called Kurt, back at Charlie's, had—from what Charlie herself had said—rambled on about fog. Ryan didn't trust coincidences, even in this random, arbitrary and seemingly totally haphazard life. His psyche nudged him, whispered that there might be something odd here, something worth following up. The old coot hadn't just been talking about any old fog, and if Charlie was to be believed neither had the guy called Kurt. Common sense, however, informed him that there were ten thousand natural fogs in the Deathlands per week, somewhere or other, and probably this Kurt bird was vision-ridden from fever—a fog with claws? Come on!—and probably this old coot here was crazed from having been forced into performing grisly and unnatural acts for the delight of that sadistic bastard Strasser. Still, from A to B to C, his mind mused—and what *were* the "possibilities"…and who were "they" and what had "they" done to him and what was a "Redoubt" and why did he talk so weird?

The explanation for all this was probably worth much less than a half pinch of nukeshit, thought Ryan, and right now there were other problems on the agenda, which needed to be solved urgently.

He stared up at Jordan Teague, atop his pyramid, cringing into the wingback chair with a mad and pop-eyed look about him.

"R-Ryan...?"

The word came out as a hoarse raven's croak.

"Teague, you fat bastard! You're the best target I've seen in years! Even a blind man could take you out!"

"Ryan! Jesus! What're ya doin? What is this? W-we gotta talk, fer Chrissake!" The bulk blubber of him was quaking like a jelly in a high wind. "Th-this ain't the way to do business!"

"You're in deep shit, Teague. I swear I'm gonna give you to the cannies. Bunch of them could live off you for a month."

"M-my God, Ryan! Ya gotta tell me...I'll do anything...gotta tell me what ya want! I'll do it...I'll do it!"

Ryan was disgusted. However many faults Teague had—about a zillion, if one were to count—however many monstrous deeds could be laid at his door, at least there'd been a time when he'd been in control, at least there'd been a time when he'd commanded a certain amount of respect as a hard man who'd carved himself a niche in the Deathlands and stayed put where others had fallen. This abject caterwauling and cringing in ludicrous terror was appalling, made him simply a bladder of lard worth nothing. Less then nothing.

Ryan put up the LAPA and pumped three rounds into the top step of the pyramid, just below Teague's twitching boots. Teague yelled, tried to turn himself into a fat ball, as the bullets smashed straight through the construction, bursting more glass the other side.

Ryan laughed as he realized the pyramid wasn't solid.

"Hun! The base! Flay it!"

Hunaker caught on. She reached for the MAC-11, rolled onto her stomach again, aimed for the second-from-bottom step and squeezed off a withering blast of rounds that turned her immediate target into an explosive spray of blown-out wood chips before powering subsonically through the hollow interior and ripping out the other side, only slowing marginally as they zip-drilled the flesh, sinew and bones of the man crouched there. The guy was shoved over bodily by the punishing impact, most of the MAC's mag transforming him into a mere torso from which blood sprayed.

The second man, yelling in panic as he, too, cottoned on, jumped from cover, M-16 hammering wildly in Ryan's direction. But Ryan was on full-auto now, and his fire line caught the man and followed him, slamming him back against the mirror wall in a twisted body tangle, unstitching him, opening him up as he smashed into the glass, soft pointed bullets and glass shards erupting him into a red rag doll.

There was a microsecond's silence and then Ryan was on his feet and sprinting back to the curtain, throwing it aside and bawling for Koll. Koll came running, his own LAPA held out.

Pointing, Ryan snapped, "There's a door back there—check it out. Look for an old guy. Long hair, black gear. Nail any goons, but don't nail him."

He turned, brandishing his piece at Teague.

"Down, and make it snappy, fat man." He said to Hunaker, "And for fuck's sake do something about those goddamned women. *Anything!*"

He watched as Jordan Teague clambered down the steps of the pyramid. As he reached the floor he pulled the blue robe around him defensively. It didn't meet in the middle. Ryan went close, poked at the sagging gut with the LAPA's barrel. Teague's beady little eyes shone with fear.

"You fat double-crossing bastard," Ryan hissed. "I oughta take you apart."

Teague wheezed, "I ain't done nothin', Ryan."

"That," said Ryan icily, "as someone said to me not too damned long ago...someone who's now *dead!*" And he spat the word at Teague, who waddled back two steps at the violence of the sound, "is a double fucking negative."

"I...I dunno watcha mean, Ryan!" Teague squeaked.

"It means, fat man, you *have* done *something!*"

"Please, Ryan..." The man's voice was a pleading whisper, and there were tears rolling and bouncing down his cheeks. "Tell me."

"You had our train nerved out, and you've got the Trader. And now I have you!"

Teague's face shook, triple jowls quivering like a turkey's wattles. He muttered, "Uh...yeah. Cort did... say..." Then he croaked, "But I was against the idea, Ryan, against it. Ya gotta believe me."

"You wanted the train for nothing—you simply iced the whole..." A wildfire of fury boiled through him suddenly and he rammed the LAPA barrel into Teague's stomach, yanked it back, flipped it and smashed the butt into the throat of the tottering, gobbling figure. Teague fell back with a strangled shriek, sprawled ludicrously half on, half off the bottom step of his pyramid throne, clutching at his neck, his face scarlet. Ryan flipped the gun again and held it down at Teague, aiming at his gut, his finger tight on the trigger, his face squeezed into a frozen mask.

From across the room, though it seemed like much farther, he heard Hunaker say softly, "Ryan."

He breathed out slowly, lowered his piece. He said tightly, "When this is over, Teague, you and Strasser..." He sniffed air into his lungs, threw his head back, breathed again, this time gustily. He said, his voice less taut, "Who's the old man?"

"Old man?" Teague's voice was a broken gargle.

"Old man, old man!" snarled Ryan. "The old buzzard you called Doc."

Teague shook his head feebly.

"I dunno, Ryan. He just...appeared. One day. Came into town. Year back, maybe longer."

"Who is he, what's he do, where's he from?"

"Dunno. Dunno nothin'." The words came out fast, a panic-stricken stream. "I thought it'd be a laugh, you know, to have him around. Cort don't like him, makes him...do things. Said he was a doctor, acted real strange. Still does, goes off in a fuckin' dream, talks...I dunno, 'nother language. Long words. Some guys did somethin' to him, took him off from someplace. But he never said where, when, why. Can't understand the guy sometimes, talks to ya like he's talkin' to a buncha kids. Shit, I dunno, Ryan—that's it.''

"What about this fog?"

"Oh, yeah. He's lookin' for a fog." Teague tried laughing, but then thought better of the idea. "Thass what he says, lookin' for a fog, special kind of fog. I dunno what the hell he means, Ryan. He says that on the other side life's better. He's burned out. Rads've eaten his brain away."

"Didn't look like he had the Plague to me, Teague."

"No, no. He's fit enough, yeah. Brain-fucked is all."

"Those two balls. Eggs."

"S'all he had with him, Ryan, when he came into town. Y'gotta believe me. Didn't have nothin' else. Some kind of metal, goes crazy when you take 'em off him. Cort gets off on doin' that, takin' 'em away from him. Guy has a fuckin' fit."

Koll suddenly reappeared. His face was set.

"Nothing out back, but there are lights heading up this way."

Samantha the Panther came through the curtains.

"J.B. says . . ."

"Lights. Yeah." Ryan gestured at Teague. "Take him out front, where we came in."

He ran back to the entrance hallway, then up the stairs to the second story. Rintoul emerged from the shadows and pointed to a room. Ryan padded across to where J.B. was hunched against a window frame.

"Two trucks and a buggy. Could be Strasser."

Ryan peered out. The arcs were still flickering, but in their nervous illumination Ryan could see what J.B. had seen. The trucks had reached the front of the house below and were stopping, the buggy sweeping in from behind. A tall, gauntly built man, bareheaded and black garbed, emerged from the front of the buggy, followed by two sec men.

"Yeah."

Strasser was staring around, peering to the left and right as though looking for someone.

"And they don't know we're here. He's looking for the guards we iced."

Ryan rerigged the LAPA and brought out his SIG-Sauer. He sighted on the roof-mounted spotlight of the buggy and put a round into it. There was a crash of glass, a sharp metallic clang and the light went dead. Strasser jumped, his head jerking up as his hand reached at his coat.

Ryan shouted, "You're dead first, Strasser. Whatever happens."

Strasser stared upward, his skull-like face expressionless.

"Ryan. Might've guessed you'd still be loose. But what can you expect when you employ imbeciles."

J.B. muttered, "I'll go down. Get Henn and the rest. Get the door open."

Ryan called out, "You killed a lot of our people, Strasser."

The bony man shrugged but said nothing.

"Tell the trucks to beat it, and tell them not to mess up when we come out. Get your men out of the buggy."

"Why should I do that, Ryan?" Strasser's voice, like his face, was expressionless.

"We got Teague."

Strasser pursed his lips, then shrugged again and nodded slowly. He began to turn away.

"And don't move from that spot, shithead."

Strasser stood still, pointed at the trucks, began talking quickly to the two men with him. One of them went to the buggy, his voice a mutter of sound. Ryan watched as goons began climbing out of the buggy, five in all. The trucks revved up, backed off from the house and turned, disappearing down the driveway into the darkness beyond the arc lights' beams. Ryan could see their headlamps cutting into the blackness. The men who had come from the buggy began to back away from the vehicle onto the grass.

"J.B.!"

Below him he saw light spill out from the opening door and he turned and raced back across the room, into the corridor, down the stairs, the SIG still clutched in his right hand.

"Let's go."

He shoved the SIG at Teague's head, and Teague whimpered as they moved out of the house toward Strasser and the buggy.

"We go to where the Trader is, we go to where the train is, and then we go."

Strasser said, "Fortunes of war, Ryan," His hands came out in a wide-armed shrug. "So near, and yet so far. Ah, well . . ."

There was something wrong here, but Ryan couldn't figure out what it was. He knew Strasser. Strasser was too cool—far too cool. Then in the same moment that he saw muzzle-flash from the buggy interior, Teague's head exploded like an overripe fruit, spraying him with blood, brains and homogenized bone. The double crack of the shots came a microsecond later. Teague lurched, collapsed into him soundlessly, and the dead bulk of the man shoved him groundward, knocking the SIG from his grasp. There was another, longer, burst of fire and a crazed yell from behind, then Strasser was screaming, *"Hold it!"*

Ryan heaved at Teague, rolled him off, as icy phantom fingers insinuated themselves into his stomach. What a jerk-off, he thought disgustedly. Then Strasser was above him, a handgun gripped in his gloved hand, its barrel inches from Ryan Cawdor's good eye.

"Don't twitch. *Shithead*!" The gaunt man's voice was a crow of delight and malevolent triumph. "Thought you had an ace, hmm? Tough titty. Now you're going to be telling me about all those ingenious boobies you have." He laughed softly. Chillingly. "Jordan was redundant, Ryan. So are you."

Chapter Nine

THEY HADN'T BOTHERED to take his watch, and the thought pounded his brain like hammer blows that time was running out . . . running out . . . *running out*.

But they'd take the SIG, the LAPA, his grenades, the contents of his belt pouches and the four sticks for the LAPA. All the obvious stuff. And although they'd left him his belt, they'd checked it thoroughly.

But they had not checked his boots, his thick-soled combat boots, and they had not checked his long fur-lined coat. Oh, sure, they'd gone through the pockets, all of them, the obvious places, but once they'd finished that task, under Cort Strasser's gimlet gaze, they had handed it back to him.

"Where you're going, Ryan, you might get cold. And we wouldn't want that."

Very funny.

And they had not checked his scarf, the white scarf of thick silk he'd found in a trunk in an attic in an old abandoned house on the borders of the Swamplands down south. It was a fine scarf, an elegant scarf, a scarf that had once surely belonged to a man of substance who had used it for those very special occasions in the old days. Those way back, pre-Nuke days. The silk was so smooth and so thick and so heavy. Especially so heavy. Especially now.

But they had left him that, probably because it had no meaning to his searchers, since the concept of "dressing up" for those very special occasions was utterly alien to them, something that had no meaning whatsoever. The way they stank, it was clear these guys hadn't washed in years, let alone dressed up.

They had not taken J.B.'s hat, either, an error they might come to regret. While they were being searched—upstairs, here in what once had been the Mocsin City Bank and Loan Facility Corporation building—J.B. had obligingly taken off his old, wide-brimmed fedora, held it upside down, the crown gripped in his left hand, and inserted the fingers of his right hand to flick up the sweatband, just to show there was nothing concealed behind it. The guy pulling weaponry off and out of him, denuding his pouches, groping at the lining of his brown leather jacket, now ran a finger around the inside of the hat suspiciously, peering intently at it, staring up at J.B.'s impassive, bespectacled face, a face made all the more funny looking because the specs had been salvaged from some surviving product dump years ago and distorted J.B.'s features. And shrugged. And watched J.B. press down the sweatband again and plop the hat back on his head. And returned to the far more important business of searching him for concealed cannon, bazookas, a howitzer stuffed down his pants. Shit like that.

Foolish man.

Strictly an amateur.

Even so, even allowing for the stupidity of Strasser's goons, the blinkered comprehension of Strasser himself, Ryan had to admit that this spot was a tight one, and it would need more than merely a modicum of luck and a good stiff breeze to get them out of it.

His ranks now were drastically depleted. That treacherous burst of fire from the concealed marksman in the buggy had left him J.B., Hunaker, Koll and Sam. And as a wild card, Hovac, waiting at Charlie's—though a pretty damned useless one, all things considered, as Hovac had no means of knowing where they were, what had occurred, and in any case was hardly in a position, even if he did discover their whereabouts, to rescue them. All he would know was that they were late for the rendezvous and time was ticking away.

Time.

Ryan had no intention of checking his watch because that would give Strasser the idea that there was some kind of time factor here, some kind of cutoff Ryan knew about that he didn't. But at a rough calculation Ryan figured that maybe two hours had passed since Hunaker had entered Charlie's with the grim news.

And that in turn meant they had roughly two hours to get their shit together and out. Say one and a half, in case of accidents. Not a lot. Not one hell of a lot.

Easing away from the wall he was lounging against, Ryan said, "You know, we can still come to some kind of deal on all this."

Cort Strasser laughed.

"You're in no position to bargain, Ryan. You're mine. So is your train. All mine."

"You got us, but you don't have the train. Touch the train and you lose it. You lose the lot, Strasser. You think we wire up the odd booby here and there to keep off predators? The old spark bomb to give a guy a shock? If you want the truth, every damned vehicle in that train is set to blow if you so much as breathe on it. I tell you, it's like a house of cards. Tamper with one vehicle and the whole lot goes. It'll be the biggest blowout since the Nuke."

Strasser laughed again, but the laugh was far too loud, far too bouncy.

"What a talent for exaggeration you have, Ryan."

"Try it."

"But you are going to tell me how to render your clever traps useless, Ryan."

"Not me, pal."

Strasser said, "Pain can make a man change his mind."

"Some men. But with me you're gonna have to work at it. And there comes a point with some guys where pain suddenly doesn't matter."

Strasser's skull-like face twisted up into a rictus of anger so swiftly and so suddenly that it almost seemed his dry, parchmentlike skin might tear. He thrust his head toward Ryan.

"Bravado, Ryan! Sheer fucking bravado! You're no different from anyone else."

Ryan said, "Suck it and see."

Strasser was probably correct. Maybe he was no different from anyone else. But in his past, the memory of it always kept deep in the lower layers of his consciousness, only surfacing rarely these days—always at night's end, when he would sometimes erupt out of his bunk yelling at the black horror of it—was an experience of pain and betrayal so terrible, so soaked in blood and despair that it had seared both his body and his soul. And in the searing—like red-hot steel thrust into the ironsmith's waterbarrel—it had tempered him, hardened him maybe beyond the normal human limit.

"Perhaps," said Strasser silkily, "we ought to take your other eye out."

For a second, skeletal fingers of fear enclosed Ryan's heart in a steel-strong grip, clutching, squeezing tight, sending ice through his veins. It was the ultimate terror, maybe his one single most vulnerable spot, the one threat that mocked all his courage and turned cool objectivity into gut-churning panic.

Fighting to keep his face swept of all but the most neutral of expressions, he thought, can he patch into my psyche? Is he some kind of weirdo mutie precog, a mind reader?

He rejected the thought almost at the same instant as it flared up in his mind. Strasser was as superficial in his thought processes as his men were in their search for concealed weaponry. Inside that skull was a warped and twisted brain that simply homed in on and struck at the most obvious chink in a man's or woman's armor.

A guy had one eye? Threaten to rip out the other.

It was as simple as that.

Ryan said in a voice stripped of emotion, "That won't do you a hell of a lot of good, Strasser. Frankly, once you'd achieved that you've achieved all."

"Give the sucker to me. Let me work on him. He'll squeal."

Ryan's glance flicked to his right. The room they were in was, he guessed, the lower-level annex, a part of the old bank vault system, although little remained to show it. The concrete walls had been stripped and were untidily whitewashed. In the center of the room was a block of wood, coffin-sized. Straps attached to rings set into it hung down almost to the concrete floor. Ryan could not tell what kind of wood the block was made of because of the discoloration, the reddish brown staining that was a crusted veneer on the flat surface, a rusty seepage down the sides. So much blood had drenched that block over the years that it had soaked deep into the wood's heart.

On metal hooks around the walls hung an assortment of implements: knives, saws, meat spikes, a number of what looked like old cattle prods. In one corner, near where stairs disappeared down to what was almost certainly the main vault itself, stood a small generator, a jumble of wires piled near it. Ryan saw there were electric wall sockets at intervals around the lower part of the walls; hence the hand-cranked generator, he supposed: if the mains were acting up, they could always switch to that.

More stairs were beyond the wood block, linking the room to the street-level floor above. There were five sec men by the stairs. The man who had spoken was one of these: a squat, barrel-chested guy with fingers like sausages, a bulbous nose that contained more than its fair share of destroyed blood vessels and heavy-lidded eyes. He was licking his lips, looking at the two girls. That one gets off on agony, Ryan thought bleakly.

But Strasser flicked a hand at him, an irritable motion. He turned to Ryan.

"So what is this deal? It seems to me, Ryan, you've lost your bargaining position."

"You don't have the train," Ryan repeated calmly. "I have the train. Sure it won't nuke up, but she'll blow. Nice firework display and you're gonna have your work cut out sifting through the wreckage for anything worthwhile."

"But you I have, and the Trader I have." Strasser showed his teeth in a wolfish grin.

"No," said Ryan. "You don't have the Trader, either. You put 'em all to sleep, right? When are they gonna wake up?"

Strasser opened his mouth, shut it again. He rubbed his nose gently with a bony finger.

Ryan said, "What are you gonna do when they *do* wake up? Keep putting 'em back to sleep again? How are you gonna know when they wake up, anyway? You got guys peering through the windows at them, waiting for the first twitch? Listen, when those guys wake up they're gonna be mad, they're gonna start doing bad things. How many men do you have out there, Strasser? Not a regiment, I'd guess." He added, "Maybe you have too many guys out at the mines."

"You've been busy," said Strasser softly.

"Shit, you can't keep something like that under wraps," scoffed Ryan.

"It's nothing that can't be coped with. A minor disturbance."

"Crap! This place is falling apart, Strasser. Too many years under one owner. The longer I'm here, the more the smell of rot and decay is stinking up my nostrils. Teague's been pushing stuff out east, hasn't he?"

It was not in fact a question. Strasser knew exactly what Ryan was saying, and his eyes darted nervously to his men at the bottom of the stairs.

He muttered through his teeth, "You're digging yourself deep, Ryan. Way deep. Deeper by the second."

To Ryan everything had become crystal clear. Strasser was getting out. The revolt at the mines had been the final straw. He'd probably been waiting to get rid of Jordan Teague for months, maybe years.

Strasser was standing beside the blood-soaked block. He was running a hand thoughtfully across its surface, backward and forward, staring down at the motion of his hand, his thin lips pursed. An altar, thought Ryan suddenly. An altar devoted to Strasser's own particular god of pain and torment.

He doubted that many of Strasser's sec men knew their leader's plans. An inner circle, perhaps, but not these suckers here. Maybe the guy with the red nose and the sausage fingers. He looked to be a kindred spirit.

Ryan said, "No deeper than I have to. I told you, we can still deal."

The squat guy said, "Lemme have him. I tell ya—"

Strasser swung around on him, face contorted.

"Silence!"

Ryan leaned back against the whitewashed wall, folding his arms.

Suddenly Strasser pointed at two of the guards. "Downstairs. Go fetch..." He didn't finish the sentence but just jabbed a finger at the steps that led downward. The two guards grinned at each other as they clumped across the room and disappeared, their boots echoing off bare concrete.

J.B. glanced at Ryan, raising an eyebrow. Ryan shrugged. He looked at the two girls and Koll. All three expressionless, waiting, biding their time. He was glad that these three were left. He knew their worth.

He said, more to keep the pot boiling than for any other reason, "How long you been waiting to give Teague the heave-off?"

Strasser chuckled.

"Ever since he did the same to Dolfo Kaler. Did you ever hear of Dolfo Kaler?"

"Doesn't ring a bell."

"Before your time, Ryan." Suddenly Strasser was almost chatty. He had the air of one who was prepared to chew the fat for a while. Ryan wasn't sure he liked that. The guy was pleased about something. "Kaler had a stake in Mocsin. He wasn't as big as Jordan, but he had power, contacts with the East. In the early days. But he had this thing about the Darks. He thought there was something up there." Strasser lifted his arms in a shrug. "Maybe there is. A lot of people seem to believe so. Maybe one of these fine days I should take a look around. Kaler didn't find it, whatever it was. Crawled back with nothing and got his head blown off for his pains. Jordan Teague made out that Kaler had the Plague and just blew him out. That's when Jordan took over completely. It's long been in my mind to..."

But what was in Cort Strasser's mind was lost as the sound of booted feet once more rang out, metal studs thudding on concrete out of view below. Strasser had half turned as the noise started up. Now he swung around again on Ryan, fingering the black silk stock at his scrawny throat.

He said, "It has already occurred to me, Ryan, that it will take time to squeeze you dry, and I'm aware that your close colleague Dix doesn't gab much. Therefore I thought of turning my attention to your three companions, the ladies especially." His voice had become syrupy. "And then I thought, no, you're all the same. Closemouthed. Stupidly loyal. Stupidly stubborn. The women might well take less time to crack, but even so I'm not in the mood to linger. And then I set to wondering how, uh..." He frowned slightly, tapping the tabletop with his fingers. "Well, let me see—how detached you were, Ryan, how, uh...indifferent you could be to the sufferings of an entirely neutral party. The thought fascinated me, Ryan. After all—" his tone was now pensive, even mildly quizzical, as though he were pondering some minor domestic problem that still needed handling with a certain amount of care "—we live in violent and selfish times. Every man for himself and the hell with the rest. That surely is the philosophy of anyone faced with an unpleasant and painful situation. Even so, it did occur to me to wonder if the age of, uh...of—what's the word I'm seeking?" He snapped his fingers a couple of times, frowning down at the tabletop, then glanced up at Ryan, his eyebrows raised. "Gallantry? Yeah, that'll do.

Gallantry. Excellent word. Nicely old-fashioned. Yes, I did wonder if the age of gallantry was not entirely buried beneath the ashes of the Nuke. It seemed a good opportunity to try a small experiment.''

He glanced to his right, toward the doorway that led to the vaults. When he looked back at Ryan, his expression and tone of voice were almost apologetic. ''It won't take long. Ten minutes at the most, I should imagine, once we're under way. And of course I may be making a stupid mistake, a wild error of judgment. I may well be wasting your time and mine. We shall see.''

The two guards appeared, hustling a third person up to the top of the stairs and out into the room, each holding an arm.

The shock of recognition was for Ryan far greater than the panic burn that had flared through him when Strasser had glibly talked of taking his good eye out. But the jolt he felt inside him only made itself manifest by a slight quiver of his eyes, plus the freezing into stunned immobility of his features for maybe a half-second.

But it was enough for Strasser. Unholy delight glowed in his eyes. His thin lips split into a reptilian grin.

''You know her, Ryan! A friend of yours!'' His voice was thick with gleeful malevolence. ''Well, that does make it easier.''

It was the flame-haired girl, Krysty Wroth.

RYAN THOUGHT, How did he know? How did the bastard *know*? And then he thought, know what, for Christ's sake? Looked at objectively, she's nothing to me. Less than nothing. I don't even know her. Up until this morning I wasn't even aware she existed. So okay, he's all set to torture and humiliate her, probably—knowing Strasser—in the most gross and obscene and bloody way, but so what? So fucking what?

Angry, his face set, feeling strangely betrayed, he stared at the scene in front of him. Strasser grinned like a malignant ape, the guards gazed lustfully at the girl, and the girl herself, a gag in her mouth, her rich red hair scraped back into a tightly knotted pony-tail, tensed her body against the two-handed grip of her captors. Her face, Ryan noted automatically, was expressionless. There was no way of telling what she was thinking either from her features or from her eyes. It looked as if she had somehow blanked herself out, consciously wiped herself clean of all emotion. If this was so, he wondered how long it would last.

He was attracted to her, deeply attracted. There were depths to her he had rarely seen in other women, a fact that had been clear to him in the few hours they'd been together and had talked. There'd been a possibility that she was worth pursuing. That had ended when he'd learned the shattering news that most of the Trader's people on this trip were dead, nerved out, her among them. And that had been that. What did they used to say? "Ships that pass in the night"—yeah. No big deal. No heavy stuff. Nothing. Forget it. It had not only never gotten anywhere, it had never even started.

The momentary ache had been for something that might have been, and that was only maybe, anyway. So forget it.

And now here she was, alive.

He was aware that the squat man with the red nose had been saying something to Strasser, something about him, his face alive with ghoulish glee.

Strasser chuckled. "Never mind Ryan. He's in a dream. This one'll soon wake him up. The way she'll be screaming will be enough to waken a dead man. Strip her."

Ryan watched, blank faced, as the squat man said, "With pleasure!" and walked toward the girl. He placed both hands on her breasts and began clutching at them, squeezing them roughly. Anger and loathing flared in Krysty's eyes.

Strasser said severely, "No time for that, Kelber. I promised Ryan this would not take long."

Kelber said, "Shit, sir. Won't be nothin' left to have fun with once we're finished with the bitch, reamed her out."

"Alas, no," said Strasser. "It does seem a shame, all things considered. She's certainly a delightful creature. But you are so right, Kelber, there will not be much left in the, ah . . . organic sense once we're done. But what must be must be."

"Couldn't we just use the prod?" said Kelber. "You know I'm good with the prod, sir. Got it down to a real fine art. You know I can make her jump, and it won't damage the merchandise." As an afterthought he said, "Well, not too much, anyway."

"No prod, Kelber," said Strasser, wagging a bony finger at him as though at a naughty child who must be indulged only up to a certain point. "I know you're a devil with the prod, Kelber. But no prod."

Ryan discovered his mouth was dry and he swallowed, tried to bring spit up into his throat. All this was solely for his benefit, he knew; a cruel and ghastly jest. A sickening parody of polite and civilized behavior that only someone like Strasser would get off on.

Kelber went quickly to work, himself clearly bored with all this funning around that his master enjoyed. He pulled off her boots, unzipped the green jump, and, while the two guards held her, stripped it off. By this time Krysty was kicking, struggling. But the two guards were beefy. They merely held her all the tighter, laughing at her struggles.

Kelber unzipped the one-piece body sheath underneath and peeled it slowly downward, first revealing her breasts, full yet firm, hanging free, then her taut stomach and the softly swelling roundness of her lower belly, the titian triangle of hair at her thighs sharply etched against the whiteness of her skin. He dragged the body sheath off finally and tossed it aside.

"Such a pity," murmured Strasser. "All things considered. Tie her down."

The sec man turned her and shoved her facedown toward the block, then pulled her forward along it so that her breasts were squashed under her weight against the rusty wood, her wrists thrust forward and shackled by the straps, her pelvis jammed down just above the end of the table, on the lip, so that her legs dangled over the side. Or at least would have dangled if she had only been quiet. But she was kicking wildly, violently, the heel of one foot clubbing up into the jaw of the guard who was trying to grab it. He yelled, clutched at his mouth, tears of pain suddenly running down his face, blood spraying out from between his lips. It looked as if he'd sunk his teeth into his tongue. Strasser angrily gestured at the rear straps and the two guards sprang forward from the front and controlled her, yanking her legs apart so that her buttocks involuntarily arched, rising into the air, exposing the cleft between the legs. The guards finished strapping her into position, and the guy who had been kicked breathed hard, sniffing explosively, glaring at the twitching figure of the young woman.

Okay, Ryan thought, whatever is going to happen I can't let happen. Who she is, what she is, none of this matters, none of it applies. It's no good saying so fucking what if she gets it, because I don't mean it, and I wouldn't mean it even if it was someone else strapped to that bloody altar.

He took a step forward and instantly the guard beside the doorway swung his M-16 up, his finger tight on the trigger.

Strasser said, "Ah, Ryan," as though meeting him casually on the street. "Yes?"

"Look, I dunno what all the fuss is about, Strasser. Sure I know her. She was on the train. We picked her up: she was having trouble with some muties. Other than that..." He shrugged.

Strasser said, "How interesting," and turned away.

Ryan turned to glance at J.B. It seemed to him that J.B.'s face was blanker than he'd ever seen it. He turned back. Only Strasser and Kelber were near the block now. The guards, including the one with the blood-smeared mouth, were fanned out around the room, rifle-ready. He could not have reached any of them before; now it was the same situation in spades.

Pay your debts, said the Trader. Always pay your debts.

To repay the vast, the immense, debt he owed the Trader, Ryan often thought that he would have to be in a position to give the Trader his life back, would have needed to say to him, "You're dying, for God's sake. Probably some kind of rad cancer that's eating away your gut, your bones, everything. But something can be done, and something's gotta be done." The Trader would have said, "Fuck it, I ain't going to no quack, Ryan," and that would have been that. And now he was spark-out in War Wag One, maybe slumped in a chair, maybe sprawled out on the metal floor, and wholly at the mercy, whichever way you cut it, of Cort Strasser.

And what did Ryan owe Krysty? He owed her his life. Simple as that. He could suddenly feel the sticky's slimy pads on his face, the immense sucking power causing his cheeks to expand away from his own bones. Could actually feel it, a tactile rerun, as though hundreds of tiny needles were stabbing and slashing around inside his cheeks, his mouth, his jaw, a fierce agony that would not cease until the flesh was ripped off of his skull leaving a scarlet ruin of dripping bloody pulp.

He felt himself trembling. He leaned back against the wall. Sweat was oozing out of his pores.

Strasser snapped his fingers. Kelber patted a breast pocket of his black jacket, inserted a hand, fished out a small box. At the same time the guard by the upper doorway turned and disappeared the steps to the floor above.

"Now pay attention, Ryan."

Strasser took the box from Kelber and held it to his ear, shook it gently. What he heard seemed to please him. He looked around as the sec men's boots hammered on the steps above and the guy reentered the room. He was holding a tall drinking glass. Strasser nodded to Kelber, who took the glass, then carefully opened the box. He tipped the contents into the glass. From where he stood Ryan saw a flutter of something small and dark, heard a faint clatter as whatever it was hit the bottom of the glass. Strasser took the glass and gazed at it critically, holding it up to the naked light set into the ceiling above him. A satisfied smile slithered across his face. He turned to Ryan and stepped toward him, still holding the glass up. Ryan caught a flicker of frenzied movement at the bottom.

"Fascinating insect mutie," he said. "Some kind of cross between a borer beetle and a termite. Much the same, I suppose, but this little beauty has certain characteristics you don't find in either."

Ryan stared at the glass. The thing was bigger than he'd thought, maybe as big as a human thumb, streamlined. He saw a black and shiny carapaced back, and four horned antennae quivering at the front. The insect scrabbled around in the glass, its six legs slipping on the smooth surface. It stopped suddenly, facing him. He peered closer, aware that the nearest guard had thrust the barrel of his M-16 almost to his left temple. He saw that the labrum flap over the insect's mouth hardly concealed mandibles that seemed grotesquely out of proportion to its size: huge sickle-shaped tusks, almost like horns. The compound eyes, small though they were, seemed to glitter in the light, their honeycomb of lenses directed at him.

The insect was quivering gently. Ryan couldn't get it out of his mind that he was being studied, noted, categorized. It turned suddenly, rushed at the opposite side of the glass, launched itself at the transparent walls of its prison. And fell back, its legs waving wildly. It landed on its shiny back, rolled on the instant, and became mobile once more.

"Ugly little brute," murmured Strasser, taking the glass away and staring at it affectionately. "But . . . fascinating. Doesn't like wood at all. Meat eater. But it doesn't like dead meat, Ryan. Fastidious. Likes its food in the hoof, you might say. But the really curious thing is it seems to have a positive yen for human flesh. We discovered this quite by chance when we popped one into the mouth of someone who had . . . displeased me. The insect ate its way out of the stomach. Right through the entrails. You probably noted its somewhat overlarge mandibles. Remarkable, don't you think?"

With a yell Ryan flung himself at the gaunt man, his hands outstretched to claw and tear and rend at whatever he could grasp.

And the world blazed up in a brilliant flash of light that seared his eye, exploded through his head, fierce agony lancing through his brain. He reeled, smashed to the concrete floor by the M-16 barrel rammed into the side of his head.

Something heavy landed on him. He sought to fling it off but a booted foot slammed into his head and more pain flooded through him, slashing at his nerve ends. He found that his arms were suddenly twisted behind him, his legs held to the floor under some heavy weight. Through a haze of pain and fury and disgust he heard Strasser's voice.

"Take the gag out of her mouth and stuff it into Ryan's."

His head was wrenched back by the hair and he tried to grit his teeth together but someone pinched his nostrils tight and involuntarily he gasped open his mouth. The gag filled it and he dry-heaved, his senses screaming that he had to have air. He could hear snorted squealing sounds and could only suppose they emanated from him. The fingers unclasped.

His head throbbed agonizingly. It was as if someone plunged a knife rhythmically and repeatedly into the soft core of his brain. Suddenly he was lurching forward, being shoved and dragged toward the wooden block until he was staring wildly, frantically, up into the rear of the girl.

Strasser was standing near him, beside the girl, one hand holding the glass, the other pushing one of the smooth white globes of her buttocks.

He said thoughtfully, "Now which shall it be, anal or vaginal passage? Difficult to choose. If the former it will at least mean that Kelber's animal lusts will not remain entirely unsatisfied, if for only a short time. Kelber has often been known to make the best of a bad job, Ryan. He is, I fear, not very discriminating in his tastes. If the latter, of course, I doubt that even Kelber would care to try his luck where something as voracious as this little brute has already been." He inclined his head, looked down at Ryan. "What d'you say, Ryan? Back or front, hmm? No answer? How very churlish.'' He licked his lips. ''Front, I think.''

He placed the lip of the glass against the broad full cheeks, and began to push it under the girl toward the dark cleft, tipping it gently upward as he did so.

Ryan struggled like one possessed of many devils. His head jerked back, his chest bulged. He could feel the tendons and veins on his arms spring out like corded cables. He was screaming, shrieking, but no sound came out of his mouth.

Strasser glanced down at him, smiling with his mouth but not his eyes, and tipped the glass up some more. It was now almost horizontal. The beetle began to scurry along the smooth curved path until it had about reached its goal. It stopped, antennae quivering. Then it scurried on remorselessly, at last reaching flesh, a portion of buttock fringed by coarse red hair, short and curly, just glimpsed. The antennae extended toward the white skin as though testing the air. Presumably satisfied with the intelligence it had gathered, the insect began to move slowly, inexorably, out of Ryan's sight.

Squealing, frantically nodding his head, adrenaline flooding through him like liquid fire, Ryan managed to inch himself forward, heaving those guards atop along by the sheer strength of his frenzy.

Strasser looked down at him again, regarded him thoughtfully, coolly, gauging his surrender—then rammed the glass hard into the girl's rear, at the same time flipping its mouth slightly upward, the sudden movement catching the beetle, the lip of the glass tossing it into the air. It curved high, legs scrabbling at nothing, and for a split second seemed to hang, weightless, at the peak of its parabola. Then gravity took over and it dropped. Strasser neatly caught it in the glass and beamed in triumph, as though he had just performed a particularly knotty conjuring trick. He gave the glass and the box to Kelber.

He said, "Excellent. Take him out to one of the trucks. The girl, too. Dress her. These…" He waved an arm at J.B. and the others, then frowned in thought. "I was going to say, kill them. But no. Take them downstairs. One of the cells. I'll deal with them personally when we return."

Ryan felt himself gripped under the armpits and dragged to his feet. He needed that. Right now he felt incapable of supporting himself on his own. Strasser caught up with them. The gaunt man with the skull face reached out and grasped at the gag in his mouth and tore it out. Ryan gasped, swallowed, grunted, spat out bits of rag that still clung to his teeth and his tongue and his lips. He gazed up at Strasser, his chest heaving, his eyes blurred.

He cracked, "You're dead, Strasser…dead…"

"No, no, no," said Strasser, leaning forward and tapping him lightly on the chest with a bony finger, his tone mildly amused as though he were speaking to a fractious child, "*you're* dead."

THE HEAVY STEEL DOOR THUDDED into place. The face of the man Krysty Wroth had booted, still blood-smeared around the mouth, appeared in the barred opening, another of the guards behind him.

"Think I'll have me the slinky black bitch, Ferd," said the man with the bloody mouth. "Ain't had black meat in a while."

"Y'know," said Hunaker to Samantha, "I bet that dick's prick when it's hard is about as big as my pinkie. I betcha."

The gloating expression vanished from the sec man's face as though wiped off with a rag.

He screamed, "You'll find out how big it is, bitch! Get the fuckin' prod! Time I'm finished with ya, yer cunt'll be green as well as yer hair!"

"Cute," said Hunaker. She said to Sam, "Hey, you think he knows where a girl's whoopee actually is?"

J.B. muttered out of the corner of his mouth, "Shut it."

Hunaker shut it, and shrugged. She turned away from the door with an exaggerated yawn. The man, his face suffused with rage, disappeared from the opening, clattering off up the passageway with the other guard.

"Too mouthy," said J.B.

"Fuck it. The wimp got up my nose."

"You just pray he doesn't stick the prod up your nose," advised Koll.

Hunaker snorted with laughter. She was irrepressible. She started gurgling and shaking and had to lean up against Koll to keep her balance. J.B. shot her a stony look.

"Aw, come on, J.B. Ain't the end of the world. We'll get outta this one."

"If we're lucky. Doesn't help when you feel the spike of that guy. You're gonna have to make up to him, or one of them."

"Oh, crap," said Hunaker. "Does that mean I have to promise 'em all they can manage? Like that?"

"I want at least two in the corridor."

"Why does it have to be me?"

"Preferably both of you."

"Well, okay, but it's bad theater, J.B.," said Hunaker. "I mean, I like ol' Kollinsen here, but I don't *fancy* him. Something about that mustache of his. You won't get a performance from the heart, know what I mean?"

"Thanks for nothing," muttered Koll.

J.B. said, "I didn't mean Koll."

"Oh, yeah? Me and Sam?" She turned on the black girl, nudged her in the ribs. "Hey-y-y! How did you know, J.B.? Been trying for a date for a hog's age."

"Je-sus." Samantha the Panther's voice was a husky plaint. "Look, J.B., I got no intention of showing off my box to those bastards."

J.B. stared at her through his steel-rimmed spectacles, his face expressionless.

"Sure. Let's hope the situation doesn't arise."

His voice was as toneless as his face.

The room went quiet. Into both young women's an image of the bloodstained block slid like a poisonous snake.

J.B. sat down on the concrete floor and began to unlace his right combat boot.

"Just put on a show is all. Ain't worth shit. You know it, I know it."

"Fuck it," complained Hunaker. "Just 'cause we got tits and all. I mean, why don't you guys stand there, wave your dongs around?"

"Ain't gonna do much to these guys," J.B. pointed out.

Koll said, "You speak for yourself, buster," in hurt tones.

Hunaker said, her voice low-key, harsher in tone, "You really think . . . the train? Gone?"

J.B. tugged his boot, pulled it off.

"You were there. You heard what Cohn said, what the other guy said."

He put a hand inside his boot and began working at the inner sole with his fingers.

'You think we got a chance?"

J.B. stopped working at his boot, sat back and frowned slightly.

He said, "Maybe sixty-forty."

"Yeah?" Hunaker's eyes widened. The odds were better than she'd imagined.

"To them," J.B. said.

"Fireblasted nukeshit!"

A bleak smile flickered across J.B.'s sallow face.

"Just wave those tits around. I'll give you better odds."

"Yeah?"

"Yeah. Fifty-five-forty-five. Still to them."

"Thanks a bunch, big boy," said Hunaker. She suddenly spat out, her voice squeezed tight with fury, "Just as long as some of 'em die nasty."

Sam was now beside the door, peering out through the bars at the empty corridor. Koll had joined J.B. on the floor and was pulling his own boots off. Hunaker unfastened the belt she was wearing and began to rip out the false bottoms of all her empty ammo pouches. She unhooked her water bottle, uncapped it, wiped it with her sleeve and took a swig. Then she eased the webbing around it, slid the flask out, began peeling off wafer-thin strips of a grayish and doughy-looking substance wound around it.

Plastique. Some things just never change.

She said, "How we gonna do it?"

J.B. nodded at the door.

"Blow it. Door doesn't quite fit. Opens outward, too. Makes it easier."

"Old Eagle-eye," said Hunaker to Koll.

J.B. smiled faintly. He did not mind being teased by people he trusted, and he trusted these people and knew that they trusted him and relied on him. That was all that mattered.

He stopped what he was doing—which was peeling back the inner sole of her boot to reveal a hollow cavity, long and narrow, carved out of the specially built-up thick-soled footwear—and gazed around the room.

As he understood it, this lower level of the bank building had once contained the main vault and safe-deposit rooms. In their stead, thick-walled cells had been erected, all with steel doors containing glassless but steel-barred viewing windows. The doors were not as thick as the walls but were solid enough, although the whole construction had been done by builders who had clearly skimped and saved, probably in a hurry, probably with Jordan Teague's goons cracking the whip over them.

This cell was an end room, one of a number in a long corridor that led back to the stairway. That was useful, being at the end of the passage, the farthest from the stairs. Nevertheless, sound carried. J.B. was going to have to be careful, was going to have to judge this one to a nicety, as accurately as possible.

The room was bare walled and bare floored, an oblong roughly one and a half times square. There was no furniture of any kind, no bunks, tables, chairs, anything. It was a cold concrete box, lit by a low-watt bulb high out of reach in the ceiling. The door was at one end of a long wall. That, too, was useful. It meant that when J.B. blew the door, none of them need be directly opposite it. It was good that the door opened outward, though lousy planning for what was supposed to be a secure cell. With a door that opened outward there was always the chance, during that brief time when the door was being opened and the opener was not sighting the entire cell, that the occupant might be able to jump his warder. But then, J.B. suspected, most of the prisoners held down here by Strasser's sec men would probably be in no fit state to jump a mouse.

He began picking out from his boot equipment what looked like tools for a dollhouse: match-stick detonators, plastic wafers no bigger than a fingernail, miniscule screws, a tiny screwdriver. He sat cross-legged and began humming softly and tunelessly to himself as he opened his brown leather jacket and slid down the lining with his thumbnail beside the zipper tracks on the left. Sewn inside the lining was a long leather pouch, very slightly fatter than the average cheroot. J.B. extracted and emptied it. The contents were long rods of cobweb-thin wire. He selected more bits and pieces from his other boot and settled down to work.

Hunaker stepped over to the door and peered at it.

"Hmm. See what you mean. We can stuff a hell of a lot of explosive down along here. Shit, in some places the door doesn't even touch the frame. Great workmanship!"

"Not too much explosive," said J.B., not looking up, his lean fingers dexterously coiling wire, fitting the tiny screws to the power pack he was creating. "Too much plastique, we get too much noise. Could damage us, too."

"Yeah," said Koll dryly, "and too little and all we get's a big spark and a fart and the door stays put."

Hunaker began to roll the plastic explosive into stringy tails between her hands. She held one piece up.

"Too fat?"

J.B. stared at it critically, looked at the door, made some mental calculations.

"Roll it some more, then slap it in."

When Hunaker started to stuff the material down the right-hand side of the door, thumbing it down, then along the lintel at the top, J.B. got up and jabbed a finger at a spot about halfway down the door.

"More in there. Three times what you have already. That's where the locking device is."

He went back to the center of the room, sat down cross-legged again and continued his construction work. There was a long silence while Koll tossed plastique from his own boots to Hunaker and Hunaker molded the doughy substance around the match-stick detonators, squashing the strips into cracks and crevices, lacing it around the door-frame, all the time trying to avoid Sam's sight line to the corridor outside.

"What d'you reckon about Ryan?" she said suddenly.

J.B. bit a filament of wire in two. He didn't look up.

"What about him?"

"He blew out up there."

"It happens." The wiry little man's tone was unconcerned.

"You think he's got the hots for the Wroth woman?"

"Probably."

"You think we'll see him again?"

"Knowing Ryan, yeah."

"He's been in a few tight ones, hasn't he? I mean, with you and all."

"That he has."

"Y'know where he came from originally?"

"Out east, I think."

Hunaker said, "'I think'? How long have you known Ryan? Must be ten years at least. And you don't even know where his kin are? I bet you don't even know his other name."

"Is this some kind of precombat intelligence test?" Koll said with a frown. He was replacing strips of unwanted plastique in his boots.

"Well?" said Hunaker. "Do you?"

"No."

"Does anyone?"

"Trader, maybe."

"Rumor is, he was a Runner from somewhere."

"Only muties are Runners," said Koll knowledgeably. "Muties and blacks and yallers and a few other colors, depending on where they're running from. If Ryan's a mutie, he keeps it close to his chest.''

"I didn't say he was a mutie. I don't believe he is a mutie.''

"Can't tell these days," said Koll. "What's the big interest in Ryan all of a sudden, anyhow?''

"I felt sorry for him.''

"Feel sorry for Strasser," said J.B. "Otherwise, shut it.''

In front of him, as though magicked there, was a tiny sliver of plastique on which was a spiderweb crosshatching of fine wire connected to a couple of chip housings, plus a keying device about the size of a quarter thumbnail. J.B. stared at it, his thin lips very slightly curved.

"Christ, J.B.," said Koll, lacing up his boots, "you look almost cheerful.''

"The miracles of pre-Nuke science," said J.B.

"You sure it'll work?''

J.B. stared at him blankly, then wrinkled his brow.

"Is that a joke?" He sounded genuinely puzzled.

"Uh...no, J.B.'' Then Koll said hurriedly, "I mean, yeah.'' He tittered nervously.

"They were very sophisticated in the 1990s," said J.B. seriously. "This is a neat little number. The detonators are tuned to it. All I have to do is build it, key it, blow it.'' He coughed, said vaguely, "I did throw in a couple of extras...''

He began packing away his bits and pieces, pulled on and laced up his boots and got to his feet. He said, suddenly brisk, "Here it is. I want two guys down here, at least. That gives us two auto-rifles plus any handguns they have. Could make do with one, but pray for two. They gotta be looking through the window. Doesn't matter if they don't come in. Don't want 'em in. Just need 'em looking for a couple of sec men and we got 'em. After that we move fast. If we can reach street level we've got a chance." He pointed at Hunaker. "You and me first. Grab the pieces and go." He turned to the other two. "Pick over the bodies. Spare mags, grenades, knives—anything."

Hunaker sighed exaggeratedly, then zipped down her jump jacket to open it. Underneath she wore two sweat shirts, which she tugged up for a second, exposing her breasts. They were small but full and round. A fine sheen of sweat glistened on her skin. Koll stared at her and swallowed.

Hunaker snapped, "That's about all you'll ever get, a sighting." She pulled the two sweat shirts some more, loosening them, then covered herself again. "Okay, ready for the off."

J.B. said, "Don't forget your ears."

Hunaker said, "You're as bad as the Old Man."

She went to the door and began to bawl out the barred window. She knew she had to play this one carefully, not overdo it. It would be easy to throw out the come-hither in a cutesy-pie voice, but that, right now, was not going to work. Instead she yelled, "Hey! There's anyone up there, I wanna talk! Ryan's got a booby on him, ready to blow!"

Koll muttered, "It's original."

There was silence. Koll licked his lips, stared at the back of Hunaker's head, at the green hair cropped short and tight. He glanced at Samantha, locked eyes with the black girl for a couple of seconds, raised an eyebrow. Sam leaned back against the wall and clasped her hands together in front of her. Koll noticed that she began twining her fingers restlessly. J.B. stared at the opposite wall. As usual, it was impossible to tell what he was thinking.

"Hey!" yelled Hunaker. "This is for real!"

More silence, then Samantha nodded and said, "Yeah, they're coming."

To Koll and the others there was more silence, then at last they heard bootsteps ringing hollowly far off.

A voice shouted, "Shut the fuck up, bitch, or you get hurt bad!"

Shaking his head, Koll murmured, "Uninspired. We already know that."

Hunaker said loudly, "I got something on Ryan. Strasser don't know it."

They could hear voices raised in argument, but there was no definition to the sound. Then the ringing of boots came closer, two sets, clattering down the concrete steps. Hunaker moved away from the bars. The sec man came nearer. The man called Ferd was in front, and behind him the guy Krysty had kicked, who had not had a wash and brush-up in the interim.

He was saying, "If there's some kind of fuck-up and Strasser finds out we knew about it all along he'll have us eaten."

Ferd said coldly, "You just be ready ta shoot the shit outta these monkeys. I don't trust 'em."

The man with the red-smeared mouth cautiously peered into the cell from the side. He gulped, moved around so he could get a better view, his eyes flickering to the right and taking in the slumped figures on the floor. In the split second he took in this part of the scene, he noted that although he could see both the blond guy's hands, he couldn't see those of the man called Dix, who appeared to be lying on them in a hunched kind of way. But this didn't seem to be in any way significant, so his gaze whipped back to where the green-haired young woman was lounging against the wall, her head back, her eyes half closed, her lips parted. She was breathing heavily. One hand held her shirt up and the man with the bloody mouth could see her right breast. The other breast was half hidden beneath the busy lips of the black girl who was leaning across her from the side.

The sec man swallowed again. Ferd shoved him aside and snapped, "Lemme see." He, too, stared in, but his face was darkening as he watched. He was marginally less stupid than the man with the bloody mouth and tended not to take everything at face value.

He snarled, "It's crap. There's something up." He shouted, "Hey, you!"

Hunaker dropped her head, smiled sweetly and said, "I can't hear you very well. I'm wearing earplugs."

This was so bizarre that Ferd's mouth dropped open and he said, "I don't..."

But that was all he did say that was understandable because a vicious cracking blast drowned him out. For a microsecond the steel door was haloed in orange flash fire before it erupted outward, slamming the two men back as it bowled across the passageway, clanging against the opposite wall. The man with the red mouth was punched against the wall, the back of his head cracking open like an egg, his brains spilling out like yolk down the concrete. The man called Ferd was dead already, the steel door having pulverized his face into a scarlet pulp as it smashed into him, and such was the force of the blast that he sailed backward with the door as though he were glued to it. His skull, too, hammered against the wall and fractured at the top, so that blood and brain fluid geysered in a pinkish spout. Bones in both men's bodies split and shattered as they were hurled against the concrete. The door banged down onto the floor, half covering their remains.

Inside the cell, J.B. and Koll sprang to their feet. Hunaker and Sam were already tearing cotton wool out of their ears.

J.B. dived across the cell and out through the now empty door space. Smoke and concrete dust rose like a fog in the narrow area beyond, but his eyes took in an M-16 lying some distance away and he grabbed it and began automatically checking it as he galloped along the passage, closely pursued by Hunaker.

Hunaker, too, was now armed, with the other man's auto-rifle, another M-16. She, too, was galloping. She, too, was spidering her fingers along her piece, tugging out the mag, glancing at it, ramming it back up again.

As they neared the bottom of the steps, two men appeared at the top, in the room with the bloodstained block in it. J.B. mentally crossed his fingers, uttered a brief prayer to the only two gods he worshiped, the god of good fortune and the god of ingenuity, and squeezed off a controlled burst on the sprint.

The M-16 functioned. Devastatingly. Rounds pounded at the two sec men at the top of the stairs, punched them back out of sight, their limbs going into spasm.

"Behind me! Hit the upper steps!"

J.B. jumped ahead of the girl as he snapped out the command and sprang up the steps, keeping tight to the left-hand wall. He squeezed the trigger and used up his entire mag, firing up and over the top of the steps at the ceiling, then dropping his angle of fire as he reached the room. He sprayed death around it. He dived at the floor, and Hunaker, behind him, suddenly had three perfect targets on the top set of steps—three sec men, fleeing in panic, lunging for an escape route. Her fire line caught them as they bunched in the narrow stairway, scrambling to get out. Rounds zip-stitched three broad backs, erupting kidneys, shattering lumbar vertebrae, transforming them into bloody dolls.

Apart from the two guys that J.B. had shot from below, there were two more stiffs in the room who'd caught his bullets, one on the floor, the other sprawled drunkenly across the wood block, new blood from him sluggishly pooling out and soaking into the old.

J.B.'s eyes darted around the room. He swore as he spotted an auto-rifle lying inches from the outstretched fingers of the man lying on the floor. A stubby Steyr AUG with the long barrel.

He said, "The nukeshitter had my piece!" in horrified tones.

He swiped it up and began to check it out feverishly as Hunaker threw down the M-16 she'd been holding and picked up another. She ran to the bottom of the upper steps, squeezed off a 3-round burst around the wall angle and risked a look up. No one at the top, but she could hear a babble of voices from the huge upper room and then she had to duck back as rounds flayed the stairwell above, spraying brick and concrete shards on her.

"Hell, we could've worked ourselves into a corner here, J.B."

J.B. was too busy field-stripping the AUG and muttering blackly.

"Shit, fucker only had it an hour. See that dent?" He angrily jabbed a finger at the Steyr's stock. "See that? Fucker only had it an hour!"

"Uhh . . . J.B."

"Yeah!" the wiry little man snarled through his teeth.

"Could be we're stuck down here, J.B."

"Grenade the bastards out!" he snapped viciously. "Fucking vandals."

"J.B., it's only a dent . . ."

He glared at her murderously, his eyes simmering behind his adopted steel-rimmed glasses.

Hunaker turned away from him. Sam was stuffing herself with hardware while Koll collected spare mags for an M-16 he'd picked up. He tossed a couple of HEs in her direction and said, "Hey, J.B., let's get outta here, like Hun says. You can polish yer butt later, man."

J.B. shot him a dark look but nodded.

Suddenly Sam's head jerked up. She rose from where she'd been squatting beside one of the stiffs on the floor. Her eyes widened, the whites contrasting starkly with her velvety black skin.

She said huskily, "I heard a bang."

No one made a joke, even under the present circumstances. Even when, a second later, another burst of firing clattered out from above and they had to duck to one side as lead ricocheted around the room. When Samantha the Panther said she'd heard something no one else had, it was advisable not to laugh it off.

J.B. slid a 30-round mag up into the Steyr and said, "What kind of bang?"

"Big one, and a rumble. You didn't feel it?"

Hunaker shook her head. She said uneasily, "C'mon, J.B. I don't wanna hang around down here if they got something nasty waiting up there."

There was silence. The sub gunner had ceased firing. Not even the sec men themselves could be heard. Nothing could be heard. Nothing at all.

Sam said, "And another."

"Okay, let's beat it," said J.B.

He took a grenade from Hunaker, saying, "Cover us."

Koll slid to the corner angle of the steps, poked his M-16 around and fired a long burst, and as he did so, Sam sprang to the other side of the stairway and fired, too, straight up, her body hunched, the rifle spitting lead, the sound racketing shockingly around the echo chamber of the stairwell.

J.B. and Hunaker unpinned the eggs, counted, darted forward and, almost as one, hurled the grenades upward. The two eggs sailed high and disappeared from view beyond the top step. There was a frenzied yell, a howl of terror, then light blazed down the stairwell and there was a fierce cracking double blast, followed by the sound of glass shattering, metal clanging against metal, a rumbling roar.

J.B. hurled himself up the steps as dust and smoke billowed at him, roiling around the stairwell. He hit the top and sprayed lead into the fog with the Steyr, Hunaker behind him, her own auto-rifle chattering in a wide sweep.

The room was long and wide, formerly the high-ceilinged entrance lobby to the bank. At the far end were two massive doors, each one a wood sandwich enclosed by pierced steel planking, triple thickness. The counter of the bank remained, but nothing else. Strasser's sec men had turned the place into a recreation room, with chairs, tables, closets stuffed with weapons. Now the furniture was blasted apart by the HEs. Bodies lay around, either slumped like piles of old clothes, or in contorted heaps. Long windows to the left had all blown out, the glass and the steel shuttering together.

"Holy shit!" muttered Hunaker.

She pointed at the windows. Instead of darkness, a lurid and vibrant light throbbed redly. But this was no Deathlands sky effect caused by the rich chemical mix in the atmosphere, which often transformed night into bizarre day with a glow that made the northern aurora look off color.

"That's a fire."

Then she cried out, her yell lost in a thunder of earsplitting sound. She felt herself lifted from the floor by a shock wave that slammed into her sickeningly. For a second she felt almost weightless as she flew backward through the air and then she saw, as though in a dream, the two vast doors splitting apart and bowling toward her across the room in an orange eruption. She thought they looked like cardboard doors. Then she thudded back against something hard and blacked out.

Chapter Ten

THERE WAS SOME IDIOT using a mallet inside his skull, and it was as if he was fixing fence posts. Every few seconds, *whomp!* There were also various sets of crazed characters having a tug-of-war with the muscles of his arms and legs, and there was a cretin who seemed to be marching around his body, or maybe swimming along his arteries, jabbing a knife into various key places, though mainly his ribs, as and when it suited him. Not to mention that some clown seemed to be eating into the small of his back.

"Apart from that," muttered Ryan, his voice like the sound of a rusty rasp, "I'm fine."

"Check," came Krysty's reply in the darkness of the speeding truck.

Ryan froze—physically not a difficult operation because he was hog-tied anyhow, lying on his left side like a strained bow, his wrist and ankles tightly laced together behind him. But it was more a mental shock, a freezing of the mind. What he'd just croaked out had been involuntary. He hadn't realized he was speaking aloud. He hadn't even realized the girl was awake.

He said tentatively, "I, uh . . . thought they cracked you over the skull when we got outside."

That had been when she'd suddenly, outside the bank building and in the harsh glare of the floods, managed to back-heel the groin of one of the sec men holding her. She was pretty good with her heels, he thought wryly. The guy had yowled, let her go and she'd twisted away from the second man and started sprinting across the open space toward the three black vans parked near the barbed wire. Strasser had yelled a warning, and three guys had emerged from behind the trucks and clobbered her. Ryan and Krysty had been left on the ground for maybe a half hour, Ryan getting more and more chilled by the minute, not to mention more and more panicky about the time factor that only he knew about. Then they'd been flung into the rear of one of the trucks and the doors had banged. No need for guards, Strasser had said. Waste of manpower. They weren't going to be able to free themselves to go anywhere.

"They did hit me over the head," Krysty Wroth said. "But I have great powers of recuperation."

Though it hurt him, Ryan laughed. It was kind of a choked grunt, sounding to his ears like the noise a guy made when someone poked him in the ribs. It felt like it, too.

She said, "Anyhow, thanks."

"Thanks?"

"For getting my..." She paused. "I was going to say, for getting my head off the block, but maybe for getting my ass off the block is more to the point."

Her tone was dry and sardonic. Ryan knew it was the humor of gritted teeth. You made a joke of the intolerable or else you went under.

He didn't know what to say. "Look, I should have stopped those bastards before things got too rough," he tried. "I *could* have. There were...other considerations... I'm sorry."

She said, "I know. It doesn't matter. Forget it. Life's too short."

He thought back to when she had actually been tied down to that foul block. She had not struggled, had not screamed or even whimpered. He was surprised, contemplating this, to realize that there had been a degree of serenity about her at that terrible time, as now. It was a strange yet oddly comforting aura of calm that seemed to surround her like a cloak. He hadn't analyzed it then—too many other things to worry about!—but he recognized it now as he reran the scene in his mind.

Such serenity at such a time seemed to him almost supernatural.

"You, uh . . . didn't seem too worried back there."

She said simply, "I knew Earth Mother was watching over me."

"I guess you realize your Earth Mother isn't going to save you every time."

"No, you don't understand. It's not a question of 'saving.' Earth Mother is not a physical presence. She doesn't appear in a flash of light—" she chuckled, and there was irony in her voice "—brandishing an M-16. She just *is*. At times that's comforting. There had been occasions when I've been stark crazy with fear and panic. Other times when it feels okay, feels right, feels like it's not going to work out too bad. That's how I felt then."

"How's it feel now?" said Ryan dryly. "I could do with some reassurance."

"Oh, I'd think we'll make out, don't you?"

He had to laugh again, and the minor convulsions trembled across his rib cage where Strasser's goons had put more than one boot in.

"Don't make me laugh. Please."

The truck lurched over something in the road—a rock or a pothole or maybe a small animal—and Ryan cursed vitriolically as he went up in the air and down again, landing on his wrists. Shafts of agony lanced up his arms. His shoulder blade felt seriously out of kilter for a second.

He muttered through clenched teeth, "Maybe it wouldn't be a bad idea if your Earth Mother did appear waving a piece, because unless they untie me I think we're in deep shit. I hadn't counted on the bastards lacing us up. Didn't seem necessary. Thought they were just gonna shove us in with a bunch of armed goons."

He didn't tell her that, hog-tied as they were, he thought their chances of surviving were precisely nil. Untied he had options. Like this he might as well be a fish in a barrel.

She said calmly, "I think I can get my wrists free." Her voice was oddly neutral. She said, "Where are they taking us exactly?"

"To the Trader first. I guess Strasser wants to get him out of the way before moving onto the train. Always a chance our guys may wake up, and if he gets inside the war wag and trucks before that happens, he's laughing. But no way is that talking skull gonna hijack all that matériel. Right about now, J.B. should be blasting his way out of the bank, unless the goons tied him and Hun and the others up, which I doubt."

"Blasting?" she said incredulously.

"Yeah. Strict policy. All of us, since way back, are stuffed to the gills with explosives, or at least the means of creating explosives. An idea I had years ago, worked it out with J.B. Just in case we get caught by bad guys, we have all kinds of shit concealed in our clothes, our boots, our webbing. The bad guys take our pieces off us, grenades, knives, all that. The obvious. They don't bother to look at our boots for false inner soles, or check every stitch, every button. Some of us have big plastique-cored buttons on our long coats, others have wiring sewn into special pouches. You can't even feel it. Don't worry about J.B. He'll make out."

"Now I know why your bunch is talked about like it is," she said. "As special people. Sure is forward planning!"

"It's no big deal. It's called survival. These days you need all the help you can think up."

"Right. In this wonderful country where you could probably live your entire life without getting raped, abducted, murdered, eaten...without seeing a—what did you call it? Plague pit?"

His mind flew back to the scene in War Wag One, her angry face as she argued with him. It all seemed centuries ago.

"Great memory you've got," he growled. "In any case, it's still true. But when you're in our kind of business, even when you have a fierce rep, doesn't do any harm to take precautions." He muttered, "And all this crap just proves my point." His mind shot back again to the war wag, which triggered off another thought. "How the hell did Strasser manage to get his hands on you, anyway?"

"I didn't keep taking the tablets. Your medic kept giving me tabs, said they'd calm me. I didn't want to be calmed, so I didn't take them. She kept saying it was crazy to think of heading on for the Darks. How was I going to do it, how was I going to travel? All that. So when she breezed off I snuck out and hitched a lift."

"You *what*?"

"You had two container rigs, arctic. I climbed aboard of one of them. It was getting dark, so no one spotted me. When the convoy parked I slipped off into some bushes. I watched you drive out in the buggy, thought of hitching onto that but there aren't too many hand holds. So I walked to Mocsin. Had to keep in cover because a lot of buggies started passing me, heading out of town, back the way I'd come..."

Ryan thought, his stomach suddenly souring, Yeah, backup for the guys Strasser already had watching the train, the guys watching us. Probably what she saw was the bunch that actually tranked the Trader.

"Then I bumped into some kind of patrol on the outskirts. They were all right at first. Oafish, but all right. I could handle them. What they couldn't figure out was where I'd sprung from, so I told them I was with the Trader, with you. I mean, I figured that was okay. But then they started getting heavy, pushing me around. I told 'em that if they didn't quit pissing me off they were going to be in deep with the Trader."

Ryan heard her voice change, heard a slight catch in it.

"And that was when it hit me," she said, "that maybe I hadn't been so smart. They started laughing, told me to forget about the Trader. He was finished. Everyone with him was kaput. No more Trader. I got a touch of the horrors then because they seemed so sure of themselves...."

"They took you to Strasser?"

"Yeah. He's..." There was a definite change in her voice. Now it was almost a whisper. He had to strain to catch what she said over the truck's engine rumble. "Ryan, he gives me a chill. Maybe I was stupid. I didn't really take in what you said about him, all that shit about getting off on pain, humiliation, perversion. But it's in his eyes. At times they're like, I dunno... No feeling, no emotion. Like pebbles on a beach. He said—well, among a lot of other things he said I'd be a fine taster before the main course." She laughed suddenly. It sounded like a nervous hiccup. "I guess I must've panicked because I didn't feel the presence of Earth Mother right then and there. Not at all. Not for one damned second. He had a bag with him, with...shit, really weird gear in it. Nozzles, rubber tubes, plastic spatulas, shit like that. But before he could really get busy, some guy rushed in and gave him a message. Then he said maybe I'd be more useful for the moment...unblemished.''

"Must've been when they told him I was on the loose somewhere,'' muttered Ryan.

"Whatever. After that, it was okay. I got my head together. Sometimes I can cut off. That helps.'' She said, faint bitterness coloring her voice, "I guess you think that was all pretty dumb...''

"On the contrary,'' Ryan replied. "If it wasn't for the fact that we're shackled up like this, it could have been the smartest thing you've ever done.''

"I don't get you.''

It hit Ryan that she really didn't know. Of course she didn't know.

She didn't know that Strasser had destroyed every single human being on the land wag train. That they were all, without exception, dead meat, and that but for the grace of some god or other—presumably, he thought, her Earth Mother—she'd have been wiped with them.

Not that that made much difference to their current lousy predicament.

"Strasser gassed the train. Leastways, that's what he says, and I see no reason to disbelieve him. We're all that's left. You and me for sure. J.B. and the rest, probably. And the Trader and the other guys on the convoy. They've been tranquilized, but I don't know for how long. And their survival is entirely dependent on me getting my blasted hands free, and even then it's gonna be touch and go because—''

The truck lurched to a halt, engine throbbing.

Krysty said, "Oh, *hell*!" fiercely, although Ryan couldn't figure out why she said it in quite the tone she did. After maybe a half minute the rear doors of the truck were unhitched and flung open.

"Out!" said Kelber. Then he guffawed harshly, and this made him cough, and he choked for a while. "C'mon, c'mon!" he managed. "Hurry up outta there!" He erupted in another paroxysm of hoarse, wheezing laughter. Now he couldn't speak properly—it was too hilarious for him, so he jabbed at them with one hand and two sec men vaulted up into the truck and proceeded to roll Ryan and Krysty out.

Ryan forced himself to relax as much as possible—which wasn't a lot in the time he had, about a half second—and as he hit the ground he managed to shove himself with his boots so that for a second he hopped on them before keeling over sideways. That broke his fall. What terrified him was landing hard on a shoulder or arm and cracking it. That would truly write finis, as the Lost Language said, across any possibility of ultimate survival.

Talking to Krysty, though bruised and battered and wrench-tied as he was, had had the effect of soothing him, calming him when he needed calm most. Now he felt not too bad. Not too bad at all. At least the idiot who'd been using his brain as an anvil seemed to be tiring of the sport.

Above him was a pale red moon, not full but nearly so. Up there, so he'd heard and read, somewhere, were orbital stations careering endlessly around the world. Full of old bones now, their crews long, long dead. They might hurtle like that forever, until the universe contracted. Or maybe they were sinking all the time, orbiting lower and lower as each century passed, and at a certain time would all at once be gripped by the planet's gravitational pull and would bucket down through the layers of atmosphere exploding into fireballs, raining death and destruction on a world that was choked already with death and destruction.

It was chilly. Far away, high and to his right, he caught a glitter of fire in the sky and thought: Look at that! Whatever I think comes to pass!

But it was only a chem cloud, spontaneously combusting. More clouds gathered, cloaking the moon. An eerie scarlet glow illuminated the land. Green wildfires crackled and hissed high above. A warm rain began to fall.

Strasser appeared above him, looming tall, a gaunt skeleton in a long coat with skirts flapping in the breeze.

"Unhobble them."

Someone leaned down and across and Ryan glimpsed a blade, felt his bonds being tugged at.

Then his legs were free and he groaned aloud as they straightened out in an automatic jerk and his circulation began to shift into high once more. Hands gripped his arms, his shoulders, heaved him. He staggered to his feet, wincing at the shafts of agony that flared up and down his legs.

"Pain cleans you, Ryan. Flushes you out. Renews you. That's long been a theory of mine."

Strasser stared at him from under hooded eyes. Ryan stared back, thinking, the sequence of events will be as follows. First the main train, then the convoy. I can now do nothing whatsoever about the train. Too much time had elapsed. But in my heart of hearts I knew this was how it was going to be, and this was how I wanted it. I knew that whatever happened the train must go. Better this way. Yes. But the convoy is next and that too will go. Or most of it. Because there is no way that I can do what needs to be done all at once. And the time element is so tight, so bloody tight, that there is more than a possibility that we, Krysty and I, will—

Strasser said, "I still have the box, Ryan, and we can still use what's inside it, right here and now. It makes no difference to me."

"What the hell do I get out of this, Strasser? My life?"

Strasser laughed softly.

"Hardly."

"So?"

The gaunt man shrugged.

"A bullet in the back of the skull is a far more pleasant method of dying than any number of ways that I could think of. A quick and happy release from the cares and worries of this world rather than an extremely slow, extremely lingering and extremely unhappy one."

"That's not a great deal of choice you're offering."

"No choice at all," said Strasser, "but still worth a good deal, Ryan, believe me."

The rain was getting to be slightly heavier, very large water droplets that thudded down on Ryan's unprotected head, though it was not yet a downpour.

This was scrubby terrain for the most part, although across the road were trees, a sprawling coppice that offered shelter if only he could reach it. But to get there he would have to sprint all out with only a few bushes between it and at least fifteen guys, all weaponed up, all kill ready. It could be done, especially in this light, but not with hands secured behind his back. Not even a charge of adrenaline surging through him could boost him for that length of run while his balance was shot to hell.

Strasser's truck was parked on the road, near two other trucks and three buggies. Presumably these were the vehicles that had passed Krysty earlier. The convoy was behind him. War Wag One, two container rigs and an armored truck were parked back to back in a circle, facing outward. War Wag One faced the road, which was handy. If all went well.

Beside the war wag stood another of Strasser's trucks, close to the huge vehicle. Although Ryan couldn't see it, he knew there were men inside peering in at the war wag's cab, watching for any sign of life from those inside, any twitch or jerk that would signal an awakening.

He glanced to the east. A few klicks up the road was the land wag train. Those on it would never waken.

He said, "Tell me one thing, Strasser. Where'd you get the nerve gas?"

The gaunt man gestured irritably.

"Don't piss around, Ryan. You're in no position."

"No, really. It's been bothering me. It isn't going to hurt you to tell me."

"The weirdo with the steel eye," snapped Strasser. "Now move it!"

The weirdo with the steel eye.

Oh, yes. Oh, yes, indeed.

The shadowy figure who was akin to the bogeyman mothers warned their kids about. The guy very few people had ever seen. The guy who sometimes called himself the Warlock, sometimes the Magus. The guy who was said to be able to appear in two places at once. The guy who had a liking, once in a blue moon, for suddenly appearing in far-flung locales, handing out fantastic, sometimes wildly grotesque, trade goods that no one could ever figure out how to use, and then disappearing as mysteriously as he'd come. The guy the Trader said had to be sitting on a major Stockpile, although the way he actually used whatever he was sitting on seemed to be a strong argument for saying he was off his goddamned head.

So he had nerve gas. It figured. It also figured that he should have presented it to Jordan Teague, probably on a plate. He seemed to take a positive delight in creating mischief, usually of the more malevolent kind.

"Ryan..." said Strasser dangerously.

Ryan's eyes took in Krysty, her face set, her long hair flicking at her shoulders in the light wind, both arms gripped by two heavies. There was something odd about her but he couldn't think what it was.

"What about the girl?"

"What about her?"

"What does she get?"

Strasser frowned, his eyes narrowed to slits.

He said softly, "Ryan, why are you wasting time like this? Can it be that you know something I don't?"

Ryan knew that it was time. Now. Only three or four minutes had elapsed since he and Krysty had been rolled out of the truck, but all at once he knew that he had to get free, and fast.

"Okay," he said resignedly, "let's do it."

"Well?"

"My hands," said Ryan pointedly.

"Just tell us what to press, Ryan," hissed Strasser, his face now uglier than ever in the murky crimson light. "What to pull, what to touch, what not to touch. You just tell us."

"Not as easy as that. One mistake and you're dead. We're all dead."

He could see Strasser mentally wrestling with the notion of having him walking loose with his hands free.

The gaunt man thrust his parchment-colored face close, his eyes blazing. His whisper was malignant.

"The girl suffers, Ryan, if you do anything stupid. I promise you. I'll keep the bitch alive for a year." He turned, nodded to one of his minions. "Cut 'em."

Ryan winced as a blade began scraping away at his bound wrists. The guy didn't seem to give a damn where he cut.

There was a muffled grunt of pain. Ryan jerked his head up as Strasser whipped around an oath. The sec men holding Krysty were holding her no longer. Instead one was on the ground, groaning, the other clutching his groin, his mouth sagging, nothing coming out of it but a prolonged croaking. The thought shot through Ryan's brain that she sure knew where to hurt a guy and then he realized she was free.

Not only free but deadly. She'd snatched an auto-rifle and was dancing away, firing at sec men who sought to grab her, sec men who jerked backward in sequence as lead hammered them away from her. Three down and her way was clear.

Strasser snarled an obscenity, dragging out the automatic pistol at his belt. In the bad light it looked to be vintage Colt .454CP. He squeezed off two shots, and the second whanged off the front offside wheel hub of one of the trucks as Krysty dived out of sight around its fender, still firing short bursts.

"Maim her!" yelled Strasser. "Don't kill her! I want her alive!"

Ryan couldn't locate her but knew she was on the far side, somewhere, of the line of Strasser's vehicles parked by the road. Then four men running for the rear end of the line were bowled over by a burst of fire at ground level. She was shooting low, from beneath one of the trucks. It was as though the men had been scythed.

Ryan strained at the cords gripping his wrists as Strasser began to run, and then everything stopped dead as the murky darkness of the east burst apart with a terrible fire, a vast wash of fierce eyeball-searing light, orange cored. Sprays of scarlet jetted high into the sky, great tongues of flame that smeared the dazzling illumination. The dull roar of the explosion, long drawn out, was followed by a thudding reverberation and the distinct sound of rounds popping in a frenzied and continuous stammering rattle. More explosions. More eruptions of scarlet fire boiling up into the night. A kaleidoscope of colors as different kinds of illue rounds rocketed high, spraying the sky green, red, white. The noise went on and on.

Ryan back-heeled viciously at the guy behind him and his boot cracked bone. The man's cry was lost in the thunder of sound that crashed around their ears. There was a lot of good shit aboard that train, Ryan thought. He felt within him almost a kind of pride.

He raced for the war wag. Light from afar danced on its side.

The rain was heavier now, but Ryan knew it would have no effect whatsoever. The land wags and the other vehicles in that rain would continue to self-destruct until all that was left was glowing scrap metal.

He heard a shriek behind him, a howl of fury, and the crack of shots, three in all, and he began dodging, weaving, as best he could, at the same time desperately trying to keep himself upright. His arms were still wrenched behind him and there seemed no damned give whatever to his wrist cords. Then his boot caught in an animal hole and he was flying through the air, cursing. He rolled as he landed, automatically, and cursed some more as his roll took him onto his back, crushing his arms beneath him. He rolled on, hit the huge near side front wheel of the war wag and struggled to his feet. A round thudded into the ground next to him and he dived around the side of the big MCP.

The priority was getting into the war wag, and that could only be achieved by canceling the boobies, and that in turn could only be achieved by accomplishing a feat that was damned near impossible in his present state.

But not entirely.

He scrambled alongside the looming vehicle, now with mud splashing up into his face. The heavy dabs of rain had been transformed into a smashing downpour of water almost at the bat of an eye. Here, at the rear, were heavy caterpillar tracks. At the front of these, under the chassis, was a covered switch. The cutoff. Once thrown, the circuit that commanded the boobies was dead, and he could climb aboard. But first he had to throw the blasted thing, had to ram his shoulders against the side of the MCP and reach backward with twisted-up arms and scrabble blindly for the unseen switch casing, pull it down with fingers that were nearly dead, then grasp the switch, then push it over, then stagger to the main door at the side, do likewise with the hidden lock underneath the war wag's body, then jump inside and slam the door closed, then...

Not entirely impossible—as long as he had about fifteen spare minutes, in daylight, and no one trying to kill him.

He backed into the bulk of the war wag and bent over, bowing his back. His arms rose behind him and his fingers thrust through all the mud and muck and filth that had accumulated there, on the vehicle's underside, and finally caught hold of the casing, hearing, as he did so, bursts of fire from Krysty battling it out with the sec men. Keep it up, he thought in anguish, his fingers tearing at hard gobs of dried mud. He unlatched the casing, felt inside every nerve in him screaming, his head to the right, expecting any second to see some kill-crazy guy storming around from the war wag's front, auto-rifle flaming. Instead, all he saw through the now bucketing rain was the sky still flaring up in bursts of shocking light, his ears taking in the almost continual rumble of distant detonations.

He shoved the switch, cursing fiercely until he grunted in triumph as he felt it smoothly slot into Off. It was a system that worked outside or inside—it didn't matter. That was the simple beauty of it.

But there was still the problem of getting into the war wag. Still one last switch to be thrown inside . . . that had to be thrown within minutes. Within five minutes, or maybe less than five—gotta be. Two minutes? Three? No more than three, he thought, and I can fall into all kinds of crap in three lousy minutes.

Already he was staggering back the way he'd come, toward the front. Again he bent over, eyes still glued to his right, and again his fingers felt for the switch housing. Damned thing wouldn't budge, wouldn't fall open. He wrenched it, his heart pounding, his breathing tortured into ugly grunts. He knew his fingers were by now slick with blood, though he could feel no pain. He could feel almost nothing in them at all. The casing suddenly flicked down and he jabbed at the switch inside . . .

And reeled sideways, a hoarse racking howl ripped from him as something solid smashed into the side of his skull. His arms scraped along rough metal as he crashed to the ground.

Shit, he thought, they came around the back.

He lay in the mud, breathing hoarsely, his body twisted, grimacing with the pain that was daggering through his head, slowly opening his one eye and making out two figures looming over him in the downpour. Strasser. Kelber.

Both had pieces, handguns jabbed down at him, at his face. He spat mud and water out and thought, *Finis.*

Strasser was screaming at him, shrieking insanely, beside himself with rage. Ryan got up, he couldn't make out what he was saying, and probably Strasser didn't know himself. Then Kelber was dragging him to his feet, smashing a hand repeatedly across his face.

Strasser howled, "You think you're smart, Ryan, but you're shit, you're shit, and you're going to die like shit!"

Kelber kicked his legs and Ryan staggered, toppled, collapsed to the ground, spraying mud and slop into the air. He lashed out, too, savagely, but there was no target and Strasser lunged at him, falling across one of his legs, jamming an outspread hand into his face. Ryan kept kicking, flailing around with his other foot, but it was difficult to do anything destructive with his hands still tied.

Strasser was yelling, "The box, the box! Get it out, you cretin!" He glared down at Ryan, and to Ryan the scene took on a nightmarish quality as water sluiced across the gaunt man's skull-like battered face, a bucketing deluge of hot rain hammering down on him with punishing force.

Ryan saw Kelber with the box in his hands, his fat sausage fingers ripped at the lid and not getting it right, the box becoming a live thing in his hands so that he was suddenly juggling with it, Strasser yelling frenziedly.

Strasser caught it and opened it. And Strasser thrust a fist down into Ryan's mouth, uncaring whether Ryan bit him or not, both hands now brought into play, fingers gripping his jaw, clenching his teeth, yanking Ryan's mouth open. Kelber leaned over, suddenly laughing like a madman, the box in his hands starting to tip up.

With an almost superhuman strength jolting through him like an electric charge, Ryan heaved himself from under Strasser's knees in a desperate scrabbling roll, and as he did so he felt the cords at his wrist tear and snap. He wrenched his arms around, pain blazing up from his wrists, and caught Strasser's open coat, clutched it, heaved, the panic and terror that was flooding through his system at the thought of that insect more than enough to send the gaunt man crashing into Kelber's legs. Kelber disappeared from view and Ryan smashed a fist into Strasser's gut, deep, powering it in, before pulling himself away and staggering to his feet. Only a grab away from him, a handgun lay in the mud. As he reached for it and held it, the thought flared through his brain that there was probably mud up the blasted barrel, but he was past caring.

He swiveled, firing at Strasser as he swung, and Strasser was flung back, winged, the bullet skinning one shoulder. He hit the mud, slid, scrabbled sideways on his knees and one arm like some ungainly spider that had lost some of its legs. He was soaked to the skin, filthy with mud. His teeth were bared, his eyes blazing with hate and fury at what he'd lost.

Ryan advanced two steps, the automatic in his right hand, his body aching and his head throbbing. His teeth, too, were bared, but in a terrible grin of triumph.

Strasser croaked, "Bastard! All that hardware! You must be insane!"

"Just wary of crazies like you, Strasser," Ryan said, his voice icy. "There are self-destruct mechanisms throughout the fleet. In every truck and land wag and buggy, automatically running if a switch is not thrown every hour, or as soon as a vehicle is safety locked from the inside on a four-hour fuse. If there's no one there to throw that switch—or if there is, but they're all dead—*bang!*"

He was aware of Kelber close to him on his left. He seemed to be having difficulty getting up, or so it appeared. He was on his knees, both hands to his throat, making ghastly gobbling noises. One hand went out to Strasser. It looked as though he was pleading, begging Strasser for mercy. His eyes were almost popping out of his head and Ryan could see the whites of them clearly.

The beetle, he thought—what the hell happened to the beetle when I banged Strasser into him?

And then he laughed out loud, a harsh and chilling sound even to him. So perish the wicked, he thought.

"Your friend. I think he swallowed the beetle."

Kelber, still on his knees, scrambled toward Strasser, pleading, imploring. Ryan couldn't imagine why—Kelber ought to know by now there was no help there, no pity in the gaunt man—but he could imagine those tusklike mandibles sinking into gullet flesh so determinedly that no amount of hawking and gagging would clear the filthy little bastard out. The hell with the pair of them, he thought, and fired at Strasser.

No sound but a metallic click.

No round.

He realized it was Strasser's gun and the eight-clip had been all used up. He hurled the weapon at Strasser, and the heavy automatic struck the gaunt man full in the mouth. Strasser squealed, fell back, spitting blood and bits of tooth. Ryan made to jump for him but Strasser was back on his feet again, sprinting away, clutching his shoulder, his long legs stabbing at the ground, boots splashing into puddles.

At that moment Kelber gave forth a high-pitched bubbling wail of pain and terror and stark, beyond-the-last-ditch horror. He pitched sideways, still screaming, and Ryan saw black blood welling up out of his mouth like dark chocolate. Kelber lay on his back, his body twisting and writhing, his legs kicking in the air. His screams died sloppily as he began to drown in his own blood.

Ryan flung himself around and jumped for the short ladder to the door, knowing that the seconds were clicking away, nearer and nearer to a total wipeout. He wrenched open the door and fell inside. There was a faint and musty smell to the interior. He felt a prickling at the back of his throat, but nothing more. He yanked the door shut, on personal full-auto now, sheer survival the only consideration. It was too late for the rest of the convoy. It would have been physically impossible to make safe the other vehicles. The explosions to the east had ceased, only fire consuming what remained lit the sky now, an angry orange dancing against the deeper red of the night.

He knew that the Trader would have automatically thrown the On as soon as he heard the train had been nerved out and as soon as he realized he was surrounded. And the captains of the other vehicles would have done the same. It would have been a reflex action. Therefore, the convoy was set to blow only minutes after the land wag train.

He shoved Cohn unceremoniously out of his radio chair, felt for the box under the table, snapped over the lever there. Then he dived for the ladder up to the machine gun blister in the roof. O'Mara was still in his seat, slumped forward, dead to the world. Ryan reached past him for the MG grips, canted the weapon, opened up and proceeded to flay the truck parked beside the war wag at almost point-blank range. Blazing tracers ripped into the back of the truck's cab, opening it up, chewing it apart, and Ryan could hear nothing but the terrible chatter of the gun, could see nothing but the devastation it created.

He jumped back down to the main cabin and dived for the drive seat. Ches was lying on the floor beside it, and

Ryan stepped over him and sat down. He began to play the console, feeling a stupendous relief flooding through him as the engine bellowed into life. He glanced to his right, saw flames in the cab of the parked truck, a guy silently screaming and haloed in fire as he struggled to claw himself out the open window—then that scene was wiped as the huge MCP lurched forward, gathering speed. He flicked the spotlight on, and the gloom became bright day in an instant. He saw fireflies all around him, red muzzle-flash winking in the dark beyond the spotlight's beam, and could hear the rattle of rounds on the sides of the cab. They could still kill him. All it needed was tracer at the front and the temporary screen would blow apart and him with it. He jabbed one of the firing buttons on the console and cannon fire hammered out its death song from below, pounding a buggy in front that suddenly ripped apart in a gout of white fire as its gas tank erupted. Figures fled away from his spot beam; any one of them could have been Strasser.

To one side another buggy lurched into life, and Ryan savagely swung the wheel to send the war wag barreling into it. The smaller vehicle was smashed sideways, and Ryan felt the MCP rise and yaw, crunching through a sudden tangle of steel, twisting and crushing the other vehicle beneath its ponderous weight. He swung the wheel again and felt the rear tracks ride over what was left.

Where the hell was Krysty?

He saw her, a fleet figure sprinting into his beam along the road. He sent the war wag crashing up and onto the blacktop, aimed it for Mocsin and geared it into full-auto mode. Then he scrambled over Ches and moved fast across the cabin area to the door to unfasten it. The war wag ground on along the road, medium fast, and the young woman appeared in the doorway, running alongside before grabbing Ryan's outstretched hand. He hauled her in as more bright light tore the night apart and the war wag shuddered. Ryan slammed the door shut, cutting off the worst of the thunderous explosions that were now ripping through the convoy.

"Co-driver's seat," he yelled, hurdling sprawled bodies and diving back into the chair, snapping the brute vehicle out of auto and wrenching the wheel as another shock wave from the self-destructing convoy hammered at them.

Krysty collapsed into the seat beside him, wiping an arm across her mud- and sweat-stained face.

She gasped, "Is life with the Trader always like this?"

Chapter Eleven

THE SMOKE FROM THE FIRE coiled uneasily, circling upward among the branches of the surrounding trees. The lodgepole pine burned with a crackling intensity, spitting out sap in spluttering bursts like rifle fire. Ryan lay back against the trunk of a fallen cottonwood, watching the gray pillar of smoke as it disappeared above him, vanishing long before it reached the top of the forest.

The wind was rising, bringing the stinging taste of a cold blue norther. The patches of sky that he could see through the trees were raven black, torn across every few minutes by the jagged silver lace of lightning. Above the crackling of the pine logs he could hear the far-off rumbling of thunder in the tall peaks of the Darks.

In the clearing around him were all the survivors of the massacre at Mocsin, sitting or lying sprawled. There had not been the time or the opportunity to save anyone outside of War Wag One. Even as Ryan had driven away, heading north and west through the sleeting rain, the heavy vehicle had rocked and twisted against the explosions of the rest of the train. The time bombs had all done their work successfully, just as they'd been designed to.

The big combat carrier now stood fifty paces away, on the edge of the rutted track. In the quiet, he could hear the clicking of the armor plate as it cooled in the evening chill. There were four or five men still on board, carrying out essential maintenance checks. Loz was clearing up after the meal of heated stew and beans. Cohn was running around the dials of his radio of many parts, trying to pick up news of pursuit.

The rest of the survivors were all around Ryan, some already asleep. Something rustled out among the pines, and Ryan's hand dropped to his pistol. Abe grinned at him from the far side of the fire.

"Only a marmot."

Abe had the best eyesight of anyone Ryan had ever met, except for muties. Ryan relaxed and lay back again, trying to ease the tension from his sinews. It had been a bad couple of days.

"Real bad," he muttered, hardly aware that he had spoken aloud.

"Very true," nodded Hovak to his left. She had the strained look around the eyes that they all had from the effects of the gassing. Her speech was slurred and the whites of her eyes were tinted pink. But she'd been luckier than some. When Ryan had finally stopped the war wag two hours out of Mocsin and helped Krysty to collect everyone together, seven of the crew hadn't made it, their hearts and lungs stilled by the nerve gas.

There was enough of a crew to operate the war wag, but if they came into a heavy combat situation, they'd be short on firepower. Ryan ticked them off on his fingers.

Apart from those in the vehicle, there were he and Krysty. The fire glinted off her vermillion hair as it rolled about her neck and shoulders where she slept on the opposite side of the clearing. Ches, the driver, and O'Mara were next, heads together, talking quietly. Kathy lay, smoking a crudely rolled tobacco cigarette, next around the rough circle. Rintoul, Hooley and Lint, were all either sleeping or sitting up and looking vacantly into the darkness.

In all he made it twenty-four. It wasn't a whole lot to tackle the Deathlands.

The glitter of firelight off steel caught his eye and he saw the chubby figure of Finnegan, whittling away at a broken hunk of the dead cottonwood with his razored butcher's knife. The man saw Ryan watching him and held up the piece of wood for him.

"Recognize the bitchin' bastard?" he asked with a grin.

Even in the poor light, Ryan could make out in the rough planes of white wood the gaunt features of Cort Strasser.

That was a debt to lay on the table. A debt that would get settled one day, Ryan had no doubt. Though their situation was dismal, with so many friends and good comrades dead and stiff behind them, it was a damned long way from being desperate.

"Ryan."

"Yeah?"

"Here."

He rose and stretched, feeling the tightness of his muscles, picking up the LAPA and moving to squat down at the side of the Trader.

Over the years Ryan had seen a lot of men, good and bad, go and buy the farm. Some of them had been wiped away in the blinking of an eye, and others seemed to have death standing silently at their shoulders for weeks before the scythe had fallen.

He'd never seen that midnight reaper more clearly than he saw him now, in the gloom behind the Trader.

"That you, Ryan?"

"Yeah."

"Everyone fed?"

"Sure. You want anything?"

Trader shook his head. "Not less'n you can call back the dead. That mongrel, Strasser. We'll regroup and get us some more good men, Ryan. Then go back and wipe Mocsin off the earth."

"Sure. In time."

Trader nodded his grizzled head. The gas still had him in thrall and he coughed, his shoulders quivering with the effort. His face turned away from Ryan and the younger man heard him bring up saliva. As Ryan had already observed several times in the past year, the spittle was flecked with bright blood.

"Thirty years since me and Marsh Folsom found them war wags. Now that fire-blasted scab done 'em in. Just that one left." He coughed again, then straightened, pasting a thin-lipped smile unsteadily in place. "But one's enough, eh, Ryan?"

"Maybe. I wish J.B. was with us. Right now his miserable face'd look like the risin' sun."

Trader sighed. "They come and they go, Ryan. Heard someone say 'bout bein' here today and gone tomorrow. I seen better than fifty summers and winters come and go. I lost count of the dead."

"The dead's yesterday. Our worry is tomorrow. You certain we should go into the Darks?"

A flash of lightning seemed crimson against the pink-gray sky. The tumbling roll of thunder lasted several seconds. Behind Ryan, Rintoul threw another couple of jagged logs on the fire. Inside the war wag he could hear someone—Cohn, he thought—whistling. Trader was right. One was enough, when you had comrades with that kind of spirit.

Trader nodded. "Too many reasons, Ryan. All you told me these last days. The girl's story 'bout her folks. Then that man . . . what's his name?"

"Kurt? One hid up in Charlie's?"

"Went up in the high country. Saw a fog. Then that old guy at Teague's, one you say they called Doc. He told 'bout what you could find. Called it a Redoubt. Heard the name before. And he said the fog was a way out. That right?"

Ryan nodded. He was close enough to the old man to catch the dry, sickly odor of his breath. Like the scent of an open grave.

"So we go up there and see what there is," Ryan said. "How long will it take us?"

"No more trouble from muties, stickies or Strasser, and we can be up there close to the tree line day after next. You got guards out?"

"Sure. Two on a ranged perimeter, crossing in and out. Due for a change in about ten minutes."

"Good. Give me a hand up. Want to go lie down in my bunk. Sleep that gas away. You wake me if . . ." Another grin, this time more convincing. "Sure you will, Ryan."

The Trader stood, gripping Ryan's wrist to steady himself. Gripping it so hard that the marks would still be livid-clear the following morning. Ryan watched him go, seeing the way that pride held the old man erect, stiff backed, all the way through the lowering trees to the steps of War Wag One. Pulling himself up and then vanishing into the cramped interior.

A touch on his shoulder made him start and he turned to stare into the green eyes of Krysty Wroth. "He's dying," she said, voice flat and calm.

"I know it. He knows it. And now I guess you know it."

"The others?"

"They don't know nothin'." He blinked and hissed through his teeth in irritation at himself. "I keep meanin' to stop that. I mean that they don't know anythin'. I've seen the blood when he coughs."

"How long's he got?"

"Year. Month. Weeks. How do I know? I'm not a medic. And Trader won't see one."

Ryan realized he was still carrying the LAPA and he tucked it back into the looped rig inside his coat. The girl stood by him, running a hand through her mane of dazzling hair, and Ryan watched her. In the flickering light of the campfire he had the momentary illusion that the red hair had a life of its own. That it had some odd sentience. It was almost as if it responded to her hand, moving in long fronds about her fingers.

"Got to check the guards."

"I'll come."

"Yeah. Be company."

They moved away from the circle of light and into the damp coolness of the forest. Normally Ryan did not like the woods. Man couldn't see far enough. Man was vulnerable among these trees, their trunks and branches tortured and twisted from years of growing in wild weather and the extremes of toxic foulness. All sorts of muties, human and animal—and something in between—lived among these trees. But now they were moving north, into the high mountains.

"Be in the Darks in a few days."

"Peter Maritza had some old maps," Krysty said. "Back before the Fire. This was called Montana."

"I heard that. Time was I knew the names of almost all of 'em. The old States. Now I forgot 'em, don't need 'em no more."

He stopped and whistled. A low, insistent sound that carried through the darkness. After a moment they both heard a whistle in reply, from their left, close in. And then another, from the right, farther away. Ryan put his hand to his mouth and whistled once more, a double trill that faded away.

"They'll be here soon. It's Jim and Meg. Wait here and don't move around, or you might get shot. End of a sentry spell and the finger gets white on the trigger."

The girl appeared first, a rifle under her arm. She was tall and skinny, with a gray forage cap pulled low over her eyes. Ryan knew she wore it that way to help conceal her baldness. She nodded to him and to Krysty and went silently past, heading for the camp. Jim was on the outlying patrol and he came in at an easy lope, rifle at the high port.

"Near shit meself, Ryan," he said.

"What's up?"

"Heard somethin' over there, thought it was a bastard sec man of that bastard Strasser. Then I heard it again, in the brush. I was just goin' to rake it apart with this babe here, and out it comes this bastard wolverine, big as a shepherd dog, mutie teeth all curled in its lip like tusks. Thought it was goin' to gut-rip me."

"Send Henn and Lint out for the next spell," Ryan told him. "If Strasser's on the trail, he could be here before dawn."

"When do we leave?" Krysty asked as she and Ryan watched the gray-clad figure of Jim disappear into the darkness.

"False dawn, that's when. We'll put some more distance between us and Strasser."

The girl moved to stand closer to Ryan, her hand reaching out into the gloom and resting for a brief moment on his right arm. "What do you think we'll find up there?"

"Fog. That's the only thing that's sure. Only thing they all talk of is the fog." He stared out through the trees, listening to the faint but insistent sound of fast-running water. "My guess is the fog hides somethin' from the old times. Somethin' they wanted kept hid, so they set this fog like a dog to guard it. Whoever 'they' are, they're long burned. Or chilled. But their dog's still there. I seen what it can do. I saw Kurt. He was like a man that's been through a mincer and then set on fire."

"Can we make it?"

"War wag holds plenty of gas. Food's fine. Touch short on men. And women."

"The Trader?"

"Soon. I just wish J.B. was here. And Sam and Hun and Koll. All good people to have at your back."

The wind was rising again. Off to the east Ryan saw something flare high in the sky, a vivid purple, crimson at its edges. One more piece of nuclear junk sliding back into the earth's atmosphere, burning up on reentry.

"Listen," said Krysty.

"What?"

She shook her head, her hair still luminous even in the blackness. "Quiet, Ryan. I can... Someone's coming."

The gun was in his hand, faster than a thought, his finger tense on the slim trigger. Good though his own senses were, Ryan had been around long enough to know that a lot of people had better.

"Where? How many? Creepy-crawling?"

"Southerly. Several. No. Moving fast and noisy. I guess five or six."

"How far off?"

"Difficult in this wind. Among trees. Maybe a klick or two."

That was close. Too close.

"Go warn the others. Now!" There was a bite to his words like the cut of a whiplash, and Krysty turned and vanished from his side.

Ryan headed toward the south. His life depended on the girl being correct. Half a dozen unknowns moving fast toward them. Odds were it was Strasser and an elite of his sec men, pushing quickly after them, hoping to wipe away their escape.

A hard rain began to fall on Ryan, slanting through the upper branches of the immense stand of lodgepole pines all around him. It sluiced through, turning the ground beneath his boots into a quagmire of mud and leaf mold. He knew now that his greatest hazard was running straight into the attackers. If there was to be any surprise, he wanted it on his side.

Holding the LAPA at the ready, he dropped to his knees behind a fallen tree, steadying his breathing, wiping rain from his forehead. If he'd grabbed one of the laser rifles with the night-sights he'd have been in better shape.

He knelt and waited. The Trader said that a man who cried over spilled milk got blinded by his tears.

By now Krysty would be back at the camp. The fire would have been stamped out and most of the party would be inside War Wag One, manning the entrances and gunports. There would be four outside, covering each compass point, watching for the attackers, ready to give him covering fire. If he made it back.

Fifty-five gifts of instant leaden mortality for the group of hostiles coming toward him with three extra sticks inside his coat, ready to slot in.

If they were muties with dark sight, he would be in the greatest danger. Then it wouldn't matter much if they were armed with flintlock muskets; he'd still be in a load of trouble. That thought made him tuck the weighted white silk scarf out of sight under the coat. He hunched and waited.

The lightning hit a tree less than a hundred paces away from him. He flinched, closing his eye against the instant blindness. The brutal thunder enveloped him, numbing his senses. He licked his lips, tasting the harsh, metallic flavor of ozone. If the attackers had been close enough, they could have taken him like a light-dazed rabbit.

"Scorch it to hell!" he cursed. Rubbing furiously at his right eye, seeing only a crimson mist, he blinked again and again. His head was lowered against the driving rain as he desperately fought to clear his vision.

He peered cautiously around the bole of the tumbled tree.

And saw them.

"Six. Seven," he muttered. All wearing the black waterproof slickers favored by the sec men from Mocsin. Hooded. High black boots. Oddly, not one of them was carrying a weapon at the ready, though he could make out rifles slung across the shoulders of some of them. It looked as if two of them were wounded, leaning on the arms of others.

They seemed more like refugees than a raiding party.

Either way, Ryan was going to wipe them from the face of this place of nukeshit and soul death called Earth. He set the LAPA on automatic and readied himself, bracing for the kick of the gun. At a range now of less than forty paces, he could take them all out in one savage raking burst of fire.

More thunder and lightning issued from a swirling sky that now glowed red in the west. Ryan waited, picking the moment when all of the enemy would be out in the open at once.

At thirty paces the sec men stopped and the leading figure turned around, pointing toward where Ryan waited. He tensed, even though he knew they couldn't possibly make him out in that weather and light. The pointman turned back, throwing off the shiny black hood. Another slash of silver lightning showed Ryan the face. And the hair.

Green hair.

"Hunaker! Hun, over here!"

The woman stared through the rain, mouth sagging with surprise. "Ryan? Ryan, you old bastard! Ryan!"

She ran toward him, then stopped and stared at him, and to their mutual embarrassment, she began to weep.

Chapter Twelve

DAWN WAS ABOUT an hour away.

The rain had stopped and the electrical storm had passed, grumbling its way to the south of them, leaving a quiet night. All the new arrivals had been fed and found bunks in the war wag.

Only J. B. Dix remained awake, talking to Ryan, telling him what had finally gone down in Mocsin. Around them, in the slumbering forest, the sentries still patrolled. They would all be on the move by first light.

J.B.'s report was characteristically terse.

"Convoy blew, knocked us all to hell and back. Sam an' Hun was laid out colder than a ten-year winter. I got my shoulder bruised some. Figured it was broke, but it's not. Girls came around and we got out. Koll found the old man, Doc. Gotten scrambled brains, Ryan. I don't know about him at all." J.B. stopped and shook his head, the glowing embers of the dying fire glinting off the steel-rimmed glasses. In the half light, his face looked more sallow and pinched than ever.

"Where d'you pick up Charlie and the guy they was huntin'? Kurt? He looks near dead, Kurt."

"Him and the Trader both. I looked in on him. Can't be more than days now, Ryan."

"Yeah."

"Fishmouth Charlie and Kurt was on the edge of Mocsin. She was near carrying him. We stopped with them to draw breath. Kurt was mumbling about when he was a blaster with McCandless up in the Darks. Claimed he knew the way to find the fogs. Said there was a big, big secret up there. A Redoubt, he called it. Figured we'd bring him. We liberated these clothes from some of Strasser's killers. There's been a small fight. Few bodies around."

Ryan guessed from J.B.'s taciturn description that it had probably been a desperate battle, but there was no point in pressing J.B. for that kind of detail. It was the results that mattered to the weapons master, not how they were obtained.

"I figured you'd gone this way," Dix continued. "Strasser's bound to come after us. He went ape-crazy. Saw him twice but I couldn't get a clear shot at him. I think our bombs fired the whole town. A rising wind did the rest. I looked back and Mocsin was most gone."

"You made good time," Ryan said. "Another few hours and we'd have been gone and in the hills. You'd never have caught us."

"Rock and a hard place, my boy," Dix said cheerlessly. "Managed to beg a couple of buggies from some sec men who didn't need them anymore. Ran out of gas three, four hours ago. Been on foot since then. Had to be the Darks."

"Yeah," Ryan replied with a nod. "It's the Darks."

They sat in silence for some minutes. J.B. had retrieved one of his favorite thin cheroots from his locker in War Wag One and reclined on the cool earth, gazing into the smoldering coals of the fire.

Ryan broke the silence. "Strasser will guess it's the Darks."

"He can't have much of a force left," Dix muttered. "Either he catches us real soon, or he doesn't catch us at all."

"I'll rouse everyone. They can catch up on missing sleep over next day or so, if we keep out of trouble. I'll get 'em out and start the show."

The sky was noticeably lighter to the south and east, but it was streaked with dark, oily smoke that showed up against the red tinge of dawn. Something big was burning out of control. That would be Mocsin.

Behind him, Ryan heard the familiar noises of the war wag coming to life. Everyone knew his task and his place. Inside the vehicle there would be little talk, beyond the routine checks of switches and contacts. It was something that J.B. had introduced to the Trader, stressing the importance of everyone knowing not only his own duties, but the jobs of at least two other members of the crew. And time and again that insistence had saved all their lives.

Standing outside the vehicle, Ryan knew precisely where they were all positioned and what they would be doing. Ches in the driver's seat, eyes ranging over the dials, automatically checking fuel, pressures and temperatures. O'Mara in the MG blister, dry-firing the piece, making sure of the ammunition. Even Loz would be busy, stacking away all the pots and pans, seeing that in the heat of a fight there would be no cooking knives or cleavers flying around inside the armored cabin.

And the Trader?

Normally he would be at the helm, here and everywhere. A gruff question perhaps, and a firm hand on a shoulder. His eyes flicking all about, giving a word of praise or a word of criticism. But now he was lying on his bunk, asleep from the drugs Krysty had given him. It was the first time in all the years that Ryan had known him that the Trader had agreed to take any medication. Which said a lot about his condition.

The out-ranging guards had fallen back from their perimeter and had been joined by a man and woman from the war wag. Each of them stood watch at a corner of the huge combat vehicle, scanning the blank walls of the forest all around them.

Ryan found Fishmouth Charlie changed from the black uniform into a pale fawn coverall, a brown denim hat pulled down low over her thick, curling hair. In the first pale hint of dawn's light, he could make out the tiny, pouting mouth and the goggling eyes that had given the woman her name.

"Ready, Charlie?" he asked.

"Sure am. Regular little army the Trader's gotten himself. Didn't find 'em too friendly at first, but they kind of accept us."

"How's Kurt?"

"Not good. Figures everyone's out to kill him. He knows you're headin' into the Darks and he keeps mumbling 'bout the fogs there."

Ryan rubbed a long forefinger down the side of his nose, glancing back over his shoulder at the nearest entrance to War Wag One. It was about time they were off and moving in case Strasser—

Blood and splattered brains blinded him for a moment. Sharp fragments of bone from the shattered skull stung the side of his face.

"Hellblast," he hissed, half turning, ducking as he did so. He was conscious of the sound of the gun. A high-velocity rifle, fired from a couple of hundred paces away, among the screen of trees. It had fluked a hit on poor old Charlie at his side. Probably one of the countless M-l6s he'd seen around Mocsin, hefted by the sec men.

Such thoughts took him a splinter of frozen time. More lead ricocheted off the side of the war wagon, leaving a splash of silvery metal to the right of the nearest door.

"Lights!" Ryan yelled, realizing what a great target the golden rectangle was. But someone inside, no doubt J.B., was quicker, and the lights went out even as he shouted the warning.

The firing became heavier, all concentrated on Ryan's side. In the false dawn he saw the muzzle-flashes and he snapped off a burst from the LAPA, not waiting to see if they had any effect. Charlie's corpse was still at his feet, twitching, arms and legs flailing in the residual movements of death mimicking life. The bullet had hit her through the right side of the cheek, angling upward, dislodging one of her bulbous eyes, exiting near the top of her skull, and flipping the cap off in a welter of blood.

Ryan ducked low, wincing as a shot from the darkness hacked up a burst of mud and water barely inches from his left foot. Already there was the deafening racket of death from the war wag as everyone poured lead into the forest, giving covering fire for Ryan and the four guards to scramble back inside.

Three made it.

The fourth, a skinny, balding man called Jed, was hit in the back of the right leg as he reached the doorway. His fall blocked the door. Ryan cursed, diving sideways into the mud, sliding on his stomach into the comforting shadow of the war wag. Jed was down and screaming, thrashing in his pain, rolling away from helping hands in the doorway. A second round smashed into his chest and he hurled away his laser rifle as he coughed out a spray of arterial blood.

"Ryan!" screamed a voice from his left, on the blind side of the vehicle.

It was Samantha the Panther, crouched by the front wheels, beckoning to him. He waved a hand, getting a flashing grin in return. Jed was down and done, struggling to get to his hands and knees, blood trickling steadily from his open mouth. Ryan saw someone appear near the edge of the trees, much closer to the war wag, and throw a metallic ball toward them.

"Grenade!" he bellowed, burying his face in his arms, cushioning himself against the shock. But the slope of the land took most of the force of the blast. The man who'd thrown it, visible in the black security uniform, made the mistake of hesitating to watch the success of the small bomb. A stream of fire from the starboard MG blister hurled him against the bole of a towering cottonwood, rolling him into the undergrowth like a bundle of sodden, bloodied rags.

Ryan took his chance to scuttle under the combat wagon, grabbing Sam's lean, muscular arm, hoisting himself into the comforting security port, kicking the door shut behind him. Inside it was the usual organized bedlam, orders shouted and a constant stream of data yelled at the man at the control center.

"You cut that a little fine, friend," said the Trader, glancing over his shoulder.

Ryan could not hide his surprise at seeing the Trader up and running the war wag from his accustomed place. But this was no time to make polite inquiries about his leader's health.

Maybe later.

"I just made out Strasser," called Finnegan from the starboard observation slit.

"Waste him," said J.B., from his side.

"Can't get a clear shot. There's about twenty of 'em here."

"More this side, too!" came a voice form the far flank of the war wag.

The slamming of bullets against the armor was deafening, but Ryan could tell that the attackers had nothing heavier than hand weapons. Problems would come if they got in closer and started using limpets or impact mines under the wheels.

"Movin' out," said Trader, calm as ever.

"Movin' out," responded Ches, engaging the gears, bringing the throbbing motor to full-powered, roaring life. Ryan hung on to a bracket as they lurched away from the ambush.

His eye caught Krysty, farther forward, managing a thin smile as she winked at him. Realizing, in the heat of the combat, how glad he had been to have her with him, safe and unharmed.

"Got an ace down the line at six of 'em settin' up a launcher," said Hovak from her mortar position high up.

"Do it," ordered the Trader. He turned to the slit at his shoulder and watched.

There was the whoomph of the heavy mortar being fired, and the war wag rolled to counter the blast. For a second or so everyone fell silent, waiting. Ryan had once read an old book about submarines, and he guessed it had been like this waiting after a torpedo had been released and was running.

"Right in the cross hairs," yelped Hovak triumphantly, banging her gloved fist on the side of the seat. Ryan joined in the general chorus of cheers at her success.

Ryan picked his way to the stern of the war wag, moving Rint out of the rear observation port. Setting his eye into the soft rubber socket of the backward-facing periscope, he used the self-centering gyro system to focus on what was happening back at their camp.

The sec men were coming out of the forest, seeing their prey escaping, their ambush failed. At a word of command from the Trader the shooting had ceased, and the war wag rolled on northwest, then westward on the crumbled remains of a two-lane blacktop.

Ryan adjusted the focusing screw, turning the milled edge until the faces of their attackers swam into sharp detail. He saw the usual brutish, vulpine expressions that he knew from Baronies and communes all over the Deathlands. Small men with a taste for cruelty.

He ranged along the line, stopping at one of the sec men who pushed through to the front.

"Strasser," he breathed.

The high-definition, directional mikes at the back of the war wag were out of action, but he did not need them to know what Strasser was shouting after them. The whole set of the man's body told it all.

The gaunt body, taller than any of his men, agitated with anger. As Ryan watched him, Strasser pulled off the visored cap and threw it in the mud, kicking it with his boots. Rain glistened on the bald skull, trickling over the thin cheeks, into the ghost of a mustache. Ryan grinned with wolfish satisfaction as he saw there was still blood clotted around the police chief's mouth where the thrown pistol had struck him.

Strasser was shaking his fist at them. Far behind him, in the fast-brightening dawn, Ryan could make out a monstrous column of greasy smoke rising from the tomb of Jordon Teague.

The ruined tomb of Mocsin.

As THEY DROVE STEADILY toward a kind of safety, the Trader took to his bunk once more, the rush from the action leaving him drained and sallow. Ryan organized the crew into their usual rotas, as far as was possible with their shrunken force. Only then did he find a quiet spot and sit down to relax. After a while Hunaker came to join him.

"Have a word, Ryan?"

"Yeah. What?"

The woman seemed oddly ill at ease, rubbing her cropped green hair, adjusting the slim-bladed knife on her hip.

"Come on, Hun. What's got you? Still feelin' for Ange?"

"No. Well, some I guess. She was a sweet kid and I figured we might... Oh, burn all that, Ryan, it's over and out. That's not what..."

"What?"

"When we was back in Mocsin, me and Sam an' Koll an' J.B. was talkin' and we—"

"Hun. You want me to pull your helldamned liver up through your neck?"

"No. Why d'you—"

"I'm tired. Just *say* it."

"Sure." With a rush, like a swimmer entering cold water. "We was talkin' 'bout you and we thought nobody knows what your name is. Ryan. Just Ryan. Got to be another name. Not even J.B. knew it."

Ryan grinned at her. "That all?"

"Yeah. You don't mind me askin' like this?"

"No. Why should I? It's Cawdor. Ryan Cawdor. Not a secret, Hun."

"Ryan Cawdor. That's not too special, is it? So how come you never told nobody before?"

"I guess because nobody ever asked me before."

They smiled at each other, a look passing between them that held a certain kind of gentleness as War Wag One, now the only war wag, ground deeper into the Darks.

Chapter Thirteen

KURT DIED JUST BEFORE SUNSET on the next day.

The flight from the blazing carnage of Mocsin and the horrible death of his only friend, Fishmouth Charlie, finally and irrevocably tipped the balance of his mind into madness. The war wag's medic, Kathy, did what she could, loading him with sleepers, but it was obvious that the shrieking had taken him over.

"Claws an' teeth! Claws an' teeth!"

Over and over and over again, even when the drugs were shutting down the lines. Even when his eyes were closed and his pulse had eased, still the peeled lips kept moving. The charred skin of the face twitched as though worms crawled through the muscles around his mouth. Always the same. Always about the fog that he'd seen, long months back, on his terrible journey into the peaked wilderness.

"Claws an' teeth."

The two-lane blacktop had given way to the broken and weed-infested concrete of a wider highway. It made for generally better motoring for the war wag, enabling Ches or Hunaker to drive on at a steady pace. All the doors were open and clean air flowed through the vehicle, purging it of the stench of sweat and death. Ahead of them, the mountains grew closer and more threatening. Their tops smoked with windblown snow.

Now and again they had to slow down because of the results of the great holocaust a hundred years before. Many times the solid road turned into corrugated ribbons of distorted stone from the effect of the nuking. Bridges were often down, embankments collapsed.

''Claws an' teeth.''

Once, with Ches at the helm, face taut with concentration, they maneuvered along a ledge through an earth-slip, with less than a hand's span either side. On the right a wall of glistening gray mud, speckled with fragments of dolomitic limestone. On the left, a long, long drop to a tumbling river. The Trader was still spending most of the time in his bunk, his coughing fits audible to everyone in the war wag. J.B. and Ryan Cawdor shared the leadership of the party, taking six hours on and six off.

Apart from the Trader's declining health and Kurt's raving madness, the war wag was running smoothly. Every cog turned as it should, and everyone knew his or her role. Krysty was wise enough to keep out of the way, offering help when she could. The only other outsider was the stranger called Doc.

Once they were safely away from Strasser and his murderous sec men, J.B. and Ryan told Koll to bring the old man to them in the nav room.

''Here he is.'' He deposited the shambling wreck at the door.

''Leave him be. Close that door, Koll.''

Doc's fingers knotted nervously like newborn rattlers. It was the first occasion that Ryan had been able to find a little time to speak to Doc and Ryan studied him. There was something about the man...something in addition to his brain-blasted condition that Ryan could not put a finger on.

"Sit down," said J.B., motioning to one of the steel-and-canvas chairs.

"I am most obliged, sir. Most obliged."

"You're called Doc? And Teague and Strasser treated you like shit."

"Indeed, I fear that there is considerable truth in that terse observation, Mr...."

"Cawdor. I'm Ryan Cawdor. This here is J. B. Dix, the weapons master on the war wag."

Doc made a courtly bow, removing the battered hat from his thinning gray hair, which hung around his shoulders like an unhealthy growth on rotting meat. His boots were cracked and worn. The shirt was faded to the palest of yellows and his coat was torn and smeared with what looked to Ryan like gobbets of pig shit. Yet, despite all that, the old man had style.

"I'm delighted to make your acquaintances, gentlemen. Forgive me that I'm not able to show my gratitude in a more positive way, but I am temporarily a little short of funds, or I would not have hesitated...hesitated to...to seek...I fear..." His hand went to his brow and he attempted a conciliatory smile. "The words have somewhat trickled away from me down the culverts of time."

Ryan stood suddenly, intending to pass Doc a mug of water. But the old man recoiled, hands flying to cover his face against the blow.

"No, don't...!"

"Doc, I'm not goin' to burnin' hurt you. Chill that kind of idea. This isn't Mocsin."

"Ah, Mocsin. Sweet pearl set in... Do you know what Mr. Teague and Mr. Strasser made me do if I displeased them in aught?"

"We don't want to talk about that," said J.B. "We're more interested in the Darks."

But Doc wasn't to be sidetracked. Once his mind set off, there was no checking him. Not until his thoughts reached some blind corner and then lurched into a siding.

"I was taken to the pigpens. I...I who was once... But I disremember that." There was a momentary pause. Then he continued, in the same, deep, rich baritone voice and the peculiarly old-fashioned way of speaking. "I was stripped and made to attempt carnal union with our porcine brethren." A ghost of a smile, revealing the excellent, strong white teeth. "Perhaps sisterhood is a better turn of phrase. Only when I had succeeded in such a union was I allowed free once more. This happened many, oh, so many times."

J.B. took off his thin-rimmed glasses and busied himself polishing them. If the old man hadn't been so damned tragic, Ryan would have smiled at the unusual sight of J. B. Dix lost for words.

"How did Teague get his blubberin' claws into you?" asked Ryan.

"I believe... Ah, I fear me that such things are lost in the far-off mists."

The door opened and Krysty appeared, the brightness of her hair flooding the nav room with crimson light. "Kathy says Kurt's goin', Ryan."

Very faintly Ryan heard "Claws an' teeth" from the main part of the war wag.

"I'll be along. Thanks."

Doc bowed at the appearance of the woman. But Krysty did not notice.

"Should I absent myself, Mr. Cawdor? Cawdor... I have the feeling I have heard the name before, but I confess that I think that about many things. The price of my age."

Ryan realized that the old man's brain was nine-tenths scrambled. It was amazing after what Strasser's evilly fertile imagination had done to the old man that he still lived and functioned. But there was no hope of getting any worthwhile or reliable information out of Doc.

Maybe one day?

"You can go, Doc. Talk to you again, huh?"

"It would be my pleasure, sir." Nodding to J.B., he added, "Mr. Dix, my best wishes."

In the doorway, the old man paused. "Did I understand you to say something about our ultimate destination? Our ultima Thule, perhaps, is what you call the Darks?"

"It is." Ryan caught J.B.'s eye. Maybe this was one of the glimmerings of sanity.

"Known, I believe, as one of the great parks of the nation. One nation, in ... How did it go? Glacier, that's it. That was the name of the Darks. Great hills, ice tipped. Ravines dark as graves. Water pure and clear. I think I have been to the Darks more than once." The man's brow furrowed and the eyes became veiled, their milky blues vanishing under a thin membrane.

"Doc? Go on."

"I fear I can no longer 'go on,' as you put it, Mr. Cawdor. There is nowhere to go. But in the Darks there were many wonders. Wonders of F to G and G to H and on from alpha to omega, they told me, but I saw only ... Saw what, I wonder. Ah, well."

Shaking his head, Doc walked through the door, reaching behind him and softly closing it. J.B. looked at Ryan.

"I'd have said he was crazed as an out-brain mutie. Then he ups and talks like he did just."

"You think it's all mutie talk?"

"Who knows?" J.B. shrugged, reaching for his leafy, crudely packed cheroots. "One of these days I'll give these things up. I'm told they'll kill me." Through the billowing smoke he reviewed the situation. "Seems from Doc, and Kurt and Krysty, that there might be somethin' secret up there. Maybe..."

"Maybe what? Come on, J.B. What?"

"This talk about *moving*. Suppose there really was a transmitter of matter. I've read about things like that in old books. It was fiction, of course, not fact. But if there was... I've seen them called 'jumpers' in books. Worth thinking on, old friend. A way of getting from Deathlands to the Western Islands in the wink of an eye. Or from the Baronies out east to beyond the Big Black Water. That, instead of weeks of danger in a war wag. Think on that."

Ryan stood up. "I've got to go see Kurt."

As he moved into the corridor, he could hear the screams of the dying blaster.

"The fog. Claws an' teeth!" But the voice was now weaker.

Out of one of the ob slits, Ryan stood and watched the setting sun on the left side of the war wag. The sky was dappled pink, streaked with shades of darker, menacing maroon. There was a big wind starting up outside and all the doors had been closed, but it was still possible to hear the muted whistling of the gale. Banks of trees all around them crowded up the edges of the ruined highway, most of them with their upper branches stunted or broken by the weather.

Once the doors were battened and bolted and the ob slits locked shut, the voices in the war wag became quieter and the oppression became a tangible thing, sitting on everyone's spirits.

Now, with a man dying, hardly anyone was talking. Those on duty were busy enough, but the rest either dozed or listened to tapes through the cans. Ryan eased his way along to the tiny sick bay. Generally it was not much used. In a firefight there were rarely any wounded.

Krysty was sitting on the edge of the bunk, wiping Kurt's forehead. Even in the past few hours the man had sunk. The mouth was relaxed, the eyes open. Even the babbling had finally stopped. The eyes followed Ryan as he moved into the room.

"How is he?" asked Ryan.

It was Kurt himself who answered. "He's near finally fucked, Ryan."

"Looks that way."

He was conscious that someone had come in behind them. Out of the corner of his eye Ryan recognized the shambling figure of Doc.

"Better here than back in hellsuckin' Mocsin, Ryan," said Kurt.

"Yeah."

"Man could choose worse company than this to die in."

"Guess so. Anythin' you want?"

"Mebbe a long drink and a tall blonde. No, make that...make that two of each." There was a dreadful spasm of strained breathing and the man's whole body racked upward, mouth gaping, the air hissing in his chest. Then Kurt lay still a moment, eyes fixed to Ryan's face. Finally his eyes closed and the flurried movement of his chest ceased. Ryan glanced across at Krysty, who shook her head and reached down to pull the gray blanket up over the blackened features.

"Gone beyond the river from which no man returns," said Doc quietly.

"He's chilled, Doc. The rest is crap. Life's just somethin' you lose."

"Ah, I was meaning to ask you, Mr. Cawdor, if by any chance any of your people had come across a possession of mine."

"What possession, Doc?"

"Plural, I think. There are two of them. Past tense. Were two of them. Small, gray spheroids, about . . . about so big." He held his fingers apart to indicate something roughly the size of an implode-stun grenade.

"Haven't seen them. What were they?"

Just for a moment a look of foxy cunning faded across the old man's wrinkled face. And went just as quickly. "Nothing of importance, my dear sir. Nothing at all."

The war wag bumped over a particularly deep rut, making the scalpels rattle in their shallow dishes. Doc adjusted his ancient hat, which he insisted on wearing despite being inside the war wag.

"Upon my soul, but these roads are not what they once were."

Ryan's eye opened wider. "How in the big fire d'you know what they were like before the nuke-outs?"

"Slip of the tongue," said Doc hastily. "I have read of these great roads, that is all." He rubbed his eyes with the stained cuff of his frock coat. "In the Darks, there was a dreadful fog!" His voice rose to an eldritch shriek that made Krysty jump, looking around her in concern.

"Mistake," he rambled on. "Escaped. Heads rolled. Fog like . . . like Cerberus."

"What the fuck's that?"

"A frightful hound of many ravening heads that guards the very mouth of Hades. Oh, yes, Cerberus. That was the name of the project. Once. Then it changed. Changed. A fog, Mr. Cawdor."

"A fog, in the Darks?"

"A fog. With claws and teeth. Such claws and teeth."

EVEN IN THAT PEACEFUL, desolate land, with not a single human being seen in three whole days, there was still the presence of death.

They had been forced into a swinging detour about one of the few hot spots in the region, around what had allegedly once been a town of seventy thousand souls called Grand Falls. It had been hit by Soviet missiles for its special industrial importance and power plants, and it was still a place to avoid, its ruins toxic.

Toward evening of the following day, Ryan received the message that the Trader wanted to speak to him. It was Krysty who conveyed it to him. With every day that passed the girl looked in better and better shape, all the horrors now behind her. She was wearing pale green overalls, with a bandolier of ammunition for her pistol that was crossed over with a broad leather belt that carried three leaf-bladed throwing knives. A larger knife hung on her right hip with a counter-draw holster for the automatic on the left side of the belt. The fiery hair was bright and lustrous, tumbling nearly to her narrow waist. The top of the overall was unbuttoned, showing the shadow of her breasts.

Ryan Cawdor found it increasingly difficult to conceal his desire for her. Asking himself whether it was desire or whether it was lust. The word *love* never entered his mind.

He followed her through the war wag, conscious of the click of the heels of her polished high boots and the movement of her buttocks against her outfit.

Doc was leaning against a wall near the Trader's cabin, his eyes hooded and far away. As Ryan squeezed by him, Doc spoke quietly.

"After the missiles had fallen, and the forty-fourth President was up in the 767, how did he begin his message to the States?"

Ryan pursed his lips. What went on under that craggy brow? Madness, or hidden intelligence?

"How did he begin his speech, Doc?"

"My fellow American! You understand it, Mr. Cawdor? In the singular. My fellow American!"

The cackling laughter followed him as Ryan stooped to enter the Trader's cramped room. He was met with the sour smell of illness. By the side of the bunk was a porcelain bowl splattered with blood and spittle. Torn rags, also stained crimson, lay on the floor. The Trader had always been a man of the fiercest pride, and now all that was done as his race neared its ending.

"Close the door, Ryan. I figure another two days at the most and we'll be in the Darks. I can taste the thin air. You know what to do?"

They had discussed the options, with J.B. sitting in, over the past three days, trying to cover every eventuality. Now there was no more planning or talking to do.

"It's in hand," replied Ryan.

The Trader's face was like a frail old man's, the skin taut as parchment over the cheekbones. The rad cancer was racing through him, devouring living tissue, eating up the hours.

"If there's anythin' after, then I'll be seein' ol' Marsh Folsom real soon, Ryan."

"I know it. We all do."

Trader nodded slowly. "Hear you told your name. Ryan Cawdor. Anyone recognize it?"

"No. Though Doc said he might have heard it. But he can't recall anything for more than a minute or so."

"Wish I had the time to chew over past days with him. Won't happen." Ryan thought the Trader was going to be overwhelmed by one of his coughing fits, but the moment passed. "Look 'round here, Ryan. What d'you see?"

"Spare clothes. Your Armalite. Handgun. Knives. Ammo. Grenades. Couple o' maps. Food you haven't eaten. Pack of cigars."

"That all?"

"Sure. What else should I see?"

"Get me a mouthful of water. Thanks. Nothin'. That's what else you should see. You listed it all, Ryan. It don't add up to much for better'n fifty years of livin'. Nothin' to add up to the pain of the mother that birthed me."

"What you've done isn't here, Trader. It's out yonder. Outside. You kept a lot of folks breathin' that would surely have been chilled."

"I chilled me some."

"Sure. They needed chilling. What you've done is to bring a little light to this pile of shit. Deathlands! If it hadn't been for you, then I'd have been dead. So would J.B., and everyone else in this war wag. You know it, Trader."

The two men remained silent, each locked into old memories. After some minutes the Trader reached out with a wasted, birdlike hand, and Ryan took it. Feeling the bones beneath the delicate skin, he held it gently, like a fledgling. As the war wag rumbled steadily northwest, the two old friends sat together in silence.

They were interrupted by the voice of Hunaker, crackling over the intercom. "Ryan. Ryan and J.B. Come to the driving console. Something you should see."

Chapter Fourteen

As HE MOVED FORWARD, Ryan felt the war wag judder to a halt, the engine out of gear, ticking over gently. On every side men and women had moved fast to their firefight positions, standing ready by the ob slits and weapon ports. But from the lack of urgency in Hun's voice, there clearly was no immediate emergency.

"What is it, Hun?"

"Look out front. Never seen nothin' like it. How 'bout you, J.B.?"

They squeezed in either side of her, peering through the forward screen. Ryan rested his hand on Hun's shoulder, conscious of the musky scent of her perspiration. He blinked his eye to rid himself of the sudden and unbidden image of Krysty, naked, moving beneath him.

"What is it?" he asked.

J.B., not one to waste words, simply shook his head. Hun pointed to the left, to the great jagged peaks of the Rockies jutting in toward them.

"Saw them first on this side. One or two. Feathers. Then this spooky kind of stuff."

Ryan was puzzled. Not many men had been this far into the Darks. The recently lamented Kurt was one of only a handful who had penetrated deep into the rugged fastness and survived. So who had put up all the decorations?

They were made out of branches of trees that Ryan believed were called aspens. "Quakers" they'd named them. Poles had been hewn from the silvery-green wood, with its criss-crossing black scars, then tied into shapes like the tepees that some of the double-poor of Deathlands lived in.

There were three of them, stretched across the crumbling relic of a road. The one nearest the edge was covered in a sprouting bunch of feathers. Red and yellow and golden-brown; hundreds of them. And topping it was a narrow-bladed knife of rusting iron, its haft wrapped in strips of what looked like dried leather or skin.

The right-hand tripod was leaning to the front, set close against a cliff of moss-streaked stone. Melt from a glacier, farther up the mountain, came cascading across the road in milky turquoise torrents. Tufted pink flowers decorated the poles, some of the flowers dead, drooping and falling on the damp earth.

But it was the center set of branches that caught Ryan's eye.

It was much the tallest, well over a tall man's height, blocking the trail. Ribbons of material were festooned all over it, tied in place with rawhide thongs. Small metal stars of brass and copper dangled from the silks and satins, chiming against one another.

And on the top, held in place with circling strands of green wire was— "A human head," said J.B.

The eyes had gone, and half the teeth were missing. The lower jaw dangled in a macabre leer, kept by a thread of gristle. There were still a few shreds of leathery skin clinging to the yellowed bone.

"What's that on its forehead?" asked Hun.

"Bullet hole," replied J.B.

"Looks like a warning," said Ryan.

"Do we stop, or go on, or what?"

"We go on."

War Wag One rolled forward again as Hun engaged the gears, driving straight for the center of the sets of aspen poles, crushing it beneath the heavy wheels. Ryan watched through the front screen, imagining he could hear the brittle crack as the skull was splintered, but through the armor he knew that was absurd.

In the next hour they came across three more sets of the weird signs. Both J. B. Dix and Ryan Cawdor stayed in the main control cabin, keeping the combat vehicle in a state of full fighting readiness with everyone on alert.

"How far?"

Hun threw the question over her shoulder. The trail ahead was becoming steeper, and the gauges showed a sharp temperature drop as night closed in on them.

Ryan eased the white scarf around his neck. "Not sure. All we can do is put together everything we know and add in Kurt's ravings an' what Krysty knew. Best map we have don't show us much. But if there's this Stockpile or Redoubt up there, then it's close to a place called Many Glaciers. Near as we can figure."

"We stoppin' soon?" Hunaker asked.

"Yeah. Give it another ten, then pull on over. That looks like a meadow along that river. Trees far enough back to cut down an ambush."

"What d'you think about those poles?" J.B. asked him, blowing out a perfect ring of smoke from the dark, evil-smelling cheroot.

"Warnin'. Some mutie religion trick. Maybe we're on someone's home turf. I've heard nothin' on any townies movin' up here."

Within a few minutes the huge war wag had finally pulled over for the night, and the usual sentries had been posted. Supper was cooking, and around a fire most of the

men and women in the team were making and mending—
cleaning armaments and repairing clothes.

Unusually in the Deathlands, the water was good. Ryan
walked down and sat down on a large boulder, riven by the
frosts, and flicked pebbles into the river. Alongside the
rocks were patches of creamy Indian paintbrush and
splashes of golden vetch, absurdly rich, their colors still
bright in the last shards of the evening sun. The sky was a
sullen red, streaked with wind-torn clouds in gray and
purple. Over the tops of the highest range of mountains
there was the usual silver lace of lightning.

Ryan Cawdor was not a man given to endless agonizing
and self-doubts. But on this beautiful evening he felt a rare
sense of melancholy. Things were changing. The majority
of his friends had been chilled within the past week, and
now Trader's race was damned near run. Whatever happened up in the topmost trails of the Darks, it would mean
an ending of the old ways of life that had been his ways for
over ten years.

"You look like a prickless mutie in a gaudy-house,
Ryan."

"Hi, Krysty. Guess Trader's sickness has really gotten
to me. He was almost like a father, if that don't make me
sound like a stupe."

She sat down by him, stretching out her long legs, staring at her own reflection in the polished leather of her
boots. "You don't sound like a stupe. I've only known the
Trader a short while, but he's . . . somethin' special."

On the farther side of the valley, up a slope of rough
scree, Ryan caught a flicker of movement. His rifle was still
in the war wag, but his pistol flowed into his fingers without any conscious thought, only to be holstered again
when he recognized the white blur as one of the hardy

mountain goatlike creatures that thrived near the tree line in the Darks.

A bright blue bird with a spiky crest came to drink near them, dipping its beak into the water in delicate, jerky movements. The smell of cooking stew came on the breeze to them.

"Hungry?" Ryan asked, turning his head quickly, finding that Krysty was sitting closer than he'd thought. So close that their noses almost touched and her veil of crimson hair brushed lightly against his cheek.

Her green eyes drilled into his and she half opened her mouth, saying nothing. Despite the cool of the evening, Ryan was perspiring.

It was utterly inevitable that they should kiss. And having kissed should kiss again, and again. His hand was holding the back of her neck, and her hair seemed almost to caress his fingers. His tongue thrust between her parted lips, and her sharp teeth nipped him, so gently. His right hand slipped down the rough material of her overalls, finding the zipper, lowering it in a whisper of movement. He felt the warm swell of her breast as his palm cupped it, and the nipple harden like a tiny animal. Her own hands were delving under the long coat, but the wealth of guns and the panga hindered her from reaching and touching him.

"Ryan..." she panted. "Please, can...?"

"Where? In the war wag?"

"No!" Vehemently. "Not in there. Out here where you can breathe free. Over there, in those trees beyond the river."

Caution, and the memory of those odd totemic warning signs, made him hesitate. But his desire overcame all resistance and he took her by the hand and they walked together, jumping a narrow brook, finding a space of cropped grass alongside a quiet pond. Trees hid them from the war wag, and the gathering darkness kept their secret.

It was too cold for them to strip, but she wriggled out of the overalls, and he pulled off the dark gray denim trousers, laying the LAPA ready to hand.

They were both desperate enough not to waste time on any preliminaries and he rolled on top while she guided him into her. Krysty moaned softly as Ryan penetrated her, thrusting, feeling her moistness and heat close around him. She locked her heels in the small of his back, drawing him deeper, pushing up with her hips at his steel-hard maleness.

They reached a juddering, simultaneous climax, and he lay down on her, his face buried in her neck, panting as if he had run a long distance race across broken ground. She touched him on the side of the face, kissing him with an infinite tenderness.

"That was so good, Ryan. So good that I'd like to do it again."

The second time, later, in the velvet blackness of the forest, was slower. They explored each other's body with fingers and lips, touching and arousing each other. Finally he lay back, the short grass prickling his buttocks as she straddled him, lowering herself teasingly slowly, so that the tip of his erect penis touched and entered and then withdrew. Until she smiled and enveloped him, throwing her head back as she pumped and rose and fell. The girl's mouth opened and she sighed with the pleasure of their lovemaking, her teeth white as wind-washed bone in the twilight.

The second orgasm was without the hurry of the first, and for many minutes after they lay tangled in each other's arms. The night's cold stole over them and eventually they broke apart and pulled on their clothes.

"They'll be lookin' for us," said Ryan.

"Not if they guess that we . . . Look, there, beyond that fallen tree."

Ryan followed her finger, reaching for the pistol, then checking the movement. Some hundred paces away from them, only a smudge of light against the dark trees, he saw a man. Standing silently watching them.

"Who is he?"

"Looks like a mutie." The man was old, and as Ryan's eye adjusted to the night, he could make him out more clearly. Barely medium height, with silver-white hair tied in two long braids, each with a scrap of red ribbon knotting it at the end. He wore a robe of some kind of animal hide, and it was decorated with a staggeringly complex design in multihued threads and silks. His face was dark, the eyes hidden in the deep sockets.

In the hair was a single feather, white as fresh snow.

Even as they watched him, the old man moved back a couple of paces and then vanished among the pines behind him. It was done with great grace. Suddenly the space where he had been was empty.

"Goin' after him?" asked Krysty.

"No. Could be a trap. Maybe he's the one who put them signs up, warnin' us to stay away."

They moved fast, back to the safety of the war wag. Ryan's hand never left the butt of the automatic. Nobody said anything about their absence, although Ryan caught Hunaker giving a sly wink to Samantha.

IN THE MORNING the Trader had gone.

The only person who had seen him leave was Abe, who had been on guard on the river side of the war wag. Everyone gathered around the lanky man as he reported to J.B. and Ryan Cawdor, just after dawn.

"No warnin', but he was behind me. I turns and he pats me on the shoulder, like he did when you'd done somethin' real good. Know what I mean? I says to him, like, how's he doin' and he says he's never better."

"What was he wearing?" asked J.B.

"Usual. Carryin' that old Armalite of his. Steppin' good, not stooped like he's been. No cough. Looks past me to the trees and the snow up beyond. Real cold. I seen his breath plumin' out. Says he's goin' for a walk, and not to take on if he's gone some time. That was about three, maybe four hours back." Abe shook his head, the long flowing hair moving from side to side. "He sure looked pretty to me, up and walkin' tall."

"He say anythin' at all, apart from that?"

"No, Ryan. But he did say there was a letter for you. Said he'd got a scribbler to write it weeks back when we was on the road to Mocsin."

Ryan spun on his heel to go and look for the letter. But Abe coughed.

"Yeah?"

"There's one other thing, Ryan. But it's kind of stupid."

"Go on."

Abe glanced away. "No. Mebbe in a while. I got to think on it some. Go read your note."

It didn't take long.

It was on the steel table in the corner of the Trader's cabin. The edges of the handmade paper were crinkled. The letter was stained with machine oil and what looked like ketchup smeared over the bottom half. Because of his own illiteracy, the Trader had been forced to get a writer to produce the note for him. Which may have led to its brevity and lack of emotion.

Or it may just have been the way the Trader was.

"Hi Ryan," it began.

If you're reading this then it means I'm dead. This rad cancer's been eating my guts for months and I know there's no stopping it. So this is me saying goodbye and the best of luck. If it goes the way I hope, I'll just walk away one night so don't you blasted come after me. Please. That's the Trader asking and not ordering, Ryan, old friend. We've been some places and done some good and bad things. Now it's done. That's all. I thank you for watching my back for so many years. You and J.B. watch for each other.

There was no signature.

So he'd done it. Ended his life in the same quietly efficient way he'd run it. Minutes later, as Ryan walked through the war wag, there were several of the women, and some of the men, red eyed. Samantha was weeping on the shoulder of Hennings. Rintoul was clicking his fingers in a nervous, abstracted way, and Finnegan's usual good nature had vanished.

"Break this up," called Ryan, making them jump and turn hostile faces his way. "Trader went as he wanted. Save your sorrow."

Outside in the freshness of morning the rising sun was tipping the hills to the west, turning the snow to blood. Abe was sitting on the ground, nursing his own M-16 rifle, gazing out across the river toward the forest. Ryan hunkered alongside him.

"Tell me, Abe."

"What?"

"You was goin' to tell me. Somethin' that Trader said or did. At the last?"

"No. Wasn't like that. I told you all he said. Then he just walked off, over there." He pointed with the muzzle of the gun.

"Then what?"

"I thought I saw somethin' there. Just by that ridge of light rock, over toward where that pond lies."

Ryan followed the man's stubby finger, seeing that he was pointing in the general direction of where he and Krysty had made love the previous evening.

"This was before Trader went or after?"

"Like after. I seen him walkin' away, and there was a good moon up, so he showed clear. I watched, and then I saw this thing up there, like it was waitin' for the Trader. First I figured he . . ."

"A man?"

"I'm tellin' ya, Ryan. I figured he might be one of the muties that done the feathers and skulls and stuff, so I get a bead on him, ready to ice him. Then I see the Trader lift a hand to him, and this old man lifts a hand back. They meet up and go under the trees and that's all I see. No danger, so I don't raise a warnin' for everyone. Then, the Trader . . . he don't come back."

"Tell me about this man. This old man, you said. What was he like?"

"He had silver hair in braids, one on each side. And a long coat with some fancy patterns on it."

"Anything else?"

"Yeah. I saw it through the scope in the moonlight. In his hair, the old man had a long white feather."

NOBODY EVER SAW THE OLD MAN with the white feather in his hair. Nor was the Trader ever seen again.

Chapter Fifteen

THE ROADS HIGH IN THE DARKS were as bad as anything any of them had ever seen. Bucketing ribbons of twisted concrete vanished into rivers and never came out again. Whole slabs of the hillsides had melted during earth tremors a century ago. They were looking for the remains of a township shown on their tattered maps as Babb, but the devastation was so total that they had little hope of finding it. Lakes had filled in where there should have been dry land, and tiny feeder streams had become howling torrents of angry melt water.

The greater the elevation, the slower their progress. The farther they went, the worse the weather became. The night skies clouded over and the fearsome chem clouds of nuclear detritus billowed about them, with incandescent bursts of flame searing the tops of the peaks. The great northerly winds came screeching in from the desert wastes that had once been the fruitful prairies of Canada. It took them four grindingly oppressive days to get close to the tree line, finding that great fires had raged through the pine forests, stripping the land, leaving the soil to be eroded to bare rock and ice. The dials in the war wag showed a daytime high of minus ten Celsius, with the night temperatures dropping fast to minus thirty. Add in the windchill factor and you had a land where a man would be dead within minutes if he didn't have adequate thermal protection.

Ryan was dozing in his bunk when a particularly vicious jolt woke him. As he stood he was aware that they had stopped moving and the engine now ticked over in neutral. He was on his way to the control room before Ches started calling him over the intercom.

J.B. was there before him.

"End of the line," he said.

Ryan looked out the front screen, seeing only gray ice and swirling snow. The road, if there was one there at all, was invisible.

"Not even the war wag can get us farther," said Ches, leaning back in the padded seat. "The trail's gotten way too narrow. Looks like one track in and the same one out. So there's no point goin' back and tryin' some other way."

"How far from where the Redoubt might be?" asked Ryan, biting his lip in impatient anger. To have come all this way and fail so near to their destination only added to the concern he already felt about their supplies, and Ryan was angry. Gas would be running low in about a week, and way up here in the Darks there wouldn't be caches hidden away for them. The Trader had made sure that throughout the Deathlands there were plenty of such caches, buried deep and safe. But not this far north into the blighted country.

Cohn was hunched over his mapping table and he replied to Ryan's question. "Way I see it . . . from what you said and the redhead said and most of all from what that poor bastard Kurt said, it should be ahead about a day's climb. Someplace."

"That's a lot of hellfired help, Cohn. What the hell does 'someplace' mean?"

"Sorry, Ryan. Just that my map's all worn and patched. Looks like 'Grinning Glacier,' best I can see. Steep trail over where a lake used to be. Who knows what's there now?"

J.B. turned from the screen. "Time our feet earned their living, Ryan. Let's go talk."

TEN.

That was the final number for the party, reached after better than an hour of discussion. J.B. had wanted to keep it smaller, but Ryan had pushed for more to be included. And both of them wanted to come on the expedition, insisting that the other should remain in charge of the war wag.

In the end it was Cohn, the most experienced member of the unit, who was delegated to take command while Ryan and J.B. led the trek toward . . . Toward what?

Krysty had to come, and so, Ryan insisted, did Doc. Whatever there might be up behind the fog with teeth and claws, Doc seemed to know something about it. And something was all they had. The remainder of their team were Hunaker, Koll, Hennings, Abe, the man called Finnegan and a top blaster, Okie. She was a tall, silent girl whose skill with any firearm was legendary on the war wag.

Cohn's orders were simple and explicit.

"Keep in radio contact. Twenty-four-hour watch on the emergency frequency. Four guards out, turn and turn about each hour. Full alert all the time. Keep her locked up tighter than a Baron's cred chest."

And then the most important part of it.

"If we're back, then we'll be here in four days. Call it a flat hundred hours. Unless you hear from us to abort this command, after one hundred hours precise, you push the boot to the floor and give her the gas and get out. From then on you're on your own.''

''What about a relief party?'' Cohn asked J.B. and Ryan.

''There won't be one, you stupe bastard,'' snarled Ryan. ''Hundred hours and we're not back, you go.''

''Where?''

''Watch my lips, Cohn,'' interjected J. B. Dix. ''We go. You stay. We come back in less'n a hundred hours, all fine. If not, then War Wag One is yours. And you'll be low on gas and supplies, so get out fast. Now just nod your head if you understand.''

''Sure,'' Cohn replied with a nod. ''That's fine. I'll be here like you say. And if there's problems, call it in.''

Each member of the team carried a pistol and rifle of their own choice. Each carried four grenades on the belts, a mix of incendiary, stun, implosion, high-ex, shrap, nerve gas and smoke. Each of them had a knife or edged weapon of his or her choosing, ranging from Krysty's delicate throwing knives in her bandolier to Finnegan's butcher's cleaver that would take the head off a horse in one blow.

They carried enough food for five days, with a small supply of water-pure tabs. Ammunition supplied most of the weight to their packs, along with a radio operated by Henn. No spare clothes or sleeping gear. There was no room for that kind of comfort.

They agreed that the best time to leave was around dawn the next day. Koll was designated to take charge of Doc, whose mind still vacillated between extremes of brief clarity and long spells of catatonic madness. His only response when Ryan Cawdor told him that they were planning on going toward the hidden Redoubt was to smile and bow, his hat nearly falling off. Krysty had managed to sew some strong elasticized cord for him to use when they ventured outside into the gales. He'd refused any helmet or goggles like the others, saying that a scarf for his throat would suffice.

"Suffice" was the word he'd used. Now he just asked Ryan about the guard dog.

"What dog? You mean the fog, Doc?"

"No. I speak of the canine deterrent... Ah, what memories that word brings back to me, Mr. Cawdor."

"What memories?"

A look of pain flitted across the aquiline features of the old man. "Sadly, that has escaped me, sir. But I believe there was something about a dog."

That night Krysty came to Ryan in his bunk, and they managed, despite the tightness of the accommodation, to make slow, tender love three times before reveille finally woke them.

Farewells were short and formal. During the years that Ryan Cawdor had ridden with the Trader he had seen literally dozens of relationships formed and broken in the war wag. Many formed from loneliness and fear. Many broken by death.

Ryan noticed Hun taking a long time in quiet talk with a little girl called Sukie who had only joined War Wag One from Three a day or so before the fall of Mocsin as a relief gunner on the mortar.

For the rest it was mainly a quick shake of the hand and a muttered word. Ryan had once seen a scratchy antique vid about some Westerners in a fort. Or had it been a church? There they were taking last messages to families and loved ones. That didn't arise in the Deathlands. Either your family and loved ones were on War Wag One or they weren't anywhere.

"What's the weather, Cohn?"

"Minus fifteen. Wind around fifty, from north, veering east. Some hail in it."

Ryan rubbed at the stubble on his chin. "Sounds a fine day for a short walk in the Darks. Be seein' you, Cohn."

"Good luck, Ryan. Give the bastards broken teeth." The two men shook hands and the main entry port slid open, letting in a flurry of snow and a biting wind. Ryan pulled up his goggles and exited with a jump, waving for the others to follow him. Ice crunched beneath his boots. While he waited he glanced down, seeing the mark on the right toe where a rabid dog had tried to bite his foot off. It had taken a 3-round burst from the LAPA to blow the mongrel away.

Between his feet, in a small hollow sheltered among some scattered pebbles, he noticed a tiny bunch of flowers. White petals, with a heart yellow as butter. Surviving in one of the least hospitable places on earth. For a reason that he couldn't explain, the sight of the frail plant lifted his spirits.

He tucked the weighted silk scarf around his neck, trying to fill the chinks where the wind was thrusting icy water. He took a quick finger count to make sure the group was all there. Nine. With J. B. Dix bringing up the rear as ten.

After fifty paces Ryan turned around, bracing himself against the driving gale, squinting back at where he knew the war wag was. But it had already disappeared in the general whiteout. Without a compass he knew that they had absolutely no chance of ever finding it again.

The track was very rough, often barely visible, and the weather was worse than he had anticipated. But after a half hour they rounded the massive corner of an overhanging bluff and the wind dropped dramatically.

"Way Kurt called it, there's a half day's walk to get to where the fog was waitin'."

"I am of the decided opinion that the fog will still be here and waiting for all comers, Mr. Cawdor," said Doc. His cheeks were almost blue from the biting cold of the wind, yet beads of perspiration hung in the deep furrows of his cheeks, glistening in the stubble on his chin.

"You know that?" asked J.B.

"It is an axiom of some veracity that a good guard dog never sleeps. Cerberus was assuredly of the best, Mr. Dix."

"Every piece cocked," instructed Ryan. "Round under the pin. Fingers—"

"On triggers," finished Okie, unsmiling. "We know that, Ryan."

They went on.

The road, if that's what it had once been, wound and twisted like a broken-backed adder, clinging to the edge of the ice-sheeted cliffs, a dizzy abyss plunging away to their left. At one bend Ryan held up a gloved fist, halting the party, waving them forward.

"What do you see?" asked Hennings, his dark skin pallid against the black fur hood.

"Down there," replied Ryan, pointing to where the tumbling waters of a river in flood tore over gray boulders. Visible now and again through the gusted clouds of snow were the red and brown metal bones of several vehicles. Torn and twisted, spotted with ice and blown spume. It was impossible to make out what they might once have been, but there could have been three or four of them. One large rusting chunk of iron might have been the rear suspension members of a large truck.

"Someone didn't make the turn," said Finnegan.

"Dolfo Kaler," suggested J.B. "Kurt talked about broken trucks an' all. They're what's left of Kaler's expedition after the Redoubt up here."

"Which means the fog that has teeth and claws is around just a couple more corners," said Krysty Wroth. She stood close against Ryan, shivering at the cold.

She was nearly right.

It was only one corner.

Waiting, quiet and immense. As Ryan cautiously waved the others forward to his side, the words of Doc came back to him. It *was* like some gigantic, patient guard dog. Crouched on the rutted surface of the track, among the snow-filled pits and hollows, it throbbed.

"There is Cerberus," whispered Doc. Behind them the wind still howled and the air was still filled with needled chips of ice swirling from the leaden sky. But on this stretch the wind was gone, echoing behind them but not before. Here it was preternaturally quiet.

Ryan gazed at it, filled with an awe that came close to fear. In all his life he had never seen anything like it. The fog squatted on the road, at least the forward part of it did, and behind it rose vastly above them until it merged with the sky. It was impossible for Ryan to guess its height. Despite the wind all around them the fog did not move, beyond a gentle rocking, pulsing movement that seemed to be generated somewhere within its enormous bulk. It looked as though a light glowed somewhere within it, like some settlement glimpsed at a great distance through mist.

He took a few cautious steps toward it, and the swaying increased. The whole mass moved the equivalent paces toward him. Tendrils came creeping from its base, edging along the road in his direction. They stopped moving as he did.

Hunaker threw back her hood, ice gathering immediately on her short, green hair. "Let me waste this shit with my rifle!" she shouted.

Immediately the fog reacted, swooping with its sinuous fingers down toward them, sending them all scurrying quickly back along the trail, back toward the bend. The fog reached to within a few steps of where Hunaker had been standing, then seemed to gather itself together and resume its previous condition, swaying smugly within.

"If I might proffer a small suggestion, Miss Hunaker?" began Doc.

"What? How 'bout, don't make any fuckin' noise or threaten it or even go close to it?"

"Those were my thoughts, dear lady. Those were indeed my thoughts."

While it had been just Kurt's ravings, or the mythic words of Krysty and Doc, it had not seemed as if it would be such a problem. Ryan had somehow thought that they'd walk through it or climb around it. Confident that once he saw it, assuming it really existed, it would just be a minor problem like hundreds of others, and with an easy solution. Now that he stood so close to it, he realized that this was in fact a form of primal force that functioned in ways that he had no idea about.

"Now what?" J.B. muttered.

Ryan unzipped his coat. Despite the ice and the bitter wind, he found that he was sweating freely. "Who knows," he said angrily.

Dix widened the question. "Anyone? How about you, Doc? You know about this bitching thing?"

"Not to put too fine a point upon it, young man, I am as much in the dark as you. I believe this is here to keep malefactors away from the Redoubt and the gate."

Ryan noted the word *gate* and filed it away as something to ask about later. If there got to be a later.

"We could try some grenades," suggested Okie.

"Could do," Ryan said. "Gotta think. No other trail. Not one that we could ever hope to find. It's this or nothin'. And there's no way under it. It hangs over the edge of that sheer cliff. There's no way over it. So you want to know what I think? I think one of the Barons out east's got him a chopper. If we just had that..."

"If we had a balloon we could float up and over it," said Koll. "But we don't."

So they tried grenades.

High-ex and incendiary looked the best bets. No point in wasting shrap or nerve against a fog.

The hand bombs made a load of noise and some fire. The flames seemed muffled by the fog and the high-ex did nothing at all that anyone could make out. Some rocks and ice from high above them came rolling down, pattering on the road. The fog retreated about as far as a man could spit, then came back. Back toward them, stopping at the bend of the trail, becoming a huge wall, almost as if it had been cut clean with a giant's cleaver.

Doc had sat down, drawn and pale, looking as though the confrontation with the fog had exhausted him. He felt Ryan's eye on him and clambered up, pulling himself to a standing position with his hands on the rock face.

"My apologies, sir, but all the noise and fire has quite..." The eyes cleared as though a veil had been ripped from them. "Antimatter, Mr. Cawdor. I believe that might do the trick. Implode, and the foul fiend will be undone—it will separate from its source."

J.B. banged one gloved fist into the other. "Implosion grenade. Turn that chiller inside out. Yeah. Koll?"

"What?"

"You got the implo?"

"Yeah. Couple."

"Go hurl them into the middle of that bastard fog. Right in, far as you can throw."

"Sure," said Ryan. "You got about the best arm, Koll. Go close as you can, then get the heat out of there."

Koll lowered his hood, wiping tiny gems of steel-gray ice from his long mustache. He unhooked the two implosion bombs, with their distinctive scarlet and blue bands around their dull tops.

"Chill it, Koll," whispered Hunaker, patting him on the arm.

The towering mist, with the strange pale light throbbing at its center, had retreated once more until it hung precisely where they had first seen it, countless small tendrils creeping from its base as though tasting the air for the scent of an enemy.

Koll crouched like a runner readying for a sprint, a grenade in each fist. He drew in a number of deep breaths, composing himself. Ryan stood at his heels.

"Not *too* close, Koll. No dead heroes on War Wag One, remember."

Koll nodded his blond head. Five more breaths, faster and more shallow. He powered himself up the trail, boots sending chips of stone and ice flying back into the watching group. For some seconds the fog showed no sign of awareness of the threat. Then it began to move.

Faster than before.

Koll skidded to a halt less than fifty steps from the nearest tentacle of the fog, looking up at its shimmering bulk for a second or two, as if he was hypnotized.

"Now!" yelled Ryan Cawdor at the top of his voice. Breaking the spell.

Koll lobbed the first of the implo bombs into the fog. For one sickening moment Ryan wondered if it would simply stick there, like a pebble in fresh dough, but it vanished deep within. The second one followed it, thrown with all Koll's most desperate strength.

"Back," said Doc calmly, speaking in a conversational tone to the eight others who stood near him. He led the way by shambling quickly around the bend of the trail, behind the rock wall.

"Koll!" shouted Ryan. "Get the..." but the words died in his throat and for a moment he closed his eye, turning away.

The fog had sensed the threat to its existence. The tendrils had shot from its base, faster than a shooter drawing his blaster. They slapped at Koll's feet and legs, before he could take more than a half dozen steps toward safety.

Ryan was the last of the party to move with Doc out of sight, and he saw it all. As the first coiling arm of the fog touched Koll, sparks flew from the man's flesh. Orange and blue fire sprayed out into the cold day as if from a welder's torch. Koll dropped his rifle and screamed, rolling onto his back and kicking. For the briefest of moments he managed to break free from the caressing tendril.

One fell across him, not hard, but more flames spat from Koll's body, at the top of his thighs, near the groin. He arched back, and the scream rose higher and higher. Smoke and the smell of burning filtered through the crackling air. The screams continued, thin and piercing, like a stallion's at the gelding.

Another tendril lashed at Koll's face and he raised his hands to take the impact, thrashing at the unknown power. Now there were a dozen or more of the thick gray tendrils enshrouding him, cording and swelling. Koll was lifted into the air by them, drawn toward the main expanse of the fog.

All this occurred within the eternity of seconds before the first of the implo grenades went off, followed a second later by the other. Ryan ducked away at the familiar hollow boom, bracing himself for the bizarre sucking feeling that came from the antimat bombs. He and the Trader had found a small supply of them years ago in a ravaged Redoubt close to the great swamps where once the Mississippi had rolled. Nobody, not even J. B. Dix, greatest of armorers, understood what they did. All that was obvious was that they caused an implosion and matter was pulled into a vacuum of limitless smallness.

Ryan looked back around the cliff immediately after the noise had faded. The fog was coiling and shredding as he watched. It seemed to be disappearing into frail towers that crumbled in on themselves. In less than a dozen heartbeats the dreadful monster had completely gone, leaving nothing but the cold wind and driven hail.

"Cerberus was a sentient creature, and designed precisely thus, Mr. Cawdor. Yet it was weak precisely where it needed to be strong. Now it is gone, my dear sir, and taking that poor fellow with it. Who cried so loud, did he not?"

Koll had disappeared with the double implosions. At least most of him had.

His right arm, two fingers missing, with the shoulder and neck and much of the right side of the lower skull, still lay in the middle of the mangled roadway. The survivors walked up the trail, pausing by the remains of the corpse. The missing fingers had been sliced away as though with a razor, and the rest of the torn flesh was cleanly severed. Both eyes were gone, as had the top of the nose. The jaw had been hewn through by an unimaginable force, and the flesh of the cheek and chin was laced with a pattern of tiny burns and scorch marks. The teeth were splintered to powder in the jaw.

Taking into account the massive injuries, there was very little blood.

''We goin' to leave him here like this for the wolves and bears?'' asked Sukie, trembling with shock.

''No. Can't bury him. In the river, J.B.?''

''Best we can do.''

As gently as they could, the two men stooped and gathered up the remains of the man who had been one of the strongest of the crew of the war wag. Swinging the dismembered mass once and then heaving it as far out as they could into the singing void, they watched as it fell into the river and joined the waters that flowed from the glacier way up above them.

They stood mutely for several seconds. Ryan broke the spell by turning to lead them up the trail. Now that the fog had vanished, he noticed a peculiar thing. On their side of the barrier, the road was in terrible condition, puckered and scratched. A hundred paces or so higher up it was in perfect condition. Smooth and flat, unbroken by the century of neglect, untouched by weeds. It went straight for a while, then curved sharply to the right, as though it ran into the face of the cliff.

Neat, rectangular white stones lined the side of the road, marking off the edge of the ravine. There was even the remains of a white line painted down the center of the trail. The nine men and women walked slowly along, cautiously checking all around them. Ryan stopped when he heard Doc start to chuckle.

''What in the big fire's so funny, Doc?''

''My apologies, sir, but the sight of us all stepping as if we walked upon the shells of eggs is risible. You see, the fog with its claws and its teeth will have kept everyone out for a hundred years. And those within are surely deceased. So where is the threat?''

''We're in. Someone else might be in,'' replied J. B. Dix.

"Only if they were watching and have followed us. And I doubt there are many people in this part of the Darks."

"What about them feathers and the skull and all that stuff?" asked Abe.

That silenced Doc's laughter.

Though the wind kept howling about them, the ferocious cold of the past few days was gone, and none of them put up their hoods again. Doc kept one hand on his ancient hat. The air was notably fresher and Ryan noticed that none of them was sweating now, as they had been in the presence of the fog.

Okie strode forward to join Ryan at the front of the group. Her dark hair was tied back like Abe's and she kept one hand always near the butt of her pistol. When she spoke her voice had a distinctive Eastern twang to it.

"What d'you figure we'll find in this stockpile? Gas? Bombs? More guns?"

Ryan grinned. *"¿Quien sabe?"*

"What?"

"Means who knows. Picked it up from a Mex mutie down south. But whatever's there has to be good to be guarded like that."

"And nobody to stop us," she said.

There was a faint hissing and a dull thunk. A gasp. Ryan spun on his heel in time to see Abe dropping to his knees, hands to his throat. His neck was pierced clean through with the shaft of an arrow, tipped with bright red feathers.

Chapter Sixteen

HENNINGS AND KRYSTY were first to the stricken man, while the others, weapons drawn, faced around, their blazing eyes seeking the enemy. But there was nobody to be seen. The cliffs towered above them, with pockets of snow scattered here and there. The road wound beneath them, and the sheer drop to the river was still at their other flank. Ahead, somewhere, was the mythical Redoubt.

"Where?" snapped Ryan.

J.B. pointed up and behind. "Arrow came from there. He's behind us. Or they're behind us."

"How is he?" He moved to stand where Krysty cradled Abe in her arms. The shaft, with its barbed tip, still stuck through his throat at a grotesque angle, blood trickling from both sides. The shaft was made of some sort of aluminum compound. It was streaked crimson. The feathers were the same kind as they had seen on the warning totems.

Henn looked up. "Bad, Ryan. Bad."

Abe was fighting for breath, fingers moving convulsively on Krysty's sleeve. Her bright red hair framed his pale face. His eyes flickered, seeking Ryan, finding him.

"Doesn't hurt..." he said, voice muffled with the blood that was now seeping through his lips. "But a blasted arrow, for nuke's sake! Be funny—" he coughed a great gout of arterial scarlet "—funny if..."

Another shaft came slicing through the air, pinging off the road and vanishing over the edge into the gorge beyond. A third arrow came, striking a spark as it struck the stone, missing Krysty by a hand's span.

"Got to move, Ryan," J.B. barked. "They'll pick us off."

The rules of the war wag had always been simple. If you can save the wounded, then you do it. But if you can't...

"Leave him," Ryan said. "Sorry, Abe."

If it had been some muties, especially stickies, then Ryan would have put a bullet through the man's temple. It looked as if Abe was dying, but there was a chance the attackers might save him. Better than no chance at all.

"Go," called Ryan, then strode ahead to lead the way in a zigzag, dodging run up the road.

Immediately the arrows came whispering after them, biting into the track. But by keeping moving and swerving, none of them was hit. Ryan risked a glance over his shoulder at a bend in the trail, seeing to his shock that there were about forty or fifty men after them, most with bows. Oddly, not a single one was carrying a rifle. If one of them had a light MG or even a machine pistol, they could have sprayed the road and wiped half of Ryan's force away.

They appeared to be short, squat men, wearing what looked at a glance to be leather.

"We could hold 'em here!" shouted J.B., pointing to where a fall of white rock had half closed the road.

"They might get above us. Keep goin'!"

Another hundred paces and the arrows were less frequent. And around another turn of the trail, there it was.

The trail widened to a huge plateau, wide enough for a dozen war wags to turn in comfort, with the stubby remains of a metal fence ringing it. And at the far end was a high gate, made of gleaming metal, showing through peeling paint. All around, on posts, on the walls, and on the gate itself, were the faded, illegible remains of notices.

"That's it."

Ryan had seen enough Stockpiles in his time to be certain that this was what they were after.

The gate was corrugated metal, showing that it folded back. Okie was there first, reaching and tugging at the handle, polished by the years of tearing gales.

"Locked!" she cried.

Henn was there next, throwing his great strength to help her. But they failed to shift it. The man called Finnegan and J.B. were next, all heaving and straining at the door, trying to get it open. Hun and Krysty, her overalls sodden with Abe's blood, arrived to help, but there was not enough room for them to get a grip.

Ryan brought up the rear, supporting Doc, whose legs had gone so that he sagged like a strawman, the breath rasping in his chest. Twice he had panted for Ryan to leave him, but Ryan was grateful for Doc's tip regarding the fog and aimed to keep this source of good information as close to him as he could. Despite the madness, Doc knew things. Things buried deep, maybe, but things that might save them all.

"Here they come," warned J.B., dropping to his knees and readying his favorite Steyr AUG 5.56 mm.

"Krysty," Ryan called, "you and Henn keep tryin' the door. Watch for Doc. The rest, let's chill the bastards."

With the Redoubt at their backs, the door towering sheer above them, there was no longer anywhere to run. Ryan's lips peeled back from his teeth in a vulpine snarl of anger and hatred. He directed it at their enemy.

"Come on, you sons of hellsuckin' bitches," he hissed. "Dyin' time's arrived."

The attackers had paused at the head of the trail, gathered in a group. His estimate had been about right. Looked like closer to fifty, all male. They had dark skins and their clothes were fringed and beaded in a way that recalled the mysterious stranger at the time the Trader had gone walking out into eternity. Some of them carried spears and some hatchets. Most had bows, either in their hands or slung across their shoulders.

"No blasters," said Okie. "We can take 'em all, easy as fartin'."

"I figure them for Indians," whispered J.B. "Some old tribe trapped up here, safe from raiders."

"What are Indians?"

Ryan stopped as one of the squat figures started to run toward them, waving a long stick decorated with a double row of white and brown feathers. His mouth was open and he was yelling an inarticulate cry of rage. None of his fellows had moved, but stood watching him as he charged at the small group.

"Gone crazy," said Hun.

Doc had collapsed as they reached the door, but he now pulled himself upright, peering over Ryan's shoulder at the running figure.

"Upon my soul!" he exclaimed. "A warrior of the Sioux nation, eager to count coup upon us. How very... very... something or other."

The man was a hundred paces away, the wind tugging at his long braided hair, ruffling the thongs that fringed his jacket and trousers. Still nobody opened fire, unable to believe such lunatic courage. Or stupidity.

The Indian was less than forty running steps from them when Okie leveled her M-16 and put a round through the middle of his face. The high-velocity bullet hit smack through the center of his nose, exiting in a straight line through the back of his head, blowing away a chunk of skull the size of a woman's palm, blood and brains spraying out in the gale. He stopped as though he'd run into an invisible wall, legs flailing in front of him, his trunk flying through the air until he landed on his back. His arms kept twitching for several seconds.

"Stupe bastard," said Okie, quietly, lowering the rifle.

The rest of the attackers gave a great roar of anger, but none of them tried to follow their dying comrade. As Ryan watched, they withdrew around the corner out of sight. "Now what?"

"We get the door open."

"Won't move," said Henn. "Krysty tried. She... Look at the handle."

The metal had become twisted and warped. Krysty leaned against the door, face white as the snow, her breathing irregular. She was aware of them all staring at her and managed a thin smile. "Can't do... I tried. Used all I knew."

Ryan blinked at the sight. To distort the metal of the lock like that took unbelievable strength. Then he remembered the way she had suddenly freed herself of her bonds when Strasser had held them prisoner. And he wondered about that amazing red hair that had seemed to move of its own volition. For the first time he realized that the girl had to be some kind of mutie. And he had made love to her...

"Without blasters they can't get at us," said Hunaker, squatting. "If we can't get into this joint, then we'll go back down. In the war wag and off safe as armor."

"Not that easy," interjected J. B. Dix.

Ryan agreed. "He's right, Hun. Think about it some. There's a lot of 'em. We seen maybe fifty. Could be a hundred more. They know the Darks."

"We can blast them away."

"Not if you can't see 'em, Hun. Where are they now? Waitin' for us? Up on the cliffs? Maybe they're movin' right now, right above us."

"Night's still some way off, Ryan," she argued, reluctant to let it go. "We keep careful, we can get ready, then make a run for the war wag."

It was possible. Perhaps the best plan they had. So they rested, snatching a quick meal and mouthful of water. Doc was in poor shape and he dropped asleep while they ate. Ryan and J.B. looked at the massive gate to the Stockpile, but there was no way in. Most of the other Stockpiles they had found were much smaller and the entrances yielded to small charges of dynamite. This was heavy-gauge metal that even high-explosive grenades were not going to dent.

About three-quarters of an hour had passed since they saw the last of the Indians.

Then two things happened at once.

Stones and boulders began to fall around them, rolled from much higher up, above the entrance door. And the Indians reappeared with what must have been the oldest piece of field artillery in all of Deathlands.

"What the...!" exclaimed Ryan.

"It's a cannon!" gasped Doc. "The sort they used in the war between North and South, about two hundred and fifty years ago. Must have come from some museum."

"Will it shoot?" asked Okie, taking a professional interest in it. "And what does it shoot?"

"Probably shoots a metal ball that might be filled with explosive. If it works, then we're over the falls without a boat, folks."

It worked. There was a vast plume of smoke from the bell-like mouth of the ancient piece, and they all ducked at the whistling sound as the shell came toward them. It struck the cliff about fifty paces to their left and twenty paces high, showering them with splinters of white rock.

"Let us get within," yelled Doc.

"Sure. You open her up, Doc, and we'll hold 'em off with blasters."

"Gettin' ready again, Ryan," said J.B., calm as ever.

"Let 'em have it. Try and pick 'em off around that gun," ordered Ryan.

"They got the cover. We got nukeshit nothin'," swore Okie as she fired her M-16 with rhythmic ease, the bullets skittering and ricocheting all around the heavy metal shield of the artillery piece. Two of the attackers threw up their arms and toppled over, but the rest withdrew around the bend in the trail to safety.

It was a standoff. But the odds were greatly against Ryan Cawdor and his friends. They had no cover at all. Nowhere to go. If the Indians could control the aim of their cannon they could blow them away. As he poured lead toward the big gun, it occurred to Ryan that their only hope was going to be a charge across the flat ground, under fire from the arrows. It was close to suicide, but it was all there was.

He felt a finger tap his shoulder. He spun around, nearly knocking Doc over with the barrel of his LAPA.

"Do you wish me to open the door?"

Grinning with his peculiarly perfect teeth, Doc stepped with a long, mincing stride to the side of the door and reached inside a small square panel set at shoulder height. "Shall we go in?"

Ryan's reply was drowned by the boom of the field gun. This time the gunners had overcompensated and the massive ball, pitching low and bouncing, narrowly missed the far end of the great door.

"Next time they'll get it right, Ryan," said J.B.

He stopped at the sonorous grating that came from the top and bottom of the huge gateway into the Redoubt. For a second of frozen time nothing happened, then a dark slit appeared at the right edge, near where Doc was still pulling a lever inside the panel.

"Inside!" yelled Ryan, as soon as the crack was wide enough for them to slip through.

Henn went first, then Finnegan, struggling to squeeze into the darkness. Okie and Krysty were next. Hun waved at Ryan to go, but he gestured angrily with the stubby barrel of his gun and she ran in.

"Now us, Doc. You done real good."

As soon as the old man released the control, the door stopped its movement. Behind them Ryan was aware of angry screams and shouts as the Indians saw their prey disappearing into the mountain. Doc vanished through the gap and Ryan followed him in, pausing to look back. He was shocked to see how many attackers there were now. Better than a hundred men, all racing toward them. He gave a quick burst that sent six or seven tumbling like disjointed dolls, blood bursting into the cold air and smoking on the ground from the scattered corpses.

"You can close it up, Doc, right?"

The yellowed eyes turned incuriously to him, veiled as though beeswax lay across them, and Ryan glimpsed the closeness of Doc's insanity. But the threads held together a while longer.

"Indeed. There's the panel."

"How come them bastard mongrels didn't get this open?" asked Krysty.

"Code, my dear titian girl. A simple three five two to enter and a two five three to shut her up tight again. Like so." He waved his hand like a magician pulling off a particularly clever trick, although this particular audience did not know what a magician was.

Doc's answer raised a whole mass of questions, but now was not the time. Ryan, with the door grinding tight shut behind him, had a chance to take in their surroundings. Of all the Stockpiles he had seen, this one was the largest and the strangest. Others had been what the name suggested: places where enormous, even staggering, quantities of food and supplies were stored. Like mighty warehouses, packed with ... who knew what?

But this was different.

Dim lights came into hesitant flickering life and Ryan figured they had tripped some kind of beam, still active, perhaps of uranium, that switched on the electrics of the place.

Sometimes you found corpses. Mummified and dried, like the husks of cocoons after the butterfly's gone. The air tasted familiar to him from breaking into similar establishments, sealed for a century. Dry and flat, with a hint of iron.

"There another way out of here, Doc?" asked J.B., reloading the Steyr.

"No." There came a cackle of laughter that often signaled one of Doc's period of craziness. "Not like you mean, Mr. Dix. Oh, dear me, no."

"This ain't like no Stockpile I ever seen," muttered Hunaker, glancing around at the huge curved roof. The room was in fact an immense tunnel, the ribbed metal ceiling like a cylinder above them that curved away into a dense mass of largely empty shelving.

"That, ma'am, is because it is not a Stockpile. Oh, there were many of those, most still hidden beneath swamps or earth slips or hot spots. But this is a Redoubt. There are many of these also, but I do not believe many have ever been discovered. They would appear valueless to those who do not know." He shook his head, the stringy hair bobbing about his scrawny shoulders. "And those who did know are so long gone."

"Make sense, Doc. We're trapped in here. If that's the only door and those sons of bitches are waiting for us . . . then how do we get out? Are there food and arms in here?"

"No. Perhaps some water, but it will be brackish and foul. Perhaps some eater tablets. No arms. That is not the purpose of the Redoubt."

"Then what is, Doc?" asked Ryan, hunching his shoulders against the oppressive feel of the place. Buried underground with nowhere to run was a bad feeling.

"This is the gateway to Hades, Mr. Cawdor. Look upon the wall where Cerberus himself stands watch. The gateway to the river to the deeps to the darks to the high mountain. All is dust . . ." And he turned away, tears streaming down his lined cheeks.

J.B. caught Ryan's eye and shook his head. "Let it lie, friend. No more help there for a while."

"We can't go out," Ryan said, "so we best go in."

Hun took Doc's arm, leading him along in the middle of the shrunken party. First Ryan, then Okie and Henn. The green-haired girl and the old man. Krysty and Finnegan. And J. B. Dix at the rear.

Eight of them, bearing the faint torch of the future, into the past.

RYAN LED THEM PAST the picture that had caught Doc's gaze. Garishly painted with a crude skill like a comic book illustration, it showed a slavering black hound. Three heads grew out of a single corded neck, their jaws wide open, fire and blood gushing between yellow teeth. The eyes were crimson, the colors bright despite the creature's age. Underneath, in an ornate Gothic script, was written the single word: "Cerberus."

Apart from that one picture, the place was bare. Ryan had seen Stockpiles that had been ravaged, but they were always a total shambles with rotting food and torn containers everywhere. This was different. It was as if a team of men had carefully gone through the entire place, stripping everything off walls, removing every stick of furniture. Nothing remained.

Nothing beyond the stale, flat air and the echoing sound of their own boots.

The walls remained curved, with strips of corrugated steel supports running clear over the roof. Behind them Ryan heard the distant sound of a shell hitting the closed door, but he knew the door to be strong enough to withstand anything short of an antitank shell.

They headed inward, toward the bowels of the mountain. The tunnel that they followed ran straight for several hundred paces with about a dozen chambers opening off it. Each one was stripped bare. Some of the walls showed the faint marks where cabinets or desks had once stood against them.

Out of habit, Ryan flicked on the rad counter clipped to the inside of his long coat, by the lapel. It murmured and cheeped a little, with the background crackling it always gave out in the Deathlands. But nothing here to worry about.

Nobody spoke as they moved cautiously on. There was a deadliness in the Redoubt that oppressed the spirit. Doc was mumbling to himself, a quiet string of nonsense. Ryan wished to the bottom of his heart that the old man hadn't lost so much of his mind under the tender care of Teague and Strasser. He was absolutely certain that Doc held the key to limitless secrets. How could he have known about the fog and Cerberus and the code to the door that had saved all their lives?

"Should I call in to Cohn?" asked Henn. "If we go much hellfired deeper they won't be able to hear it."

Ryan shook his head at the suggestion. "No point, Henn. That door and this concrete will stop anything gettin' out."

The corridor reached a T-junction. It was a momentary temptation to split the party, but Ryan elected to keep together. Eight wasn't a big enough group to divide and then hope to survive a firefight. Despite what Doc had said, there might be another entrance. Or the Indians might be able to force the main door, now that they had the added incentive of pursuing them inside.

He led them to the left, wandering along a snaking passage for some minutes until it ended abruptly in a rockfall. It looked as if half the hill had come bursting in through the roof.

There was a doorway partly buried under the stone, and Ryan scrambled up to push it open. It moved back uneasily on warped hinges and he glimpsed light and some wooden pallets. "Somethin' here," he called.

"Old stores. Left behind," said Doc.

Ryan beckoned for Krysty and J.B. to follow him, leaving the others immediately outside; there was no obvious danger of a fight, and they would give warning of any attackers. It was a corridor with a rounded ceiling, made of rows of stressed metal ribs. On the right were dozens of stacked boxes, with a few more piled loosely on the other side. At the farthest end he could see the red and silver of the sky, patched with purple chem clouds; the end of the cave was open to the world. Some of the boxes had been opened, and Ryan and J.B. began to investigate. Krysty walked to the opening, less than fifty paces away.

"Blasters," said J.B., sitting on one of the containers, peering at a bizarre weapon by his feet. It was like a large pistol with a massive ammunition drum that had chambers for a dozen rounds.

"What the hell does that fire?" asked Ryan.

"Seen a pic of one. Colt M2-0-7, 40 mm gren launcher. Twelve different grenades. Laser sight and high-low propulsion system. I might come back for it once we've scouted around."

Ryan had taken a gun from its box, wiping the grease off on the sleeve of his long, fur-trimmed coat. "Nice. Close assault blaster, Heckler & Koch 12-gauge scattergun. Night scope and image intensifier. Be good 'gainst stickies in the dark." Reluctantly he laid it back in its box. "Yeah, might take some of these babies on the way out. If we get out."

Krysty appeared cat-footed at his side, her hair reflecting the fiery brightness of the sky behind her. "Not gettin' out that way. Land slip's taken off the edge of the whole mountain. Clean as a knife. Drops clean down to the gorge, and that's a long way. Not a hope."

They turned away from the small Stockpile and rejoined the others in the corridor. Ryan told them briefly what they'd found and that there was no way out.

"I believe I had already mentioned that probability, Mr. Cawdor," Doc said with a grin.

Ryan ignored him. "Let's go."

They retraced their steps, and Henn moaned about carrying the radio.

"If we ain't usin' it, then why in blazing shit am I humpin' it on?"

Finnegan patted the tall black man on the backside. "Ice your asshole, Hennings. You got the radio and I got my big gut to carry."

The other branch of the corridor went a couple of hundred paces, then forked like a sidewinder's tongue. The lights had failed in the one end but burned brightly from the roof along to the right. "That way," said Ryan, leading the others.

As they went, they checked off all the rooms, on the chance that one of them might contain some clue, some indication of what had happened in this place.

Hun picked up a torn piece of card tucked in behind one of the plastic doors. Holding it up to the light, she read the faint pencil lettering.

"Forty-Niners over the Dolphins, twenty-four to twenty-one," she read. "Now what the scorch was that? Some kind of firefight casualties?"

She tucked the scrap of paper in a pocket of her overalls.

The corridor ended abruptly. A door of vanadium-type steel ran ceiling to floor, its surface polished and gleaming, throwing back their own reflections as if it mocked them. There was no sign of any lock or control, just smooth walls on either side.

"Try that other way. Where the lights had gone out," suggested Hunaker.

Doc waved a careless hand. "Waste of time, my emerald-locked elfling. That corridor curls all the way around the Redoubt complex and returns behind that rockfall. There is nothing there."

"Just how d'you know all this, Doc?" asked J.B. "Maybe this is the place and time to tell us."

Doc's cunning eyes turned to J.B. "This is a place and a time, sir. But not *the* time or *the* place. When that might be, I do not know. It is beyond my control."

"You knew about the main door to the Redoubt. How about this one?" asked Ryan. Casually he allowed the barrel of his gun to move toward the old man.

Doc noted the gesture. "Ah, Mr. Cawdor...a threat. Over the years I have become overly familiar with threats."

"The door?"

"It is the last door before the gate."

Ryan closed his only eye, fighting for control. There were times when a great scarlet mist drenched his senses and an entirely insensate rage possessed him. There was the temptation to take this doddering imbecile with his antique clothes and rich baritone voice, take him and rip the seamed old face from the skull. Things were tough on Ryan now. The realization that Krysty Wroth was probably a mutie had already shaken him. He'd fallen in love with a mutie! Once this was over he would need to clear his mind on that one. But for now...

"Can you open the door, Doc?" in a voice calm as buttermilk.

"If I were within, then it would be a matter of the utmost simplicity."

"Within what?" asked Finnegan.

"Inside the door, stupe," hissed Henn.

"It cannot be opened from out here."

Ryan looked at J.B. Suddenly both of them chorused, "Over, under or around."

It had been one of the Trader's pet sayings when confronted with a problem that could not be solved directly.

"Over's impossible. Under, as well, without digging gear."

"Go back and radio the war wag for help?" suggested Hunaker.

"What about goin' in the side?" Ryan asked. "In that room there. Maybe the walls aren't as thick. Worth a try."

The room was a bare office with only a grease mark on one wall showing where someone had sat and leaned back against it.

The first high-ex bomb broke the outer layer of the walls, exposing hollow cavities of concrete and rusting iron rods. The room was perfect to contain and compound an explosion. More grenades opened up a great hole in the far wall, clean through to the other side.

The smoke and bitter fumes took some time to clear in that underground expanse of still air. Ryan and J.B. went first, checking that the main structure was not about to topple in on top of them.

"Looks good?"

"Yeah. I'll call the— What was that?" Ryan's acute hearing had caught the faint rumble of a distant explosion, hollow and metallic.

J.B. had heard it, too. "Main door?"

"Could be. If it is, we'd best find a good ambush spot. We'll need it. Else those bastards can starve us out."

The others joined them. "Hear that?" asked Krysty. "They've managed to blow the main door."

"We'll stand and fight," ordered Ryan. "Only choice we got."

Doc coughed. "If the gate is still functioning, then there is that option. The makers said it would last a thousand years. But others have made such a boast and been proven wrong."

"What is this nukeshittin' gate? Where is it?"

"It is the alternative way out of the Redoubt. And it lies through that hole."

They all scrambled through successfully, though Finnegan managed to tear his sleeve on one of the jagged pieces of twisted metal. Inside, the rad counter on Ryan's coat began to cheep and mutter to itself a little louder, indicating a marginally higher count of radiation. But it was not enough to worry them, and Ryan switched the device off.

It was like nothing any of them had ever seen.

Great banks of dials and flickering lights, red, green and amber, with thousands of white switches. Circuits hummed and crackled, and loops of tape moved erratically in a row of machines. Occasionally they had found Stockpiles that held ranks of electrical machines that none of them could figure out. But this was something else.

"Through there," said Doc, pointing with a bony forefinger past the consoles to a doorway.

Again Ryan led them through, into an anteroom. It had a polished table on one side and four empty shelves on the other. Beyond it was another door.

"The gate is there. In that next room. Are we ready for it? It is the gate of gates. From this point the hills will become more and more shallow, but the valleys will become more and more deep."

"We lost him again," said Hun.

Once Doc's mind began to wander like this, it might be hours before they got any sense out of him. By Ryan's reckoning it would take the Indians about thirty minutes to track them down.

Ryan opened the far door, hand on the butt of his pistol. And faced yet another door, made of what looked like smoked glass. There was a neat panel by the side of the door with a variety of numbered and lettered buttons, some glowing brightly. Above it was a notice in angular maroon lettering.

Entry Absolutely Forbidden to All but B12 Cleared Personnel. Mat-trans.

"Matter transmitter," said J.B. wonderingly, taking off his glasses and wiping them. "Damnedest thing. I'd heard they had somethin' like this."

"How does it work?" asked Krysty, running her fingers over the smooth glass of the door.

"Who knows? Chance is it doesn't work at all. When the long chill came, they was workin' on a lot of clever things like this. I read they were close to..."

Doc pushed past them all, sweeping open the door and bowing low. "Here be dragons, lords and ladies. Enter and leave."

It was a chamber, six sided, all the walls of the same brown tinted glass. The floor was patterned with metallic disks, raised very slightly. The pattern was repeated in the ceiling. The opening of the door triggered some sort of mechanism and a few of the disks began to glow faintly in a seemingly random form. A faint mist appeared in the room, swirling and darting. Ryan drew a slow, deep breath, remembering the fog outside. Was this the same? Some deadly trap by long-dead hands....

Doc stepped in, beckoning them to follow. "Around and around the little wheel goes, and where it stops... Come in."

Nothing more happened. The mist coiled about the cracked boots, rising no farther than the knees. More of the disks were gleaming with a silvery light, and Ryan could hear the faintest of humming sounds.

"Hell, why not?" he said, and stepped in, followed by all the others.

With a cackle of manic glee Doc immediately leaped and slammed the door shut so hard that the room vibrated.

"Off we go!" he yelped, voice rising to a banshee wail.

The hum rose to a whine. The lights flashed a pattern that dazzled and forced the intruders to close their eyes. Ryan was aware that the fog had thickened, climbing all about them, filling their lungs. He coughed, unable to breathe. There was a dreadful pressure in his ears. For a moment it felt as if a huge fist was reaching inside his head and squeezing his brain like a sponge.

His body grew light, and he knew that he was passing out.

Ryan's last thought as he fought his way into unconsciousness was that he should have killed Doc days ago.

Even that was swallowed by an impenetrable blackness.

Chapter Seventeen

RYAN OPENED his eye.

There was a mild pain across his temples, like after a night of drinking home brew. His pulse was up and so was his breathing. He lay still, aware of a tingling sensation at the tips of toes and fingers. He lifted his hands and touched his face, feeling a faint numbness. And his black, curly hair bristled with static electricity. He closed his eye and opened it again, blinking up at a ceiling of patterned metal disks that glowed. A glow that was fading even as he looked up at it.

He tried to work out just how he felt. His stomach swirled as if he'd been riding War Wag One over the bumpiest road in all Deathlands. And his brain relayed the curious sensation of having been sucked into itself and then dragged through a vacuum before being rammed back into his skull.

But he lived.

Whatever that bastard machine was supposed to have done, it had failed. The trap had not been properly sprung. Maybe over the decades the gas or poison or whatever had lost its power. He thought again that he ought to kill Doc. Now, without any further hesitation.

"Ryan? You all . . . Mother, my head aches."

Ryan sat up, looking around, seeing all his comrades either slumped unconscious or showing the first signs of recovering. Krysty blinked and sighed.

"How d'you feel?" he said.

She licked her lips, brushing a hand through the tumbling hair. "I've felt better. What was it? Death trap went wrong?"

"Don't know. Doc knew about it, the old . . ."

"Where are we, Mr. Cawdor?"

Ryan drew the LAPA, finger on the trigger. "We're still in the Redoubt and we're all alive. Trick didn't work, Doc."

"Trick? Upon my soul, but it is no trick. And it *did* work."

"What? Knocked us on our asses, that's all."

Doc was up, tottering, steadying himself with a hand on the streaked glass of the wall. Everyone was now back to some degree of awareness.

"What color were the walls of the gateway in the Redoubt, Mr. Cawdor?"

"Brown and . . ." Ryan's jaw sagged a little. "Fireheat! These are green. They've changed."

"No. We've changed. The gateway worked. We are no longer within the Redoubt in the Darks."

That was enough to bring them all to their feet. J.B. doubled over and retched as though he was about to throw up, but nothing came.

"Not in the Darks no more?" he gasped, wiping a gloved hand over his mouth. "Where, then?"

"Ah . . ." The triumphant smile had vanished. "That is one of the many problems with the gateways. Not always reliable. Depends on destination setting."

Whatever had happened while they were all out cold, Doc's madness had deserted him and he spoke clearly and intelligently.

"They started here about a hundred years back, trying to transmit matter. They began with a pair of small metal balls. Light gray metal balls. They got them to travel a few centimeters. And they went on from there."

While he listened, Ryan moved around the room. The walls were certainly a changed color and the air tasted different. Not flat and dead as in the Redoubt. Was all this possible? Had the fog been a luci-gas? Was this all some chem dream?

"They wanted to use it for military purposes. But the big war stopped that good. By then they'd set up a network of these Redoubts, each with gates. Send and receive, and some big mistakes. Horrible things did happen."

He stopped as though his mind was lodging on unbearable memories. Ryan reached to open the door, but Doc waved a hand to stop him.

"Not yet. Nearly done. Gates can be set as this one was. But all codes are now lost, lost forever. So it's a gamble *where* and *when* you get out."

"But . . . some of these gates must have been destroyed in the fighting," said Ryan. "What would have happened if the controls had been set for one of those? Then what?"

"Most in the wilderness areas were destroyed. As to your question, I suppose that possibility represents the final frontier!"

And he laughed.

"You crazy bastard," spat Hun, moving toward him with her fist clenched.

"Leave him be," ordered Ryan, stopping her.

"Let's go see where we are."

"I am obliged, Mr. Cawdor," Doc said, relapsing once more into the archaic way of speaking. "Most of all I would dislike having to strike a lady. Next I would dislike being struck by one."

The door opened easily.

Opened onto a room of the same scale as the one back at the Redoubt. Any of Ryan's doubts were dispelled when he saw a table knocked over on its side and two of the shelves slipping lopsidedly. A long crack ran down the wall, deep enough to insert a hand.

In the next room, the consoles whirred and lights danced, but there was an undertone of grinding and Ryan could smell a frail scent of smoldering. Of a fire that slumbered somewhere within the machinery that surrounded them. He could see all eight of his group reflected in the smeared metal of the door that he knew would open on a blank passage. To the right of it there was a green lever in the down position, with the word Closed printed beneath it.

Ryan grasped the lever and pushed it up to the Open position. It moved easily, as though it swam in a greased slot. For a moment nothing happened, then the grinding of gears, and then the door began to slide back.

Everyone yelled at once.

The moment that the thin sheet of filthy water came gushing through the widening crack at the edge of the door, the shouting began. Water immediately flowed about their feet, carrying innumerable wriggling creatures with scaly skins and ferocious rows of tiny teeth.

"Shut it!" shouted J.B., but Ryan had already thrown the lever down again.

It seemed to take forever, but the door finally hissed shut, and the water stopped.

"It's fuckin' hot, Ryan," said Henn, kicking with his boots at one of the reptiles that had fastened onto the sole of his boot.

"It came all the way from top to bottom." Krysty's shocked voice said it all. The Redoubt where they had finished up was under water. Maybe under shallow water, maybe under whole fathoms.

"There is a thirty-minute automatic reset on the gates," said Doc. "If we make haste we should . . . should be back in the Redoubt in the Darks."

They splashed through the filth of mud and water, crushing the seething life as they moved. There was a step into the actual trans-mat chamber and the slime had not penetrated it. They all stepped in, and J.B. reached to close the door.

"Hold on. If we're goin' to pass out," said Ryan, "I guess it's better if we sit down first."

They sat in a ring, Krysty opposite Ryan. Their eyes met and he winked at her. He enjoyed the hint of a smile on her full lips. And she was a mutie!

The door closed and once again darkness clawed its way over Ryan's mind, blanking it out.

The moment of wakening was less painful, the headache gone, but the feeling of disorientation was still as strong. It was as if every atom in his body had been juggled around and clumsily reassembled.

Ryan opened his eye.

The walls were brown glass. By the texture it looked armored. It was not possible to guess its thickness.

"Come on, people," Ryan said. "Doc? You know how to reset this machine?"

"Yes, indeed, Mr. Cawdor. But I must repeat that it is a random element. All instructions and codes are gone these many, many years. I can alter the setting and then it will be in the laps of what gods we worship.''

"I worship this," said Okie, holding up her M-16.

As he checked that everyone had recovered, Ryan wondered yet again about Doc's range of knowledge. Lots of it could have come from some hoard of old books or vids. There was no other sensible explanation. But he knew so much. Spoke as if he'd been here before. Been here a hundred years ago!

They were back in the clean, antiseptic anteroom. Ryan tugged the door open, hearing the faint whisper of sound that told him that it was air locked.

He pulled harder and it swung open.

The master control room now held a dozen or more of the squat, muscular Indians.

Okie reacted fastest, and Ryan winced at the stream of bullets that burst past him, knocking down five or six of the attackers in a welter of blood.

"Don't' fire!" screamed Doc's voice. "Damage anything and we'll never jump again!"

Ryan reached for his heavy panga, drawing it from its stitched leather sheath, thrusting at the face of the nearest of the Indians. It cleaved through the open mouth, splintering teeth as it did so, and lodged itself in the cervical vertebrae at the back of the man's neck. Blood gushed, hot and salt, into Ryan's face, nearly blinding him. But the man was down and done, screams bubbling through the choking flood of scarlet.

Around him the most desperate battle raged. Okie used her gun like a club, smashing one man across the side of the head, kicking him hard in the groin as his hands went to grab her.

Henn and Finnegan had both drawn their knives, automatically fighting back to back, the steel of their blades making a deadly web that snared any of the Sioux who tried to get within it.

J.B. had his delicate knives, one in each hand, the thin blades opening up hideous gashes like lips in the stomach of the man attacking him. As the man reeled away, crying like a scalded kitten, Hun used her own broad-bladed dagger to slit his throat. Blood from the jugular pattered onto the concrete floor, making it slick and treacherous.

Krysty ducked and weaved against a taller Indian, her hair seeming to foam back and forth in the man's face, blinding him. But she did not carry a long-bladed knife, and she was in desperate trouble. Meanwhile Ryan punched a grinning face, knocking it away from him, and raised the panga as he closed on Krysty's attacker.

The impact jarred Ryan's arm. But the steel was honed enough and weighted enough to hack clean through the skin and flesh and bone of the neck. The head, eyes staring, tongue moving, rolled and bounced among the fighters' feet, while the body gradually slumped to the floor as though reluctant to submit to death.

"Thanks," she panted, trying to back away to join Doc near the door through to the gateway.

"Anytime."

Henn was staggering, blood streaming from a cut along the side of his thigh, with Finnegan holding off a pair of the Indians, each armed with a triangular ax.

"Make for the door!" Ryan yelled, going to help Finnegan cover Henn's retreat. Hun got there first, stabbing the nearest of the attackers so hard that the steel snapped and she withdrew only the hilt, grinning at the shocked and puzzled expression on the bronzed face of the man she had just killed.

Doc, Krysty, Henn and Finnegan were through into the anteroom, watching anxiously as their friends still battled on. Nine or ten of the Indians were down, dying or dead. But four more had come in, two armed with bows and arrows.

"Back!" shouted Ryan again, pushing Hunaker in front of him, parrying a lunge from a feather-tipped spear, turning and spilling the man's guts in loops of greasy intestine around his feet.

Okie stood, legs braced, to one side of the doorway, the M-16 steady in her hands, waiting a chance to open fire at the enemy without harming the electrical equipment in its serried banks.

J.B. followed Hun through, then Ryan was in the doorway, tapping Okie on the arm. At the far end of the control room, more of the Sioux came pouring in, screaming and shouting. An arrow hit the wall at Ryan's side, and he snapped off a 3-round burst at the man who had loosed it. The rounds kicked the man onto his back, knocking others over with the violence of his dying.

Another arrow clipped Okie's right shoulder, pinning her to the wall by the material of her jacket. "Bastard!" she hissed, reaching and snapping the shaft of the arrow, and throwing it contemptuously on the concrete. Then she ripped in half the man who had wounded her. His body jerked and danced, held up by the force of the bullets that stitched him apart. As she took her finger off the trigger he fell sideways, crashing into one of the consoles, where sparks flew and a siren began to howl deep in the recesses of the Redoubt.

"That screws it," hissed Ryan, grabbing Okie and pulling her after him. There wasn't time to close the intervening door. The rest of them were already in the glass-walled chamber, beckoning to Ryan.

More arrows sliced by them, one plucking at the hem of his coat. J.B. yelled for them all to get down. The ar-

mored door began to close the moment they were all inside.

Ryan was last. A final shaft missed his left elbow by a
hairsbreadth, hitting the control panel to the gateway,
splintering one of the numbered buttons, breaking the
plastic cover, revealing all the mass of tangled multico-
lored wiring beneath. As the door closed, Ryan's last
glimpse of the Redoubt in the Darks was a worm of smoke
inching from the damaged control.

An arrow pinged against the glass, but the thick plate
held fast. The fog rose about them and the metal disks
glowed brightly. Ryan felt himself being sucked into the
maelstrom and fought against losing consciousness. But
the physical disturbance was too severe, and the darkness
swamped his mind.

RYAN OPENED HIS EYE.

As before, his seven comrades were lying all around him.
J.B.'s glasses had become dislodged from his thin nose and
lay on the floor. Finnegan was snoring, flat on his back,
revealing a mouthful of teeth that overlapped and jostled
one another like a view into an excavated graveyard. Hunaker was curled into a fetal ball, eyes blinking as she began to recover. Henn held his leg, the blood still trickling
steadily from it. Okie was also bleeding, crimson rivulets
threading from between her fingers as she clamped her
hand over the superficial flesh wound in her shoulder. Her
other hand held the M-16 tight. Krysty was sitting up,
shaking her head to clear the mist from it. The front of her
overalls was soaked with blood from the Indian that Ryan
had decapitated.

Doc was groaning, with a small pool of yellow bile near
his feet. As he sat up, he looked toward Ryan. "Upon

my... I am becoming too old for this sort of foolishness, sir. Indeed I am.''

"If they wreck the Redoubt up in the Darks, then what if we tried to get back?"

"Not a wise idea, Mr. Cawdor. I will alter the setting so that the automatic return is negated. That is, if we should decide not to remain here."

"Where is here, Doc?" grunted Hunaker, standing up.

The glass was a pale gray color, and as Ryan stood he noticed that there was a network of very fine cracks lacing the plate. He took a deep breath. The air smelled bad. He could taste the oily flavor of methane on his tongue, and some other, bitter chemical.

"Don't like this. J.B., you come with me. Rest of you stay here. Doc, you'd best alter the control."

"You do appreciate that I can change them so we don't return, but I have no control over where we might eventually finish up?"

"Yeah. Just do it, Doc. Ready, J.B.?"

"As I'll ever be."

As soon as they left the trans-mat chamber, Ryan sensed something was wrong. Gravely wrong. The bitter flavor of the air was stronger and it was very warm. The door to the anteroom was already ajar. There was no furniture there at all, and the walls were marked with deep gouges and scratches, with smears of burned ash across the ceiling. The outer was also partly open, showing nothing but a great darkness.

"Don't like it, Ryan," said J.B.

"I know what you mean."

Ryan moved to the door and peered out. The darkness was not total. The sky glowed an unimaginably deep red, with flashes of lightning scattered across it. But each bolt of lightning stayed in place for several seconds as though frozen there. Distant thunder rumbled. The land seemed flat and sandy, from what they could make out in the strip of light that spilled out through the open doorway.

On a sudden deadly impulse, Ryan flicked on the small geiger counter in his lapel. Immediately it began to crackle and click louder than he'd ever thought possible.

"It's a hot spot!" said J.B.

"There's enough milli-rads here to fry a war wag. Let's go."

As he turned, Ryan glimpsed something moving out in that seared desert. Something blasphemously huge, lumbering toward the remnants of the Redoubt. He hadn't made out the shape of the entity, except that it had seemed in that single glimpse to have no true shape at all.

With the knowledge of that horror at his heels, Ryan pushed J.B. ahead of him, past the banks of machines, many silent and blind. He saw the others, gathered in the door of the chamber, and the look on his face propelled them into instant action. Guns sprang into hands.

"No. Just get out!"

"I've altered..." began Doc, but Ryan elbowed him aside, pulling the door and slamming it shut behind J.B. and himself.

The lights came on and the thick mist rose about their feet.

"Here we go," said Krysty softly. "Where to this time?"

"Somewhere better," Ryan began to say, but he felt the suction of his mind and the atoms and molecules of his body being displaced.

But even as the displacement occurred, and in spite of it, Ryan Cawdor knew with a profound and gratifying certainty that, in fact, they had already achieved, truly achieved, what he and Krysty had set out to do. They had broken from the bonds that were at the heart of the

Deathlands, they had entered the forbidden places, deep into the Darks, and they had found ... something, something other than their dreary experience in the Deathlands, something that by its very newness spelled hope for a different life, a different future.

That was what they had always yearned for, quested for, put their lives on the line for. Now Ryan and his woman and J.B. and their warrior allies and the strange character called Doc were free at last of the deadening reality of the Deathlands, free to live anew even if the new life was hazardous and unknown.

Through love and through death they had come this far, and they had seen so much, and now they would conquer....

And the darkness fell once more over them all.

Epilogue

RYAN opened his eye.